EASY MONEY

BY THE SAME AUTHOR

Westchester Bull

Hot Stuff

EASY MONEY

by Sam Koperwas

William Morrow and Company, Inc.
New York   1983

Library of Congress Cataloging in Publication Data

Koperwas, Sam.
  Easy money.

  I. Title.
PS3561.064E2   1983   813'.54   82-14399
ISBN 0-688-01550-6

Printed in the United States of America

First Edition

1 2 3 4 5 6 7 8 9 10

BOOK DESIGN BY ALLAN MOGEL

For Evelyn, with love and friendship.
And for Harriet, the only other woman
in my life.

ACKNOWLEDGMENT

I would like to thank the
John Simon Guggenheim Memorial Foundation
for their generous support.

EASY MONEY

Chapter

1

Del Plato had on his lawn-mowing Hawaiian shirt with surboards and sunsets, a pair of Wrangler cutoffs that still smelled of camphor flakes, and his ripped sneakers with purple laces that all the black guys at the academy gym loved to razz him about and call his jig shoes. No socks. Del Plato also had his police-issue blue-steel .38, which he carried uncomfortably in a stiff cowhide shoulder holster concealed beneath his Hawaiian shirt. No matter how he rearranged his weapon that morning, it would not fit properly. Every little thing was giving him a hard time.

Del parked his car in the driveway of a store selling used golf balls. He had to slam the crumpled car door twice before it would close. As he banged the door shut a second time, Del Plato noticed his lips had pulled back awkwardly into the type of idiot grin a person would have if, for instance, a wet newspaper had been delivered in the morning, or say someone parked in your spot. He realized he was in a bad mood.

Del Plato had been living in Fort Lauderdale for nine years. Each and every winter, grinning stoically, he had been

witness to the same discouraging scene. Too much traffic. Too
many college kids and vagrants and traveler's checks. South
Florida just after Thanksgiving meant tourists making left-
hand turns from the right lane, buying chocolate-covered
coconut patties and miniature orange trees. A new season
of rubber alligators, and coconut heads of Groucho, Teddy
Roosevelt, and drunken Indians.

Del checked his watch to see just how late he was. His
watch looked exactly like a Seiko chronograph. When Del
Plato grabbed it for sixty dollars off someone in Homicide, the
watch had even been neatly packed inside a Seiko box. But
from the start the watch kept funny time—there was some suspicious spelling on the back—and Del was fairly certain it
wasn't the real thing. Now he called the watch his Fako and he
had nothing to do with anyone in Homicide.

As he crossed the street, he noticed Breed's car on the corner, parked near the alley. Breed's car was a brand-new foreign job, with six stereo speakers and metallic paint, a
five-speed gearbox, and doors that for sure you didn't have to
slam twice. Flaming decals tore across Breed's hood. It was the
kind of automobile kids collected in miniature and put under
their pillows after prayers. Sometimes when you stopped and
looked around, you saw that things simply did not seem fair.

Del Plato had been up late the previous night, drinking
Dubonnet red which had turned up—surprise, surprise—inside a guest closet, of all things. Del had been hunting for a
fresh towel at the time. At night he liked to explore his new
home, going through cupboards and personal effects. Del
rented the place, so he thought of it as his apartment—a two-
bedroom home west of the Sunshine State Parkway, in a development of single-family units at affordable prices where only a
few years before there had been a sprawling broccoli farm with
cows and ducks and abandoned vehicles that didn't have any
wheels or doors. During prime-time TV, he had started to
drink instead of taking a shower, and then he ate cream cheese
sandwiches with cucumber slices and lots of pepper, didn't
shave, and in general spent a long evening doing many things
he now figured he had every right to do. Who said he had to be

clean or go to sleep? An *Outer Limits* was on, one Del had seen before. He dozed through that. But then he was remarkably alert through *Rin Tin Tin, Noche a Noche, Petticoat Junction,* and a movie that the TV section had warned him about.

Was this new life so bad? From time to time during the night, Del asked himself this question, sipping wine with ice. He could keep the hours of an insomniac, drink whatever had been left behind in closets. But when a religion program unexpectedly appeared on the screen, he suddenly bolted straight up and went directly to bed.

Early that morning, however, the alarm woke him from a very scary dream, and for a long while Del Plato was in a slight panic. He didn't know where he was, he couldn't remember what had been going on in his dream, he couldn't find coffee. Then he splashed cold water on his face and reminded himself in a fuzzy but stern tone that he wasn't a drinking man, he had never been a drinking man, and just because he was on his own now was no reason to start acting like a man who drank. Right? Del Plato swallowed three aspirin with some Dubonnet red. Then he got dressed. Shirt, shorts, he could care less.

Since Denise had called it quits, however, his personal appearance was getting more than a little out of hand, Del had to admit that. Looking at himself in the bathroom mirror that morning, he decided nobody would believe he was only twenty-nine years old. He looked lousy and at least forty. He needed a haircut. And what kind of outfit was he wearing anyway? A business appointment, first thing on the agenda, and he shows up in jig shoes and short pants with mothballs in the pocket.

Early in their marriage Denise had picked up matching vinyl luggage with Green Stamps booklets, just in case Del would ever decide to go somewhere for his paid vacation instead of the usual car rides to Cape Canaveral and Disney World, or five-day fishing trips with his police friends. She made him pack away all sorts of old clothing—paint-splattered jeans and socks that fell down, stretched-out athletic supporters, shirts with frayed collars and collars nobody wore

anymore. They all went into a valise. But now Del was beginning to recycle this stuff—torn sneakers, cut-down Wran-
glers—which had been crammed away for years with his men's
magazines and gift-boxed cologne, and Denise's bridal veil and
her college yearbook. There was even an old dashiki stashed
away in there—a huge shirt with tribal colors and a lion—
which he had bought for four dollars from the back of a van
outside Briggs Stadium, just before a doubleheader when the
Tigers went ahead and took two from the Yankees, those bastards. The shirt was still good and he felt it should never have
been written off. Del saw this as a prime example of the differences between him and Denise. She liked to squirrel away things
of sentimental value in the garage, which she could then poke
through every few years and sigh over. Del liked to use things
until they were no longer usable, and then give them away
to bums or charity. Some things he would never forget anyway,
shirt or no shirt. McClain and Coleman, Horton and Kaline,
a doubleheader sweep of the Yankees, those bastards.

But right now Del was way behind schedule, there was the
taste of aspirin stuck in his throat, and he realized he was
probably going to be in a foul mood all day, no matter what.
*Although, just how were you supposed to feel anyway, if your
wife sent you out of your own house with sentimental clothing and her lawyer's business card? And this is after what,
after—*Del did some quick arithmetic to check—*nine married
years, and a child too. There's a child involved here, don't forget that.* Del Plato concluded it was no goddamn wonder he
snooped around in closets and slept with his mouth open and
was turning into material for Alcoholics Anonymous.

Back in Detroit, when he was down with a cold—a deal
that could last the entire football season—he would try to
make himself better with plenty of liquids and sunny thoughts
of Florida. As a teenager, he was taking a self-improvement
course based on psycho-cybernetic principles, and had completed an A-plus paper on how basketball players could improve their shooting by simply concentrating on a few orange
basketballs swishing through the net. Del had been to Florida
only one time, during his junior year of high school, Fort Lau-

derdale Beach, where he passed himself off as a sophomore
from Notre Dame and was thrilled to actually shoot hoops outdoors in February and sleep on the sand. He had brought back
a set of salt and pepper shakers and guava jelly for his mom, a
pipe shaped like a porpoise and a nail clipper with a map of
Florida for his dad, and a beer mug with a whistle on it for
himself, not to mention those bright images with which he
would try to stop his sniffles back home. Del would conjure up
scuba divers and a temperature in the eighties—which he
could see as a real deterrent to Detroit germs—or he might
envision a water-skier, for instance, someone with a solid tan
and one foot in the air, giving off a lot of positive psycho-
cybernetic energy, and then zoom even closer into this picture
to discover that this daredevil was himself, Del Plato, tied to a
speedboat, a healthy hotshot in the warm blue ocean, with no
sign of congestion or fever.

Now Del Plato lived in Florida and tried to work out
three times a week. For nine years he hadn't been sick. One
day soon he was going to see what it was like to water-ski.
Maybe he would give scuba diving a shot.

Waiting in the alley for Del Plato to arrive, sitting on the
edge of a metal trash barrel, was Jewboy Breed. Breed wore a
shiny Philadelphia Phillies warm-up jacket that shimmered in
the early sun like spoiled meat. He was drinking a Yoo-Hoo
and reading a sheet of newspaper that had blown into the
alley. It was local news, obituaries and zoning plats, and high-
school scores. At the sound of footsteps, Jewboy Breed glanced
up, nodded pleasantly to Del, and continued reading. He liked
to keep up with the news. Breed was toying with the idea of an
elected office. He enjoyed talking to old people and Hispanics
and having lunch; he enjoyed graft in every form. Breed had
been living in Miramar for twelve years, near a swamp of
gumbo trees. These were called tourist trees because the bark
was always red and peeling. Breed also considered himself a
native of South Florida. He could remember back to when
Meyer Lansky first began having breakfast at the Singapore,
when there was no cable TV.

They were in Hollywood, but the wrong Hollywood, and

down the street was a gas station that had been converted into a doughnut place, a shoe store paying highest prices for gold and silver and graduation rings, a tax accountant, a junk yard that bought aluminum by the pound, a discount store with specials on sugarless soft drinks. There was a used-car lot with gleaming cars and yellow price tags on the windshield, along with cute selling points—I'VE NEVER BEEN DIRTY, THIS LITTLE PIGGY STAYED HOME, BUY! BUY! BUY!, TAKE ME TO THE BEACH. Palm trees lining the street, after the high winds and heavy rains of hurricane season, were topped now with shrunken, tightly curled fronds and small green coconuts all bunched together, which gave these trees a paranoid appearance, as if they suffered from some floral form of shell shock.

On one side of the alley was a medical-supply store, with stainless-steel equipment and an early wreath of holly in the window. On the other side of the alley was Happy Harry's Decor Discounts. The storefront was painted pink, with a pink flamingo in profile above the entrance. Red-and-white pennants whipped from a cord that was tied on one end to a telephone pole. The other end of the cord was tied to the flamingo's beak. Above the door to Happy Harry's was a sign in orange Day-Glo—NOUS ACCEPTONS TOUTES LES MAJOR CREDIT CARDS. They were near the beach. The air in Hollywood smelled of salt water and tanning butter.

"My tongue happens to be killing me this morning," Breed said for openers. He was checking over the Yoo-Hoo label for ingredients. "Genuinely killing me. Irish, I'm suffering this very unique agony. I don't know if I should tell you, though—that's the thing." Breed's eyes were brown; his hair and his mustache were the color of unwatered grass. He had the look about him of a person who, in a supermarket, would stroll right into an express lane with way more than ten items in his shopping cart. "How about yourself? You feeling good this morning or what?"

Del Plato, staring out the alley, was still thinking about the upcoming crush of tourist season and about Happy Harry's Decor Discounts. Strictly out of habit, just to keep his hands busy, he removed his weapon to inspect the trigger assembly. Otherwise he had a tendency to pick at his finger-nails or set the hands of his Fako to the correct time. Chamber, hammer, sight, spin, click. When he tucked the gun back into his shoulder holster, it was still uncomfortable.

Jewboy Breed put down his empty pop bottle and winced as he pinched his tongue. "Anyway, this damage, last night I pulled some muscle in my tongue or something, a ligament. That ever happen to you, Irish? Probably not. Probably you have no idea what I'm talking about."

Del Plato had his eyes on a Jet Liner. It hummed monot-onously overhead, making a slow descent into Fort Lauder-dale-Hollywood International. He wondered about the people aboard. Where were they from? Canada? Michigan? South America? Del could close his eyes and imagine people filing out of airplanes, renting autos, and immediately screwing up traffic. Perhaps that had been his bad dream the previous night.

"What an ordeal for me, Irish. What a crazy encounter. For sure this is nothing you ever been through. I come home, maybe two in the morning, it's very late, and Gail wakes up. Snap. She's awake. And instantly she has me pinned, in-stantly; she smells something on my face. First she's asleep, then she's wide awake and full of accusations, and she's sniff-ing at my face. Del Plato, I was mortified. What could I possi-bly say?" Breed removed a Ring Ding from the pocket of his shiny warm-up jacket. He squashed the wrapper into a ball and let it drop. "But this honey I destroyed my tongue with, let me tell you, she only wants to be a cheerleader for the Dol-phins, if you can imagine that. Constantly watching TV, watching football. And this is for the halftime shows, for the dance routines. That's why she watches. For the hairstyles, to check out the latest costumes."

Del Plato didn't want to hear it. He lightly kicked the barrel Breed was sitting on, and the sharp rattle of metal echoed in the alley. "No details for me, J.B.," he explained carefully. "Right? We go inside. Finish your breakfast and let's get this done."

Breed was cupping his hands over his nose and mouth to see if he could smell something that would get a person out of a sound sleep at two o'clock in the morning. "What happened is that I told her one time I let Joe Robbie himself slide for a traffic summons or something—some asinine story that I of course made up on the spot. The upshot of which is that he now owes me one, Robbie does; he carries my shield number in his wallet. The man only owns the entire football franchise. Del Plato, tell me the truth, am I talking about a stroke of genius here? I think I couldn't have said a more perfect thing to her. . . . So now what I have is this pulled fucking muscle in my tongue, or a ligament."

Del Plato was paying no attention. He was rubbing his temples and thinking about his automobile. He wondered when he would finally take it through a car wash, or maybe do something firm and buy a new one. The car had been a wedding gift from Denise's father. It was a tan Dodge station wagon that went back to the Johnson administration and had been repainted twice, with push-button transmission, furry dice on the rearview mirror, and a large Italian good-luck horn. The mileage meter had given out somewhere on the third time around. An embarrassing vehicle. You had to slam a door two times. Denise naturally drove a better vehicle. Del was in the frame of mind to bat this stuff around. What else? Denise had the stereo, and the Sony color. Certain things he had neglected to take—baby pictures of Keri, his Al Kaline glove, socks that didn't fall down—came at Del Plato in a barrage, without warning, like a late-afternoon sun shower—his 1600-watt hair blower, a key to the safe-deposit box, power tools, his James Bond series.

"I also have this lovely girl's phone number, Del Plato, my friend, in case you suddenly recall that you used to play strong safety for the Dolphins or some such lie, if you see my point. Do you see my point? Irish, in addition to being very good-looking, this particular chick is certifiably insane. Other people would say thank you. Other people would not kick garbage cans so early in the morning."

Del Plato took out his car keys and jiggled them for no

reason, then put them back in his pocket as Breed finished eating. He looked at his shorts and his ripped sneakers with purple laces. It was beginning to bother Del Plato that he hadn't been more careful in dressing.

"Doesn't this get on your nerves?" he asked Breed. "Tell me honestly, J.B., doesn't this get to you after a while?"

"Be a little more explicit."

"This stuff. This crime."

Jewboy Breed stood up, wiped his mouth, and stretched lazily. As he did, there was an unexpected snap inside his chest, a loud one, which made Breed look down and prod around with his fingers.

"There's no challenge to this cockeyed life," Del Plato told him. "That's one thing. For another thing it's probably not even worth our while, this small-time criminal crap."

"You're not very cheerful today. I've been noticing."

"We get what we want, J.B., sure. I don't deny that. But our goals, that's what I'm talking about. They're too low. Where the hell is our competitive spirit?"

"Beats me," said Breed. "Get to the point." He pinched a rib, poked around where he thought the vital organs might be.

Del Plato nodded and stared out the alley. Across the street was a chiropractor's office, as well as a barbecued-rib joint that had gone out of business. New cars hummed by.

"It's all your perspective," said Breed. "You get philosophical on me, Irish, then I'll point out you got a serious problem with perspective if you can talk that way about what we do. Because actually shakedowns are fun. For me, anyway. I thoroughly enjoy shakedowns like this. Our petty crime, man, if you can appreciate it, can be a very heightening experience. No shit. Seems to me your problem is one of attitude. And don't lose sight of the fact that you've also got this red ass today."

Del Plato folded his arms over his chest and acknowledged this with a grunt that was neither here nor there. Then he said, "My guidance counselor gave me tests when I was in high school, said I would make a good optometrist. Thirty thousand a year to start, wear a tie to work. But I was eighteen

years old at the time. What did I want to know from optometry when I had this tremendous shooting touch from the base-
line? I was a schmuck who dribbled between his legs, shot a
hundred foul shots every day, and had to chase the ball himself. But now it doesn't seem fair, J.B. I'm putting in twelve-
hour shifts because some eighteen-year-old schmuck got it into
his head to become a basketball player. I fall asleep in the
movies. I'm one thing and I could have been another."

"When I was eighteen years old," Breed said, "all I
wanted to do was get laid. I'm thirty-six now, and I'll be honest, all I want to do is get laid some more. Some things never
change, Irish. Go and figure."

"Maybe I could help people with their eyes. Maybe I
would like to be a sort of doctor, wear a lab coat. But now I'll
never know what it's like to pull down thirty, forty grand a
year, call things by their Latin names. For me, it's something I
regret, a lost opportunity. All because some schmucky kid sold
me short."

"Call me shallow," Breed said, "but in my life it happens
to play an important part and it always has. If I get laid, I'm
happy. If I don't get laid, I keep looking around until I do."

"An eighteen-year-old jerk, with sneakers and a jump
shot, who looked down on optometry. There's really no justice.
Now I live far enough from the station house that after work I
can think of three hundred ways to improve my life, but when
I finally get home I forget them."

They walked out of the alley to the front of Happy
Harry's Decor Discounts. The front doors were foiled with silver. Cast-iron grates and stickers with pictures of snarling
guard dogs were on each window, along with a number to call
in case of emergency.

"Although I do think I see the drift here," Breed was saying with no enthusiasm. "Bigger and better, in other words.
We could stand to be a little more upwardly mobile according
to you."

"I think we should rob something. I think we should rob
something and make a lot of money doing it."

"How middle class, Del Plato. Doesn't that sound middle
class to you?"

"An awful lot of money, J.B. Not this nickel-and-dime extortion we do, with a hundred dollars here and two hundred there. Enough of that. Let's think big now. I'm very serious."

It was already hot. Del Plato shaded his eyes in front of the furniture store and stretched above some gold lettering on the window to look inside. A very large man was in the process of demonstrating to a customer the tubes of pink neon light hidden below a platform bed. When you pressed a button, the bed glowed like a spacecraft that could defy gravity.

"I've been tossing around some ideas with Hooven," Del said. "I really need some confrontation. With all this routine, I'm going nuts. I need a score."

"Hooven. Wonderful."

"The man has these connections. We rely on him enough as it is, so there's no point talking that way. Whether we like it or not, we need him."

"Yeah," said Breed, "but even those eyes of his. There's something there, Irish, and I can't stand it. A sneakiness or something. You ever notice? What's the word I'm looking for?"

Del was still shading himself from the sun. "Sneaky," he said. "Shifty. Untrustworthy. I don't know." He checked the street for innocent bystanders.

"Come on, it's similar to shifty. Help me out." Breed also took a peek inside the furniture store. He had been improving his word power through the *Reader's Digest.* In the glove compartment of their patrol car, Jewboy Breed kept a pocket dictionary along with his stomach pills and gum and maps. *"Furtive,"* Breed said after a moment. "That's it. *Furtive.* Fucking furtive eyes. That weasel look."

"It's so easy to criticize. I don't understand your attitude with Hooven, I really don't. It's you, J.B. You're the one with an attitude problem. We have a business relationship with the man, it's simple as that."

"I can't stand the sleaze. Is that equally simple or what? Joe Hooven. *El Slimo.* With those furtive fucking weasel eyes."

They opened the door to Happy Harry's Decor Discounts and a bell in the shape of an orange tinkled gently. Del Plato patted his wallet and his badge and entered first. Happy

Harry was seated with his customer, fooling around with buttons on a pocket calculator. "Fiddler on the Roof" played from a floor sample. Enormous wall units of Formica, chrome and glass, wicker and Lucite, made for long thin aisles and little to steal.

"Don't talk to me about the wood family," Happy Harry was telling his customer in a gruff voice. "This is Florida. In Florida you want your Formica, your chrome and glass, your wicker, your Lucite. Pardon me for being blunt, but face reality. Gents, don't go away; I'll be with you momentarily. You know what wood does in this climate? I'll tell you. Wood warps. It chips, it splits, it cracks, it rots. Come back when you're ready to buy and face reality—do us both a favor—because right now I see no sale."

Happy Harry weighed at least two hundred and eighty pounds and his hands looked like they could crush small change. He had a very pleasant smile. A picture of himself with that same pleasant smile was taped above the cash register. It had him in profile, with his eyes wide and his teeth pressed together as though he had been caught after a piece of food had fallen from his mouth. On each furniture price tag was a smaller Happy Harry photo.

"And when you finally decide to face reality, I'll make it easy for you to buy. I'll take cash from any country. I'll accept Visa, Master, Sears, I don't care. I'll take postage stamps. Ha, ha. Forget wood. This is Florida. Live like a Floridian."

When his customer had left and the front door had closed and the bell in the shape of an orange had stopped tinkling, Happy Harry hummed along to the radio as he walked across his showroom floor to where Del Plato and Breed were examining color schemes on a huge credenza.

Lately, Happy Harry had been having trouble locating customers with ready cash to spend. He talked to people in restaurants and in the sauna, and everybody had stories—some oil-rich South American, or the British, or a man as plain as you or me who had one day filled a twenty-foot cabin cruiser with narcotics and now went around buying Lamborghinis and five-bedroom numbers on the Intracoastal with an Adidas satchel filled with green. Happy Harry was still optimistic whenever someone opened his door, but mostly what he had been seeing were old people from Lansing or young couples already behind on their finance payments. Even his South American buyers were on a fixed income. As he took a close look at his next customers—Del catching a quick snooze and Jewboy picking chocolate from his teeth—Happy Harry decided that these two were not carrying Adidas bags of money either.

Del Plato spoke first. "I'm Officer Laurel, and this is Officer Hardy. Let me get right to the point. Why don't we go back there to your personal office, sir, where the telephones ring? Why don't we do that right now? My partner will lock the front door for just a little while."

"My office? Well, my office, gents, what a mess . . ."

"We're fully aware what kind of mess. We also know that you run a half-sheet bookie operation for Tommy Parrajo. We know exactly what kind of activity moves through here. I realize, sir, this is quite a shock to you, but let's take one step at a time for now and everything may not be so bad as you might imagine."

Breed said, "I never knew that before about wood. Gail is always polishing, and we never had a problem ourselves, so that really throws me there, with wood. I would never suspect." Breed pulled open various drawers, just nosing around. "When I get home, Happy Harry, for sure I'm checking out this wood theory more thoroughly."

Happy Harry leaned against a sturdy piece of furniture and crossed his legs, as if he wanted to appear adult about this thing. In a serious tone he explained to Breed that the humidity did it to wood, the constant humidity. Also he said he didn't know what in the world they were talking about.

"Stay calm," Del Plato told him, "act casual." Del also had his legs crossed and was leaning on furniture. They looked like men discussing T-bills, or fluctuations in the prime rate. Del snapped open his wallet to flash his shield. "Now let's see that back room. Please."

Happy Harry stood his ground. "I'm in the furniture

business. Let me get this off my chest. For thirty years I've worked ten hours a day, six days a week. I did a condo for Buddy Hackett and for an entire Central American junta. The wives of the generals even sent me letters. They exchanged recipes with my wife." Happy Harry spoke firmly, although the color had completely drained from his face as if some kind of elementary-school science project had just taken place. "This field is my life. Don't make hasty mistakes with me, gents. I'm not a greenhorn refugee, and I'm not without influence. In my time I've very possibly done custom selections for your superior officers. I'm a hardworking man and I deserve better. Besides, don't you need a search warrant?"

Breed excused himself and walked away to lock the front door. Del Plato wanted to know if Happy Harry had the slightest idea of what a search warrant looked like.

"I sell furniture. Go talk to Jordan Marsh or Levitz if you want to show off. They don't have blood pressure and pills under the tongue like I got."

Del Plato drummed his fingers on a TV stand of Lucite, currently reduced from three hundred dollars. "You still don't know how lucky you are," Del said quietly. "Other Metro law enforcers would come in here, and they would do something drastic to get your attention. Without doubt. I've seen it happen." Del removed his car keys and carefully scratched his initials into the TV stand. "Drastic measures, sir. But we're not like that, Officer Hardy and myself, and you should be more appreciative."

"What are you doing?" asked Happy Harry, checking the price tag of his ruined merchandise. "Is that nice, what you just did?"

"You have some aspirin?" Del asked him. "I've got this headache now that's right on the verge of getting much worse. For some reason I'm not myself today."

"I told everybody Miami Beach," moaned Happy Harry. "Miami Beach. Sun, the ocean, dog races."

"Another thing I was curious about," Breed added as he came back down a narrow aisle, "although this is probably a funny request. But I feel I can talk liberally to you. Is Happy your *real* first name, or is that just a nickname? I assume it's a

nickname, but the reason I ask, because there's Happy Rocke-
feller, Happy Chandler, and I'm curious if that happens to be
a genuine first name."

The furniture man fidgeted. His smile was exactly the
same smile as the smile on his pictures.

"Not that we would necessarily give our child a name like
Happy," Breed pointed out, "but Gail and I agree it's good to
know what's available—which names are coming back and
what are the possibilities. We plan on having a family very
soon."

"Congratulations," said Happy Harry. "There's nothing
like children."

Del Plato took advantage and was already at Happy
Harry's office desk in the back room. Two ladies with telephones sat behind a Plexiglas partition. Del nodded hello. One
lady had dark-red curly hair and the other lady had light-red
curly hair. Del was browsing through incriminating yellow
legal pads as Breed joined him with Happy Harry.

Thinking about what a professional he was already—a
young age and what hadn't he seen at least once—Del Plato
gave some serious consideration to Breed's notion of an attitude problem. Maybe Del had an attitude problem. Maybe it
was his damn attitude, always looking to come out ahead, always unsurprised. Maybe he would have to get his attitude in
gear.

It was not an easy time for him. Obviously he wasn't himself. He had taken crisis intervention at the academy and
knew for a fact he was undergoing a difficult transition. People hurled themselves from terraces and drank Clorox because
of what he was going through. When Denise was asleep each
night at nine o'clock and then out of the house all day, Del
realized something was up. He sensed some drama unfolding
in their relationship. She changed her hairstyle and left him
notes on the refrigerator: BUY WINE. FIX THE DISPOSAL. WON'T
BE BACK. But what was he supposed to do? They had never
been much for those involved and wrenching dialogues. They
had always gotten along.

He had first met Denise at the airport, where she was applying for a job and he was in training for full-time duty. They went to a cafeteria for Jell-O with fruit slices and were married two months later. For nine years they had been sensitive enough to each other's looks and pauses and carefully worded reproaches—"Do you think that's a good idea, hon?"—so what was he supposed to say when she all of a sudden wrote notes and gave him looks? Denise flew to Quebec with Keri and called him from her father's factory to say that the kid would have to miss school, Del would have to pick up stuff from the cleaner's and eat out a lot.

Small sacrifices were probably in order, unspoken agreements. Del Plato felt he could handle it. He was ready to be accommodating, apologetic as well, ready to get the ball rolling on some reconciliation. But Denise came back from Quebec and changed the locks on him, and before he knew what was going on he was in a Days Inn with Green Stamps luggage and nothing on TV. She had an entire game plan to work against him. And in the motel room Del Plato felt for the first time a tremendous weight of lonesomeness, a lump just sitting there in his stomach, heavy and sad, like one of those half-sunk warships in Pearl Harbor. A number of times Del repeated to himself how lonesome he was, so he wouldn't overlook the significance of his situation. His wife had left him. *I'm so lonesome, I'm so lonesome.* Then, feeling even worse that first night in the Days Inn, Del sat up suddenly on a corner of the empty bed and went through some exceptionally emotional shudders that completely bewildered him. What the hell was going on? He thought he was coming down with something— an early stroke, or a nerve disease that had been dormant all this while inside his genes, where no one could see it. Del pressed his wrist to his forehead and shook some more, and then fell into an audible stage, where he let loose strange gaspings and unbidden sounds that also worried him no end. What was it? Jesus. Crying was something Del Plato never did, not ever, and it was so hard for him now. Choked harsh sobs came out, like someone was squeezing him from behind with one of those techniques when food is stuck in the wrong pipe. Was this the way people behaved when they were low? It was awful.

But then Del stopped the whole thing almost as soon as it had begun. He figured that just what the hell was this anguish anyway if not a loser's attitude. Right? It was the way a loser would face up to some strife.

Cut it out, Del Plato, he had to tell himself after a few terrible groans. *Cut this crap right now.*

The furniture man, in the back of his store, was meanwhile assessing the pros and cons and it looked to him like he was in for it now. Happy Harry admitted his guilt. "At this point, gents, I'm offering no resistance. You got me. But I'll have one question to ask, and please be honest when you give me an answer. If I go to jail, will I lose my eight percent mortgage?"

"I see a count or two of illegal betting," Del Plato said stonily. "I see conspiracy of bookmaking."

"I'm on the board of directors of my condominium," sighed Happy Harry. "They'll let guests walk around with no wrist tags if I'm not there, they'll vote for a kiddie pool. You can't arrest me, gents. Maybe I'm guilty, but I have dining rooms to deliver. I paid in advance for a gambling junket to Freeport. I can't leave yet."

Breed was also looking through yellow pads, examining point spreads. He used to bet football heavily, but had to let it go when he found himself able to name the starting backfield and head coach in each major conference, college and professional, and also give you a team's percentage against the odds line. He read tout sheets and devised new statistics instead of eating. Breed threw himself into projects, developing obsessions the way other people develop the mumps—something he would surrender to entirely at first, but then battle back and defeat, and eventually become immune to forever. Previously Breed had been through serious bouts with the martial arts, vitamins, hi-fi, chain letters, and gourmet cooking.

On Happy Harry's desk were scattered sports sections, underlined teams, a list of phone numbers, a blackboard with dollar figures.

Happy Harry had been trying to monitor the expression

on Del Plato's face. He was at the same time trying to place his
hand over evidence with which they could murder him in a
courtroom. Happy Harry appeared dazed. He was dwelling
over this run of bad luck. He was getting old people and factory workers and now police, and none of the international
trade, none of the big spenders. He had location, the right
prices; he advertised. But he was in no position to refuse when
hoodlums had approached him to make book and offered him
a telephone with ten buttons. A man had to make a living,
after all.

"At one time I had a decent business back north," Happy
Harry explained to the out-of-uniform officers. "Everybody
asked me what I was moving to Florida for. In Florida everybody's on vacation, I told them. Terrific tans, good pizza and
seafood, those tiny swimsuits. Automobiles stay clean. I saw a
Miami like in the postcards."

"This is not such a serious business," Del Plato said in the
way of consolation. "We're reasonable guys, if you give us the
chance."

"But ambulances every five minutes, two-hour waiting
lines on every golf course, waterfront property you can't
touch. That's also Florida." Happy Harry still had a faraway
glaze over his eyes. "Every month a hundred and fifty dollars
for the electric bill. And try to wait for a bus."

There was a brief, uneasy silence. Air conditioning
droned, lights hummed. "The Impossible Dream" came on, an
all-strings instrumental.

"Once you start with handcuffs, my car is not worth two
cents," said Happy Harry. He was making sad noises, as a
person would whose grocery bag had just fallen apart in the
street. "My wife is a wonderful person, but she doesn't know
about oil. She never heard of battery water."

Finally Breed stepped forward to explain the situation
plainly. "Here's the deal, Happy. What we would like is a
bribe. Something in the way of a comfortable payoff, to put
things in a nutshell. Got that?"

"Five hundred dollars a month sounds reasonable," Del
Plato told the furniture man. "Think of it as another rent

payment. Call up Tommy Polio, and tell him that Officer Laurel and Officer Hardy were here. He knows who we are. Mention the five hundred dollars. Just don't be nervous and don't be foolish, and when we see you next time, we'll be in and out in two seconds. Where do you keep that aspirin?"

Happy Harry took an extra-deep breath. His eyes slowly began to focus. "Nobody takes my fingerprints? Nobody reads me my rights?"

"This is America," Del Plato told him.

Slowly, Happy Harry opened his desk drawer. Del shook two tablets from an aspirin bottle and swallowed them without water.

"Five hundred a month," said Breed, "and if we can work it out, a nice coffee table of some kind. Gail would love a coffee table. Irish, tell me something, Denise ever bug you like that, with interiors and stuff?"

"I have a headache."

"How about you, Happy?" Breed asked. "By the way which one is your wife?"

Happy Harry waved sweetly through the Plexiglas partition, and the lady whose hair was slightly less red waved back with a telephone. "Twenty-seven years next month," said Happy Harry. "For our twenty-fifth anniversary the kids sent us to the Orient for three weeks."

"Lucky dog. Pick out something Gail would like. No wood."

Del Plato examined random sports results. It was always the same. Hooven gave them information, they walked inside, some wheeling and dealing, and that was that. Business. Easy business. Too easy.

"Tell me, gents, what is this called? Does it happen often?"

"A shakedown," Del explained. "We do it once, maybe twice a week, much too often, practically all the time. Ask Mr. Parrajo."

When Del Plato and Breed were outside a few minutes later, the street was empty. The sunlight caught them at a funny angle and threw hollow-gray shadows on the pastel walls behind them. From the road came a dry, metallic down-shift of gears. Trash removal. Breed made a sour face as something came up inside. He pounded his stomach and reached into the pocket of his satin Phillies warm-up jacket for a vial of hydrochloric acid pills, which aided his digestion.

"Gail doesn't know I still eat crap," Breed said. "I don't have the courage to admit it to her—we're on this health binge now. She goes to the supermarket, it's three bags of groceries that cost maybe ten dollars total and there are no preservatives, which is well and good of course, but all that stuff gives me gas. I just wish I could explain it to her. I mean we all live and we die anyway—that's pretty much the way I feel about it—so there's really no rationale for artichokes and steamed celery for dinner. Not in a broader sense."

Del Plato said, "I graduated Southeastern Florida Institute of Criminal Justice, right, top of the class almost, and I had no idea I would take bribes. What went wrong? I put in eight hundred and twenty training hours, and it never once occurred to me that I might be wasting my time. I was first in my class in physical training. I was way up there in written exams; I worked hard." He picked camphor crystals from his pocket. "But now it seems I'm just coasting, and it bothers me.... I'm always in neutral. These days I don't get pumped up. It's not that I'm bored exactly, but I am dissatisfied, and even more than that I don't know what's going on."

"You worry too much," Breed said. He snapped out his nickel-plated Llama .25 to click through each chamber. "You'll be one of those old people who wander in the street with their bedroom slippers on. I can see it coming, Del Plato." His gun had scrollwork on the grips, still slick with oil. Breed idly picked at strands of thread and dirt that clung to the barrel. "What are you telling me, Irish?"

"I was thinking of robbing the jai alai fronton at Olympia," Del said. "I need it. A real heist, a challenge. When I was talking things over with Hooven, just ideas, it seems that he knows someone who used to work there with the money, at Olympia."

"Do me a favor, don't talk to me any more about Joe Hooven. Do that for me. Because he's a condom, your friend is, you know it as well as I do; he's a Baggie. And it's bad enough we have to give him a percentage of these shakedowns, Irish; I will not involve myself in armed robbery with Joe Hooven. I refuse."

Del Plato's eyes had suddenly become fired. "Right here," he said. "All this Florida for us to beat." Del swept his arm in a wide arc. He felt a little foolish with this gesture, but what the hell. A New World explorer might have done the same thing on discovering this land of coconuts and souvenirs. "I'm taking Olympia. I'm stripping it clean. I can do it."

"Beautiful," Breed said. "What's with this winning shit all of a sudden?"

Chips of glass and bits of shattered asphalt glittered in the sun. Across the road and beyond the dry palms and the high-rise developments was the ocean. Del caught a glimpse of it between buildings and he could picture the rest, red and white sails on the flat blue water, a short stretch of sand, fast billowing clouds. And birds, circling birds, and slow waves to tumble gracefully and run up on the beach. All this Florida, right here.

Breed walked to his car on the corner and got inside. Del walked beside him and leaned on the driver's window. Behind them were low white warehouses, wild orchids, scrub palms sticking up among the Spanish moss and pampas grass that rimmed the service road, and thick weeds that milked when they snapped.

"I'm seeing a doctor now, Irish. My tongue." Breed rolled down his window. His car had a maroon interior and a steering-wheel cover to match. Barry Manilow came on the tape deck. "You know what really gets me, Del Plato? That Gail has such a sharp sense of smell. It's so weird; it kills me that she knew what it was right away. I give my wife an awful lot of credit."

Del was wrestling with responsibility. He knew what he was doing. Did he know what he was doing? Olympia. Money. Unfamiliar territory within him itched for the robbery, for weapons and hot-blooded action, drawing him toward a payoff the way shreds of metal are drawn to a magnet, the way old people home in on the section for day-old bread.

"Tonight I'm meeting a nurse," Breed said, picking at the maroon-colored steering-wheel cover. "Some busy schedule I have. This one likes to give enemas. I don't know what it is, but all these women with problems find me attractive."

Del Plato said, "I'll repeat myself. I'm drawing up plans with Hooven to rob Olympia Jai Alai Fronton. I'd like you to be there, Breed. It could net us maybe sixty thousand each if we do it right."

Breed turned down Barry Manilow. "Not with the Baggie. No way. I have to decline on this one. You know what I'm saying? Because he's the kind of prick who knows bits and pieces of enough languages to bum a cigarette from just about anyone in the world. And we don't need that."

"You get married," Del said, after a moment of deliberation, "you raise the family, that much I know. You don't wear stripes with checks, you don't send cash through the mail—I understand all that. But still I want to rob this jai alai. With you or without you, J.B. What is it? What's wrong?"

Breed said, "Is this going to be a while? I'll shut the engine."

"Do you know what I'm talking about?"

"I have no idea."

"It's really something," Del said, "isn't it?"

"Maybe I see your point, Irish. What you're saying is that you're fucked up." Breed was watching a girl walk by. "Anyway, with my nurse later, what do you think? Should I ask if she has a friend?"

Del Plato just looked at him.

"Yes?"

Del was wondering what he had to do today. Wash the car, buy socks.

"No? Make a decision, Irish."

Del Plato curled his fingers over the rolled-down window. "I'm going to ask you something serious. When Gail makes a salad, does she sometimes give you lettuce that's brown on the edge? You know what I mean? Or does she throw that part away? I'd like to know."

"Sure, brown lettuce. You're in some mood."

"It's all these little things. I mix up my wines for instance. Bordeaux, Burgundy, I'm always on the spot. That mean something to you?"

"It means you're a head case, Del Plato." Breed was covering his eyes. "I see it clearly. Lettuce is brown and you have this trouble with wine, so you turn to robbery. Makes sense."

"I come out terrible in photographs. That's what I'm saying. I get lousy seats in the theater."

Del Plato shielded his eyes from the glare and glanced around him. He was searching for something concrete, something definite, something he would probably recognize—no, definitely recognize—if only he could find it. An explanation, a reason. It was so hard to tell.

Breed said, "How's this? I been going to the same mechanic now for a few years. The other day I run short of cash and go to give the guy a check, and he still asks me for two pieces of ID. How fucking annoying is that? Am I on the right track, Del Plato?"

Blinding sunlight bounced off the tinted glass of newly leased real-estate offices and beauty salons off West Dixie. Del took note of what was there. A florist, discount shoes. Electrolysis and blank windows. It was the same in Perrine, in Hialeah, through Boca and Jupiter. Chattahoochee patios and the stony stucco fronts of buildings. Florida.

"I follow your drift now," Breed was saying, warming up to things as he played with the fine-tuning controls of his tape deck. "I'm talking lettuce and personal checks here, and other stuff too. Wine, for example." Breed drummed his fingers on the steering wheel and was having a good time. "I love it, Del Plato. I'm eating this up."

Del started to walk away toward his own car.

"Figure out a way to screw Hooven. I'd join you then."

"I need to do something already. I'm going crazy."

"Me and you," Breed was saying, "basically we're the same, Irish. You work hard and so do I. We're the same. You veg out in front of the tube at night, a little marital discord . . . Am I right or what? But Hooven is different. He sleeps till noon, Joe Heavy; he orders food in French. His fucking sunglasses cost more than my best suit."

"I don't intend to get caught, J.B. I don't intend to louse

up on this heist or to lose, whether you're with me or not.
When I was a baby, my mom put me in this baby contest and
even then I came away on top. I've been winning and pushing
ever since."

"More winning shit." Breed fired up his car and began to
inch away. "What's with that? I don't understand."

"The point is," said Del Plato, "the point is that I'll always have to deal with lettuce that's brown along the edge, I
realize that. I see my future. I'll always come out bad in snap-
shots. But still I've got to do something. I have to try."

Breed nodded and stared and shrugged. Then he drove
away. Del Plato remained for a moment on the deserted sidewalk.

They would go for it. He walked across the street and
started his push-button Dodge. As Del Plato drove away
slowly, that's what he was thinking—*they would go for it.*
Himself, Breed, Hooven. They could pull it off. Why not?
Why shouldn't they? It could be done. Absolutely.

He turned up a wide street, which looked to Del Plato as
though it might lead him to some major, recognizable road.
But there was construction going on, with orange pylon cones
and mechanical arms waving safety flags, and soon Del had no
idea where he was going. Which direction was south? Where
was he? Street names were totally unfamiliar, every corner
was named after some president—McKinley Court, Taft Terrace, Tyler Place—like a lousy history quiz. And the commu-
nities made no sense. Lakeview Villas. Red Bridge Estates. He
saw no lake, no damn bridge, no easy way out.

It hadn't been a good day. Del made a sudden, screeching
left turn for no apparent reason. He took another street, pushing the gas. When he didn't know where he was going, he
drove faster. The radio off, two hands on the wheel, relying on
speed and intuition to get him back.

Chapter
2

Monkey cages were fixed up with silver garlands and angels and little Christmas lights that blinked from red and orange to blue and orange. *This is nice,* Del Plato told himself, looking around the park. He took a good grip on his daughter's hand, and they watched the flashing lights, red and orange, blue and orange. They were visiting Monkey World, and Del was reading off information from a small wooden sign posted in front of a cage of gray monkeys, brown monkeys, and sullen monkeys that looked like they were not going to buy all this holiday spirit, no way.

Del told his daughter the monkeys eat red berries. They reproduce in captivity, and in some parts of the world are considered a delicacy. How about that? He asked if she were hungry. She said she had no appetite, thank you.

This is nice, Del Plato said to himself again. He checked the time on his Fako watch and looked around once more for Hooven. He was wearing his T-shirt that said I DO NOT BRAKE FOR ANIMALS. What had he done with Keri before this business of getting together every other weekend? Washed the car with her, pulled weeds. The park was nice for a change.

A Santa Claus jogged by in running clothes. He pointed this out to Keri. Wasn't that cute?

A guard with a bullhorn said not to touch any of the monkeys or throw objects. The guard's face had a bored look that seemed as if it would never go away, and square stubbled cheeks right out of the Flintstones. He was wearing a rumpled khaki uniform and a pith helmet. One look and Del Plato had the man pegged. An ex-cop. What else? Of course the guard was bored; of course he needed a shave. The poor sucker owned a station wagon, a quarter acre off some muddy canal, right, a teenage kid who had drug problems and problems with spelling. To Del Plato this was all perfectly clear. A few stocks, no accidents or moving violations in the past three years, a dentist appointment only when something hurt.

Myself in ten years, Del also thought. Couldn't it happen? He closed his eyes and ticked off the arithmetic until retirement. Nine years, five months. An ex-cop. He could also dress up like Rama of the Jungle and warn you not to touch any monkeys or throw objects.

Del checked the time once again, searched the crowd for Hooven, and also reminded himself not to be so impatient and not to be so goddamn nasty about everything. What was with this bitter outlook? Where the hell had that worked its way into his personality?

When he was younger he had been a good-natured guy, Del Plato, the best-natured person around, always looking for a pickup game or a part-time job, or some door to hold open for someone else. He would call people long distance just for the hell of it, give pocket money to the less fortunate on every corner. But now he was a cop, and something of a crook, and going through divorce. At times he could almost feel the remaining good nature seep out of him, like air from a slowly leaking tire. How had this happened?

Monkeys in cages were ducking thrown objects. There was too much noise for Del Plato, although nobody seemed to be actually talking, and even the monkeys didn't appear to be doing much when you really looked. They scrambled and chattered and swung around until you caught them at it. Then they stared back mutely, like juvenile delinquents, as if wondering why it was never somebody else who got picked on.

Pausing in the shade of a high bottlebrush tree, Del sneaked another peek at the time. Two o'clock, right. So where was Hooven?

He twisted the green top off a strawberry and handed the strawberry to Keri. She said thank you and placed it in her other hand, where she already had two others. Everywhere there was activity and quick junglelike movement. Not surprising. Del saw it as the type of commotion you could expect in a place where lions or bigger monkeys might suddenly pop up. It was hot and damp, and the trees grew huge, with thick leaves and all sorts of hidden dangers. All these jittery moves—greens and grays and browns together—combined into a surging wave of distraction.

Keri found something interesting inside the cage of rainforest monkeys and kept staring that way. Del looked too. He wanted to take an interest—they would have something educational to talk about. What did she see inside the cage? What did he see?

He noticed Keri was wearing a new polo shirt. It had cowboys on horseback chasing mustangs. Del turned her around so he could look more closely at the pictures—clean-shaven cowboys with smiles like movie stars, colorful horses snorting wildly, lassos. Del gave his daughter one of those smiles like the cowboys had. Her birthday was coming up. Keri would be—what?—seven or eight years old. Go with seven for now. And what could he bring to her party? Or would he even be invited? Possibly not. Possibly it was one of those separation deals where you weren't even invited to a birthday party when your daughter was seven or eight years old. Del pinched off another strawberry and at the same time was wondering who had bought her that shirt. Denise? The new boyfriend? Would a new boyfriend pick out a shirt like that?

They walked to a different cage, surrounded all the while by shrieks and monkey yells, and flashes of monkeys swinging among the branches. Tails, feet, teeth, fur. He let Keri hold the box of strawberries while he felt around for something to give his daughter. Suddenly he felt fatherly, overwhelmed with this wrenching burst of fatherliness and concern for his little girl. Was she getting enough green vegetables? Was she hanging around with the wrong crowd? He saw her in this terrible vision of nine-year-olds, who would play with matches and mispronounce words, and carry those big radios, and spit. He felt nervous and more than a little empty, the way he figured other fathers probably felt when they were living alone in large rented houses and could see their children only once in a while. What would Keri remember about him anyway? That he took her to Monkey World?

When she was younger, Keri had his complexion and posture, and his way of taking things without asking. Now she was picking up her mother's features and was polite as well— how had that happened? Del Plato felt another part of him drifting away.

What could he give her? Del looked down at his clothes and then fumbled around inside his pocket. What? Finally he came up with a twenty-dollar bill and a bullet and a packet of mints, which he pressed into Keri's free hand. She had strawberries in the other.

"What's this for?"

"Just to have."

"Thank you, Daddy," Keri said, and put everything in a small beaded purse she wore over her shoulder.

He kneeled and picked up his daughter to give her one of the old up-in-the-air powerful squeezes that would leave her breathless with his love. She hugged him in return, trying not to get any strawberry on him, but the brief contact wasn't enough, not for the emotion he was feeling right then. Keri had given him a hug that was over there on the anemic side. Right? He pinned it as a hug her mother would give. It was the type of greeting for some fairly close relative you met at weddings and funerals. Maybe also to a father who didn't know where to take you on a Saturday.

Del thought of Denise, and for the moment he could picture her perfectly, wearing a simple white blouse, nothing special at all, but on Denise it looked terrific. He imagined her as a photograph, framed above his stereo or stuck on the refrigerator door by some cookie-shaped magnet, like Keri's better schoolwork. She had a very smart forehead, Denise did, a forehead which gave the appearance of a lot of brains on the other side. But lines were beginning to show—is that why she was giving him the boot?—and for what, what did she always worry about? About all the wrong things. That's the way Denise was, and had always been, and much chance Del Plato had of changing anything.

Even when they were in their rush to get married, two displaced people caught up in a strange climate, she made a ton of calls to her father in Montreal, but only to ask about factory workers and the weather, and how the Canadiens' defense was holding up. It was infuriating to Del Plato, now that he thought back to some of her early concerns. After all, something had hit him very hard right there in the airport cafeteria, amid the orange and turquoise seats and the sugar packets with pictures of vegetables and airplanes. He had taken a good look at this person sitting across from him—with her smart forehead and pretty eyes—and he knew right away this was a potential wife for him, this Denise from up north who was looking for work. Her hair was in some knot that probably took time and quick wrists in order to get just right, and Del also loved the idea that girls from Detroit would never know how to braid their hair in this French-bread fashion. She was a quick eater and he was too—so much in common. She liked the Jell-O and the little pieces of fruit wiggling inside. They both always seemed to be in a hurry, and had a mutual mistrust of nuns, dating back to experiences in parochial school. And just like that they were together in South Florida. They tried some restaurants, learned the names of streets and incorporated towns, and then they went to City Hall for a license—the two of them swept up in a confusion of romance, and a mix-up of space and time and new careers, not quite comfortable in this busy coast of sunset and sailboats and high-rise condos unless they were with one another.

So what had she been worried about all the time? Why all the anxiety? It was her enthusiasm that got to Del Plato more than anything else, and hurried him to get married. Sure, he had just met her, he was still a trainee cop, he hadn't even started on a Florida suntan, but what about this boundless spirit with which he was eating Jell-O? You didn't run across that every day, and maybe not more than one single time in your whole entire life. The way she leaped at things and was so pleased with her decisions, like what she chose to wear or order or which movie to see.

Separated for three months now, he was still overcome at times with that bounciness Denise had brought with her everywhere. It touched him, the way light from a fizzed-out star still spills through the sky. She was so happy to get pizza with extra cheese. How many people could be like that?

Keri worked her way out of his grip and stuffed her cheeks with strawberries. Del Plato was mopey, thinking that even after a marriage has gone sour there were parts of it you couldn't do anything about. They would survive, like those car batteries that will spark an engine after being frozen or set on fire. *Some things you could not kill. For instance, there was some of the love you felt for a person who no longer wanted to live with you, who sent you out of the house with an embarrassing car and old clothes. Who wouldn't invite you to a daughter's birthday party. Who was taking up with some goddamn boyfriend.*

Through his sunglasses, the glare was still strong. An ice-cream cart was pedaling past, and Del Plato flagged it down. The boy selling ice cream wore a camouflage suit and a pith helmet.

"How about a cone?" Del called to his daughter.

"I don't want."

He turned to the ice-cream boy and ordered two Popsicles.

"Daddy, I don't want."

"She don't want. Change our order to toasted almond, Jungle Jim. Two of them."

"Dad-dy."

Del wiped his sunglasses with a napkin from the ice-cream cart. He unwrapped his toasted almond bar and ate it in huge bites while Keri drifted away from him toward a high cage with skinny monkeys inside. Eating ice cream, Del tossed around the idea of whether or not he was having a good time. *Yes, I'm having a good time. No, I'm not having a good time.* Either way he tried to think of someplace he might rather be, but nothing came to mind. He checked out a few of the skinny monkeys that were rolling around in the hard dirt or dozing, and if these were distant cousins to the general public, Del figured that was reason enough to take these monkeys into secret labs and pump them full of nicotine and birth-control pills and Pepsi. Whatever went on was okay. Big fish eat little fish, right? He was already thinking hard about where to take Keri on their next Saturday; he was getting impatient with the time.

He asked Keri just how old she was.

"Seven. I'll be eight on my birthday."

The Monkey World park smelled of popcorn and spilled soda and animals. A monorail glided overhead, humming with high voltage. Inside another cage with twinkling lights on the outside bars, some monkeys swung from an automobile tire that was hanging by a steel chain. Keri was standing beside the cage. A monkey with a bitten tail stuck its hand through some wide metal grating and gave Keri one of those zoo stares. Right away she hustled herself away from its reach, but then Del was over in an instant to nudge his daughter close to the bars again. She was just staring back at the monkey.

"Go ahead, Keri. It won't bite." She pushed back against Del Plato. "It's okay, I'm here. Come on."

Finally she fed the monkey a strawberry. The monkey immediately held out its rubber paw for another.

"No more," Keri said. Suddenly she began to cry. She jiggled the box of strawberries just out of the monkey's grasp.

Del didn't know what was going on. Was she crying? "Come on," he said, "what's this teasing? Nobody taught you to do that."

"Well, I don't like it to touch my fingers." She hid the strawberries behind her back and made angry faces at the monkey. She told the monkey to take a hike. "Stop doing that," she said. The monkey's hand was just out there, open and waiting. "Make him stop, Daddy."

Del sat on a concrete bench that had advertising for

splanch homes. The homes were only minutes away from shopping and a bus; now was the time to buy. Beside his shoe a pigeon was pecking at roasted peanut shells.

One at a time, Keri tossed strawberries inside the monkey cage. When there were no more strawberries, she heaved in the empty container. Then she threw in her unopened ice cream.

Del Plato glanced up at the people walking past. He decided nothing was going to get him upset. He could put up with all kinds of stunts from everybody. His wife who had showed him all this enthusiasm and then went to sleep during prime-time TV, his daughter who acted up with monkeys, Breed who was obnoxious, Hooven who was more than an hour late. Del looked at all the baby strollers and Instamatics passing him by in Monkey World, bright faces tilted up to the white sun. For a while he tried to imagine where each passing family might be from. Plaid shorts, thermos coolers, clear plastic bags filled with oranges and orange peels. Wide white belts, white shoes, sunburns the color of lunch meat.

When Keri came back to the bench, Del said, "You're not having a very good time, are you?"

She shrugged. Del wondered what that was supposed to mean. *Yes, I'm having a good time; no, I'm not having a good time.* Keri played with the money Del had given her.

"Next time we could go to Alligator World. They wrestle alligators in the swamp. How's that sound? You could feed your ice cream to the alligators."

"It's okay here," Keri said.

"It's not okay if you're not having tons of fun. Wipe the tears out of your eyes and then tell me you're having tons of fun."

"I don't like it if they touch me. That's creepy."

"Right."

He was thinking that in another few years he might not even recognize her. Keri was probably getting bigger each week, definitely more polite. She was acquiring new clothes and new habits. What would happen? Denise would marry this new dork she was seeing, or a different one, and Del Plato would be left with a few fuzzy photographs and a drinking problem. He'd have a crummy disposition, and almost ten more years on a job where he could get killed or psychologically scarred at any moment and where he was looking at some serious trouble with his back from sitting in a patrol car all day.

Keri rested beside him on the stone bench. Sunlight worked its way through the interlocking vines and branches above them, viburnum and black olive, and small white tree petals floated down with a breeze. They watched a few gorillas lumber about slowly, scratching and stretching inside their cages, and still more or less looking like folks you might hug weakly at a wedding or funeral.

"Mommy said you'll always be my father."

"Makes sense. I would expect her to say that, or something like that. Me always being your father is just the kind of thing your mommy would say." He searched his daughter's face for any features of himself. "It's a nice thing to say, I suppose. Although I can see what's coming next."

"Ethan said the same thing to me."

Del Plato turned away. He was up against an Ethan. *Who had a name like Ethan?* "Sounds to me, kid, like just the kind of thing your mother would tell this guy to say. You get that feeling too?"

Keri shrugged and continued looking down.

"What's his name again?"

"Ethan."

"You like him?"

"Sure."

"Right. What else are you going to say? What does he buy you?"

"Things." Keri swung her feet back and forth and began to pay attention to some scuff marks on her sneakers. "For Christmas I got a hundred-dollar gift certificate in a sports-stuff store, and they give you a free key ring and something else. I got a football with somebody's name on it. I got new blue sneakers with white stripes—they're at home because mommy doesn't want me to wear them yet. And he teaches me how not to throw like a girl."

Del nodded. Sounded like a reasonable guy. He wondered how you would go about murdering someone like that. Run him over? The push-button Dodge might not make it. Rent a car? Del asked his little girl what she was planning to pick out from the sporting-goods store for a hundred bucks. A bike or something?

Del leaned over and put his face up right against hers. Their noses were touching. "How about me, kid? You like me? Think carefully."

"Sure," she said. Keri slipped the sunglasses off his face and tried them on. "You're okay, too, Daddy."

"Also makes sense. I mean I give you twenty dollars for no reason at all, I take you to Monkey World, of course I'm okay." He gave her another one of those beaming smiles and put an arm around her. "And I tell you what. Because I'm your father, and because we all agree I'll be your father forever and always, I'm also buying you another toasted almond bar right now. Fair enough? Am I a great guy?"

Keri giggled and gave him back his sunglasses. She smoothed the hairs on Del Plato's arm and then held his arm.

Del thought, *Life is so funny. The way the old ball bounces.* Everything suddenly seemed so true to him, and important—all these sayings that popped into his head. *The best things in life are free. That's the way the cookie crumbles.*

The pigeon, still pecking at peanut shells, was too close to his foot. Del shook his leg to move it away. He thought he could feel the remaining good nature bubble out of him. Soon he would be thirty-five years old and then forty, and then he would become an ex-cop with Fred Flintstone jowls who told strangers not to touch anything.

He turned his attention to tourists—balloons and beer hats and faces. *Where do these people come from?* Why couldn't they drive better? Keri helped him keep count of all the wide white belts walking past.

He looked down again at the pesky bird by his shoes. Maybe it wasn't even a pigeon. Maybe it was some kind of native wildlife, a sandpiper or an egret or a flamingo, whatever the hell they had down here in South Florida. Del Plato stamped again and the bird hopped away with a flutter.

His heart felt very crowded. It was packed full of emotions and longings, like some sort of colloidal suspension of strong, sad feelings that were probably bouncing into each other and would never settle down. If he tapped his heart, it would thunk like a jar of mayonnaise. *What would an Ethan look like? Not only that, but an Ethan who bought gift certificates with a key ring thrown in for good measure.*

Del smoothed back his hair as Keri slid off the bench, and when she was no more than a few steps away, he suddenly blurted out her name. She turned to see what was up. "Yes?" But Del had no idea why he had called her. His stomach felt hollow. First his heart was too full, and now he was empty, as if some vital organ inside him had decided on a whim to go for a walk. He wanted very much to ask his daughter something, or perhaps Del Plato just wanted to look at her.

At bedtime, whenever he was home, he used to make up stories for Keri—purposeful stories, about the little girl who forgot to put away her tea set, or the lovely young princess who was afraid of the dark. Now Del Plato had to feed monkeys with her, he had to ask how old she was, he had to give her money and crap from his pockets.

"Who bought you that shirt?" Del finally asked. Keri looked down at herself to see what he was talking about. "Did Ethan buy you that neat shirt?"

"I don't know."

"Did he get you that for Christmas?"

"Mommy picks out what I should wear. . . . Daddy, can monkeys be allergic to strawberries? We have this boy in class who used to live in Boston and his mother had to come because he traded lunches and it had strawberries inside."

One of the guys he played hoops with at the gym, Medlow, had divorced his wife and then got married again to the same woman. Was that out of the question? Medlow told the gym regulars he had done it for tax purposes—his accountant had advised the idea—but no basketball player believed a word of it. Fast Calvin on the other hand got married to someone else who did a better job of ironing his shirts and had Johnny Walker waiting for him any time he got home, and no questions. Bigfoot got divorced and stayed divorced. James Lloyd, who had lost weight, was getting divorced and was staying divorced.

Keri meanwhile watched the pattern of flashing Christmas lights—red and orange, blue and orange. How good could this business be for her? How many guys could she call her daddy? At least she might get some better grandparents out of the deal—there was a bright side for Keri. Denise's father sent twenty-dollar toys or returnable clothing on every occasion, which was probably fine for someone who lived in Montreal and said over and over he had no desire to die in a plane or travel for two days just to see a daughter and granddaughter whom he could as easily speak to every Sunday morning on the telephone. But Del's own father wasn't even in the picture for Keri. She had seen Grandpa Del Plato and the second wife only one time, when Del's dad had called up out of the blue to say he had a mobile home now in Lakeland, where the Tigers held spring training, and was in town to see an exhibition game against the Yankees, those bastards. Could he at least see his grandchild one time? So what could Del do? He couldn't say no. And then what? Not a toy, not a crocheted sweater for the kid, not even box seats. Maybe she would luck out this time with grandparents. Folks who gave a name like Ethan would very likely come to birthday parties and chip in toward a decent education.

Del closed his eyes and leaned his head toward the sky, a little bored and as impatient as ever. He stared directly into the sun for a few long seconds, daring himself. It was a stupid thing to do, staring into the sun. His eyes got hot, and in his vision the sun became indistinct, moving around up there inside a haze, slipping this way and that like a pop-up in a tricky wind. He was a family man and he wasn't, a cop and also a crook, a good guy and not really such a good guy. When he opened his eyes and shut them, everything took on a sort of lavender hue. It was like the smoky light inside some nightclub with topless girls and a comic, and Del even had those little pops of flashbulbs going off.

Life is funny, Del repeated to himself. *That is so true, so absolutely right. And God helps those who help themselves. A walk is as good as a hit.* Everything he could think of was wisdom, the experience of generations. Human beings were smart and they knew smart things, and they said smart things to each other, things that would hold water after years and years. *No taxation without representation. What goes up must come down.*

He spotted Joe Hooven then, finally, on his way to the bench where Del was sitting alone.

Who else but Hooven? Long blond hair that was shiny and flat, linen slacks, big sunshades with a pastel frame and somebody's initials. Only Hooven. Del made a big point of tapping his Fako watch as soon as Joe Hooven sat down beside him.

"I'm late? Tell me about it," Hooven said in the way of an answer. "With traffic now?" He slouched entirely too low on the bench, in some kind of loose and sullen posture that Del Plato simply wasn't in the mood for. Then Hooven asked if everything had gone smoothly with the furniture, hitching up his linen slacks so they wouldn't stick to his legs in the heat. "You look like a tourist, man; I just now noticed. Put a little white junk on your nose, hey, you'd be perfect."

"It's Joe Hooven," Del said after a while. He was hoping the conversation would not continue this way. He felt some more of his good nature blow away in a puff. "Hello, Joe Hooven."

"Man's on a bench, catching up on some rays, unbelievable." Hooven looked at Del Plato for approval. He decided not to push it. Del was a decent guy, but sometimes he got into these funky spells and then the man could not take a joke at all. One time he owed Del Plato a few dollars, no big deal, and when he tried to pay it off with bootleg cassettes of Barry Manilow, the man right away went into a funk. "What's with this Monkey World?" Hooven wanted to know. "Look at this, I got monkey shit on my good shoes."

"I'm here with my little girl."

"A little girl? Hey, no shit, I didn't know that." Hooven immediately snapped out of his slumping posture and smoothed back his hair, as though he were about to be intro-

duced. Putting his hands in his hair was Hooven's way of
showing a keen interest in things. Whenever he was excited, he
went for his hair, which had been shoulder length or longer
ever since the time someone had asked him after a fill-in gig if
he was with Steely Dan or the Allmans. He washed it every
day with herbal shampoo. Long hair also made him look laid
back, Hooven thought, and sort of gentle, like a folk singer.
People wouldn't figure he had a gun. "Which kid is yours?" he
asked Del Plato. "I never see you as like a family man."

Hooven put his hands into the pockets of his linen slacks
as Del Plato pointed out Keri. She was getting braver on her
own. She shook hands with a monkey and then smelled her
hand afterward.

"Cute girl. Really, what a doll. I got a kid too, a little
dude. Bet you never knew that, man." Hooven jiggled loose
change as he spoke, and collapsed again into that slouch.
"Must be four years old now. Me and the old lady got into like
various directions and all. They're living in Houston now, I
think. What's her name, your little girl? Kids are so great."

"Keri."

"That's fine. Mine's Jagger."

Hooven had very bright yellow hair, hair that a child
would draw with yellow crayons. On the middle finger of his
guitar hand, he wore a ring that had a gold unicorn with ruby
eyes and a small diamond mouth. "We named him when I was
like involved with my music and shit. For Mick Jagger?"

Del Plato pulled some crisply rolled bills from his back
pocket. He rested against the concrete bench and stretched his
arms and at the same time passed the money.

Hooven discreetly palmed the bills and fitted them into
the pocket of his linen slacks. Then he reached for his wallet
and removed a baby picture for Del Plato to look at. In the
picture, Hooven's kid was asleep on somebody's lap, wearing
tiny moccasins and holding a celery stalk.

"Looks like O.J. Simpson," Del Plato said.

"Nah, looks like me, man."

Hooven had been living with the same cute girl for five
years, off and on, on and off, but after the baby was born and

she suggested it might be a good idea for them to get the piece of paper which made it okay for the rest of society, Hooven all of a sudden got cold feet. Not that what she wanted was unexpected or without reason. After all, he had coached her through the hard times and right through delivery. He had kept her away from wine and tobacco and salted pretzels; he had tried to be sociable with husbands who were present at breathing classes; he had been good.

But then Hooven started to pick fights with her for no reason. He just did not want to get married. In his scheming way, he hoped she would eventually have enough of his senseless bickering and then cry a whole lot and leave. It would be a clean if slightly bitter separation. He criticized the way she heaped things in a supermarket basket without comparing prices, the way she served Red Zinger tea before the water had completely boiled.

This went on for months. Entire weekends would pass with him wearing headphones, rolling thick joints, while she ran up the phone bill in another room or picked up on the alpha waves a small child could give off in its crib. At last she clutched Jagger fiercely one day, pushed him into the baby pouch and fitted him on her back, and said she was going to Houston, where her sister had a house and a car she could use. Hooven removed his headphones and gave her $190 and two ounces of pot, which he had set aside for precisely this occasion.

But that last month's phone bill when it came in was enormous, and he called the Houston number to say a thing or two. Actually Hooven was stuck for lyrics on a tune he was writing, brokenhearted times, and he wanted another jolt. Also, he wanted to see how things were coming along. She was fine, Jagger was fine, would Hooven send the makeup case that was in the middle drawer in the bathroom, and also her diaphragm, which was in the drawer below that.

"When I'm rich," Hooven told Del Plato beneath a tree in Monkey World, "first thing I do is buy a farm somewhere, with lots of neat kids all over the place and some together animals, man, ducks and Irish setters, and sheep and shit. Hey, even a few of these baboons. It's what I could really do." He took back the photograph of Jagger as a baby and replaced it in a window of his wallet. "Like the material bullshit is important to me now, per se, but I could settle in with something close to the ground and natural, Del Plato, honestly I could."

Del took off his sunglasses and wiped perspiration from the bridge of his nose. He squinted up toward the sun and asked if Hooven knew anything concrete about Everglades National Park, where the alligators were. It was supposed to be a nice show for children and such.

"Like we go ahead and do the Olympia thing," Hooven continued, his voice rising slightly. "We do it and it's cool. Then I float off on a forty-foot ketch and drift with the sea, man, a couple months of nothing. Screw this money game, this buying and owning shit. Put up the sails and flow with it, man. Be free. A video recorder, some Carta Blanca trailing behind. Del Plato, it would be ideal."

"Well, I don't know about Olympia Jai Alai yet. I like it, Joe, and I don't like it. What I don't like mostly is that nothing is planned, nothing is on paper. I have lots of trouble with abstract ideas, and what I need and what Breed needs before we commit ourselves to anything is a definite blueprint. You have this friend who used to work there, and he knows this much and that much, which is okay to get us this far, right, where we can talk with the possibility of moving ahead. But we're in a different situation, J.B. and myself—we have careers and family ties to consider. And what we have to do is be very certain, or at least reasonably certain, before we walk in and fucking rob a jai alai joint."

"I don't actually know what you're saying. Are you saying I'm like not risking as much? With Tommy Polio? Well, don't say that anymore if you are." Hooven breathed in and out rapidly and brushed back his hair. "We can wax Olympia, man. . . ."

The pigeon or sandpiper or flamingo that was eating peanut shells at Del Plato's feet moved to Hooven and poked around there at crushed soda cups and clumps of gum.

"I also said I like the idea," Del Plato added. "I'm all for something major. I'll just have to ask you to work on the specifics, to map out the actual movements and what we have to do exactly."

"Okeydoke," Hooven said. "I can relate to that."

"Also, there's the fact that Breed hates your guts. We'll have to work on that as well."

Hooven nodded his head at hearing this, and for the moment took on a studious look, as though someone had asked him for directions, or one of those problems involving percentages. "Sounds to me like Breed's tough luck, not yours or mine," Hooven then said. "Although how does he like hate my guts?"

"He just does."

Hooven nodded again. He said that was cool.

Del Plato decided he should be spending more time in the sun. He could almost feel his skin take on a healthy color. All these people coming down, on vacation, investing, eating, purchasing, they had to know something, and this was it. What was the story with South Florida? Whatever they said it was. Sun, number one. And sand, and what they chose to show on postcards—big fish, clean buildings, grapefruits, seashells.

Del Plato asked Hooven what he thought about responsibility, if he ever gave it much thought. "I mean in a general way, Joe. Because lately I've been thinking it over, how we're all getting a little older, how we're not kids now." He blew on his sunglasses and looked at Hooven. "How old are you?"

"Twenty-seven," Hooven said.

"I'm up there too. We're not kids."

"Twenty-five," Hooven said. He was doing arithmetic on the palm of his hand. "For sure we ain't kids. Hey, why do you think I want Olympia? I pump my man, Jackie Molson, who used to work inside Olympia, it's because I see what people sometimes got to do. We all got like responsibilities, man, pressure and shit everywhere we turn. I know that." Hooven shook his head sadly. He twirled his hair around a finger. "I can't believe I'm twenty-five already. And where did I get twenty-seven, where did twenty-seven come from? I caught myself, man, I was fucking that close to being twenty-seven years old. Strange? Unbelievable, I'll tell you."

"I'm resigning from the force," Del Plato said. "Very soon

I'm doing that. I enjoy police work so far, I really do, but it's not for me, not a career. Where's my future? I can describe every day if I stick it out with police work. I know all the things I can do and can't do, everything I can buy and can't buy."

"I'm doing all right for twenty-five," Hooven pointed out. "Look at me. Not too bad. Even if I was twenty-seven, man, even then I'm not too shabby."

"At times I love it," said Del Plato. There was excitement in his own voice and Del Plato was tuned in on that. "There's a lot going. You sniff the air when you're in uniform, and you can get this flavor when there's danger, a special aroma. It happens with me. It smells like dinner. Sometimes you breathe in somewhere, and it can be Chinese food, or Italian. Danger can smell that way, very recognizable and very strong. It fills you up, Joe, the way good cooking does. And I like that. I like to be smart, to be aware of all these secret recipes not everybody knows about."

Hooven bobbed his head from side to side like one of those hula dolls on the backseat of a car. He had no idea what Del Plato was talking about, but to him it sounded honest, and that was all right.

Del Plato was busy thinking how one thing actually does lead to another. Another true saying. Didn't that cover it all? *One little thing leads to another little thing, a big thing leads to a bigger thing.* It was the rock-hard knowledge of humanity. *You live and you learn. Right? Some things were true in the past and would always be true, sticking around for generations, because that's what made the world go round. You get what you pay for. One thing leads to another.*

Del asked if Hooven's ex-girl friend liked living in Houston. Hooven didn't know. He was waiting for a Christmas card.

The park bird returned to Del Plato's feet. Peck, peck, peck. This was without question a pigeon, Del saw that now, absolutely.

"Anyway," he said to Joe Hooven, "smell the air. What does it smell like to you?"

"Monkey shit. I told you, man, I got it all over my good shoes."

"No," said Del Plato. "It smells like danger." He touched his nose. "Remember, I can tell these things."

Hooven sniffed carefully. Then he rubbed his hands and rubbed his face. He wasn't concerned with danger at the moment, or what it smelled like, or any of Del Plato's crap. Hooven was caught up with when he could play in front of a paying audience, when he wore his shirt out of his jeans and nobody had to ask him why his hair was so long, when he could down two of any pill in the world and sound like Morrison, or Rod the Mod, or anyone on the charts.

For some time Hooven had worked on the Lauderdale strip with three other cats who also wore their shirts out of their pants and had lost a lot of weight. They played other group's tunes and did drugs backstage. He felt close to these musicians. They were people Hooven felt he could live on a farm with, or float off with on the ocean's currents. But first one band member dropped out to sell office equipment for a firm that paid him to relocate and gave him a Cordoba. Then the drummer stopped attending sessions, only to show up one day with a seersucker suit, a haircut, a fiancée wearing a two-carat lavaliere, and his own mobile-home dealership in Tucson. These were dudes who had balled complete strangers, who had shared their lines of coke and taken turns picking up the tab in diners. They had sworn to work the earth with their hands and feed the poor and nail some more chicks. They were never going to get married or vote or wear a tie.

Besides Hooven, the only remaining original band member was a dissolute and especially scrawny keyboard player named Trig, who wore guinea T-shirts and the same pair of boots. One time Trig had attempted to get into the *Guinness Book* by eating nine Black Beauties and then playing the Evel Knievel pinball machine for ninety-six consecutive hours. But even Trig admitted he had been taking courses in economics and poli-sci for two semesters. He knew what grain was selling for overseas, and the process by which crude oil was actually broken down into gasoline.

Hooven put on a smile for Del Plato and brought himself up to date. "You're crazy, man," Joe Hooven said, putting two and two together in his own way. "You're ready for Olympia, that's what you're giving me. I'm saying to myself, I'm saying, 'What the fuck is he talking about, with sniffing, with danger?' But now I like see what's coming off next."

Del was still thinking about the connective thread running through all he did. One action logically and pretty much automatically led to another—the chain of events. The limits of right and wrong had simply been stretched. Del Plato shot upright on the bench. He cheated, lied, and took things, but could still consider himself a basically honest man. He would never kill without good cause, for instance, or tailgate, or stiff a waitress. It made so much sense when he concentrated. One thing really followed another.

Joe Hooven folded his arms and said, "I got to ask you something, man. You interested in robbing Olympia? I'm curious."

"I suppose I'm interested," Del answered. "I mean all things considered, I'm still here. Right? I'm talking to you."

"You suppose. What a funny dude. Hey, we could go for Fort Pierce, or Miami even. Only you really got to do more than suppose, man."

"The only drawback," Del said, "when you look at it from my point of view, is why would we want to go into this thing with a hustler and a jerk like you? Nothing personal, Joe, but it's a major obstacle. I mean, it's such a sketchy deal, and how much can we trust you anyway?"

One thing leads to another. The old web of things. I take payoffs as a cop, so I can rob jai alai frontons. Everything is simple.

"For one thing," Hooven was saying to him without malice, "I'm not a jerk. I got rent payments and both feet, hey, right on the ground. For another thing, don't call me names again. I don't go for names." He was counting each item on his fingers. "Another thing, talking about Olympia Jai Alai now, the joint is a mark for us. Olympia is a—quote—an easy caper. Man, I got the details, all the little like minor points without which anybody else would fuck the entire thing. Necessities and shit? Like where the money goes, like who holds it, like what time it gets carted away. And for another thing," Hooven said, tugging at split ends, "man—the last thing?—I think we should just go in, get the thing done."

"Specifics," Del Plato said. "Diagrams. Synchronized watches, Joe."

"You'll do the place without me. I ain't telling you more until it's a deal."

"Look, I'm sorry I called you names before. But I'm going back to my partner, and Jewboy is one of those guys who's going to want the whys and the wherefores. You know the way he is. For some reason he can't stand you, but I won't do this without him, so we got a problem. Give me something to win him over, a fact or two, Joe. I'd hate to go in there like the Three Stooges. Right? I'd hate to be embarrassed."

Hooven patted Del Plato on the shoulder and said it was okay about the name-calling—everyone gets out of line from time to time. "Olympia Fronton, man, the daily handle can be like half a million dollars. For sure we walk away with a few hundred thousand, minimum. You need a fact for the other dude? I got a badge to get in, man. There's a fact. I can get into the counting room at Olympia, Del Plato. I can't say more than that." Hooven stood up and arranged himself, his slacks, his hair, his shades. "I can get us inside. I've been there."

After a few seconds, Del had his eyes closed again to the sun. He opened them to watch Hooven leaving.

Del's mom had passed away when he was seventeen. After taking the bus home from basketball practice, he found his old man reading the paper in the kitchen instead of being at work. "Your mother's in real bad shape," his father had said. "I suppose you been noticing." Del hadn't been noticing at all. When had this been going on? "That lady from downstairs called over to work, I drove to Saint Luke's. . . . What is it you do when you come home, you eat or something? Later I'll drive you over, or take the car yourself, why don't you? You're a big kid now, and I think you'll be learning to take care of yourself, because what else can I say?"

The doctor at the hospital was a nicely graying man with

deep-set eyes and a smart-looking pen set clipped to his breast pocket. "I used to play some round ball myself," the doctor told Del Plato. "Hook shots from the pivot, two-hand sets. In college I once fouled Cliff Hagan in the act of shooting." He showed Del the chart at the foot of his mother's bed and took her pulse. Del wouldn't look at her; he kept staring at the sheet, at the doctor's pens and distinguished hair. "Naturally it's a different game today, what with the jump shot and the overall progress, but you can't tell me a Cliff Hagan would not be a star, even today."

His mom had been going through some rough times with a problem inside her, the doctor explained, putting his hand on Del's shoulder and making eye contact in a very coachlike gesture. A television was suspended from the ceiling. Del didn't mind looking at the doctor's eyes, anything but his mom on a hospital bed with a problem inside her that could make a doctor talk to him this way. His father would keep working at the plant and Del would have to join the Air Force. That's what Del remembered about being in the hospital. Cliff Hagan could make it, although maybe not. Del just didn't want to join the Air Force. He could even recall what had been on the television screen. Jack Nicklaus was trying on pants. What would he do in the Air Force? He was so close to tears right there, with the handsome doctor and hook shots, expandable waistbands on TV, fighter planes that could crack the sound barrier. Where would the Air Force send him, and why did he have to go? What were the Pistons' chances?

In Monkey World, someone with a long boom mike attached to a camera was taking moving pictures. A baby was crying, straw hats bobbed along. Soft drinks, canes, white pocketbooks and white open-toe shoes. Del found it amazing, this swarm of human beings from Canada or Michigan or South America. Pretzels, children, paperbacks. White caps with gold anchors, a restaurant guide. *The wisdom of generations started right here; here was the source. Don't bite off more than you can chew, and as long as you got your health.*

Keri was standing beside him, looking up. He had forgotten about her. She rubbed her foot back and forth on the con-

crete, squishing ants, while one hand was near her eyes, block-
ing the sun.

"Ready to leave?" Del asked.

"Okay."

Two boys walked by, twins, with orange-and-turquoise
Monkey World pennants. Their father followed a few steps behind, carrying a small transistor tuned to the Gators, all the
way from Gainesville. A bus beeped in the parking lot.

Del touched his daughter's cheek and said, "I told that
man I would be here today with my number-one kid, my favorite daughter. You don't mind that, do you?" She continued to
look up at him blandly, and he wiped his face with the inside
part of his T-shirt and then fixed his sunglasses. "You feel like
eating something? Let's pretend it's your birthday now, right
this minute, and I'm taking you out to a fancy meal. I'm talking anything you want now. Name it and it's yours."

"It's not my birthday, Daddy."

"Pretend. Try to keep it under five dollars."

Keri was walking from one side of the bench to another.
"Daddy, do you know Ethan?"

Del said he hadn't had the pleasure. They began to walk
among the crowd of visitors, and when Del reached for her
hand, she tightened up. He looked at Keri and was surprised
to find her crying again. He touched her shirt, the cowboys,
the horses, and ropes. Who had bought the shirt? Why was
everyone so sensitive? Her cheeks gleamed in the falling
sunlight. She was so pretty, his daughter, he didn't want her
to cry.

"Honey, what's wrong? Tell me."

"I don't know."

"Are you insulted? I met that man here. Are you angry
for that?"

"I don't know."

They continued walking, and although Del Plato was trying to keep a pleasant face, he was very confused. What was it
with people? What did he do to make them cry? He took her
hand firmly and for a second Del thought he might lose his
temper with Keri. They followed the crowd to the cars.

"It used to bother your mother; I pulled the same stuff on

her. Business, kid, shitty business, and I feel terrible now.
Have you stopped crying yet? Things seem important to me
and I just do them. I don't always think. Look, sweetie, I'm
sorry. If that's the thing that's bothering you, that I met a guy
and didn't spend all my time with you, then I apologize. And
if it's something else, then I'm sorry for that too, I really am."

She stopped and searched through her little handbag for
a tissue. Keri had a twenty, some mints, a bullet, two dimes
and a quarter, a stubby pencil, some coupons, her mother's old
wallet with a broken snap, Donald Duck, a paper clip, a pack
of Chuckles. No tissue. Del found a clean-enough napkin on
the grass and she blew her nose in that.

Del scooped her up and put her down in a different spot.
She still weighed nothing. "What didn't you like about the
guy I was talking to? Tell the truth, was he a little creepy?"

She sniffled one last time and showed a smile. "He was
cute, Daddy."

"Cute?" Del Plato was squeezing her hand. He let go because he was afraid he might be squeezing too hard. "Cute?
You mean cute like Ethan? Is Ethan cute?"

When she didn't answer, he picked her up again and
whirled her around. Around and around. Actually, she was
built pretty solid; he couldn't just hold her up there forever.
Keri giggled wildly and he kept it going, twirling her in the
bright sunlight. A smiling crowd gathered behind them to see
what was happening. Keri clawed at him and she couldn't stop
laughing. Del Plato was also laughing. This was pretty good.
Do other fathers do this in the park?

And Del, clutching her, wanted to ask more. *Cuter than
me?* he wanted to ask. *What happens now?* he wanted to ask.

But instead he could only press her and hold her, and
dance with her out in the open—a couple of nuts, right—
round and round, until his vision blurred, until he could stand
no longer. And as he lost his feet—out of breath, excited, grinning and panting—Del gave it up and collapsed with his girl
to the ground.

Then people edged slowly away. The show was over. The
man with the transistor radio turned it up. The Gators had

scored. Del Plato dusted himself off and helped Keri to her feet. She had a rip in her jeans and a possible scrape.

He was dizzy, and vaguely aware of a buzz all around him. Del saw himself as if from a very great distance, maybe from even up there with the sun, looking down on the colors and sounds and families. From where he was he could see things clearly. He was going to commit a crime, a big one. And he was not going to enjoy this divorced life, not in the least, not at all, not one little tiny bit.

Chapter
3

Ricky Hopper stung a few high notes and told the late-night crowd to enjoy the evening, enjoy their mates and dates, and to enjoy the magical musical sound of the Ricky Hopper Solo Revue, featuring the costly Hammond organ and the costly mini-Moog synthesizer. He told the crowd to enjoy their lives, the air they breathe, and especially to enjoy the wonderful and relatively inexpensive drinks offered at the Frisco Lounge.

At a dark table near the rear of the Frisco Lounge, Del Plato was saying, "I haven't had this much fun since the Monkey Jungle." He was looking at the San Francisco wallpaper—cable cars, the Golden Gate, seals, Chinamen.

The woman he was with lit her own cigarette again and casually brushed ashes off Del Plato's shirt. "Don't be sarcastic. When you're sarcastic like that, you remind me of Maurie, thank you very much." She finished the last of her Tanqueray and tonic, her third or fourth. "And besides, I think he really knows his business up there. For instance, the way he did 'Man of La Mancha' a second ago. And especially he tells those jokes. Like Don Rickles." She brushed ashes off her arm. "Not Don Rickles. The other one, from *M*A*S*H*, the actor." She snapped open her makeup kit and it lit up. "Anyway, we all need a sense of humor."

Del Plato was thinking, if he had a sense of humor, he would get up and sit at another table. He had put away three or four Rebel Yells. When he leaned forward, his hair kept falling into his eyes, annoying him. "How about another round?" Del asked. "Who's Maurie?"

"Oh, boy, Maurie, talk about Maurie. That was my first husband, Maurie. What a mistake. Maurie, Maurie used to clean his ears with my hairpins. What kind of marriage is that? I look in the medicine cabinet and I find wax. I have no sense of humor about my first marriage." She wiggled her fingers at a waitress and asked for another TNT and another Rebel Yell. "Plus that he was sarcastic. Which is the whole point about Maurie, if you follow what I'm saying." She pursed her lips in the mirror and puffed her cheeks. "But you're cute. Not like Maurie. See? So really, honey, don't talk like him."

On stage, Ricky Hopper was wearing a red shirt with white buttons, a white belt, red-and-white checked slacks, and white shiny loafers without socks. He dedicated his next tune to Cheryl. Ricky explained that Cheryl was this knockout blond waitress at the Frisco Lounge with these gorgeous eyes and these heart-stopping knockers, whose pants he was trying desperately to get into.

There was a small dark dance floor, and Del was watching some kids out there. He couldn't tell what kind of dance they were doing; he couldn't tell what song Ricky Hopper was playing. Del assumed he was very loaded. He was caught up with trying to remember the name of Maurie's ex-wife, who was sitting across from him. *Margie,* Del thought. *Margaret.* He said to her, "You're a knockout; your eyes are gorgeous." Del was feeling drunk and a little proud of himself for being so sarcastic. "Your whole appearance is heart-stopping. Let's go somewhere."

She brushed ashes off her hand. "Alan Alda," she said

suddenly. "I couldn't think of his name before. From *M*A*S*H*, the funny one."

Mandy, Del said to himself. *Marcie, Margo.*

Del looked her over, thinking it was a good time to leave because he didn't want to drink any more or talk any more or listen to Ricky Hopper on the costly Hammond organ. Hooven was late; Breed was nowhere to be found; Del Plato was getting a headache; whatever her name was was dressed in a gauze outfit with most of the buttons undone. He guessed she was thirty-three, thirty-five, gold on her ankles and wrists, around her neck, gold earrings, gold pins, rings. He pulled her chair closer and put his arm around her.

Marlene. Marlo. Marsha.

The waitress who was not Cheryl brought their check and Del glanced casually at the addition before stretching a crisp fifty across the tab. "You're some knockout," he said again, but she was already putting away her cigarettes, Mindy or Maggie, smoothing down her filmy blouse. Del picked up his drink again as he waited for change.

She asked him what line of work he was in. Del said he was a ballplayer, semiprofessional.

High-hat droplights threw down skinny bright beams. He was looking for the waitress. Ricky Hopper broke into "Some Enchanted Evening" and the stage spots went from amber to blue.

Then, from nowhere, Hoover walked right up to their table. "Having fun?" he asked nicely. Hooven had on a velvet sports jacket and cologne. "Hey, I saw you leaving and all—I figured I'd say hello, ask how everything was going."

Del Plato frowned. He was looking at another section of wallpaper. Candlestick Park, fishing boats, redwoods, a different view of the Golden Gate.

"Pretty lady you're with. I'm not like looking to mess up your moves."

"Then leave," Del told him.

Hooven kept standing. Del tried to get a close look at Joe Hooven's eyes to see just how furtive they were.

"Looks like my friend might be getting lucky for a

change," Hoover went on. He pulled up a chair and took a cigarette from Maurie's ex-wife. "We just came from jai alai, myself and this other friend, who is at the bar now. A dynamite
sport, jai alai. What's your name?"

"Margie." She stirred her drink with a finger. "I've been
to jai alai once or twice, but gambling doesn't really do that
much for me."

"An exciting game," Hooven said, "if you're aware of the
intricacies involved. I'll meet you there one time, Margie, explain the intricacies."

Across the table, Del Plato was nodding his head. *Margie*,
he repeated to himself. *Right*. He was still waiting for his
change.

"I guess you're a friend or something," Margie said,
brushing cigarette ashes off Hooven's sleeve now. "Are you a
ballplayer too?"

"Hey, I'm a musician," he said with enthusiasm. He got
comfortable and swept back his hair. "Don't I look like a musician?"

"This is Al Martino," Del said, a little too loudly. He was
grinning thinly, very sorry he hadn't left earlier. " 'Spanish
Eyes'? Here's the man."

Margie frowned and blew ashes off her bosom. "Just like
Maurie, I swear. Maurie number two." She leaned toward
Hooven and flipped away the hair that was falling on his
shoulder. "They don't wear it that way these days. You should
get your hair cut, honey, styled or something. In my shopping
center I have this girl who does wonders."

"It's this band, actually," explained Hooven. "Girls go for
wild hair and all. The Allman Brothers, if you ever heard of
us. You go for music? You listen a little? I'm Duane Allman."

"I figured a musician," Margie said. "With all that hair.
Do you have albums out?"

Del Plato put away the last of his Rebel Yell. He didn't
like to drink so much. Once, after strawberry daiquiris he and
Denise had whipped up in a blender, Del remembered a maneuver Breed had bragged about and tried to coax Denise into
an unfamiliar posture. She shot him such a look that right

then and there Del Plato made a silent vow to watch his boozing. Now the waitress was in no hurry with his fifty dollars, and spinning mirror globes suspended from the light panels were also beginning to get on his nerves.

"Who was the one with Cher?" Margie asked Joe Hooven. "That wasn't you, was it? The hair was the same, I remember that—too long and unstyled."

Del decided that Melanie, Maryanne, she wouldn't give strange and guilt-inspiring looks to a husband with private requests. He was wondering how he would feel. There she was, bye-bye Mavis, waving smoke from Joe Hooven's eyes, dusting ashes from Hooven's knee, see you around. *Jealous, yes or no? Hurt, yes or no?* "Personally," she was saying, "I could not for the life of me see what a superstar like Cher, with those hips, was doing with a musician."

Del Plato continued tapping to the music, listening closely for the beat until finally he recognized it. "Raindrops Keep Falling on My Head." He drummed his fingers, and when the waitress at last came back with his change, Del wearily pushed away from his seat and stood up. It was more difficult than he had imagined. The lights, in particular, kept spinning.

"Let's go, Joe. Business time for us. Happy Harry sent you a nice birthday present, you know. A hundred eighty dollars."

Hooven gave the woman a smile calculated to keep her a few minutes. "What's her name again?" he had to ask Del Plato as they bumped past unbuttoned shirts and neck chains across the Frisco Lounge.

"Melissa."

"Seems she's hit on me, Del Plato. Hope it's no problem, man."

Ricky Hopper, sipping from a highball glass, told the crowd that Cheryl was not treating him right. He wasn't going to be hurt by her again. So his next tune was being dedicated to Lorraine, who was also a shapely cocktail waitress at the Frisco Lounge. And besides, according to Adolpho—the knowledgeable bartender at the Frisco Lounge, who fixed those wonderful and relatively inexpensive drinks—Ricky would have a much easier time scoring with Lorraine, who came across for just about anyone.

When Del and Hooven got to the bar, Breed was waiting for them. "My man, Irish," Breed said, twirling a glass of club soda. "I hit a perfecta tonight, Irish—a hundred forty American dollars."

"Attendance, seven thousand and change, a handle tonight of over three hundred thousand very large ones." Hooven had a rum Collins on the bar and was eating the fruit slices. "Easy access and plenty of exits. You ever meet my friend Jackie Molson? He used to count money at Olympia, last year. Hey, we used to jam together, me and Jackie Molson."

"Your well-connected source," Del Plato said. "All the necessary details, the whys and wherefores, the logistics of money."

Del Plato went into his pants pocket for a stack of crinkled bills held together with a rubber band. As Hooven put his rum Collins back on the bar, Del removed a twenty from the pile and pushed the rest of the money into Hooven's free hand.

"One hundred eighty," Del said. "Minus twenty. You can pay for your girl friend's drinks."

"Look, Del Plato, no ill will. Someone smiles at me and I smile back; it's my nature."

"Your nature is to get on your knees for construction workers," Breed said. "Your nature is to unzipper Little Leaguers."

Hooven closed his eyes and said, "This got nothing to do with you, man. Jesus, you people got no appreciation."

"I see," said Breed. " 'You people,' " he repeated. "Is that a racial remark? Just to clarify things in my own mind. You see, it kills me that you get a one-third share, Joe Hooven; that devastates me, and I'm anxious for the least little excuse to break your face."

"No, it's not a fucking racial remark. Look how upset you're getting me. Let me be more precise. By 'you people' I mean yourself and Del Plato. You people, you and Del Plato, you show very little in the way of appreciation. That's my entire point." Hooven picked up his drink again. He was trying to talk calmly, but his voice came out sounding grating and clipped, like the noise silverware makes when it's caught in the disposal. "And you people, while we're at it, you also look so much like cops it's fucking ridiculous. No decent clothes to wear, is that it? You come into a lounge and everybody in the world knows the rollers are out. What did you do, you drive up in the squad car?"

Breed was looking at his clothes. He had on a knit shirt with a zipper front. He was pulling the zipper ring up and down.

"We'll make this fast," Del Plato said, speaking in an even tone, and very distinctly as well, which was a pleasant surprise. It was nice for Del Plato to know that he could be bombed but still coherent. "We'll meet next time in a Burger King or something, Joe. For whatever reason, your hundred eighty dollars from Happy Harry, your hundred eighty dollars from the Quaalude factory in Hialeah, all the extortion. At least they don't give you this live-music shit in Burger King."

Breed said, "Gail bought me this shirt on sale. What do you think, Irish? Be honest, it doesn't look so hot. It doesn't, does it?"

I'm so drunk, Del was thinking. *I shouldn't drive; I shouldn't even be allowed to stand.* He was smirking foolishly, trying to remember just what he had in mind that last drunken time with Denise. He got a kick out of it, the memory. How wide and shocked her eyes got, like someone with a real big phone bill.

"What we should talk about," Breed was saying, "what we should discuss, with clear heads and a disregard for any personality clashes, is a new split. A new way of splitting up these payoffs. Because, as was pointed out, can Irish and myself use some new silk shirts, or what? Apparently we could stand for some menswear improvement—maybe get some slick hats like the nigs wear. Whatever, it's basically a difference of opinion on how we share the money. And you can't be a Baggie about this forever, Joe Heavy."

Breed was standing beside Hooven with his arms folded. Breed checked with Del Plato, who swayed to music from the costly instruments.

"We need to negotiate," Breed explained. "It's just that to me it doesn't seem we're on equal footing. A three-way split, as matters stand now, is very fair for the rambling man. However, for the Metro officers, not so fair. I'm explaining my viewpoint, rambling man. Are you listening?"

"Fair for me, not so fair for you."

"Irish, how about you? Something to say in our behalf?"

"You're the one driving this car."

"So here's the solution. Twenty percent for the initial information. Now that to me sounds more like people who have respect for one another. Where one is in no way fucking over the other two. *Equitable* is a good word. Equitable is what I'm talking about. And ten percent thereafter, for each subsequent visit that Irish and I make. We see Happy Harry again, five hundred dollars, then fifty dollars cash goes to Joe Heavy, we give cheerfully and with mutual respect."

Breed's grammar improved whenever he got angry. He always felt there was something intimidating about really proper usage. You wouldn't want to get into any sort of long thing with someone who knew the difference between *affect* and *effect,* for instance, or wise up to a guy who could suddenly slip into the subjunctive. Breed would try to speak more clearly and distinctly, rising to some superior form of language as he lost his temper, as though he could scare off the opposition simply through the fierce and unassailable strength of his diction.

"Irish, I could use some support at this point."

Del looked at the ceiling and smiled. "Now there's an alternative," he said. "Twenty percent for Joe, ten percent for Joe."

"So there you have it. Honest opinions. Because otherwise, and I'm sure a rambling man like you knows what I'm talking about, otherwise these things get bottled up, animosity builds. It's human nature."

Hooven finished his rum Collins and cleared his throat. He said, "I'm laughing. I'm hysterical laughing. Because, fuck you both, fuck you people. Without me—hey, *you* pay attention now—without me, you have nothing. Without me you have like zero. No gas barbecue and no color TV, no electric crepe-maker. Not without me. Look, I'm the one who finds things out, and that is everything."

"Joe Heavy. Keep your voice down, Joe Heavy."

"You ain't the only dishonest cops in town, believe me. So stick it with your twenty percent and stick it with all your animosity bullshit. Sit on that. Don't insult me."

Breed swallowed his ice cubes. "This is fucking incomprehensible. I cannot make any sense at all of this shit. You have no defense."

"There are three of us involved, man; we divide things three ways. What's hard to understand?"

Breed said, "Before we go further, there's one thing I would like to have out in the open. It concerns you, rambling man. You see, I'm a very straightforward guy, a direct kind of person, and I want to be very honest. I think you're a complete asshole. Also, I cannot tolerate the way you talk. I hate your fucking guts, Joe Heavy."

"I respect your candor," Hooven said with a remarkably well-tempered manner. "Only call me an asshole again, I'll knock you down one time, and when you wake up you might even be lucky and your clothes will be back in style."

Del Plato paid for their drinks. He was still smiling. *What a team.*

Breed was looking at his marked-down shirt again. "We're sworn officers of the law—that's what gnaws away at me more than anything—and here this maggot is calling all the shots, our silent partner."

"That's good, look, that's a good one." Hooven was still pumped up, and his voice was up again like a rocket. He flashed his ID. "I'm a maggot. Hey, a good joke, that you have the *nerve*, that you have the balls where you can like call me a maggot. That's great. Look at this, I got Carte Blanche here, you jerk. I got American Express. In *gold.* I got these charge plates from department stores that wouldn't even let you in the door. So tell me about your salary; tell me who's doing better. I got the Diners Doublecard."

Breed said, "Why am I associated with such a moron?"

"How about you, Officer Del Plato? Come on, show me your Sears card; show me Penney's."

Ricky Hopper, on his feet, smoothed the crease in his red-and-white checkered slacks and told the crowd that he had been around, everywhere, all over this world. He had been to Mexico and Club Med in Martinique, three times to Baltimore, and with all his travels he was able to discover something about people that was worth sharing. Ricky explained to his crowd that people—especially those "people who needed people"—well, they were the "luckiest people in the world" and there wasn't much more to be said about it. But he could still sing about it.

Hooven twirled his ring and said, "If you dudes had any class at all, hey, you would be thanking me instead of hassling me."

"Sure, I got a present," said Breed, "our thanks, our appreciation. Barry Manilow, you like him? You love Barry Manilow? I'm giving you a Barry Manilow cassette. Step outside with me to my car and it's all yours. You like him or you love him?"

"And Ricky Hopper," Del said. "All yours."

"Because you're not only a Baggie, rambling man, you're a lubricated Baggie. A French tickler. In the world of Baggies you're second to none, and I was thrilled with that line before about how you were knocking me down. That was also delightful."

Del was seriously thinking about another drink. Hooven looked back at the dark table in the rear of the Frisco Lounge to see if Marcie or Margie was still there. Del followed his glance and there she was, Hooven managing to catch her eye from across the floor, Hooven waving. She puffed away cigarette ashes from her napkin and held up her glass in return. *Margie,* Del Plato thought, *Margie.*

"Down to business again," Breed said after a while. "Stupid business. Silent-partner business. This is so discouraging to me."

"West Miramar," said Hooven. "Listen for the salient points, Officers. I have to like move along, if you know what I mean. Off Four Forty-one, there's a pet store this time, Florida Exotica, something like that. This guy Arriz is the one there, Cuban, and like all kinds of contraband traffic comes in and out. Nobody knows a thing about this yet—Narcotics at this point is completely out of the picture. So Metro could go on the cuff and it would be a very simple procedure."

Breed looked away. He drained his club soda, even though it was already empty. "What exactly are we talking about? Let's not be so slickly smooth here, seeing as how you're so reasonable and all and how you have to like move along. Are we talking about stolen property or strictly drugs, or what? Humor me."

Hooven turned to Del Plato. "Tell your friend Bill Blass that it's strictly cocaine. This is Little Havana money, and from La Seguasera. Mr. Tommy Polio again. Pot too, but they don't keep it there."

"Oh, Bill Blass, good for me. Talk straight," Breed snapped. "How come you're talking and I can't understand you? They don't keep the pot there, or they don't keep the other dope there? Which is it?"

Hooven was still facing Del Plato. "They don't keep the pot there," he said very slowly. "Any other questions, Officers? Hey, please don't hesitate. This pet store imports various things from South America. Tarantulas, vipers, vampire bats, that's the way they smuggle. Burlap sacks or taped cartons—WARNING, VENOMOUS REPTILES. Who's going to stick his hand in that? So when they get a shipment, Florida Exotica, it's maybe four boa constrictors, two scorpions, a twenty-foot python, and twenty-four ounces of pure coke."

"One other thing," Del Plato said. "One question. That gold American Express card before, how do you get one of those? I like that one very much."

"You can ask with a straight face. It's not for policemen,

Del Plato. Not for you, no way, and not for your buddy." Hooven pivoted to leave. "You can be on the take forever and you'll never have enough."

"Just curious."

"I'll take twenty percent on this one," Hooven said. "Okay? Because who needs this same shit coming up again, for one thing, and for another thing, let's just say, hey, that I'm really a reasonable guy."

Hooven turned and started toward the table, but then he stopped, and Del Plato looked too. Madeline was talking to an offensive lineman. Sun-bleached hair, washed-out shorts like offensive linemen wear, an eighteen-inch neck. She was drinking a fresh TNT, about to flick a clump of cigarette ash off the big guy's shoulder.

Hooven shrugged, put down his own drink, and said, "My biorhythm chart showed that today was very high for me sexually. I wouldn't want to like waste it. I'll see you around, troopers. Wish me luck."

"I wish you get cholera," Breed said. "Go home and flog your fish. With your biorhythms and your Bill Blass."

A nice-looking waitress walked by, collecting empty glasses. She smiled sweetly at Del, and for an instant he fumbled for names. Then he heard himself asking, "Is your name Lorraine? I was hoping to find Lorraine."

"The rambler," Breed said. "Did you see that before? His whole wallet was all credit cards." Breed took out his own billfold and looked inside. Then he massaged his stomach and took a pill. "I'm distressed now, Irish. I really am."

"We're doing all right," Del Plato reassured him. He tapped the bar with his fist. "Knock on wood. We're okay; we can't miss."

"It's disheartening, Del Plato. Our silent partner has us walking into armed robbery."

Am I too drunk? Del asked himself. *Should I go for more? Where's Lorraine?*

"With his friend Jackie Molson, who used to count money at jai alai. What's armed robbery, Irish? Twenty years and up?"

Del hesitated at the exit of the Frisco Lounge to double-check the change from his fifty. He was still listening to the music. "Moon River," he finally decided. Then, as a cocktail waitress who just might have been Cheryl smiled brightly and told them to come back again, he stepped outside with Breed into the breezy, dark parking lot. There they rubbed their eyes and yawned, and parted ways to look up and down for their cars.

Chapter
4

A few days later, Del tried to wake up with cold water on his face, followed by hot water, but that didn't work. Then he tried it with hot water and cold water, followed by a splash of Skin Bracer. Denise was in the kitchen, lighting a Vantage for herself on the stove coils and reheating a pot of strong coffee, which had been there a while. She had come to Del Plato's rented place that morning mainly for her record albums—songs in French, golden oldie collections, *Saturday Night Fever*, everything by the Stones. When he had moved out, grabbing this and that without much thought—who knew then what you would need in a new house?—by mistake Del had packed some of her favorite records along with his own things.

Across the street from Del Plato's rental, a yellow bulldozer crushed its way loudly over dry, rocky soil and planks of unused wood that had been left out in the rain, trampling over small cypresses and brittle thornbushes and an enormous mound of empty beer and soda cans which the construction crew had been building up for the past few weeks. There were concrete blocks stacked nice and neat, good lumber, ladders, white pipes, and surveyors in white T-shirts with orange helmets and engineering boots, who drank coffee from a thermos or pounded layout stakes into the rough, flattened ground. On the plot of just-leveled land adjoining that one, a different yellow machine was noisily sucking up water that had gathered at the bottom of a concrete-lined hole.

The hole was going to become a sunken living room. Del Plato could already picture it. He was half-watching the construction crew at work. Café au lait carpeting and shiny furniture in the Oriental style. With framed needlepoints and a hooked rug. A couple of trophies, a wine rack filled with bottles of wine. Who would move in? Professional people? Del sort of hoped it would be folks he could wave hello to in the morning, knowledgeable people who could tell him what to do about chips in the patio and broken sprinkler heads, where to go for wallpaper and how to get a decent butcher who wouldn't take meat into the back room where you had no idea what he was doing to it. It was important to get along with your neighbors. Just as long as they weren't cops. Del had about had it with cops.

He had rented his new place from a man with the Drug Enforcement Agency, South Florida operations. A cop. Del had spotted the ad pinned to the roster-room bulletin board. There was a raffle notice up there—WIN A TRIP TO ST. PETE OR A SIDE OF BEEF—along with the usual green index cards with a ten-speed bike for sale, a Python Colt with fifty extra rounds and ivory handgrips, a high chair and stroller, golf clubs. And also the house. DEA, CRRNT ASSGN GULF COAST, RCNT DVRC, $400 FRNSHD. So Del immediately gave the guy a call. Del badly needed a place to live, and four hundred a month was only a hundred or so more than he could afford, which wasn't too bad, considering. Del had been sleeping in a room he rented by the week, next door to a young couple who listened to "Stairway to Heaven" at 6:57 every morning, and he was spending all his free time along with his gas money in the Pillow Talk Bar & Lounge across the street, where he ate Cheez Doodles and drank Michelob on tap, watching the Atlanta Braves on cable out of West Palm.

The DEA man's place turned out to be a find. Two bedrooms, a covered carport, a wet bar, cathedral ceiling, sunken
living room. All of which was right up Del Plato's alley. What
he didn't want was a high-rise apartment where you did your
laundry in the laundry room and you had to press the floor
buttons in the elevator when people asked you to, and where
strangers would probably come right out and question you
about just what it was you did for a living. Del wanted something close to what he had before, nothing more. A place like
what he had been living in with Denise for nine years. Where
you didn't have to say good morning to your neighbors and
they would still keep an eye on your crabgrass problem and
put out your trash barrel if you forgot, or turn off your headlights if you had driven home ossified.

This two-bedroom job was it for Del Plato; the place was
perfect, absolutely. It was just that the DEA man himself had
turned out to be such a prick, wanting two months in advance
and a full month's security on top of that. *Although, what the
hell else could you expect from a cop? Right?*

On the stereo was *Saturday Night Fever* with the volume
down low. Del had quickly turned the volume down low, on his
way back from the bathroom with Skin Bracer on his face. Denise had put her record on with the volume up high.

He joined her in the kitchen. They sat at a white
wrought-iron dinette table with white chairs that had come
with the place. The furnishings were whatever the DEA man's
wife didn't want to take with her. Del Plato began to cut up a
grapefruit. He was wearing his yellow terrycloth bathrobe
that had a yellow sash and an embossed S with a crown over
the breast pocket. Del had picked up the bathrobe on their
Disney World and Ocean World trip with Keri, along with a
stack of yellow towels and a postcard assortment of Sheraton
lobbies and swimming pools. Denise wore a short-sleeve top
with a silk-screened palm tree and a round white tablet, and
lettering that said Fort LUDErdale.

"I could have been with a date or something," Del told
her. "Usually people call up when they're coming over. It's
customary to give a guy some notice, right, husband or no husband." Across the street, the bulldozer started up again, claw-

ing rocks, pushing debris, and Del had to raise his voice to be heard. "That would be embarrassing, wouldn't it? I mean if you walked in here, no phone call, no notice, and I was with someone else. You were lucky this time, Denise, I have to tell you the truth."

"I didn't think to call." She glanced around the new place to see how he lived. There wasn't too much furniture because the DEA man's wife had decided to take most of it.

Denise got up to poke around the kitchen. Everything in the four-hundred-dollar-a-month house was just the way Del had found it when he moved in, with his suitcases and his alarm clock and some of Denise's records. Above the dinette set was a colorful poster of a Paris café, with waiters in white aprons and waxed mustaches, and there were some small framed photos of café food—croissants, wine, apples, cheese. There was also a sign the DEA man had put up himself, held in place with white thumbtacks. DO IT. JUST DO IT. Below that was a nutritional chart and a bank calendar.

Denise opened the refrigerator. She wanted to see what Del Plato was eating. Del looked too. What did he have? He saw orange juice and mustard, baking soda, a box of Little Debbies. A.1. Steak Sauce, taco sauce, Saucy Susan, the sixteen-ounce yellow American cheese, individually wrapped. Napkins, a lime, cream cheese. Del figured that was a fairly average refrigerator. *People bought pretty much that sort of thing, didn't they? Except for the napkins. What were they doing inside the refrigerator?* He had to remember to get those napkins out of there.

When he went down the aisles now in the twenty-four-hour supermarket, Del bought everything that seemed familiar, putting things into his cart if they looked in some way like what he might have bought before, or what a guy was supposed to buy when he was only watching out for himself. Del figured other single men might go in for king crab legs, or a jar of capers, exotic bachelor food. But Del Plato just wanted ordinary T-bones and porterhouse. None of that faggot skirt steak for him. He wanted Pepsi, deodorant, aspirin, cookies. Maybe a green vegetable. Because what would happen if he let himself go? He would drink too much and eat wrong, and watch

Walter Pidgeon movies when he was supposed to be sleeping, and probably wind up with some vitamin deficiency or calling in to those call-in programs.

After Denise had closed the refrigerator door and given him some kind of blank but significant look, Del said, "We won't get back together, will we?"

"What?" She made a motion—all that clamor across the street. "I can't hear you."

"We won't get back together."

"No."

Del rubbed his eyes. For some reason he couldn't seem to snap out of it. Why was he so tired? "I won't ask you again," he told Denise. "That's the last time I'm asking." He yawned into his hand and realized he had been shouting. So he repeated it in a quieter way. "That's the last time I'm asking, Denise."

She smiled and drank her coffee. Del didn't think it mattered too much if she had heard him or not.

Denise said, "It's weird to be here; I'm so uncomfortable. Do you feel that way too? It's meeting someone you know so well for such a long time, only you can't get it out of your mind that the last time you parted it was on less than the best of terms, which is what happened with us. Don't you think? I'm at a loss, Del. With what to say. I'm trying hard not to say anything unpleasant."

What would he do, would he go back if he had the chance, if she went along with that idea? He had to consider Medlow again, who had remarried his first wife and now couldn't even talk about it at the academy gym. Medlow the pivot—the big man, the board crasher and intimidator. Probably there was nothing wrong with that, Del Plato figured, but still it seemed this was the kind of thing a big man would not do. Not a true intimidator, not an authentic board crasher. Bill Russell would not marry the same woman two times. Kareem wouldn't. Two times? Chump City. Now, whenever somebody made the least little remark on the court, Medlow would bounce the ball off his foot or lose it out of bounds. It was such a touchy subject. The whole thing lacked common sense.

Denise had brought with her two issues of *Sports Illus-*

trated, an underwater scene Keri had done in school, and some loose keys to which she couldn't find a lock. Also a net bag filled with grapefruit she had picked off the tree in the back-yard of their old place.

The grapefruit tree was why they had chosen the house. Theirs was a two-bedroom townhouse, with a two-car garage, a wet bar and cathedral ceiling, a raised living room. And a grapefruit tree. Del and Denise went to closing on it not long after they had returned from a brief honeymoon in the Keys, where Del went out on boats for marlin and Denise won an award for shuffleboard, and they developed a taste for cock-tails that came out of a blender. They had seen the house and made an instant decision on it. They thought long range. De-nise was just beginning to get sick in the morning, developing an aversion to solid food and coffee, so they had to think long range. Del would get a lawnmower at Sears, Denise would pick breakfast right off the branch each morning. Del could hang a hammock out back—one of those wide South American ham-mocks in which a whole family could swing away an afternoon.

Across from Del Plato, Denise was examining her skin at the breakfast table. She poked her forearm to check the tone. "Two more men tried to pick me up yesterday," Denise told him. "At the pool. I won't mention names, but you know who they are. It's amazing, suddenly I'm so popular."

"Well, you look great," Del said. Then he wanted to know who, exactly, had been coming on to her by the pool.

Definitely she couldn't hear him. The racket was too much, bulldozers in the morning. "I have nowhere to get the sun," Denise continued. "It's too far for the beach, and I re-fuse to sit on a lawn chair. And I can't use the pool anymore, not with those neighbors." Denise stubbed out her cigarette and got up abruptly to drop it down the disposal. "They bor-rowed tools from you. Their children still come to the house and don't put away any of Keri's toys. I think it's just awful, Del. I'm shocked each time it happens."

"You'll have to get Ernie to buy you a sunlamp. It's Christmas, right? Let the boyfriend buy you something."

"Ethan."

"Tell Ethan to buy you a sunlamp."

A flatbed truck carrying a cocoa-brown bathtub and an almond bathtub stopped across the street. It was so sunny outside, fins of color flashing through the window and the sky. Fireproof metal studs began to go up on one of the plots of land that had a buyer's deposit safely in escrow. Walls and a roof, two bathtubs, another home.

Del was thinking about the hammock. It was something he had never managed to find a place for in the backyard. Where was it now? In the garage, more than likely. Folded up in a hard-to-reach corner, along with the can of spare gasoline, pesticides, a rebuilt carburetor, Keri's outgrown car seat. Suddenly it took on an immense importance to Del Plato: the hammock that was never hung, the unhung hammock. No wonder they were splitting up.

Denise was saying something he couldn't make out. Del moved closer, watching her lips. What? He tapped his ear to show that he couldn't hear her. Then he smiled and came over beside her and gently squeezed her hand. She withdrew her hand and sat down again. What was this? Now she didn't trust him either? What were you supposed to do when they were building houses across the street and you were trying to have a conversation?

He happened to notice Denise still wore her thin wedding band. She had it on her right hand now. Del looked at his own hand and saw that he had his ring on as well. The idea had never even come to him to take it off. He asked himself, right there, why he was still wearing his wedding ring. Because he had never thought about taking it off, that's why. And he wasn't going to take it off, or wear it on the other hand. He decided he was the type of person who would put on a wedding ring and keep it on, no matter what. He was going to do all his shopping in twenty-four-hour supermarkets; he was going to keep his napkins inside the refrigerator if that's where he had decided to put them.

And probably, Del figured, probably he was going to get married again real soon. He was also that type of person. The thought made him a little sad. He wasn't going to stay single very long. Other guys would go for flashy small apartments, where you could bring a date and get down to serious business right away, and where you didn't have to spend a lot of time dusting or noodling around with vacuum cleaner attachments. Other guys would eat king crab legs and sell *both* wedding bands. But not Del Plato. He was going to pretend he was still married or something, renting a house that was much too big, needing a haircut, leaving napkins in the wrong place, putting lame moves on his own separated wife, for Christ's sake. All she wanted was her goddamn records and to see how lousy he was getting by without her, and he was touching her already, putting hands on her and smelling her hair in the kitchen.

What a perv, Del said to himself. *I'm such a vermin.* He was no different from the tool-borrowing husbands. He was worse. He was almost as bad as Breed.

But her hair was so glossy that morning. Del bent close again. Denise's hair smelled of cream rinse. She had washed her hair before coming over, that was something. What brand, what kind of cream rinse? Del couldn't think of it, although he had used it too. Cream rinse was another item he would have to get for himself.

"I'm not myself," Denise said after a moment. Her throat was raspy from too much shouting. "I'm not sure how I should talk to you now. I'm not sure I'm handling this well. I don't think I am. I don't really feel anything, Del, that's the problem."

"No problem. We'll make it up as we go along, don't worry about that. What else are we going to do, right? We'll do the best we can."

And what had she kicked him out for anyway? He was supposed to dump *her.* Del would forget her for some new thing. That's the way it was supposed to work. Ask anyone. Some fresh thing, with no stretch marks and a different kind of cream rinse. Del was thinking of a whole new ballgame. A receptionist, something like that, who took sociology at night and who wouldn't make such a big deal about *Saturday Night Fever* or songs in French, some honey who owned a healthy pair of headlights pointing straight ahead.

Denise sat directly across from him at the dinette set. Del Plato was eating grapefruit slices off the tip of his knife. They were both looking out the window, where even more trucks groaned up the street, carrying piled sods of grass, muddy machinery, hoists and sledgehammers and rough-sawn cedar.

"I was scared to death of what I saw," Denise was explaining to him. "Why I left. It still frightens me. I kept seeing these nightmare images which you'll never understand, not really. Myself with two or three kids, with fuzzy slippers on in the afternoon and I'm not dressed yet. Signing report cards, whacking weeds. I stick in the diaphragm every Saturday night. I didn't want that person to be me. So I left. I took Keri and we went to the airport. But then, when I was up north again, with my father, it wasn't better. What could we possibly say to each other? I told him I wanted a divorce, and he thought I was talking about something else. It was very funny, really, because neither one of us knew exactly what I had in mind. He thought it was some intellectual pursuit, like I was going for a doctoral thesis, so he was all for it. My father told me to go ahead and do what I had to do. But I didn't know what I wanted to do. I hit the panic button and I left. It was hostile up there, Del. My father means well but he kept asking Keri how old she was. And always asking me if I needed any money or warmer clothing. Every morning up there I was smoking two joints. It was pathetic."

A crane had come from somewhere, huge and black. It lifted Sheetrock and steel tubing. Yellow cement trucks churned and growled.

"Everything is you," Del said. "How about the practical side. How about looking at this from my point of view? Who'll do my shirts now? I can't iron, Denise. And I can't cook a thing if it's not on the barbecue. In this house I've been eating nothing but pizza and cream cheese sandwiches. I realize you weren't happy before, but I happen to have my brown shoes in our old shoe-repair place, so this situation is much deeper than just you. I'm the one who has to find a new mechanic now, and a new druggist. I'm the one who had to move out."

"I keep searching for a reason," Denise said softly. Building noises drowned her out. Del sat closer. "Sometimes I can put the words together very clearly and I know exactly what I'm doing and why I'm doing it. Only I forget the reasons, and I can't think of anything right now. I thought there was another side to life, Del. A side I'm not getting. That's as close as I can come. I suppose basically I was looking for someone who would crack jokes and take me to the movies. Which isn't a lot to ask. Someone who would think the world of me."

"I thought the world of you. I let you balance the checkbook, didn't I? That shows respect, Denise."

"It's hard to explain, but I wasn't having a very good time. I'm not having an especially good time right now. I wish I knew what to say."

"I know you, Denise. You're saying exactly what you want to say."

She opened the morning paper and turned to the movies. Del Plato silently finished his coffee and his grapefruit, and got up slowly to switch off the music. He didn't know what to say either. Denise had come for her albums; she was welcome to take them all as far as he was concerned. Where did she develop this taste in music anyway? Who listened to songs in French? How were you supposed to have a good time when you were dealing with songs they didn't even sing in your own language?

He flipped on the FM instead. They were giving temperature readings for other parts of the nation.

He had his disappointments too. His job, for one thing. He had chosen a career, right? Del Plato had examined all sorts of possibilities, and what had he chosen? He had chosen police work. And for a reason. The starting salary was okay, but more important was the fact Del could go around keeping the world more or less together. He would do it through law and order, which was the basis of the whole country, which was what the government and Wall Street and all of industry were founded upon. Del Plato had aced Techniques in Criminal Behavior, and when he was sworn in for duty, Del *knew* he was coming into something special.

And at the beginning it had all gone smoothly. He was doing work based largely upon courage and reliability, dependable work in an important field. And he had fallen for an attractive woman who had a way of saying even the most ordinary words—words like *orange juice* and *sneakers*—in that French-Canadian inflection, so her voice always came as a pleasant and sort of exotic surprise. Other men married more fragile women, who couldn't use a self-service pump or drive at night, who you had to carry around through life like a delicate piece of crystal. Women who maybe wouldn't have nightmares about two or three kids and fuzzy slippers, but you couldn't really trust them to assemble Lego blocks or pay the bills on time.

And for so many years—almost nine—their hearts had been fairly full, crowded with the accumulations of a time together, and lots of love, which were things you couldn't just chuck away or donate to St. Vincent de Paul thrift shops.

But there was something that gnawed at Del Plato. It was his line of work. He was only doing his job when things were wrong. Could Del Plato replace stolen money, or give back a life? He never could see the right side of society. His training took him away from that. In all his years on Metro, Del couldn't recall being witness to a single real crime while he was off duty. But on duty he wouldn't see anything else.

In the rented living room, the radio continued giving bad news for up north. Snow in the air for the mideastern region. A high in the twenties for the Windy City and the Great Lakes.

Del Plato went into one of the rented bedrooms and came out a moment later with a red TWA flight bag he had prepared for Denise. In it were his life-insurance policy, his Public Safety Department policy, property and liability insurance, auto and national flood insurance, both safe-deposit keys, the house deed, five hundred dollars inside an envelope, both bankbooks, and twenty-five shares of some mining stock Del bought because one afternoon at the gym Medlow and James Lloyd had been all over him to buy it. James Lloyd had passed a test and was selling stock on the side.

Denise looked down at the red flight bag without opening it. Then she carried it to the front door and left it there.

"I'm not sure I feel anything," Denise said. "I'm empty.

It's the same as when we were having a fight. I wouldn't feel anything then, I don't now. I'm shrinking inside."

Del was looking up at the kitchen wall, at the pictures of food and the basic color scheme. He was wondering about the DEA man's ex-wife. Did she ever pick fresh fruit in the backyard? Did she say *orange juice* in a new and exciting way?

"It's a matter of quality, I think," said Denise. "Our marriage was economy class, and it becomes a question of what you're willing to live with the rest of your life. Don't you see? We were living in the clipper section, where they cut out the frills on us. When you go first class, Del, there's only one way, and nobody is getting it better than you. That's what I believe. But when you go Super Saver, or any of those gimmick names, they're always holding something back, and I got tired of that."

Del was paying close attention. Despite the noise, and the fact that Denise had to shout to be heard, Del understood completely what she was getting at. But still he was thinking about himself.

Why had he gone ahead and married so young? He had no idea of what he actually wanted out of a marriage when he rushed into it with Denise. He just wanted to be married, that's all. To have a spouse and be able to check off the box for Married when he was filling out a form. An apartment or something that smelled strongly of disinfectant and good cooking, that's what Del was after. A place where you could get a good hard shower and find a few cold ones waiting in the fridge, with an oven that could clean itself and someone who would tell you if you needed a haircut. People fell in love and got married. What could be more true than that? What more could a person need?

His old home in Detroit, Del could remember that only vaguely, and only if he concentrated real hard. Otherwise his early years were a blur. He could picture neither parent very clearly, not his bedroom and not the furniture and not his childhood friends.

His first car, that he could remember. A tan Dodge sedan, with push-button transmission and furry dice dangling from the rearview, and Saint Anthony watching the road. As a kid he had collected hood ornaments—rockets and swans with orange wings, and silver horses on their hind legs. He could also recall perfectly, absolutely, the schoolyard where he had spent hours each and every day, up and down the concrete court, where weeds grew in the cracks and puddles could remain for days, with chains for nets rattling with each basket, dead spots on the backboard where rivets had come loose or rust had eaten through, bent rims and a faded foul key. Also Del remembered the sky-high feeling of being good—a winner all the time. It was something that could stay with a person forever.

"When I first met you," Denise told him, "I was so impressed. Handsome, tall, and, even though you were a cop, you still knew all of 'Alice's Restaurant.' It was what I needed, Del ... I can love you for so long, almost nine years, but then gradually stop loving you. And love someone else. I love Ethan. It's true, but how can that be possible?"

Del Plato looked up. The electric crepe-maker hung from a nail in the wall. The bank calendar was turned to the wrong month, with the birthdays marked off for people Del didn't know, and a doctor's appointment. Del was seeing the DEA man and his wife now, and they were a couple. The DEA man's wife, what would she look like? Del saw her as someone with beauty-parlor hair and Ultra-Lashes. She and her husband would watch television, sitting on the comfortable chairs she didn't leave behind for Del Plato. She might do the crossword puzzle in back of a *TV Guide,* but then what happens? The marriage slips, and soon the house is up for rent, partially furnished.

Did the DEA man leave his wife everything inside the safe-deposit box, or had he poked around in there first?

"When I was a kid," Del said, "I'm just remembering this now, I was a kid and I was coming home on the bus. It's an example of how there's a wrong time and a right time for emotions, and how they can screw you up. I'm fourteen or fifteen, and me and two friends had been out sledding. All of a sudden we're coming down the street, carrying our sleds; we're off the bus. It's that wind you can't really forget, winter back home, and then there's this crowd in front of my house, and I don't even see it, all these people, until I'm right there. Something is wrong. I ask a cop what it is—I'm shivering like crazy in the cold—and he tells me the show is over. The big blue overcoat, earmuffs, a cop. 'Some Mrs. Del Plato,' he tells me. 'They go, kid; happens every day.' Just like that. It's my mother, right—Mrs. Del Plato. She's gone; it happens every day. And when I look around I'm suddenly alone, because my two friends, they've taken off down the street."

Denise watched the construction crew working outside. They were pouring in a concrete foundation on the corner, hammering together a roof beside that. "I'm sorry," Denise said loudly, "but I can't even picture you being fourteen or fifteen years old. You're telling me this awful story, and all I can think about is why you never told it to me before. You never talked about yourself, Del. You never went out of your way to appear interesting."

"Anyway, it wasn't my mother. My aunt had come for a visit, and it was her. Mrs. Del Plato, my aunt. And I was disappointed when I went upstairs. I felt cheated. They had set me up for it: my mother is dead; it happens every day. But when I climb the hallway steps, which takes me forever, I know what I'm going to see up there and I'm mostly afraid of how everyone's going to look at me, what I'm supposed to do, but it turns out that my mother is right there. She's on the phone. 'Change your shirt,' she says to me. 'We have a tragedy.' I was feeling a hundred crazy things at the same time, and no way of knowing what was the right thing to feel."

"Is that a true story? Or did you just make it up?"

"It's true."

"All the time we were married, Del, and in love, you kept too much inside yourself. Nothing came out, nothing escaped. I hope I'm making myself clear to you. On a special day, what I got from you was a card with a seagull on it. 'Happy Birthday, your loving husband.' That could drive a person crazy, don't you see? 'Happy Anniversary, your loving husband.' You were satisfied; you had what you wanted. But what did I have? I had a husband with no complexity and no history, a husband with nothing to say."

Del Plato was looking out his front window. He was wondering about his lawnmower from Sears, which was still in the old garage. Denise didn't use it, did she? And Del was paying a guy twenty-five dollars a month to take care of the lawn in this rented house, so maybe he could get the lawnmower over here. He needed it more than she did. Right? He was wondering also if he had the makings of a complex person or not. Probably he was as complex as the next guy. Certainly Del had as much in the way of history and things to say as Ethan did. What did it matter anyway what Del wrote on a card? What kind of thing was that to be holding against somebody?

"Why is it only now you tell me these stories?" Denise asked him. "It makes me furious. After I stop caring, after nine years, after you move out and I have this flight bag filled with stuff, then you suddenly decide to develop a personality. It isn't fair."

"We're getting divorced," Del said. "I suppose that's why." What, was Ethan somehow deeper, with his gift certificates and adultery? A stepfather, was that complex?

Workers were going at it with power tools across the street. The weltering started and stopped and started again.

"Anyway," Del continued, "it was the cop back then who made some impression on me. The way he could be so unaffected by the whole thing, that appealed to me very much. Obviously the man had seen it all, and at the time I thought that was terrific. I suppose in a way I still do."

The radio continued in the other room. Citizens and commentary. A radio voice talked about another successful tourist season, Motel Row booked solid through spring break, a growing international flavor to South Florida.

"I think you have to meet Ethan," Denise said. Construction noise began once more and she had her hands over her ears. "Under different circumstances, you might like him," she shouted.

Even with all the insistent banging, Del could still hear Denise and even hear the radio. Sea bass were running from Deerfield to Golden Beach. A bale of marijuana fell from a twin-engine plane into somebody's patio fountain. At Inverrary a seventy-eight-year-old man shot a hole in one.

"His racquetball is really improving. I can't imagine you're interested, but Ethan is the club pro, lessons all day long. He won the open division in downtown Miami and in Boca. He's seriously considering a professional career. You probably don't care."

"Move in with him," Del said. "Keri likes him."

"His lawyer says not to."

"Ethan has a lawyer. Good for Ethan."

"A business manager actually."

Two workers in hard hats carried a coil of steel-wrapped conduit. Men with masks sprayed white stucco from a tank. From a distance came the dull, flat thumping of new groundwork.

Del said, "We're going through a rough time, me and you. It's only natural we're a little uneasy."

Sunlight scattered off the metal skeleton homes, and for the moment Del Plato had only a fractured vision of workers without shirts, a riddled white light of motion. He couldn't think. A shrill whistle sounded loudly across the street, and after that he couldn't hear. He was feeling something, but it was one of those confused feelings again. Was this anger, some kind of sorrow, another goddamn headache?

"You're too smart for me," Del Plato said. "You always were."

"Too smart to stay married to you."

"If we can still be close, Denise, if we can find some way to do that, I'd like to give it a try. For Keri, of course, but also because we've been through that much, me and you, and neither one of us has very many people we can really turn to."

"There it is again. This new side to you. What makes you think we can talk, Del? Why is it so different now that we're not together?"

A whistle blew again across the street, followed by jackhammers, heavy equipment, drills.

Denise shouted. "I don't trust you anymore. This is ridiculous."

She went to the front door and picked up her TWA bag of valuables. She was leaving. Del Plato waved. In her eyes, he saw what could have been anger.

It was over. He was certain of that.

You fucked up a marriage and this is the way you had to pay for it. You stepped out of line once too often and they threw the book at you.

"Denise . . . ?"

She turned from the doorway, gazed back at him.

"Will we work this out? I'd like to try."

"Sure."

"Denise, I'm serious."

"So am I."

"Say it then. Come on, promise me."

"We'll work this out."

Chapter
5

Jewboy Breed made sure he was standing a safe distance
away before he tapped the side of a dimly lit glass cage
with a penny held in his hand. Tap, tap, tap. Inside was a
twenty-five-foot snake that refused to move. Jewboy was origi-
nally from Philadelphia, and the only actual snake he could
recall having seen was a slithering chartreuse one that somebody had let loose during a 76ers' game, which had wriggled
through the bleachers until a Spectrum usher threw an empty
Schmidt's carton over it. This big snake inside the glass was
various shades of green and looked very much like a nice rug, a
department-store rug, all coiled and laced with intricate patterns. Breed wanted to know exactly what kind of beast it was.

"Anaconda," Del Plato said. "Read the sign."

Breed pressed his face to the tank and tapped again. Tap,
tap. "Does he bite?" Breed asked.

"Kills by crushing. Read the sign."

Breed was in full uniform and so was Del Plato. The glass
of the snake tank went up six feet, with gray round rocks on
the bottom, a small stream that trickled from a hose, and the
stump of a leafless tree.

The coiled snake had two thick lumps about a third of the way down its length. Wrapped around a branch of the tree was another anaconda, smaller, also with nice shimmering patterns that would have made attractive wallpaper. It had only one lump in its throat. Tap, tap, tap. The smaller snake was staring fiercely with hard black eyes at a mouse that was shivering behind a rock. Tap, tap. Tap, tap.

Del Plato had made it out to Florida Exotica after having spent five hours in court that morning, and now all he wanted to do was take off his patrolman's dull-black shoes and drink soda. He would rub the toes that ached. He figured he could also go for some TV, and some of that fresh fruit Denise used to bring in from the yard. Did that seem like too much to ask?

Breed was still tapping and trying to get the attention of these giant snakes. Jewboy made sudden karate-chop moves in front of the glass, saying "Here boy," and "Boo," and "Come on, big fella," but neither anaconda wanted any part of it.

Del himself had seen plenty of snakes, all sizes and colors. With his lawnmower he had mangled a few garters and even one small water moccasin that had slipped in from the canal. Denise absolutely refused to take out the trash after sundown because of snakes.

From the back of Florida Exotica, a short man with perfectly combed hair was looking with some amusement at the two officers in their blue-gray uniforms. The man wore mirrored sunglasses and a tight tank top with gold spangles. His hands were cupped loosely together, and when he bent over he might have been whispering something into the space between them.

"Did that guy just do something?" Breed asked. "I thought I noticed something odd."

"Hard to tell," Del Plato said.

"Because I'll be honest, Irish, is it extremely gross in here or what? A dog without a leash makes me nervous; cats make me reach for my stomach pills. Gail brought this cat home once, a hundred-and-twenty-dollar animal, cleaned itself like a psychopath. A week later I stuck that fucker right in the trunk and dumped it in the woods. They drink milk and sit in

your lap, tell me about it, but let them alone for two minutes
and those suckers come back with pieces of bird in their teeth."
Breed massaged his stomach to quiet things down inside, rubbing his belly in small gentle circles the way you would put an
alligator to sleep. "The point being, Del Plato, that these are
your more or less domesticated creatures which still manage to
get me all fucking shook. So you can imagine how I feel when,
here we are in this Amazon pet store, and the guy back there is
having a conversation with his hands."

Breed and Del Plato moved next to the scorpions, which
were all mixed together, brown and yellow and albino scorpions, scuttling and dragging their stingers. Breed peered
inside. Tap, tap. There were scorpions under flat stones,
others crouched in the sand, some poised with their tails
curled in the air.

"I don't mind telling you, I'm less than thrilled."

"This is business, Jewboy. Get a grip on yourself."

There were vampire bats, poison snakes, fish with teeth.

"Thank you for bringing me here, Irish."

There were black widow spiders. Each was in its own glass
cubicle, like an office worker. The black widows lounged
around on thick, messy webs, very ungraceful webs, full of un-
sightly clumps and dangling threads.

Del Plato was watching the guy in back. His hands were
still cupped loosely together and he was nuzzling close to
whatever was inside.

Breed said, "He's doing it again. This is a delightful experience, Del Plato, fucking Del Plato. You don't mind if I wait
outside."

Del was just watching the guy in back of Florida Exotica
and he was getting that feeling, where he could sniff the air
and tell what was for dinner. This was *his* feeling, the Del
Plato sense, and his intuition was acting up. Del had been
drifting off, but now he snapped back into things.

The storeowner in back turned his hands upside down and
continued whispering into the space between his fingers. Del
asked if he was Arriz, Arroz, Arroyo, something like that.

"Maceo Arriz." Between his hands, he blew gently and

then he gave a broad smile. "You'll understand if I don't shake hands. Like surprises, Officers?"

"I'm gone," said Breed. "I'm sorry. He's got something in his hands there, and he's asking if we like surprises." Breed clenched his teeth and patted for his stomach pills.

Del had to go with his feelings, and his feelings were that something definitely was up. What? Maybe trouble. Probably trouble.

Here was the pet shop, Del told himself. *Drug smuggling would be mentioned, just as Hooven had explained, and then monthly payoffs. What was the big deal in that? This action was strictly routine.*

But Del couldn't shake his feeling. Part of his job was to be alert, sure, but this was also the way he was, someone who tuned into his awareness and then listened, the way you would listen to a car mechanic's explanation of what was wrong if that mechanic wore overalls with a nametag, or the way you would listen to real-estate advice from a broker with an especially deep tan. Del felt like he was in touch. In a diner for instance—one of those places with red booths and a suspiciously long menu—he would search deep inside for his intuition and order from there. And in a full-court game, Del would rely on that same inner voice to tell him when to crash toward the hoop rather than pull up for a fifteen-foot jumper off the key. He liked to think that he could live natural, close to the ground, by his senses.

"I do not like surprises," Breed was explaining to Arriz. "There are tons of things I'm not enthusiastic about, but more than anything, I don't like surprises. If you open your hands, I'll be upset."

"In the market for anything special?" Arriz asked, opening his hands for just an instant and then closing them up fast. "We'll be glad to help you out."

Del was trying to piece together what was bothering him. There were purple neon lights, huge jungle plants with wet leaves and spooky veins, parrots with price tags on their feet.

Breed said, "What's this *we* shit? I caught that business with *we*. Irish, tell this geek please that I've had it up to here with animals. I'm going to empty my service revolver into him, *and* his hands, and then I'm going to open them up to see what he's got there."

Arriz uncupped his hands as soon as Breed was finished. A tarantula strolled easily from one palm to the other. It was the size of a hamburger and the same color. Over a wrist it stepped, casually, across a forearm, ten hairy legs inching higher. It came to the bend of an elbow and paused there, as if to check the view. Arriz blew amiably on the tarantula's fur and gave it some sweet talk.

"Tell me this is normal, Irish. Be truthful."

Arriz was stroking the tarantula's back. It shivered slightly and began to move again.

"Because personally I have my doubts. I question the normalcy of this entire setup here. From a reasonable perspective, Del Plato, just take a look at this. Okay? You got these hairy bugs from outer space, you got snakes that could swallow a linebacker. I think I'm raising some sound objections."

The tarantula continued climbing. Up the pet guy's shoulder it went, up his neck.

Breed had one hand near his weapon. "Let me ask you one question. What was your name . . . Arriz? With what's walking all over you now, that bites, doesn't it?"

"When he has to. Actually they make fine pets."

Del was tingling, waiting for something to happen. Outside it grew darker, with rumbling black clouds that choked the sun. A television was playing somewhere. Del Plato couldn't see the screen, but he could hear it. *Bowling for Dollars.* A mother of two was going to try her luck. Her special interests were calligraphy and precious metals. He could hear the hissing and low growls of things in cages.

Once, with Denise, he smoked some pot that had acquired an unappealing yellow mold from having been forgotten in the attic for a very long time, and Del developed an acute sensitivity from being high that was similar to the perception of danger he was experiencing now. Completely wrecked from the exotic pot, Del became alive for the very first time to battalions of white corpuscles and small antibodies inside his own body.

They were staging a full-scale war against vicious and vaguely Oriental-looking flu bugs going around that time of year, with barricade-storming and sophisticated matériel, and the only thing he could do to keep from going bananas was devour a super-deluxe pizza and half a box of Trix, not to mention the Lido cookies they had been saving for company.

Now Del knew he was on top of things inside Florida Exotica. He was crackling with signals like a shortwave. He could hear rain acting up outside, Breed's stomach making noise, the tarantula breathing on the pet guy's neck.

"I'm going to take a wild guess," Del Plato said. "Here we go. My guess is that you were expecting us to come by this afternoon. You were waiting for police at your door. That's my brainstorm. How's that sound to you?"

"Wow," Arriz said, pulling the tarantula off his cheek. "I'm impressed."

"There's more. Somebody told you we were coming. There's no contraband on the premises, no drugs, nothing illegal. You were prepared for a visit. This is just a hunch."

"I'm calling up Johnny Carson right now," said Arriz, "that's how impressed I am. Mental ability like that, it's some talent." Arriz placed the tarantula on the back of his hand and it climbed up his arm again. "Don't stop, you're batting a thouand so far."

There were sudden claps of thunder, the lights buzzing, creatures slithering, the hum of a slight headache coming on. The mother of two rolled her first ball on the Jersey side and knocked down five pins.

Breed had wandered off to a Gila monster's tank and tapped there with the same shiny penny. "Irish, what's this orange one over here? I think I like this one."

"Read the sign."

The tarantula climbed again to Arriz's neck and curled there for a while. Del was getting very edgy. Outside the rain came down with a hard steamy sound. The woman's second attempt was on the headpin and the audience applauded.

Breed was relatively comfortable beside the leathery Gila monster, which was lapping water from a Tupperware bowl.

Pieces of lettuce were all over the floor, and Breed figured any-thing that went in for salad couldn't be all bad. Gail's hun-dred-and-twenty-dollar cat hadn't gone *near* a piece of lettuce.

Suddenly the front door was thrust open. Three men came in—one, two, three—stamped their feet to shake off the rain-drops clinging to their hair and to their clothing, and then they pointed their guns. Wind swept into Florida Exotica, swirling gusts that made the tropical leaves shiver.

Del Plato was almost smiling. *I knew it,* he thought. He put up his hands. *Didn't I have this one pegged right from the start?*

Breed said, "Fuck this," and also put up his hands.

The gunmen seemed to have it worked out. Two of them took places on the near side of the store while the remaining one, shuffling away from the rain that continued to sweep in, guarded the front door. The one on his own was Joe Hooven. He was trying to hold his aim steady while brushing raindrops off his velvet jacket.

"At least this doesn't come as a total surprise," Arriz said from behind. "With that nightclub mental ability you must have known Mr. Parrajo was anxious to make your acquaint-ance."

Hooven, frowning, asked if you could do anything with velvet if it got wet in the rain.

Del Plato sized up the opposition. Arriz was behind them and would probably stay there. Hooven was Joe Hooven—you couldn't tell what he would do, especially if his clothes were in jeopardy. Another gun-pointer was a skinny kid with a silk-screened T-shirt that said SHE'S ONLY ROCK 'N' ROLL. The third one was a hefty character who kept either yawning or scowl-ing, it was hard for Del Plato to tell.

A fourth man rushed into Florida Exotica and closed the door behind him. This was Tommy Polio, wearing a nice blue suit, a three-piece job including a snappy vest of alternating blue checks. Tommy Polio also had a shiny scalp covered with clots of dried blood and clumps of surgical stitches. He pulled over a reticulated metal cage with parrots inside and sat on that. There were stitches that went up diagonally above each

ear in a series of short and long thread, like a Morse code of
flesh wounds. More stitches made swooping perpendicular
patterns across bony parts of the skull, some in back, some in
front, short, tight stitches connecting into longer arcs. Tommy
Polio's head looked like a map of overseas air routes—New
York to Athens, Los Angeles to Tokyo and back.

A few feet away, Del Plato and Breed were standing with
their arms upraised. Breed kept glancing behind him, checking on the tarantula, which was still somewhere on Arriz. Jewboy didn't believe for one second that line about how they
make great pets. A tarantula didn't even look like the kind of
thing you would stick in your trunk and drive out to the
woods. Cats, okay, he could see where some unsuspecting people might be fooled by the purring and the twine unraveling,
and maybe let some demented feline into the house, where it
would bring its dead and possibly suck out a baby's breath,
one minute sleeping and slothful and the next minute crazed
with lust and blood. Cats had a good scam going; Breed could
understand how certain civilians might fall for it. A hundred
twenty dollars for something that would spit and yowl and
lick itself all over. But these tarantula babes couldn't possibly
turn a profit.

Tommy Polio, this well-tailored man with stitches, spoke
up. "You know who I am," he said in a voice that could
straighten out the worst delinquents. "You know why I'm
here. Don't waste my time; I won't hurt you more than I
have to."

Del Plato said, "How's it going, Tommy?" and tried to put
his hands down. But the gunman who was either scowling or
yawning made a noise from somewhere deep in his throat—a
grunt, or perhaps a kind of snore—"Hrumggh, rrzzemm," and
Del chose to keep his hands up because, even if it was a snore,
Del pegged it as a threatening type of snore, absolutely.

Hooven, waving his gun haphazardly, was just all honked
off at his ruined velvet. And the kid was nodding his head to
the beat of some rock and roll tune, not even in a proper position to discharge his weapon with authority. Del Plato was
slightly pissed that he had to deal with such amateurs. He was

anxious for some hard-edged mothers who knew how to sight down on a catch.

"I had a hair transplant," Tommy Polio explained. He winced as he touched a tender cluster of stitches in the vicinity of some northern air corridor. "I should never have let them slice me up with hair transplants. A Gambino wouldn't sit still for that. Am I right or wrong? But vanity—my wife said do it, it would make her happy to live with a full head of hair. So what did I do, I did it. Maybe one of those Gallo brothers would have gone in for this hair, but none of your top names, not a Lansky. So what am I talking about? ... I'm listening. Any ideas, speak right up."

There was a complete silence inside Florida Exotica. Suddenly nobody was moving. There was rain and quiet breathing.

What's this? Del Plato thought, perking up a little. *Some sort of stratagem? Some competition?*

"Maceo," said the boss, Tommy Polio, in his usual shouting manner, "I'm calling on you. Start us off."

Arriz had come hesitantly from the back room with a jar of crickets in his hand. "Was that a parable, Mr. Parrajo?" he asked in a slightly shaky voice.

"Good, Maceo. Not a parable, but I'm making an analogy. The hair transplant was four thousand, which is a lot of money. Yes or no? ... Yes or no?" Everyone said yes. "But what did I do? I cut my losses. I looked at the facts, and I came to a decision. So what's my point?"

The gunmen coughed, then shuffled, then moved from one foot to the other or aimed their guns at Breed instead of Del Plato, or Del Plato insted of Breed. Thunder continued to rumble and rain kept smacking down.

Arriz had placed the tarantula in a glass tank beside Breed. The tarantula was quickly weaving a slanted web of thin, shiny silk, crisscrossing threads that were all anchored at various corners. When its web was finished, the tarantula packed the excess thread neatly inside its abdomen and then struck a crouching pose in the web's center.

"I'm talking all the time for what, for a point. Come on,

this isn't hard." Tommy Polio's voice boomed through Florida
Exotica and even the most venomous-looking animals seemed
to slink away. Tommy Polio began to thump his foot against
the metal parrot cage he was sitting on. "I'm waiting!"

Del Plato's hands were getting tired. He played ball twice
a week, both ends of the court, an hour and a half of hard work,
and he couldn't even keep his hands in the air.

"What's my point?" Parrot beaks were coming a little too
close. Tommy Polio thought he felt a nip or two back there. He
kicked the cage with a backward swipe of his heel and the parrots were sent squawking in a flurry of rain-forest feathers.
"Felix, so what's the main idea?"

"Hrrggungh."

"Hector from Orlando?" Tommy Polio was impressed
with the quality of feathers scattered all around. He kicked
again, just for the hell of it. "You're my soldiers. You march
with me and you're underworld figures! Help me out, Hector."

"Huh?"

"What am I talking about?"

"I dunno." Hector from Orlando had his head down and
was looking very hard at the splash of lettering across his
chest, as if the answer might be on his T-shirt. "What? I
dunno, Mr. Parrajo."

Tommy Polio covered his eyes and shook his head in dis-
belief. He explained that Hector from Orlando was a nephew,
in and out of military schools, trouble with grades, but family
was family and the kid was there to learn the business. Del
Plato and Breed said they understood.

Jewboy also saw an opening. He waved his upraised hand.
"I think I can sum up your analogy, Mr. Polio. I'm pretty sure
what you're saying, basically and fundamentally, is that you
learn by your mistakes. People learn through experience."

"Excellent. What was I asking? Was I asking for something hard?"

Arriz unscrewed the cover of the glass jar he had brought
from the back room. He reached inside to stir up the crickets.
Then he opened the lid of the tarantula tank, whacked the bot-

tom of the jar, and the crickets jumped inside. For a moment
the tarantula stood up on all its legs before slowly settling
down again. Crickets hopped everywhere, wildly, like they
were at a party.

Del Plato also took a stab at it. "You don't want us into
your operations, Tommy; that's what you were driving at with
how you cut short your losses. You want us, no offense, out of
your hair."

"Someone with brains," Tommy Polio shouted. "And no
offense taken, for sure. Which one are you? Let me get it
straight. Are you Officer Laurel or you Officer Hardy?"

"I'm Starsky," said Del, feeling good. He put his arms
down at last and draped one on Breed's shoulder. "Me and
Hutch here are pretty sharp, no question about that."

Tommy Polio got up and walked forward to tap the apartment complex of black widows, just as Breed had done to the
snake cage. Tap, tap, tap. The top floor of spiders began to stir
and jerk and weave new thread.

"If there's one thing I hate more than anything else,"
Tommy Polio said, "it's a sense of humor. That gets me. We
have guns, and you start in with Starsky and Hutch. I have no
patience for wit; I have no patience for jokes."

Del Plato was standing beside Jewboy Breed, both of
them keeping an eye on the action inside the tarantula cage.
All the crickets had gathered in a sort of wagon-train circle,
and a few of them jumped out as scouts. The tarantula
was poised on its web, legs tucked in, pretending to look like a
toupee.

"You two jerks are into my payroll, into my operational
system, and the thing is this, the thing is that I'm tired of it.
Who I want is the one feeding you information. I got fifty, I
got seventy people working for me in this city, and at least one
of them sucks. Very direct now and very plain, I'm telling you
what I want. I want my informer. Someone sells me out, that's
who I want. I want a name."

"It works two ways," Del Plato said very calmly. He felt
light, buoyant. It was almost an effort to keep his feet on the
ground. "Look at the way you were prepared for me and my

partner to stop by this afternoon. I was thinking that we also have a serious problem with informers. Tommy, I'm as concerned as you are."

A cricket scout was checking out the tarantula's web, poking at strands of thread. But the tarantula wasn't moving yet. The cricket inched higher, feeling with its antennae. Nothing. Another inch. Everybody was watching now. Slowly the tarantula began to rise up on its legs.

"I think we can work out something," Del Plato said, still bouncy. "A compromise, Tommy, a little horse trading."

Tommy Polio told Del to shut up for a minute.

The web was stickier up high, and the cricket was slower in lifting its feet from the vibrating silk, pausing here and there with cautious antenna checks, as if about to enter some tricky intersection. It stepped on this thread, that one, and finally the wrong one. Suddenly the tarantula attacked. Tightroping down the web, in an instant it was all over its victim. The tarantula's abdomen doors flashed open and the cricket was flipped over and tied in a small bundle. Then the tarantula's jaws came out and two pincers swiftly pierced its pray.

"I'm waiting for a name," boomed Tommy Polio. "I want my traitor!"

Del Plato, filled with energy and ideas, was considering other tough situations he had been in. Always there had been some way out. In the course of duty he had disarmed perpetrators with the same disregard for personal welfare. Eight years he had done his service for Miami Metro. Officer Del Plato, doing his duty. He talked down hot Hispanics and snapped-out mall shoppers. He soothed sullen teenagers, arrested ethnics of every origin, gave directions to tourists.

"Look," Breed said to Del Plato, "that man has a legitimate bone to pick with you, Irish, and the moral thing right now is to tell Mr. Polio whatever he wants to know. Just spill the beans and let's go somewhere else. They got fucking bugs in here that assassinate you."

Tommy Polio sighed impatiently and fooled with the buttons on his vest. It was obvious he was the restless sort—someone who couldn't sit very long with a meal. He might pull out his own transplanted hair so there would be nothing left to comb.

"My partner is getting divorced," Breed explained to Tommy Polio. He took a pack of Junior Mints from his shirt pocket. "Irish gets very animated and irrational when the odds are stacked the other way. Just watch what he does. I'll bet he gives you a complete stonewall routine. It wouldn't surprise me."

Actually Del wasn't at all sure what he would do. He was curious to find out. He listened to the rain outside, waited for things to fall into place.

"Go ahead," Breed was saying, "cut off his finger. He won't make a sound. Get one of these boys to hit him on the head with a gun. He would not fall down."

"What I'll do," Tommy Polio said in his extra-loud fashion, "I'll propose a deal. Here goes. I knew two cops would be crowding me this afternoon for another payoff, and the way I knew is Jackie Molson. You know him, this Molson? He sold you out. He's *your* traitor." Tommy Polio rapped his knuckles on the black widow spider community. They scurried up and down their low webs, bouncing the sticky silk. "To me this Molson is nothing, a name, a lowlife I never met. Also I don't care about you, Laurel and Hardy, Del Plato and Breed. From you all I want today is one important thing, and that's why I have my soldiers here with guns. I want my traitor. Felix wants my traitor. Joe wants my traitor. My nephew Hector from Orlando wants my traitor." He banged the spiders again. "I told you. Now you tell me."

No one spoke. Tommy Polio waited a few long seconds before he called over Felix and Joe Hooven. Then he pointed to Jewboy Breed. "Stick that one's hand in the spiders."

Hooven was the one most surprised by this, and very uneasy. He felt he wasn't the one for intimidation and goon work. If the man wanted goons, he could go out to the schoolyards or hire more relatives. Joe Hooven was a musician, not a thug. Looking very unhappy, Hooven removed his velvet jacket and folded it neatly with the lining on the outside before taking a few cautious steps forward.

Felix wasn't at all unfamiliar with what to do. He handed his weapon to Arriz for safekeeping and said, "Uurrallgggh. Friggzzmm," and then came up to a sneaky position behind Breed.

"Tell me a traitor! Give me the name and I won't have my soldiers put your hand inside."

Del Plato moved slightly away to give everyone some room. He asked Arriz if the black widows would be fatal. Arriz adjusted his sunglasses and said probably not a single bite, but if they kept Breed's hand inside, then the spiders would massacre him for sure. Del said that's pretty much what he had figured.

"Tell me who!"

"You got goldfish?' Breed asked. "I'll put my hand in some goldfish, but with this spider business I'll have to object."

"Who!"

"Those things really bite, don't they?"

"Who!"

Breed pointed a finger directly in front of him. Joe Hooven was standing there. "Him," said Breed. "This homo right here. He's your man; take him away."

Tommy Polio slammed the spider tank with the flat part of his hand and the black widows began running up and down like crazy inside their little condominium units, weaving and pouncing and tugging their nets.

Hooven discreetly massaged his heart because he thought it had stopped working.

"Who!"

Breed pointed next at Felix, and said *he* was the one, that miserable traitor, that spineless villain.

At this point Del Plato figured it was time. He stood up nice and tall. "Say we're plugged in," he told Tommy Polio in a tone that suggested reason. "Say you're right about us buying information from people in your organization. Every month you pay us off, we look the other way when there's bookmaking and contraband all over, and we all profit nicely from this arrangement. Me and J.B. do well, and you also do well. But if it wasn't us, someone else would be on your pay-roll—the county sheriff's office or the DEA—lots of people are out looking for crime. You know us, Tommy. You know we're not greedy; we take what we can get. But you start dealing with these other law-enforcement agencies, and the unknown factor exists. Maybe they'll want a percentage, or maybe they'll be after promotions and throw a collar on the whole deal—you don't know what kind of instability you can run up against, Tommy. You should be happy you finally met us. You can see that we're fair—we're businessmen."

Tommy Polio considered this only briefly. He thumped the spiders again. "I made an offer. His hand over there, I won't put it in the spiders if you tell me what I need to know. Fair, you talk about fair, what could be more fair than that?"

"Sounds good to me," said Breed. He pointed to Hector from Orlando. "There's the bastard. Stick *his* hand in the fucking spiders."

Del Plato felt as if he could simply wave his arms or something and put an end to the whole thing. He could snap his fingers and be somewhere else. Outside in the rain, for instance, just like that, in a jiffy. He could be on *Bowling for Dollars* if he wanted, rolling a string of strikes, raking in the loot. He could be on the hardwood court, wearing his jig shoes and ahead of the pack, floating in from the foul line to stuff one in with both hands. He could reach out and take away all their guns as if he were snatching away matches from the hands of small children.

Del wondered seriously if there might be something wrong with him. It seemed to him highly unnatural to be so unafraid. Probably he was a little sick. That would be a logical explanation, he decided.

Del Plato wanted to know more about Jackie Molson. "I'd be curious to know what it was worth to him. We'll take care of Jackie Molson in our own way, but how much would someone go for to sell out his friends?"

"Five hundred dollars," said Tommy Polio. "I paid that kind of money to meet you. But the thing is this. I'm still waiting."

Del's breathing was beginning to go out of rhythm. His respiration came in sudden deep puffs, like someone in a troubled sleep, dreaming of bats or creative financing. What should he do? Should he fire a weapon, start a brawl, say sarcastic things about Tommy Polio's hair?

"Let me put it another way," Tommy Polio said, banging his knuckles against the spiders to keep them active. "Say there's a far-off land, and this sultan is there—a wise sultan. He can't complain, this sultan; he's doing well. What happens though is that with all his lieutenants and his vicars, his viziers, one of them gets greedy. And the good guy, the sultan, he finds out, and to put it plainly, the guilty party, the vizier, he's put to death. Am I right or wrong with *vizier*? But everybody else then, they all live happily ever after." Tommy Polio was checking his reflection in the glass of the spider tank. He patted down some unkempt stitches. "Joe, let me ask you something now. The story I just told, that mean something to you?"

"Sure does, Mr. Parrajo." Hooven coughed nervously and made a weak grab for Breed's wrist. "Hey, really, you can't believe what these cops are telling you. They just keep blowing it out—you got to see that. Because none of us would like dare do anything, Mr. Parrajo."

"Is it clear how much I want my traitor? Yes or no?" The gunmen all said yes to Mr. Parrajo. "In my story, Joe, let me ask you another question. What do you think happened to the greedy vizier? Was his death a quick one, or was it slow and painful?"

"I'd have to go with quick, Mr. Parrajo, just off the top of my head. Because that sultan sounds all right to me, and maybe he'd even let that vizier cat go, you know, if the guy maybe promised . . ."

"It would be painful, Joe. How do you think my sultan would have it arranged?"

"Hey, I really couldn't say, Mr. Parrrajo." Hooven continued to struggle, tugging with half a heart at Breed's wrist. Hooven had to do what he was told, but he was also afraid of pushing Breed too far. Breed was such a lousy sport about things. Hooven would much rather have been sticking Del

Plato's hand into the spiders. "If this vizier got to get his plug pulled, maybe his car gets blown up or like that."

"First he would be tied up, and then parts of this double-crosser's body would be severed. Do you know why a traitor would die that way?"

"Because you know that in a million years we would never do anything, Mr. Parrajo, nothing funny. Me and Hector from Orlando was just saying the other day, honest to God, how you treat us really right, with bonuses and all.... Hey, Hector, isn't that right? We were saying that stuff, right?"

"As an example, Joe." Tommy Polio pounded the spiders. "For other viziers and underlinings, so no one else gets greedy. And because in my story, the sultan I'm talking about happens to enjoy that kind of torture." Tommy Polio whacked the spiders. Everybody jumped. Lightning sizzled outside. "Stick his hand in there," said Tommy Polio.

Felix took a grip on Breed from behind. Joe Hooven stepped forward to get Jewboy's hand, and Hooven's face had a surprisingly stern look on it. Hooven circled with caution, like a wrestler facing an opponent who was known to go out and pull all kinds of cheap shit—strangle holds and blunt objects concealed in his trunks, false pleas for mercy. Hooven threw a few dekes this way and that, flipping the hair out of his eyes, looking for an advantage.

Breed calmly explained that a joke was a joke—ha, ha—but very shortly he was going to get extremely ticked off.

Del Plato thought he might be watching something on TV, an action series in which the good guys have to make their escape against huge odds. How do they pull it off this time? But he couldn't shake the sensation that nothing could happen. He was drifting and free, as though everyone else were underwater and he wasn't. They had to push against tons of force simply to walk or sit down or make a threatening move. All that Del Plato could see was slow motion. These other people were submerged. He was on air.

Do it, Del Plato told himself. *Just do it.*

Hector from Orlando put down his gun to help with Breed. They had a problem getting Jewboy under control.

Arriz puffed his chest, blew a kiss to his tarantula, and also stepped forward.

"That crooked vizier, that thief, he has to pay! I want him! He owes me!"

Do it. Go on, do it.

Del raised his arms. Suddenly everyone froze. It was wonderful.

Just the least little bit, that's how much Del Plato pushed, or so it seemed to him—his wrist, his fingers, a nudge—and the entire condominium of spiders began to topple. So slowly. Down, down.

Down.

Nobody could move. Del seized Breed and pulled him toward the front door. It was really and truly slow motion. Still nobody was reacting. The multi-unit glass tank was going down, down. What was everyone doing? When would they finally move?

Crash!

Glass cracked and shattered open. Black things were suddenly loose and on the move.

Del Plato was already out the front door with Breed. They stopped to watch for a moment. There was plenty of time. They stood in the rain to witness the mess.

Felix stomped spiders with one foot and hopped up and down on the other. "Oorowgh," he snarled, leaping after a big one.

Hooven said, "Oh shit," and slapped around for his gun. He wasn't going to get spider junk all over the soles of his shoes. No way. And Arriz could only shriek at seeing his merchandise scurrying here and there. Tommy Polio's soldiers were stomping at will, and Hooven pumped a few rounds into the carpeting. Florida Exotica soon reverberated with thumping feet and savage yells, like the floor show of a Polynesian tourist trap.

Del Plato had his crummy old Dodge on the corner and they were going that way through the rain. Winds careened off the shore. Wet, torn leaves blew past them. Del Plato really wished he owned something more zippy in which to make this getaway. Why should Denise get to keep a better car? They weren't even divorced, just separated, nothing official, a mutual agreement between married adults, that was all. And here he had to escape from gangland figures in a piece-of-shit automobile that cost an arm and a leg each time you had to fill it up, that needed new shocks and considerable bodywork, a new tail section too, for crying out loud.

Tommy Polio thundered out the door after them. "Run away!" he roared. "Run, you jackals!"

The car sputtered and the engine did a sort of shimmy but did not start. Del wasn't surprised. What was he supposed to feel like anyway, driving this heap? He started it again. Finally it caught, and he gunned the motor loud. He would have to get a new car. He'd leave this one way out in the woods, where Breed had ditched his cat.

"I'm waiting for something!" Tommy Polio's voice came booming. "I won't rest! My traitor! I want him!"

Chapter

6

Del Plato waited outside with the motor coughing. He was afraid to shut off the engine. Del figured he had already been through enough adventure. He watched the front steps, where kids were wading for small change in a fountain. The radio had only AM, another sore point, and for the whole evening they had been playing strictly oldies stuff—"Duke of Earl," "Palisades Park," "Please, Mr. Custer." Del did not like oldies stuff, not at all. It was today that counted. Here and now, present tense. Del also didn't like kids taking money out of fountains when they should have been home studying for college or something, but he was inside the car, listening to pimple commercials and people winning fifty dollars' worth of groceries for admitting they listened to stations with pimple commercials, and just what the hell was Jewboy doing up there for so long anyway?

Del Plato was watching the front door because Breed was supposed to be bringing down some nurses. But he'd been up there maybe twenty or twenty-five minutes already—maybe half a goddamn hour—while Del was downstairs in a car that

113

you couldn't turn off, with kids swiping wet coins that people had made important wishes with—maybe peace on earth, for Christ's sake. And what about this stupid radio? With all the oldies bullshit—songs that are supposed to make you remember things that are not coming back again and you might as well forget anyway, like pizza at fifteen cents a slice and sharkskin suits and multiple orgasms. What was going on? Del punched the steering wheel and hurt his hand doing it.

After the pet-store encounter, they had driven directly to a 7-Eleven. A sign posted in the front window said ONLY 2 STUDENTS AT ONE TIME. Jewboy rushed to the phone booth with quarters while Del hurried inside for a six-pack of Lites and tuna salad sandwiches.

"First I tried the cheerleader," Breed explained after getting back inside the Dodge and popping open a can, "but nothing doing on that end. Which is unfortunate, because I can't overemphasize what an exceedingly attractive woman this is, Irish, and on top of that she is completely crazy. Totally berserk. You're my friend, Irish; we've been through all sorts of shit, and I would even have let you go first."

Del had never ever been with anyone he considered crazy. During his nine years with Denise he had been with only two other women, and both had urged Del to get a divorce and marry them. One was a neighbor with a degree in the humanities, who was also seeing another man at the time, and the other was an energetic woman in real estate who had sold the house to Del and Denise and who still sent season's greetings. Neither of them had been even remotely berserk. Both, in fact, had been pretty glum throughout the entire affair—going through motel rooms the way you would go through maybe a hospital ward, inspecting sheets and things, very quiet. Neither one had been exceedingly attractive. Del stopped seeing the industrious real-estate lady when she told him with obvious pleasure that all her four-year-old wanted for lunch was "monster cheese." Del admitted this was cute, but afterward decided she rarely showed half as much pleasure in the motel bed, no matter what kind of twists and unusual turns he could come up with, no matter how much change he dropped into the jiggle machine, and that anyway if you fooled around on the side you didn't necessarily have to hear about monster cheese. He broke it off abruptly with his humanities-degree neighbor when the word *suicide* came up three times in her conversation.

Breed, however, was very animated now and was continually poking Del Plato whenever punctuation was called for. "My nurse, Irish—and pay close attention to this so you'll always remember who your friends are—my nurse was watching *Masterpiece Theatre* with her roommate, who is also an RN. I mentioned my nurse to you, didn't I? It's ten minutes from here. Step on the gas, Del Plato. I told them both to wear their uniforms."

Del Plato had a change of clothes in the trunk, and in the men's room outside the 7-Eleven he took off his patrolman's uniform and put on his sleeveless basketball jersey with the number 23 on it, his cutoff gray sweatpants, and his ripped sneakers with purple laces. No socks. Breed left on his uniform pants but took off everything else, including his shoes, stripping down to a T-shirt that said IT'S BETTER IN THE BAHAMAS.

Outside the nurses' dorm now, drumming his fingers on the dash to "Running Bear," Del inspected his appearance in the rearview mirror. He didn't look too bad, did he?

Del recalled a time in Detroit—*Jesus, was it really that long ago?*—when he and a buddy from the church basketball squad had driven downtown for some fun you had to drive downtown for, and Del wound up getting lucky with the cashier at a Walgreen's. They had stopped there for cigarettes and the latest ball scores. Del told the cashier—a teenager with a kerchief in her hair and plucked eyebrows—that she had really nice eyes and a figure that wasn't half-bad either. It was a completely unrehearsed line that came to him with surprising ease. She ate it up and let Del drive her home. They smoked cigarettes, and then she showed him where to park behind a small, dark factory that made automobile floor mats. She unbuttoned her blouse and beat Del off inside his pants while the radio played "Duke of Earl." The cashier thrashed inside his pants and his poor fish got terribly mauled and cut

by his partially open zipper; he had scabs for two weeks. But
he had walked up to a downtown girl, and he had been in control of things, and getting your crank yanked by a cashier
with no eyebrows had to be a pretty good deal in anybody's
book. Also, Del had completely forgotten his basketball buddy,
who was left in a pretty seedy section with only public trans-
portation to take him home.

Finally the nurses came down the dorm steps wearing
their starchy whites, white sensible shoes, and a medical-supply bag with a bright and reassuring red cross in the center.
One nurse was very black and leggy, which Del was able to
take completely in stride. After a day like this, if mix and
match was on the agenda, well, he could go for that too. The
black nurse was trying not to get her hair wet from the fountain spray.

Breed put on his patrolman's cap and sat in the back with
his black nurse. She said her name was Sasha. Del offered
either a beer or half a tuna sandwich. His date for the evening
was Charlotte, who said she hated *Masterpiece Theatre* and
was from Winnipeg, and she had to pay taxes in two countries.

Without even giving it half a thought, Del went directly
with the percentages and took a sure shot. He told Charlotte
she had really nice eyes and a figure that wasn't half-bad
either.

"*Star Trek* was just going on," said Sasha from the backseat. "You know that show? I love it, I really do. Especially
when they do all that science talk, with dilithium crystals and
solenoid reactors. Don't you love it? Scotty's my favorite."

"Mr. Sulu is the one *I* like," Charlotte piped in. She had a
round face and pale-blue eyes that were open too wide, as
though she had just sat on someone's hand. It made Del suspect there were glasses upstairs. She wore a generally bewildered expression, like someone hunting down baggage in an
airport terminal. Del figured this was just his kind of girl.
"Mr. Sulu is the only one who looks *happy* out there," Charlotte pointed out. "He's glad to be in another universe, seeking
out other life-forms on a five-year mission. I also like Mr. Scott,
and admire his loyalty to the *Enterprise,* because he's the one

everybody depends on when all of a sudden you scan a Klin-
gon fleet command or a runaway planet. But Mr. Sulu *smiles.*
He's a friendly man. I think that's very important when
you're in outer space."

"They're educational programs too," said Sasha. "You
follow *Star Trek?* There are monsters who are really your
imagination, and God, and people who can never fall in love.
Always something different."

Del Plato, driving seventy-five miles an hour back to his
place, snapped open another pop-top and offered it around.
Charlotte moved a little closer beside him in the front seat and
said, "No, thanks." She opened her medical-supply bag. Inside
were two bottles of Boodles gin, a whole lime and clear plastic
cups. Also some fat joints held together with a rubber band,
pills inside an aspirin bottle with a child-proof cap, a change
of underwear, some orange sour balls, a game for youngsters of
all ages called Don't Tip the Waiter, an enema bag, syringes
and stuff, and a *Star Trek* novel in paperback.

Del asked if he could have one of those jays right away.

They got to the rented house and Del Plato let Charlotte
press his electric-eye garage-opener. They went in through the
empty den. Del picked marijuana seeds off his tongue while
the nurses unpacked their medical bag for cocktails. Then he
went over to thumb through his record collection and see what
kind of winners Denise had left him.

Other than the stereo cabinet, there was no furniture in
the living room. The den had two blue director's chairs Del
Plato had found on a shelf in the garage. He moved the outdoor furniture inside for a dining room—three chairs with
green-and-yellow straps, a lounge chair with green-and-yellow
straps that could convert to four horizontal positions, and an
aluminum table with a green-and-yellow Cinzano umbrella.

Charlotte was examining a coffee table the DEA man's
wife was supposed to have taken as part of the settlement. It
had a wide variety of matchbook covers and foreign coins beneath the glass. Reading the coffee table, Charlotte named the
various restaurants she had already been to, and others where
she had plans to dine. Sasha flipped on the tube to see if she

could catch the end of that particular *Star Trek* episode, with
rocklike creatures who live much longer than we do and who
communicate by very advanced methods of thought waves that
probably Einstein couldn't even get down on a blueprint. But
since it was already time for some movie in black and white
during Burt Lancaster week, Sasha instead set up gin with
lime in clear plastic cups and also set up the children's game
on the umbrella table, brushing green-and-yellow fringes from
her face.

Del liked the way things were going. He mentioned this to
Breed, who said, "Irish, we're the same people, you and I, and
you have to realize that. We're two of a kind. We have no one
to rely on but one another. You work hard for a living, don't
you?"

"I do," said Del Plato.

"So do I. I work hard and I also like to play hard. But explain that to a civilian, Irish, or a wife. Tell them what we go
through each day. All the violent crime we endure, the constant public dissatisfaction, the athlete's foot we pick up in the
showers. You can't minimize the drawbacks, Del Plato, you
cannot do that. You see what I'm driving at?"

"Vaguely."

"Watch out for your loyalties, Irish. We're scheming
something—me, you, and Joe Hooven. Me and you come first.
The faggot comes last. Way last. Because of reasons previously
brought up between you and me and too numerous to mention." Jewboy waved across the bare living room to Sasha. He
made enema signals to her. "Also," he told Del Plato, "don't
drink too much. You have to drive us all home later."

Del Plato took the nurses on a tour of the rented home. He
showed them day-to-day things, commonplace but integral,
things he had probably never noticed or paid enough attention
to while he was with Denise. Very likely that was the reason
Denise was now seeing a man who gave his daughter gift certificates and key rings for Christmas, and the reason she had
taken all the decent albums so that all he could play was left-
over stuff like *The Rascals Greatest Hits* and *Tango Time!* and
Favorite American Legion Marches. Who knew about dish de-

tergents before, or frozen lemonade? But that's what he showed the nurses on his tour—spare vacuum cleaner bags and extra light bulbs, empty jars and coupons from the Wednesday paper, an electric toothbrush.

From room to room he led them, while Breed assembled Don't Tip the Waiter with instructions geared for a third-grader. Del Plato pointed out linen closets with plenty of storage space, the bedroom drawer where the DEA man kept his insurance policies and bank statements, the sign above the dinette set that said DO IT. JUST DO IT.

"What a great color for the carpet," said Sasha, sipping gin. "You could spill and no one would know."

Charlotte thought the ceilings were terrific. Nobody could bang down if you had a party at two in the morning.

He showed them another bedroom, only half-covered with a wallpaper design of old-time newspaper advertisements. CA-DILLAC SEVILLE $911, GENTLEMEN'S TAILORED SHIRTS FROM IRELAND, A STOVE WHICH COOKS WHILE NOBODY IS HOME. On the floor were remaining rolls of wallpaper, a step stool, and a bucket of paste which had turned to something you couldn't lift with one hand.

Del felt as if he might have been the President guiding friends or the press through East Wings and Madison Rooms, a modern and self-assured President, whose First Lady, okay, was currently estranged, but still he could answer any question and even iron collars without much trouble. *This,* Del Plato decided, *was how people lived. In houses, where they knew what was what and where to find it. With a list of emergency phone numbers. With canned goods in the pantry and extra coffee.* He had whizzed past so much with Denise; everything had been mere scenery. What had he been doing then? What was so important? She had every goddamn right to boot him out and keep a new car. Could he have found the Fantastik or a feather duster in his own house, or even the postage stamps?

Jewboy Breed clapped his hands for attention and explained the rules of the game. A cardboard waiter in a tuxedo rocked back and forth on flimsy supports—a big-nosed guy who looked like he made a lot of undeclared income—and the idea was to place cardboard food on the waiter's tray. If your piece of food made the waiter drop anything on his tray, you lost that round, and you had to remove an article of clothing.

"It's strip poker," Jewboy explained. "But when I play poker, I like to play for money. Say you deal yourself a full boat, or you shoot the works and you draw to an inside straight. Sometimes all you get is a sock, or a hair barrette. You know how annoying that can be? This way it's a game, and it's all in good fun."

Del went over to put something on the stereo. But what? Finally he made a selection. *Tango Time!*

Charlotte gave the waiter a pepperoni pizza to start off the game; Breed tossed in a lollipop. He told the nurses about this run-in, that very afternoon, and it was the man right there, Del Plato, who had pulled them out of some deep trouble and had probably saved Jewboy Breed from spending the rest of his days on a life-support system.

"I guess I saved him," said Del Plato with just the right kind of matter-of-fact tone. He asked if those were aspirin inside the aspirin bottle. Nobody seemed to mind the hot Latin beat in the background.

"There was incredible tension," said Breed. "I knew the only thing to possibly restore us would be a couple of sexy registered nurses."

Charlotte and Sasha exchanged glances. Sasha poured more drinks and passed another joint.

"I knew you led an interesting life," Charlotte said softly. "It's just like this one episode where the captain was held inside a hollow asteroid, and they were going to probe Kirk's brain with a machine that looked like a scary Mr. Coffee. It would have sucked out all his intelligence and changed the color of his eyes."

It was Charlotte's turn, and she added some alphabet soup. Distracted with her story, she tipped over the waiter's tray, spilling soup and a sandwich. She had to unbutton her white nurse's dress and step out of it. She was wearing white pantyhouse with no undies and a bra that hooked together in front.

Del started on gin with lime out of a clear plastic cup.

"Spock couldn't do a thing," Sasha said, adding a cheese-burger to start the next round. "He's a complicated man. Spock has these religious and moral problems you can't believe. But at the last second it's Scotty who finally gets the diode generator working, and they break away from the force field with a warp factor five."

Breed upset the tray with a strawberry tart and removed his T-shirt that said IT'S BETTER IN THE BAHAMAS.

Charlotte was adamant about the fact that there would have been no *Star Wars* without a *Star Trek*, and she didn't even notice or care that a small pale nipple was peeking out. Del Plato noticed. He stood up slowly and staggered to the stereo for side two of *Tango Time!* The flip side introduced castinets and threw in a quick *cha-cha.* Del told himself that three hundred years from now he was going to remember this night. He was wearing his basketball outfit and playing strip-tease games with two nurses who could give each other mean-ingful glances. These were women who could put a guy on the spot. Right? And it was up to that guy to meet the challenge.

They continued boozing it up and loading down the waiter with heaps of stuff—malteds, spinach, lean pastrami. Everybody was snapping fingers and bobbing.

Sasha soon enough was down to her muted white panty-hose and one white shoe. Charlotte had only her pantyhose and a shoe. And Breed was out of the game, down clean in record time. Jewboy was also shaking his head and giggling, mostly because Del Plato hadn't taken off a single thing. Drunk, and hoping more than anything to wrestle either Charlotte or Sasha to the mat, Del still had to play the game to win. He chose his food spots carefully, the way a smart pitcher works the corners of home plate, inside and outside, spaghetti here and a glazed doughnut there. He couldn't help it.

When it was her turn again, Charlotte tipped over the en-tire full-course mess. She sighed, snapped the waistband of her nylons, and smoothly peeled them off, together with her one remaining shoe. They toasted her for losing. Then things picked up in a hurry, as Breed leaped and took Sasha to the

floor with a blind-side tackle. He was going for the white ho-
siery, which actually came off much more easily and smoothly
than either Del Plato or Breed might have imagined, considering the length of the nurse's legs and the disoriented state of
everyone. Charlotte, with no clothes on, changed the stereo
herself. She chose the American Legion favorites, doing a
proud march to "You're a Grand Old Flag." It filled Del Plato
with a degree of patriotism and craving.

Breed asked Del Plato if he was having a good time. Del
let out his breath and said yes, he was enjoying himself, certainly.

With an electric toothbrush in her hand rather than a
baton, Charlotte smiled broadly and flashed her eyes, and
marched back into the thick of things with perfect, high-step-
ping majorette form. Sasha untangled her incredibly long legs
and also fell into step, twirling the enema bag. She *loved*
marching music. The two nurses pranced through the living
room, pumping and strutting and completely naked.

Del Plato, with a goofy grin, had his teeth set gently together. Denise should see this now. Did her sweaty boyfriend
ever bring the good stuff and pot inside a medical bag? Did he?
Did he give half a chance to John Philip Sousa?

He stripped completely in two seconds. Then, marching
in place for just a few beats to get the rhythm right, he
snapped his arms high and kept those knees like pistons, and
put a real smile on his face to join the happy parade.

Do it. Just do it.

They circled the empty living room and paired off. Jewboy had Sasha in a position that Del Plato had only seen before on the back of a playing card. Del nudged Charlotte into
the spare bedroom, with the half-finished wallpaper, where she
told him he looked a little bit like Sulu, after he had steered the
Enterprise through a deadly meteor shower, with boulders the
size of a municipal building hurtling at thousands of miles a
second toward them. Kirk and Spock and even Bones were all
in sick bay, down with some intergalactic measles or something, instant death all around in a hostile solar system. But
he was able to guide them through, safe and sound, and every-

one aboard owed it all to him, and what could she ever do to repay him? How could she thank him enough—show him some small bit of pleasure, after that bravery and daring all alone in the wild cosmos, where it was just the two of them and the stars, and the electric toothbrush she had marched into the room with?

Del Plato said maybe, for starters, they could try something he had only attempted once before.

Some time later—hours?—there was a knock on the bedroom door. Sasha asked permission to beam aboard. Del Plato had no voice. He could only nod. Sasha came in, carrying the medical bag. She began to rummage inside, then smiled very nicely.

Later still—hours?—Breed knocked to see how things were going. It was time to leave. Del was driving. He found Del Plato sitting against a half-papered wall, staring at the ad for the new Cadillac, which cost less than a thousand dollars. Del lay there stunned and silent, like someone pulled from a wreck. Jewboy had to call out his name a few times, and in the end had to shake Del Plato and bring him a beer before there was any kind of response.

Chapter 7

The setting sun outside was rich and round, as pink and ripe in the sky as an exotic fruit. But inside Olympia Fronton there were only tubes of fluorescents dimmed by overhead panels of crackled glass, and the weird white light from betting windows. Hung on the lobby walls were framed glossy photos of the jai alai players posing with a shiny helmet, a cesta, and a stern Basque expression. Customers waiting for the next game on the afternoon program chewed their pencils or counted their money, or carefully examined the photographs to see where an earlier bet might have gone sour.

Joe Hooven was waiting for the man at the food concession counter to bring him some Cuban coffee. Long ago Hooven had gone out with a Spanish chick who carried a five-inch switchblade and knew how to shift gears without stepping on the clutch. She taught Joe how to count in *español* and rank someone out, and she had a way of saying his name—José, José—from somewhere deep in her throat, without moving her lips. On their dates in *latino* sections of Miami, he admired the way stocky and swarthy dudes—with fierce black stubbles and expressive eyes that reminded him of Eli Wallach in *The Magnificent Seven*—would order tiny cups of sweet, muddy coffee and belt them down like shots of red-eye. Now, Hooven ordered *café cubano* whenever he saw it.

The last game of that afternoon's betting program appeared on the tote board, and Joe Hooven wondered about leaving town, an option he was forced to consider. What was the weather in Houston? He could always go there in a pinch, look up his ex-girl friend and the kid. In Houston or anywhere else on the map, he could tune up the strings on his blond Rickenbacker and pull down fifty or eighty bucks a night, tax-free cash. Hooven liked to think of himself as an air plant, able to survive on oxygen alone if he had to.

Because if he stayed in Lauderdale he would have to square it with Del Plato and Breed. How could you square things with people like that, who had no understanding of what a man had to like put up with when he was working for a Tommy Polio? Would they give two shits about the pressure Hooven was under? No, they would not, the pricks. They would try to rough him up, and be sarcastic to him.

Hooven had a rolled-up jai alai program in his hand, $340 in his pocket, and 80¢ for the coffee. He set the coins on the counter. When his thimble-sized cup of Cuban coffee came, Hooven gulped it in a single swallow. Then he wiped his mouth with his fingertips.

"*Gracias,*" Hooven said. "*Muy bien.*"

"Sure thing," the concession man replied.

Hooven wore a nylon jacket with an emblem of a large motorcycle on one sleeve and an American flag on the other sleeve. So far this was not a Joe Hooven day at Olympia Jai Alai. One, three, five, and eight were his favorite jai alai numbers, and he had just scattered a hundred dollars' worth of no-good tickets from the previous match, all possible combinations of one, three, five, and eight. He was down a total of three hundred dollars, give or take a little. He had bet four races and lost four. Three hundred dollars, small potatoes. Hooven told himself he had done worse, no sweat, although he didn't care to remember exactly where or when that might have been.

In his shirt pocket he had fresh quiniela bets for the game going on. One-three, one-five, one-eight. Three-five, three-eight. Five-eight. Five dollars each ticket, thirty dollars total.

Hooven was not going to Houston, no matter how hard the other two would come on for what had happened in Florida Exotica. They had no jai alai in Houston.

He watched the number-two team in blue serving to the number-three team in white. Hooven was surrounded by stubbed cigarette butts, empty cups, dropped wrappers, and losing tickets. He fluffed the thin, neat ripples of his narrow-wale cords and leaned on the orange concession counter, watching the action on a closed-circuit screen. If Del Plato and Breed didn't want to go ahead with Olympia, that was fine with him. They could continue being cops. He would play music. Top-forty tunes, or even that dumb-fuck disco thumping. Joe Hooven would always pay the rent and have a little extra for a good time.

Number three went ahead and beat the two team. It was only the first round. The deep man in blue prepared for a return off the side wall, more than a routine play but nothing fancy, only to have the ball slip out of his basket and roll off the open end of the court. He was a well-known player, with his picture in a prominent position in the lobby, so fans did not boo him as much as they might have. The fronton smelled of sweet Cuban coffee and cigars and a faint trace of marijuana. One point went up on the main scoreboard for number three.

Team number four came trotting off the bench, green jerseys.

Hooven was more interested in a college-looking girl who had her hair brushed to one side and wore loads of handmade jewelry from the sea—shark-tooth earrings, an abalone bracelet, a necklace of pink-and-orange coral. She looked like she might have been at home inside an aquarium, with bright pebbles under her feet and an underwater castle to swim through. She was scrambling along the tile floor of the lobby, flipping over tickets that had been thrown away. She was careful not to soil her flowered skirt, which had lush gardenias and a slit all the way up one side. Other people also watched the girl. Her outfit did a nice job of highlighting her tan. With one hand she searched for winning combinations among the discards, while she held her skirt closed with the other.

From where Joe stood, he could hear the pelota carom off the back wall a split second after he saw it in black and white on the monitor. He thought that was pretty neat, the way technology could do things with your head. He was interested in what was going on in this race—a quiniella bet could bring back a healthy return—but points doubled after all eight teams had made an appearance, and that's when a game was usually decided.

One of Hooven's lucky numbers had run out to a quick lead just the race before, with the front man throwing wicked kills and the back man tossing the pelota deep each time. But when points doubled, their rhythm was suddenly broken. They came out gesturing and glaring at one another like motorists with tangled vehicles. At one point they collided, and lay prone on the court. Hooven's team won no more points. As he went for coffee, he reluctantly let his worthless tickets fall one at a time, leaving a hundred-dollar trail behind him.

Hooven took a walk to the back row of the arena seats, just for a different look at things. Three was still on, playing the five team now, in black. He listened to their jai alai cestas whistle through the air, the conventioneers and old people and the regulars rooting impatiently for their numbers. Many of the red-cushion seats were still empty because it was a beach day. Usherettes stood to the side and chatted with one another, discussing the best real-estate bargains in Broward County, the best stone crabs, comparing eye shadow. They wore skimpy red uniforms, with high heels and seamed stockings and frilly underpants.

He went back to the lobby, and right away noticed the college girl again, who was kneeling for another handful of dropped tickets. Hooven pretended to do something with his shoe and managed to catch a nice flash. The concession man had told Hooven that some security personnel wore uniforms, but others did not. They were there mostly for pickpockets and drunks. A man in a business suit, for instance, was security. Hooven's man had pointed him out casually. "Don't look now, but the gray suit, straw hat, he's security." Hooven took a look. The dude looked like Bing Crosby. The college-looking girl with shell jewelry was also security. The concession man had seen her snap the cuffs one time, and other times give hand signals to the armed guards at Olympia.

Hooven asked what they like did all day, and how many of them could there be in this joint.

"Security. No one steals the pelota, or a vending machine." Hooven's concession man put a pot of coffee back on its hot plate and the metal steamed and sizzled. "For me, it's like the old days, when that anarchist peasant was coming in. You tell me how many there are, my friend. Anyone can be security."

Hooven considered putting on a move. He thought the girl had let her skirt open just a little on the side once she had seen him looking from across the lobby floor. But he realized this was a bad idea. Some people at Olympia Jai Alai already knew him as Jackie Molson. A good idea would be for Hooven not to get recognized, or make himself too well known.

He went back to the arena seats. It was comfortable watching jai alai, it could have been any time of the day. Three was still going strong, up against the six now. The number-six team wore yellow. An usherette asked him if he needed something, a drink perhaps. Hooven said he was okay. Now he was suspicious of everyone.

He figured he would win this particular race because he had bet almost nothing on it, thirty dollars. Things like that happened on a day that was not a Joe Hooven day. His luck was rotten, his karma was from hunger, his Mercury and important planets were probably jacking off on the job. Hooven tried to think of really bad days, exceptionally hopeless days from which he might take some comfort if it turned out that his three—with this lead—could somehow find a way to lose this game for him too.

Once, someone had turned him on to coke cut with strychnine, and Hooven had stared at his reflection in the bathroom

mirror for at least six hours, thinking he was watching a foreign film, and a long one at that, a film he was not going to recommend. Another bad time, he had taken two ludes at a
backstage party and found himself being kissed on the lips by
someone who smelled of Old Spice and needed a shave.

But the worst day of all for Hooven, hands down, had
been a certain sunny day about three years before. Going over
the details again made Joe feel a little better about the three
hundred dollars. He was alone that day—a brilliant South
Florida sun, boats on the Intracoastal, car radios blaring—
Hooven only recently on his own, no band, no chick, no kid.
Some dude with a 450SL and a terrible habit of talking to you
as if you were standing in another part of the room was giving
Hooven a hard time about a quantity of pot that Hooven
hadn't exactly paid for. At the time Hooven was waiting tables
at Piña Colada World, making good tips. But he was already
thinking of cutting out for Tucson, or Houston—anywhere he
had connections—when the 450SL pulled up and the dude
walked into Pinā Colada World and just gave Hooven a look.
A look. Then he got back in his car and was gone.

Hooven knew he was in hot water. It couldn't have been
much later—a few minutes, an hour—when the next thing he
knew, three huge guys managed to trap him in a place without
witnesses. Three immense dudes, the kind who tell you to sock
them in the stomach as hard as you can and then have a good
time laughing over your mashed knuckles. One of them wore
one earring and had a chain in his back pocket. He explained
that he had pushed the earring through himself, with no ice—
he just jabbed it through there—and if Hooven didn't fork up
the money, he would take the same stud earring and push it
right into Hooven's dick.

Joe accepted this with a little shiver, but calmly, the way
you accept news of root canal, or a new transmission. There
was little he could do about it, per se. Then the three huge guys
went ahead and worked him over—with the communicating
grunts and the efficiency of furniture movers—and even
through the pain, Hooven was thinking this was a day he
might sometime look back upon for its complete and total lack
of luck.

Soon afterward Joe Hooven joined organized crime. He met the wrong kind, and after a series of interviews in the office of a gas station, he was eventually introduced to Tomás Parrajo, of the underworld, to whom he offered his services. Surrounded by brake pads and oily tools, spare parts and boob calendars, Hooven pledged loyalty, obedience, and said he damn well knew the score.

When Del Plato arrived during the second round of play, Hooven's three team was still on a blitz. They had gone through six teams and were a sure shot. What Hooven needed now was for one of his other numbers to come in. Just a point or two from his other positions and he would cover any combination of three.

Del Plato was out of uniform and all by himself. No Breed. Hooven felt his luck turning for the better already. But then Jewboy was there too, from out of nowhere, and Hooven's heart did a slight flutter, as though he were back in Piña Colada World again, threatened with an earring. Breed had been down on his hands and knees to get a peek up the college girl's flyaway skirt.

They caught up to him by the concession counter, near the soft drinks. When he saw Breed approaching, Hooven turned his back.

"Look who's here," Jewboy said loudly. "Is it who I think it is? Yes, it is, it's Joey." Breed was blowing into his hands and rubbing them together, as though spotting Hooven had given him the chills. "What do you know, Joe? I'm asking him right now what he thinks of my new attire, because if there's one thing this rambling man is an expert on, I'd say it's style." Breed pulled up his slacks and lifted his feet to reveal a new pair of socks. They were cappucino, with bold stripes. "Dior," Breed said, not without pride. "I wore these just for you. Check it out, fuckface."

"Very nice," Hooven assured him.

"Very nice. No shit."

Del looked around, as if for ideas. Here was Hooven, but what was he supposed to do with him now? "What happened back there?" Del Plato asked.

"You mean at the pet store?"

"Did he just say something?" Jewboy Breed began pacing in a small circle, wringing his hands like a mad scientist. "He just said something, didn't he? You asked him straight out what happened, I heard you; you asked him very nicely in English, and he said something like, 'You mean at the pet store?' With that voice of his. Joe Asshole."

Hooven had practiced what he was going to say, but now that they were in front of him, he was at a loss for words. "You got a right to be pissed," Hooven explained. He was hoping his air-plant qualities would pull him through. "I would never stick nobody's hand in that spider shit, man; you got to know that for a fact. I swear it. The last thing I would do is like hurt you guys."

"Might be the last thing," Breed told him. "So far I love this. Keep talking."

Del Plato was thinking that everything was more than it seemed to be. He asked Hooven to tell them about Jackie Molson. Del was keeping his voice down, being good.

"What's there to say, man? I'm sorry."

"But your boss knew we would be there, Joe. That can never happen. Never."

"It never will again, Look, man, you seen what that Mr. Polio is like. He suspects me. Not only would my career be ruined, okay, but I would also have to like fear for my life. All that shit he was talking, he's *serious* with that. Throwing dudes in Biscayne Bay, putting someone's balls in a blender. He can do that shit and it wouldn't mean a thing." Hooven was twirling his hair and trying to keep the pitch of his voice down. "So when he was looking funny at me, man, at *me*, hey, I had to tell him you would be there. I *had* to. I admit it."

"You admit it," Del said, shaking his head. What were they supposed to do now? Go out and buy a Cuisinart and stick Hooven's balls in that? What?

Breed was no help, staring across the tiled floor at the slit in the college girl's skirt. Del looked too. The skirt was wild jungle flowers. She moved the right way just then, and they caught some golden upper thigh, perhaps even a lucky shot of cheek. Del wasn't sure. So much depended on the underwear.

With those high-cut panties, Del thought—*the kind that just cover up this and that and would fall apart in the dryer—it might have been cheek.* And even if it was only high thigh, that was nothing to shrug off either.

Del took a deep breath. "What do you admit?" he asked Hooven.

"Through Jackie Molson he knew about the pet store, but it wasn't like a real setup. Not the way I was giving you all that room to cut out of there, man, because I am not dumb."

Suddenly Breed whirled and jammed his elbow deep into Joe Hooven's belly. Hooven doubled over and shook his head. He tried to find his breath, remembering black days.

"You skirt the fucking issue," Breed said. "What's crucial is that you did something, jitbag, and you shouldn't have done it. Irish explained that. Tommy Polio looks at you, and you give us up? Does that make sense? It's irresponsible, Joey." Breed helped Hooven stand up straight. "But what irks me more than anything, probably—although this is strictly me speaking, as an individual—is that you're more afraid of Tommy Polio than you are of us. I don't see how that can be possible."

"If I didn't do something to gain his trust, man, then where would I be? In a swamp, and my life would be over. And if I went ahead and told you what was going down with the pet shit, okay, then the crazy man would know more than ever someone was feeding you the right stuff, man. And there I am in the swamp again." Hooven was talking with both hands guarding his midsection. "I took a calculated risk, man."

Breed took a pill. He would look only at Del Plato. "Irish, he's getting to me real bad. I'm going to have some kind of temper thing."

"Everything turned out cool, and the man like trusts me now, which is no small thing. We take him off for a lot of bread, each week, and if I can keep the heat off me for a while, really, then that's the thing we have to do. Because if I say I'm with you guys, then I'm with no one else." Hooven went ahead and left his stomach unprotected to show his good faith. "Man, we been through so much already."

Del Plato felt the weight of responsibility. He was dealing with irrational people. If anything was to turn out reasonably well, he would have to bring it about. No one else.

"It's my fault," Hooven was saying. "Okay? The whole accident at the pet store was because of me. But I didn't mean for nothing bad to happen. I saw what was coming down on me from all sides—this pressure?—and telling Tommy Polio was like the only thing I could do."

"We'll drive him out to the woods," Breed said. "We can leave him there, this Baggie. I know a good place with mosquitoes and alligators, and outdoor cats."

"Nobody got hurt. I tell you the truth and shit, man, you got to respect that. Mr. Polio was all over me. He can't like listen to reason the way I know you guys can."

Del Plato sucked up his breath and dipped his shoulder, then snapped a straight right jab into Hooven's midsection. Hooven let out all his breath at once and sat on the tiled floor, rocking back and forth. Del Plato was looking at his clenched fist as though it were something you couldn't turn your back on for even a second.

"Irish, that was very good. I'm proud of you, that instinct." Breed tapped Joe Hooven on the shoulder to get his attention. Hooven was reaching for a program booklet or something to slip beneath him so his slacks could stay clean. "Joey, what do you think of my partner here? Tell me the truth, rambling man, was that something else or what? You were talking, asshole, and then he knocked you down."

"Yeah, man, what did you hit me for?"

Del Plato shrugged his shoulders. What did he know?

"Saint Irish," Breed announced. He helped Hooven to his feet and touched Hooven's clothing, testing the material as he brushed him off. Breed was relieved to discover he wasn't the only one who could throw his weight around. "Look at my slugger now. Who would ever have a negative hunch about this Del Plato? Teachers were probably crazy about him, with that polite tone of speech he has, and all the answers he knew. With that shy smile, and his fucking hair always in place." Breed dusted off Hooven some more. "Hit him again, Del Plato. Go with it. Get in touch with yourself."

Del had to take a stroll. He went to get something from the concession stand. It *had* been a good punch. And Joe Hooven was just the kind of guy you threw punches at. Del had no regrets. You did what you had to do, and some people were like that anyway. They had a way of walking, or some look about them—furtive eyes, for instance—that spelled out victim. It was a fact of human nature. Some people found money in the street, or could buy clothes without even trying them on, and some people had their wallets lifted on a regular basis or always found hair in their food. You either hit or you got hit.

Back in his old Detroit neighborhood, there was a boy named Eugene, who invariably had his top button buttoned and all his homework done. Eugene had to give up his lunch money every day and had to have a parent take him home from school, or else kids would not let Eugene get off at his bus stop. Del Plato figured Eugene was probably a top vein man or something now with every luxury and a beeper, just waiting in his blue scrub suit for some old school chum to check in with a health problem. If you didn't hit, you got hit.

And Breed was right, teachers had been crazy about him. The answers he gave, his smile and his hair—Del was a favorite. School never intimidated him, never threw him off. He wasn't the best student, but he tried to be, and who wouldn't fall for ambition like that? Del was in his element with somebody else in front of the room and competitors in every seat. He could handle himself playing shirts and skins on the court, and he could handle himself with the academic side. Del handed in typewritten reports with footnotes and the pages stapled together. He drew cover sheets for important homework assignments—black and beige and yellow hands all clasped together above the continents for social studies, Oscar Robertson dribbling a basketball all alone in the dark for English.

But now he threw cheap-shot stomach punches in the lobby. Where did he think he was going with all this new behavior?

Del ordered a hot dog and a root beer. The concession man managed to bring the food and make change without once looking up from the floor.

Hooven was standing in the corner with his head against the wall, protecting his belly, groaning softly.

"I can't believe you would like do that," Hooven said as Del returned. He lifted his shirt to show Del Plato the red mark. "That's so unlike you, man, really. Really."

Del finished up his hot dog. One, two bites, three, all gone.

"There's no Jackie Molson," Hooven told him. "He don't exist, per se. It's a name I sometimes used to use, man. When I was younger and shit? Look, I told you already, it was through me, the whole thing back there in the spider store was me. But what was I supposed to tell Mr. Polio, man? I couldn't lay down some shit like I was the one who knows where the two cops are who rip us off. Not directly, man, because you know what that is. That's swamp talk. So I had to like lead him on, play with his head, sneaky shit. So I told him I know this Jackie Molson dude, and it's him who's got something to say."

"For five hundred dollars," Del said.

"Hey, I'm not like planning to *keep* that money, man. I got it right here, Del Plato. I got it *with* me. Here, let me give you some."

"The Baggie thinks money is the issue," said Breed. "I have to hit him again, Irish. I can't control my temper."

Del Plato was just mooning around now, wondering how this had come about. He could remember being an absolute ace of a guy—*it wasn't too long ago, was it?*—a good student and a real good basketball player, a good cop, and someone you could stop on the street for directions. He was punctual. On Valentine's Day he had always brought Denise some kind of Valentine present. But nothing was simple, and people did things for reasons nobody could understand, not even themselves. People left their husbands and broke the law. Reasons were too complicated, and explanations were not true.

At times Del Plato was able to feel like a genuine desperado, able to push spiders on gangsters and throw punches from the blind side. But there were other times—right that moment in the lobby of Olympia, for instance—when he felt completely bewildered with all this swindling and the corruption in small places. What were his motives, and what was going on? What the hell was he doing? The answers were beyond his grasp, like some of those frustrating laws of science. What the hell did anything mean? Fucking gravity, now what was that supposed to be exactly? Or infinity, and radiation from your color TV? What was the real difference between a cold and the flu? Why couldn't they invent something for traffic?

He suffered from confusion, and became mopey, feeling weak and helpless as one of those tiny countries on a classroom globe—a pink country, without natural resources or friendly harbors, surrounded by belligerent patches of brown and dark-green neighbors.

He had fallen into crime easily enough. First it was Medlow and Bigfoot and James Lloyd making no bones about it after a workout—small talk in the shower of paying off and shaking down, the logistics of taking. And then he was teamed with Jewboy Breed, who showed him the ropes of extra income, the fringe benefits of a Public Safety Department shield. It was done everywhere, starting at the top. Right? And a person had to do what he had to do, with what the pay scale was, and the lousy dental plan they offered.

In the beginning Del was surprised it didn't make him more nervous. As a kid he had pocketed candy bars and war comics, and kept Eugene from getting off at his bus stop, but this was something else. Extortion meant nothing to him. Wonderful. As it worked out, each shakedown served as another confirmation of this surprising and somehow pleasing twist to his character, leading him deeper into corruption, until there was no thought at all of turning back. Which Del Plato could see coming all along. *Once you were in, everyone had the same soul of larceny.*

Del figured it was like when he was moving the ball upcourt, weaving through defenders, feinting and bobbing and changing up on his dribble. Suddenly he would find himself beneath the basket, where he didn't really belong, in dangerous shot-blocking territory, where taller guys with sharp elbows and size-sixteen sneakers would jam it right back in his teeth. But what else could he do? Del always took his shot. Why else would he have been under the hoop?

Del Plato brought his attention back to Joe Hooven. Hooven had licked his thumb to count out $348 which had been in his pants pocket. Del Plato told him to forget it.

"No, man, no way I'm letting this slide. This don't mean nothing to me, Del Plato; it's money and I'll throw it away before this comes between us."

"Just put it back in your pocket, Joe. I don't know what to do with you."

"*Do* with me? Hey, Del Plato, just give me a break, man, that's all. You don't have to do nothing. I can't believe it that you're even *talking* to me this way, man."

The college-looking girl had nonchalantly drifted over. She was poking for change inside the pay phones and had managed to work her way within earshot. Hooven spotted her right away, and immediately scouted the lobby floor for Bing Crosby. Sure enough, *Der Bingle* was twenty feet away, casually thumbing through a copy of *How the Experts Pick 'Em.*

"Don't make like a big thing of this," Hooven said very softly, looking away, "but we got store detectives watching us now. There's that chick by the phone, man, and some dude with a suit. This is the way they work, I'm telling you."

Del took a look. "So what?"

"We don't want attention, man. You're being uncool and you're bringing on a lot of attention."

Del took a few steps back to confer with Breed, who was following jai alai on the closed circuit.

"He's full of shit, your friend is. Name one time he wasn't full of shit. He's Joe Asshole, he's Jackie Molson. The pecker can be a thousand different people and every one of them is going to be full of shit."

"Well, let's not hit him anymore. Not for now. We'll make believe we're all good friends and we're trying to pick winners. How's that sound?"

"Sounds ridiculous, Irish, that's how it sounds. He's looking to glom everything we have. And what I'm thinking, what I'm seriously thinking, is that we can't work with him, Joe Heavy." Breed pointed up to the screen, where jai alai players jockeyed for position and the ball shot by at lightning speed. "You ever watch this game, Del Plato? It's really interesting once you get the hang of it. It's like handball, only they got these baskets on their hand, and all the people keep betting money and more money."

The college girl, with a nice smile and her hair bouncing cutely, came right over to where they were huddled. She asked Del and Breed if they could possibly help her out with sort of an awkward problem. She was from Philadelphia, where she went to Drexel for the art program, and she had run out of money down here. Her friends didn't wait up for her and had already left. She was missing classes, and was only a little short.

Del Plato said that was a shame and gave her fifty cents. Breed said it was probably cold in Philadelphia, and asked what kind of artwork she was interested in. He looked to see what Del Plato had given her and matched it. Hooven came over as well, but said he carried no spare change, only very large bills, sorry.

The girl asked how their luck was holding up.

"The usual," Del said. "Not bad. We're having a good time. Good luck yourself, with school."

"Oh, that. What are your names anyway? I'd like to thank you."

"Jackie," Del Plato told her.

Breed shook hands with her and said his name was Jackie too.

"Thank you, Jackie. Both of you."

When she walked away, Hooven said their luck was very bad, actually. "I'm sure she don't know nothing, man, but hey, we been pinned. We have been—quote—singled out. That can be like a problem."

"You're a problem," Breed said. "She's going to Philadelphia, dipshit. She's got school."

"Come on, man."

"You're just full of it, Joey. That's the thing. It's what I was telling Del Plato just before. I was saying, 'Irish, your friend is full of shit.' Those were my exact words."

Del Plato saw that things could get out of control. He lightly squeezed Breed's shoulder and Hooven's shoulder, and told them both in a very reasonable tone they were here to look at all angles of a heist that carried some heavy-duty charges if they screwed up anywhere along the line. He asked Hooven if he had taken the initiative and done any actual work on the specifics they had talked about earlier.

"I'm not telling you specifics, man. No way. Because the tables are turned, Del Plato. It ain't the same. Because now I can't trust *you* people. You hit me in the stomach."

Del whistled softly and said he had to make a phone call. He asked Joe Hooven if, offhand, he knew Tommy Polio's phone number. "He had asked me something the other day, a question, and I figure this is maybe a good time I got back to him."

"You see how you're talking? Who talks like that, man? I swear it, Del Plato, I don't know what's bugging you, but you're acting more and more like Breed, you really are."

"I'll get it through information. Anyone got a quarter? I gave away all my change."

"Don't get nothing, man. Don't get nothing. You guys, you think so small, you really do."

Hooven led the way through the jai alai arena, surrounded by betting booths and guards. The money went upstairs after each game began and all betting had stopped. A guard brought each cashier's money box to the counting room, one flight up, where money counters wearing red jumpsuits without pockets, whose fingerprints were on bonded file, made large, neat piles of the day's take—wrapping, stamping, and putting it into burlap bags.

"I got a badge, man, I told you. It has my picture on it. I can work here part-time, I've done it. Only the badge is made out for Jackie Molson, man, and that's the great thing. That's where it's really cool. Because three people are doing this robbery, and one of them is Jackie Molson, who like isn't even a real person. It's unbelievable."

Del Plato didn't know how he was supposed to make heads or tails of this information. How could he go along? Guns?

Armed robbery? Absolutely not. However deeply enmeshed he was in this huge world of misdeeds, Del could still see this Olympia business was not for him.

Joe Hooven played with his hair, fluffing it up in back. "We need a diversion, man," Hooven explained, all pumped up. "One of those things where you get everybody's attention somewhere else? I seen them do it once on *The Mod Squad*—it was great. And then I like go inside with my badge and shit, and someone comes with me. It's not so dangerous. And it's a lot of money, man."

Del Plato said it was the stupidest idea he had ever heard. What was he doing? He was going right to the hoop where he didn't belong, and messing up his life even more.

"I knew you would say something like that, man, I *knew* it. Fucking Del Plato. To you everything is stupid; you don't want to do nothing lately. I'm telling you a *plan*, man," Hooven said, punching one hand into the other. "I'm telling you straight. It's thousands and thousands of dollars."

"Don't upset yourself," Breed suggested. "You're young, asshole, you got your whole life ahead of you."

"Yeah, well fuck you too, man. I don't go around and hit people. All right? That's one thing. And when I tell someone I'm doing something, man, then I wouldn't be saying it unless I was going to do it."

"I don't know what you're trying to tell us," said Del Plato.

"I'm saying you piss me off. Okay? No more and no less."

"I see."

"What do you see? You see nothing, man. I got access to this joint. We can be in and out of here in like two seconds."

"I don't see how we can go ahead, Joe. Not at this point. Not the way things stand right now. This doesn't look like anything I could agree to."

"Sure, man. You got what you wanted, I told you how it can be done. Now you'll do it without me. I'm always giving you information and shit, I'm always like Mr. Nice Guy, sure. And I get a hard time for it."

"You can't fucking bemoan this situation," Breed

chipped in. "To the trained eye, it's a joke." Breed had gone to the candy machine for some Rolaids, which he passed around. "I mean, we walk in here and there are probably easier establishments to take off. Fort Knox, for instance. It would be a piece of cake. Or the fucking Orange Bowl. We could rob that too if we're paying no attention to common sense."

"Don't talk to me," Hooven said. "Okay? Don't say another word."

Breed cracked the candy with his teeth. "Look around, Del Plato," he said. "We got this retardo plan, and we got Joey. From what I understand, is this your kind of challenge or what?"

Del Plato and Breed left Olympia Fronton. Hooven remained right where he was awhile, trying to regain his breath and his composure.

For the most part Hooven liked what he was doing. He enjoyed the life-style, and the fact that he had money in his pocket or the ability to pick up some quickly. Mr. Parrajo was a drag to work for, sure, but Hooven met chicks, he had a lot of space, he could sleep late every morning. For a young guy with no college, he was doing very well. Twenty-five years old and no family connections to set him up with mobile-home dealerships in the desert. And he had ambition, Hooven did, he always had ambition. What could these two know? They were cops who had to dress exactly alike, who knew only how to hassle people and how to hit.

He had missed the end of his game. Joe looked up at the big board to check the numbers. The three-two combination had come in. He didn't have a three-two ticket.

He figured this was some joke. The whole thing was fixed, it had to be. They waited to see what numbers he bet and then they sent someone down to make sure it went the other way.

Hooven kept looking up at the screen for the last game. He watched the new odds flashing as fresh bets were punched into the computers. He walked over to one of the closed-circuit sets, where players were throwing the pelota easily back and forth as betting continued, setting each other up for practice kills. The five-minute warning bell went off. Hooven threw his

old tickets on the floor. They scattered in the air and floated
down, and that was that.

He placed his first new bet at the regular quiniela window. Behind the glass was a Cuban woman in a blue tuxedo.
She had stiff blond hair and a blue bow tie. Hooven smiled,
brushed back his hair, and took out his wallet. He told the
cashier to wheel the *siete* for him.

"Wheeling the seven," she repeated. She moved the machine handle and punched out all the combinations of seven.

Hooven gave her fourteen dollars and said, "They tell me
seven is like a lucky number. What do you think about that?"

"They're all lucky, mister."

"Hey, I believe you, really. Wheel a three for me this
time."

Soon the players would line up for the recorded trumpet
rally and lift their woven cestas in pregame salute. They
would trot to the screened-in bull pen, and the red shirts of the
number-one team would start it off by serving to number two
in baby-blue jerseys.

Hooven checked the big board for his odds. With a few
minutes left until post time, the seven position was listed as a
five-to-two shot. His three team was seven-to-two. If three and
seven were the top final scorers, he would win two times. Hooven looked through his program to see the names of the players
on his teams.

The game would start, the hard ball smashing off the walls
and the polished hardwood, thudding from front to back. The
referee would lift his flag and call the close ones. Players
would fling themselves to the floor for saves, putting the
pressure on, driving each shot fiercely, leaping for high
bounces, running up the back wall for deep retrieves. *Chula.*
Reboté. People would scream and applaud and win and lose.

Hooven found a spot not far from the payoff window. It
felt right to him, lucky. He would keep his distance and watch
the TV screen, waiting for a seven or a three to come home.

Chapter
8

N umbers didn't lie, and as he drove in no particular hurry to the ball field, Del Plato was already resigned to the cold fact that out on the diamond his little girl was going to be no Pete Rose. He had never seen her play, at least not in uniform—the snappy black and gold of Hen-Rob's Vacuum Cleaner World Pirates—but Del was definitely expecting the worst as he neared the field. She had never been athletically inclined. Keri didn't begin taking steps until about fifteen months, and even as a toddler she was constantly having trouble with buttons. At a time of development when other preschoolers were already on roller skates and doing perfect cartwheels, she was still pushing her riding toys instead of riding them. But to Del Plato her lousy Little League statistics meant nothing. Big deal, whatever it was. No hits in twenty-three times at bat, something like that. Twenty-three strike-outs, big deal. Eight years old was no time of life to worry about playing hurt, or an inferior batting average.

The sponsor of Keri's Little League team had called at eight o'clock sharp. Del had come off an extremely late shift. He had been dreaming about a new car, one with plenty of horses under the hood and lifetime rustproofing. Keri, right fielder for the Hen-Rob Vacuum Cleaner World Pirates, was shaky on defense and a sure out every time at the plate. Could Del Plato explain that?

No, Del could not. He could not even open his eyes.

The vacuum cleaner mogul, on the phone so early, on a Saturday yet, told Del Plato that all Keri did for the squad was swish on meatballs down the pipe and make costly miscues. Two foul tips was all the contact she had made in those twenty-three trips to the plate, two weak nicks off the handle of her Junior Slugger. She didn't know what she was doing out there. One of her foul tips had caught the other team's catcher in a sensitive area, and the game had had to be delayed. The other foul tip plopped right down on home plate and just stayed there, like the ball was dead. Did his daughter think she was supposed to fan every time she was up at the dish? Did she need glasses, or professional help?

Who needed Willie Mays for a daughter? Del Plato didn't. Keri was relatively well adjusted without baseball, and for that Del was happy, with what the kid was going through and all. Here her mother had sent her real father off to some rented house, to sleep for two hours at a time. Not to mention that Denise was seeing some dipstick who probably had them all sitting nude in a hot tub. And still his Keri could endure. She didn't overeat, she didn't stutter or set her stuffed animals on fire. Big deal if the kid went down with a K every once in a while. She cleaned her room; she didn't steal or hitch rides or neglect her teeth. It was simply that Keri had no aptitude for the hardball game.

Sure, it would have been okay with Del Plato if his little girl could step to the plate and casually whack out a few ropes. But facts were facts, and you couldn't argue with zip for twenty-three. Probably she had no business wearing a number on her back, or those sunglasses that flip down off the brim of a cap. But she was signed up for baseball—Keri in right field, the .000 kid—and hitless or not, tough in the clutch or not, this was his own kid.

Keri was the first girl to play organized ball in that area.

She was the first girl to have tried. She went to the black and gold of Hen-Rob's Vacuum Cleaner World Pirates. The luck of the draw. They let her play right field, where they figured she would do the least damage.

Denise was willing to make an issue of it. Sports for girls, and for Keri in particular. Denise was all gung ho for that kind of thing.

"She'll see opportunity," his ex-wife had pointed out over the phone. He had called her that same morning after stepping from the shower with two hours' sleep. He had to wonder what Denise was to him now. An ex-wife? An estranged wife? "Let our daughter get the experience I never could," Denise told him. "Women through the ages might have appreciated an extra-base hit, believe me. But who ever gave us the chance? I'm emphatic on this. Who ever taught us how to swipe a base or gun out a runner or go to the opposite field? Don't deny our only child."

"I'm not denying anything. She's the only girl on the team, on *any* team, that's all I'm saying."

"Who's been talking to you?"

"Nobody."

"Next year we'll have others. Pitchers and catchers, cleanup hitters. Golden Gloves, you'll see. Whatever Keri goes through will be good for her. Sports builds character."

"But she can't catch. Boys resent her and call her names."

"Did she tell you that?"

"I thought I'd come to the game today," Del said after a while. "That would be okay, wouldn't it?"

"Ethan coaches her team, I think you should know. Look, Del, she plays and she does her best. I'm proud of her, no matter how much the boys resent her, no matter what that vacuum cleaner bully says about her. Don't argue with me over this."

"I'm not arguing. I'm trying to show you both sides."

"Don't show me."

One time Del had batted grounders to Keri in the park, while Denise took pictures and made encouraging remarks. The pepper game ended with Keri attempting to be brave all the way to the emergency room, where they had to rush her for

X rays. Denise drove. In the car she sat on Del Plato's lap and
watched her ring finger swell enormously. A one-hopper had
plunked the kid on her throwing hand. Del had to cut through
a turquoise ring with his wife's nail file because Keri's finger
was turning blue.

"It doesn't hurt," Keri told them in the car. She was trying to squeeze and maneuver the swelling out of her finger, as
though it were the empty space in one of those pocket-size
number puzzles. "I'll be fine. It's getting better. Let's go home
now."

Denise's father had the ring shipped from an Indian res-
ervation in New Mexico, where he had bought it with traveler's
checks right off the blanket of a genuine Navajo. The Indian
had boasted to Denise's father of having abandoned three different late-model Eldorados in the desert, leaving each of them
to the elements, like good ponies that had died on him. Del
handed his daughter the sawed-off ring, which had been her favorite. He told her to leave her puffed-up finger alone and
from then on to always try to keep her body even with the ball.

Del Plato felt his position was pretty solid on women in
sports. They could do whatever they felt like doing. In pickup
games he had played against some pretty decent ones, healthy
chicks in ponytails and Afros who could pop them in from fifteen feet and dribble between their legs. One cutie had even
knocked him down as they were both hustling after a loose
ball, a foul in anybody's book but still the right play to make
in that situation. After the game Del had shaken hands with
her, no hard feelings, and went so far as to loan her his razor,
which was something he never did for Denise. Del Plato had a
rule about shaving material. It happened too many times. You
lather up and start shaving with what you think is a blade you
used only once before and two seconds later you've got clots of
tissue and Band-Aids all over.

When Del Plato got to the field, he parked his piece of
crap beyond the range of any stray balls. It was a humid day,
rain had been the forecast all along. Right away Del spotted
the gold uniforms with the black piping and trim of Hen-Rob's
Vacuum Cleaner World Pirates. They were on one end of the

big flat lot, with another Little League game under way on the opposite corner. Areca palms and ixora bushes lined the sidewalks in foul ground, and a fence behind home plate kept foul tips from breaking windows on the street or getting lost. There were tiered wooden benches behind the fence, and a Freezer Fresh custard truck. Canvas bags with bats and balls and shiny batting helmets were inside each dugout. Ducks wandered in right field. Blue dragonflies hovered above the warped, water-stained seats. A black El Camino was parked on the sidewalk.

"Mr. Del Plato, I don't want to start off on the wrong foot with you," the vacuum cleaner guy had told him on the phone early that morning. "I'm not crazy about your Keri on my squad. I'm calling because this winter season I have a high-caliber team, to which I lend my business name and charitable contributions for ice-cream sodas and such. But my right fielder, who I have to play because they put her on my squad, lacks certain essentials. She's afraid of the ball. Every time she strikes out. Now don't get me wrong, because your Keri is a sweetheart and I don't doubt for a second she could knock them dead with bowling or jogging or some other sport, but with baseball she hasn't got all the tools yet."

Del Plato had to hold the phone away from his ear. The team sponsor spoke with that kind of urgent relentless energy of people who require only four hours sleep.

"Mr. Del Plato, let me be honest. She's stinking up my infield. What matters to me is ability and ability only. Effort matters, but not so much. I've known second place with my squad, honorable mention. This winter season we got a clear shot at all the marbles and I want it. Mr. Del Plato, this year I got switch-hitters and bruisers, and what I don't need is your daughter. I have to go with ability every time."

"Talk to my wife."

"Mr. Del Plato, I can't talk to your wife. I tried and I can't."

"We're not together at present," Del said. "I don't see how I can help you."

"Mr. Del Plato, help your daughter. Come to the game

today. See for yourself. She always tries, don't get me wrong, but what can Keri give me in the way of hand-eye coordination? I could have bonus babies out there. Mr. Del Plato, we keep charts for my squad. For the Vacuum Cleaner World Pirates I spare no expense. Here's what it says next to Keri's name. It says nothing. Are you listening? Goose eggs, Mr. Del Plato. Officially at bat twenty-three times and nothing but a string of whiffs across the board. And in the field she'll turn an everyday grounder into an inside-the-park job."

"What time is it now?" Del asked.

"Mr. Del Plato, come to the game. I do a very big business with vacuum cleaners, and if there's any way I can do something, say the word. But with your wife, Mr. Del Plato, if she stays stubborn, the opposite is also true. Give her this message for me. Do me a favor. Mr. Del Plato, let her have trouble with a rug. Let her spill on a carpet and look for a shampoo anywhere in this town. Even if she needs a vacuum cleaner bag I can make her sweat."

The stands were jammed with parents and relatives. Del scouted the seats and picked out Denise, who was sitting alone. He eased himself beside her. She was reading about home decor in a magazine as the kids warmed up before game time. Denise looked up and nodded. The sky had already taken on a thick and unwholesome color, like a budget cut of meat.

Keri was out on the dirt portion of the field, between first and second. Infield practice. They were going to try her at second base. She had her knees slightly bent, glove down, her hair tucked beneath the gold-and-black cap. Del looked all around the ball field, up and down both benches, and on the opposite field as well, but Keri was the only girl in uniform.

On the field she talked to no one. She made very small movements if she moved at all, like a defendant in front of a jury that watched everything.

The third baseman fielded and threw to first, then the shortstop. When it was Keri's turn, a bleeder was tapped her way. The ball approached, rolled up her arm, and skipped behind her. She chased the baseball, picked it up, then threw wide of the first baseman's reach.

Denise stood up to applaud. Del Plato put his head down. They got a fresh ball and the routine started again from the top.

"I wouldn't have expected you here," Denise said.

"Nice day for a ball game."

"It's supposed to rain."

"I could leave," Del offered. "Maybe I should. It's not my Saturday."

"Whatever you want."

"Then I'll stay." He glanced around at the parents of ballplayers and the wide outfields. "Which one is Ethan?"

"He's not here yet."

Denise wore her hair a new way and looked fine. It made Del think of a few years before. The good times. Then they would have had things to say to each other, and there was the other stuff too, love, after the eleven o'clock news or whenever he got off work, when they would pat each other on the back afterward and collapse to their own ends of the bed like punched-out prizefighters. It wasn't so long ago, was it?

The smell of grass and the crack of a bat got Del Plato feeling sentimental. *She was always so steady, Denise, so strong-willed, and it should have worked—it should still be working.* Wasn't he steady and strong-willed too? What was different? Had he changed, or had she changed?

Denise was still the same dress size as on that very first date in the airport cafeteria, the same woman who could hang things on the wall if she had to, even fix small appliances. Probably he was the one who had changed. That's what Del was thinking. Denise had always had her father's knack for taking care of whatever had to be done—whether it was earning a living or setting out roach motels or divorcing a husband. If he hadn't married her back then, she would have taken some halfway decent job with the airlines, or else have gone back full-time at her old man's asbestos factory in Montreal, where she would have season tickets to the Forum and be smoking Export A's.

Del on the other hand had his ups and downs. Saturday night was coming up, and what was he doing? Nothing. He

was getting nostalgic and probably a little horny. He wasn't
socializing or getting enough sleep. He would have to ask
Breed to arrange something again with the nurses.

"How's it going, Del? Truthfully." Denise was looking at
him. She covered his hands with her own, and he was thinking
what a nice gesture that was.

Del said things weren't bad. Could be better.

A motorcycle pulled into the parking area then, a red one,
with the chrome gleaming. Del figured there was probably no
grease or fingerprints anywhere on this machine, and he figured also that he knew an Ethan when he saw one. The guy
came off the bike wearing black and gold and a crash helmet
that sparkled.

This was exactly what Del Plato had imagined. An Ethan,
a new daddy who most likely ran marathons and owned four
pair of brand-name sneakers and gym shorts by the dozen. An
Ethan who no doubt did those intricate stretching exercises
twice a day and probably trimmed his mustache as often, who
washed his hair with goddamn essence of banana peels or
something and did his own mechanical work on the bike.

Denise stood up to wave. So this was Ethan, absolutely.
The boyfriend gazed up at the dangerous skies and decided to
unfold a tarpaulin cover to throw over his motorcycle, then
hustled right out to the playing field to shake hands with
every member of his team and the opposing manager.

Hen-Rob's Vacuum Cleaner World Pirates came off the
field and took the dugout area along the first-base side. The
boys put down their fielding gloves and tried out batting helmets and Little League bats. Keri took a seat at the very far
end of the bench. There she poked at the dirt with the cleats of
her baseball shoes. Ethan came over to bop her lightly on the
throwing arm.

"She knows you're here," Denise said. "She'll pretend to
be miserable just to get attention."

"How's her game coming along?"

"Not too well. But she'll get a trophy anyway. The team is
in the semifinals now."

The other club wore navy and white, representing the
Yankees, those bastards, and a firm that installed swimming

pools. The umpire for this game, wearing black-and-white ref-eree stripes, blew his whistle out by the pitcher's mound and the Yanks took the field.

Del Plato called down to his daughter. "Blast one out, sweetheart!" Keri would not look up.

She's a kid with a zero batting average, Del told himself. He wanted to talk to her one-on-one, a father to his kid. When you're eight or nine years old, he wanted to say to Keri, some things might seem important, but soon you become twelve, and then fifteen, and then you get even older, and plenty of other things come along. Algebra, and career choices. Who to marry and where to eat. What to do with your evenings, how much to give the mailman for Christmas. Straight life and IRA and lines of credit. How to use bleach properly and which side streets to take when traffic is bad. How to deal with the electric bill.

Rain was on the way for sure, lots of it. The sun had been a faintly glowing pearl behind a thin cover of translucent clouds, but now the sky began to act up and it looked crummy out. Every once in a while a dust storm would kick up beyond the deep grass and blow in.

Keri kept her position on the end of the bench. Her team was at bat, and she followed the game as if she were being forced to watch an educational program on TV. She didn't clap or boo or raise her voice. Keri's left hand was locked in-side her fielder's mitt. Her right hand was on her trouser leg, where her fingers traced black pinstripes in the flannel, as if this were perhaps the skin of some strange creature—a black-and-gold beast, with a leather claw and spiked shoes, a hat with flip-down shades—and somehow she had become trapped inside this gruesome body.

"That vacuum cleaner man had a grudge against her right from the start," Denise said. "All season she's been doing her best, but nobody takes the time to show her how to hold the bat or meet the ball. It's a shame. Every game she's on the end of the bench, not a peep out of her. I ask her if the boys say anything, but she won't tell me. When Ethan asks, she won't talk about baseball. But every Saturday morning she puts on her uniform and eats her Cheerios, and rides her bike to the

field. I don't know what to tell her, Del, but after it's gone this
far, I think the worst thing to do is quit."

Keri chewed a knot in the webbing of her glove, flexed the
bill of her cap, watched her teammates run and hit and throw.
Then it was her turn to bat, bottom of the order. With runners
on first and second, a few runs in and a couple of outs, Keri
tapped a batting helmet into place, took quick strides to the
batter's box, planted her feet beside home plate, held the bat
above her right shoulder, and swung and missed three straight
times. One, two, three, you're out. Zero for twenty-four.

The game went on, too much jumping and running, and
Del Plato had to wonder why he was there. He had played Little League ball too, sure, and had also been nothing special. He
tried to remember if he had been a loner back then as well, if it
was a thing with Del Platos to sit on the end of a bench and
chew leather. Certainly he had never gone down the tubes
twenty-four consecutive times. But then things were different
now. Keri had so much to put up with—a father who saw her
every other week, being no Say Hey Kid on the ball field, a
mom dating a biker who worked on those show-off muscles and
thought there was nothing wrong with body odor.

One team got up and the other team got up. Del found
himself thumbing his way through home decor. In no time at
all he was up-to-date on exposed brick and the Shaker style.
The few times he looked at Denise he had nothing to say. What
was he doing there? He was supposed to be phasing himself
out of this family situation, wasn't he? So a vacuum cleaner
man calls him up, so what? It was a ridiculous hour for a
phone call anyway, but here he was, in the bleachers on a dis-
mal day. Wonderful. His kid knew beans about handling the
stick, Denise was a total stranger in him now, the boyfriend
probably rubbed avocado and vitamin oil on his chest. Terrific.

Keri muffed a pop fly. Sometime later she forgot to charge
a Baltimore chop off the plate that went for a double. When
she got up to bat again, she went down on strikes. Ethan kept
rubbing her back and clapping his hands and telling his team
they had to hang in there.

Then clouds began to bunch above the field. With his team at bat and way ahead in the score, Ethan stood up between pitches and called for a time-out. He wanted to discuss with the umpire the possibility of a washout. It was decided the game had to go one more inning in order to be an official victory for the Pirates. They would have to finish their time at bat, and then the other team would have to be retired completely, weather permitting. Otherwise the game would be replayed from the start at a later date. Birds were hopping from tree to tree; people in the stands checked to see where they were parked.

Ethan chugged back to his bench along the first-base side of the field and passed along a new game plan to his starting lineup. They were under instructions now to swing and miss—to pop up deliberately or get thrown out—and to do it pronto, before the skies opened up.

But the other team saw this strategy for what it was, and came up with a different idea. Their countermeasure was to stall. They changed pitchers for no reason, relocated outfielders, got things in their eyes. Players on their bench began to whoop and holler and gallop around in a rain dance. Suddenly nobody was playing baseball. The umpire had to tell everyone to wise up already or else both teams would lose on a forfeit.

But finally Keri's team managed to get out of it. Three players found a way to do themselves in for that half of the inning. They swung wildly and ran out of the base paths. Keri had to go to a full count—three balls and two strikes—before she was able to contribute her share as well. There was a grumble of thunder in the distance and darkness overhead.

"We're looking sharp," Ethan called out, clapping and making fists. "We're hanging tough, sports fans, we're winning a ball game today. We're playing baseball now."

Keri's team took the field with a major win only three outs away, and a few heavy drops of rain already spattering down. Keri was in position between first and second, even with the bags, her feet shoulder-width apart, knees bent, elbows loose. She was on the balls of her feet, hands down, glove open.

From above came a deep, rumbling groan. Station wagons

began to start up in the parking lot, bicycles with wide tires tossed into the back.

Del Plato looked over at his wife. His ex-wife, separated wife. Denise suddenly appeared older than he had remembered. He decided he liked her hair better the other way. Down on the field, Ethan had taken off his cap and was using it now to shield the defensive signals he flashed with his fingers.

Bouncing lightly on her toes, Keri gave every indication of a willingness to go left or right, to attack the high chop or retreat to flag one down on the outfield grass. But who could tell what she was thinking? She watched each pitch, acknowledging nothing, saying nothing, doing nothing.

The first batter on their team kept taking pitches without a swing. It began to drizzle steadily. When two strikes had been called, he tapped one back harmlessly to the mound and there was one down. The next hitter figured he knew a good thing when he saw one and was going for the right side of the infield from the word go. Keri's side. The rain came down harder. People in the stands began to cover themselves with extra clothing. Denise put her magazine over her head. The boy at bat took two called strikes, tapping clumps of mud from his cleats, fixing his protective batting helmet, killing more time with his major-league-style batting glove that had the fingers snipped off. Then came another pitch, and he stroked a medium-hard grounder right where he wanted it. The ball came off the end of his bat and twisted past the mound. Almost gracefully, the baseball hopped to Keri.

She backed up on the ball—a mistake. She tensed up and put her knees together—a mistake. Del could see it coming, everyone could. Rain hissed down, cats and dogs.

It was maybe more than a routine play, but not much more. The small white ball took a true bounce, a high bounce. Anyone could have had it.

Keri closed her eyes. The ball struck her squarely on the shoulder. It skipped behind her. She fell down, got up, and went after the ball into short center field. Rain gushed down, a burst of thunder. Denise turned her head. Nobody said a word. Lightning ripped the low dark sky.

The batter rounded first base and taunted Keri with a
fake dash to second, clapping and jumping and acting obnoxious. But Keri wasn't even looking that way.

Puddles had already formed in the outfield patches. She
splashed through them and stood over the baseball after it had
rolled to a stop. The rain came in torrents—a downpour. For a
long time Keri looked down without moving, completely still.
This small wet ball was what gave her such a hard time. Then
she stooped, held the round white thing in the palm of her
hand, spun it once or twice—red seams, the small print. Then
she heaved it for all she was worth to the farthest reaches of
center field.

Denise, in the bleachers, covered her face with her hands.
It was pouring, teeming. The umpire lost sight of the ball as it
soared beyond the outfield grass, and he waved his hands to
call it a day. All over. The other team had been spared an official loss, and in a blink they were off the field before the rain
had a chance to stop or the umpire had a chance to change his
mind. They piled into station wagons and hatchbacks. Batting
helmets, bats, warm-up balls, first-aid kit, the extra catcher's
mitt, new baseballs packed in boxes.

Ethan sighed deeply, then clapped his hands and told his
sports fans to get their stuff together as well. The square white
bases were pulled up, and they dug out the pitching slab.

Keri sat down all alone at the head of the infield diamond.
Second base had been there. Her baseball shoes were covered
with mud. A shallow pond had formed around her.

Denise brushed water from her clothes and stepped down
the rows of bench tiers and out onto the field to sit beside Keri
in the loose, wet dirt. The parking lot was nothing but exhaust
fumes and red brake lights as everybody else headed for home.

After his team had been shipped off, Ethan hesitated for a
moment near the pitcher's mound, and Del Plato could guess
what was going through the guy's head. *Maybe this was one of
those personal things, and you had to leave a mother and her
daughter alone when they were huddled in the infield.* But
then Ethan did a half-jog and half-walk to meet them, and he
took off his baseball cap to place it gently on Denise's head.

Del wasn't far behind. He also took an easy jog out there.
Denise was hugging Keri and stroking her hair and the rain
kept coming down.

Del Plato was thinking how weird it felt to be out on a
Little League field. It was so tiny when you were on the
grass—everything was so compressed. When he was in Little
League the field had been huge, hadn't it? Even from in the
seats it had seemed bigger.

"We sure got jobbed today," Ethan said. He had his
hands in his pockets and was looking toward the skies. "If only
it had held up another minute. We had this one in the bag."

Keri peered from beneath Denise's arm to see who was
there. She shivered weakly and continued with a noiseless sob-
bing as she looked from one face to another. Denise took
Ethan's hand and guided it to a place beside her own on Keri's
shoulder. A few ducks waddled in from the outfield to see what
was going on.

"I hate this game," Keri moaned. "I hate it."

Ethan told her it was a tough break on that last grounder.
Slippery turf, for sure.

Keri worked her arms free and popped the buttons off her
black-and-gold uniform top. She tugged the sleeves loose, then
slammed her jersey to the ground.

"You know Reggie Jackson, the baseball player?" Ethan
asked.

Keri was busy tearing the baseball spikes off her feet. She
yanked off her stirrup socks and flung them into a deep puddle
that had formed around the second-base pipe. Her socks took
on water and slowly went under, like scuba divers.

"This is an interesting story. Reggie Jackson, when he
was about your age, had a funny thing happen to him. Seems
that Reggie was playing an important game, and there was no
score. And it was the last inning." Ethan wiped away rain
dripping off the tip of his nose. "Reggie tore into one finally,
and he knocked the ball over everyone's head. But he got so excited, as I remember this story, that he forgot what to do. And
he ran the bases the wrong way. He went to third base, then
second, then first, and when he slid into home plate he was

safe. But because he ran the bases backward, it was actually minus one run, so his team wound up losing, zero to minus-one."

Keri said, "I hate this game." She took a punch at her drenched uniform top.

"I'm trying to make the kid feel better," Ethan told Denise. "What are you looking at me like that for? I heard the story when I was in Little League and I thought it was a good story. We had Mickey Mantle when I heard it."

Denise had caught Del Plato's eye and she wanted something. He had forgotten he was there. Do something, she was telling him. Do it, just do it.

Do what? Who were these people?

Keri took a peek at him too. He was the father, wasn't he?

Del found himself plagued with doubt and indecision, which wasn't like him at all. His daughter was in a pinch here, but Del Plato felt the distance, and he didn't know what to do. Was he supposed to hold Keri and put his hand on her shivering shoulder with all those other hands? Was he supposed to pat her on the rear and give her a bogus baseball story? Or should he help her stomp on her baseball clothes?

And why him? Officer Del Plato, a man without a country, a man with two rent payments and a cold coming on, who was mud all over now, who had lost his sense of right and wrong and had nobody in the world to lean on.

And what were they all doing out in the rain? Anybody with any smarts would have been home, drinking a hot toddy in the family room—children in front of the tube, a wife preparing an unusual quiche, a husband idly adding up his net worth. Why was Del Plato out there to catch pneumonia? With his estranged wife and his hitless daughter, who would only wind up driving off in their own car to their own house, with a grapefruit tree in the backyard and all his fingerprints wiped off the wall, where some Ethan who took saunas and did three hundred push-ups a day would be waiting.

And what would Del do? He'd get into his piece-of-shit vehicle sooner or later and probably drink a beer in the rented house. Maybe he'd snoop through more drawers out there.

Maybe he would drink rum. He could drive to the academy gym and hope for a game of shirts and skins, talk things over with the shooters about sports and skirts and the new flexible mortgage rates.

Or he could invite this whole wet crew out to a nice lunch or something. That's what he could do. Get Denise and Keri and even the boyfriend out to some nice restaurant, where they could eat things and get started on a new kind of life and maybe know for sure what they were supposed to do from now on, how they were supposed to talk to one another. A place with plush carpets, where you could drop change and never find it again. They could talk about who was supposed to shoulder the responsibility now in case of emergency, like if Keri had to go for finger X rays or if there was a snake in the garage.

Denise and Keri rocked back and forth. Denise was also crying softly. Del stayed a few steps behind. But Keri was staring at him, her eyes wide, and in them Del saw—What? A lot. Respect, for one thing, and probably some fear. He would always be her father, no matter who bought polo shirts for the kid or gift certificates, no matter who made up stories to tell her. Here was a big moment, everyone on the field, the middle of a storm, and him looking eye-to-eye with his daughter.

"That last throw," he wound up telling her, "the one to center field, that was probably your best throw ever." She was listening to him, not so much to anything he said as to the sound of his voice. It was a father's voice, after all. Right? "That was a major-league throw, kid."

He was thinking that any father shouldn't have to sit with his family on the second-base pipe. What kind of relationship was he setting up for himself? His daughter played baseball, fine, but a guy with two hours' sleep and troubles of his own shouldn't have to spend his day off getting soaked. It wasn't right. A small girl shouldn't have to cry over a batting slump, a wife shouldn't have to trade words with vacuum cleaners, and once you got that much out in the open there really wasn't more to say about anything.

But then Keri broke away from her mom's grip, and took

off toward Del Plato. In her bare feet, with those small fists, coming toward him. And Del was gone. Pursued, he turned his back and was putting on the moves, dipping and darting through the thick, wet grass. Then he was laughing and she was laughing, just like that, and they all were.

"Catch him, Keri! Go! You got him now!"

Del pulled stop-and-go fakes, his daughter always a few steps behind. He did spins and twists. When Keri fell, he hung back until she was on her feet and on his tail again.

Del Plato leaped over puddles, flew through the field, scattered the ducks. He was uncaught and on top. No one would catch him. But then, laughing still and exhilarated, Del glanced over his shoulder. Trailing him, Keri had this look on her face, gasping a little, and right then and there he saw something. She was not about to give up, no way. Del Plato had been worried that soon he wouldn't recognize her, but he knew and he would always know. Keri strained behind him, fierce footsteps behind him, and Del had that tugging feeling once more. Being a father, that was the feeling. *Look at her,* Del Plato told himself, *a daughter who would hunt down her old man across a wet infield, relentless.* She would chase him forever. Keri's face was his face, absolutely.

And it was so easy. Once he thought about it, he just slowed down, and there she was, all over his back is an instant, bringing him down, with her breath hot and her little arms locked tightly around him.

And on his face Del had the idiot grin again, there in the dirt with a half-undressed daughter on his back. He was getting good at this grin, with his lips frozen in a sort of smile, and Del Plato was thinking that, no matter what—no matter what—he was still a pretty decent guy through it all.

They stayed on the ground. She had him now and neither one was letting go.

Chapter
9

"I rish, you ever been on a cruise? Me and Gail were on a cruise. Once. A gambling thing to Freeport and back. You're on a ship, and there are all these people, and you have to look everyone over, decide who you're talking to and dining with, because that's what you do on the ocean, you look for another couple who enjoy the same things you enjoy, so you don't lose your fucking mind with all the waves and five meals a day." They were driving along A1A, beside the rolling gray ocean and white motels. "When I first saw you, that's what I thought, in your uniform. This is to your credit, Del Plato. Here's a guy who might keep his mouth shut. Here's a fellow officer who might be sympathetic, who might enjoy some of the things I enjoy."

Del Plato was sitting back comfortably on the passenger side of Breed's car. He ran his fingertips along the plush seat fabric, thinking, *This is what you get for payments of two hundred dollars a month. You get only what you pay for.* He was looking out at the Atlantic, in a cheerful mood for some reason. He was expecting a trick from Breed, some sort of fast one, sit-

ting as he was in Breed's car, with the six speakers and over-
drive, as though he were inside a disreputable store, where
they might charge extra for things you weren't supposed to
charge extra for and then give the runaround about refunds.
This distrust Del Plato found oddly reassuring.

"We're a little behind schedule," Del said. "All day I've
been behind schedule." He closed his eyes as if he were thinking of something more profound than the fabric of Breed's car.

"I saw someone who wouldn't ask too many personal
questions when we were on duty, who would answer the
squawk box and let me drive the automobile. Someone who
wouldn't eat in the front seat and leave crumbs."

Del would have liked to stop the car and maybe go for a
walk—he was in that kind of cheerful, good mood. He would
take off his shoes and socks and roll up his cuffs, buy ice cream
and walk along the shore. Smile at the girls in bathing suits,
toss a pigskin with husky college boys down for the week. He
was in a mood to do Fort Lauderdale things, mindless bachelor
things. Maybe he would scuba dive, or finally try his luck on
water skis. One scoop of chocolate, one scoop of vanilla, with
the seagulls and pigeons, in his rolled-up pants, cheerful, leaving footprints in the wet sand.

"I'll tell you why we never put in to become detective,"
Del said, staring out the window at bleached palmettos and
trimmed hedgerows. The revelation had come to him suddenly.
"When we're in uniform, everything is so immediate, we're
right there. Detectives have to come in later, after the fingerprints and ambulances, after the stories have been taken
down."

Breed seemed uninterested, lost in his own thoughts behind the wheel.

They passed more motels and a cluster of trees. They were
on their way to Happy Harry's Decor Discounts, for money. It
had been Del's turn in court earlier that day, but after Officer
Del Plato had been waiting to testify since eight-forty-five in
the morning, the judge got fed up with a team of lawyers in
matching blue blazers and first thing after lunch the entire afternoon's calendar had been adjourned. Del's case had never
come up. Breed, after his shift in the squad car, had been down

at the weapons range to get in some firing time with his off-duty hardware. When Del Plato finally caught up with him, they stopped for a couple of short ones at the Quién Sabe, and Del—very businesslike and antsy after a day in court with nothing but a paperback—phoned Happy Harry to pass along the news that it was time for a little visit.

"You see someone with the *Wall Street Journal*," Breed was saying to him in the car, "on a cruise, someone who would turn you and me down for a loan, you know straight out we got very little to converse about with that type, or so one would assume. The thing is, Gail wanted a cruise, so what am I going to say when Gail wants a cruise? On this boat you got fags, you got old people. You got optometrists. You got married couples where the wife got it into her head for some reason that what they need more than anything else in the world is a cruise."

"To Freeport."

"With gambling. With a comedian at night. With Dramamine pills."

"And you didn't have a good time," Del said after it had been quiet awhile. He put his head out the car window and took in a deep breath of ocean air.

"I was out of my element. So was Gail, whether she knows it or not. If they put me on a boat again, I'm going over the side."

Breed was wearing a T-shirt with the sleeves torn away. It said WASP in huge letters. Breed was tapping a beat on the steering wheel to some tune he had in his head. "People got fifteen pairs of shoes. They order things like Cinzano with ginger ale, and chenin blanc. You tell me what we're supposed to say to people like that."

"We."

"Me and Gail, on a cruise. . . . Or me and you, for that matter."

"Ah," said Del. "Or me and you. I think I finally see what's coming."

"The cruise wear shop, the gift shop. Everyone smells like Zizanie. Everyone smells like Hawaiian Tropic. The changing clothes five times a day."

"Hooven. It's Joe Hooven again."

"Tennis on the upper deck. Everyone's been to Acapulco five times."

"I kept asking and asking myself what he's talking about. I should have known."

"Joe Bankbook." Breed also appeared to be in a relatively cheerful mood. "Out of our element, Irish. A person with whom we have nothing to say."

"J.B., I guess I never took the time to notice before, but there's such a smallness to your thinking. I mean, really, as a human being. Think about it, about how prejudiced and small you can be. It's discouraging."

They drove past ragged strips of sand dunes and scattered copra. Fishing vessels bobbed on the shoreline, and sailboats were tied to mossy, mussel-stuck docks, with stacked orange life vests and rolled-up sails. Along the tumbled dunes were thick, colorless reeds, and black stumps of waterlogged wood. Then a volleyball net, people on blankets, and the strong, thick smell of salt water.

"Fuck you, small. Your friend, I bet he's insensitive like that too." Breed began to munch on a Three Musketeers bar he had been saving in the console. "He also wouldn't know shit about human nature, he would also come out with ball-busting remarks."

Del Plato had his hand out the window. He watched it flap in the breeze. "They say one thing you develop as a cop is this ability to define character, to tell who's good and who basically is bad. Well, I'll tell you something. I been on this job a few years now and I know less than ever about character. I don't know a liar or a thief from the next one in line." His hand went up and down in the wind. "I don't know beans about character. You're right."

"Maybe you have more in common with the Baggie than I imagined. Maybe you and I are not as close as I thought. It could be I misjudged you, Irish. Maybe at heart what you really are is exactly the kind of person who could have a swell time on a cruise. With shrimp you peel yourself, with three showers a day. Fucking chenin blanc. Maybe that's the real you and I just never noticed."

The road swerved inland and widened. Framed in the windshield was the full pink sun, sinking through clouds into the lacy, lip-red horizon.

"Concerning the asshole, Irish, I still think what we have, me and you, is what they call your classic difference of opinion. How do you feel about that?"

"You don't listen to me. You don't pay attention."

"I listen. It's a matter of principle, though, with Joe Baggie, with your friend who has that personality. Because what I would like to do, speaking from the heart, I would like to tie him down on the street and run him over with my car a hundred times." Breed was driving with one hand. His right hand was over his heart. "I'm not even talking about jai alai now. What I'm talking about is our basic one-third agreement with the prick. How can you sit there and be so understanding over one-third?"

"You'd like to do something. You have a plan."

"I'd like to run him over. I just told you. You're the one who doesn't pay attention."

Del was concerned with how little he actually knew about character. Human nature. Lately everyone appeared guilty. A little guilty, very guilty—if Del was capable of it, anyone was. He could be a Del Plato who spoke politely, who did the dishes at home, who worried about his daughter—but just as easily he could become another Del Plato.

"You know we'll pay up in the end," Breed said a moment later, polishing off the candy bar. "We'll get caught or something."

"We won't get caught."

"That makes me feel better—your confidence."

"Nothing happens to us."

They went over a series of speed bumps as they came off the Hollywood Beach side and Breed wheeled into the driveway behind Happy Harry's. There were other cars parked in the shade of one wide tree. Breed pulled in by a low guardrail that was dented and buckled from careless drivers and pitted by the humidity. Breed couldn't take it when big American car doors left dings and unpolishable scratches in his metallic

paint. Dumped among the shrubs behind Decor Discounts
were bald tires and striped mattresses, pieces of furniture,
rusted buckets, a cracked porcelain sink, a refrigerator with
the door removed, the hood of a sports car.

"What would you do in his position?" Del asked. "You'd
try to get away with what you could."

"Not the point. Here's the point. We're on the shit end of
the stick, Irish, you and I. He does nothing and he gets a third
of what we do, and that's the point entirely. It's beyond what I
can tolerate. What I would love to do, what would make me so
happy, is to dream up some really diabolical way to get even."
Breed, having turned off the ignition, folded his hands over
his stomach. "Seriously, you think we'll get caught or what?
You're such an optimist, Del Plato. You go from day to day
with no concept of human nature and you think we won't get
caught."

"Did I say that? I haven't really given the idea much
thought. Maybe we will and maybe we won't. I guess that's a
better way of phrasing it for now. There's a possibility we'll
eventually get caught."

"We will."

Del turned his attention to what he should get for dinner.
Was he hungry? There was all the fish you could eat at
Howard Johnson's, but Del had already had a potent veal cutlet sandwich for lunch, in a crowded diner outside the court-
house—that special kind of counter-top veal cutlet that was
somehow immune to gastric enzymes and could lie in your stomach forever—and lately Del Plato had been going through all
kinds of concern about too much fried food in his system. He
ate enough crap on the road, didn't he? Eggroll and chili and
corn dogs. Cream cheese sandwiches with pepper, for crying
out loud, and round, Toast-R-Oven-sized frozen pizza. Even in
his own rented home he was eating crap on the road. Del could
see himself one day with Breed's stomach, taking pills, living
off vending machines like a junkie, paying up in the end.

Breed stepped out of his car. Del Plato came around the
other side, watching where he walked in the high weeds. It was
humid out, and birds cautiously circled overhead. Del found

he was less tired than he had imagined and still leaning toward an ice cream, toward a leisurely stroll on the beach.

"A casual visit," Breed said. "You remember what it was we told him last time? Was it five hundred?"

"Whatever we told him, I'm sure he'll have it ready."

"I wonder what that comes to anyway, three ways."

"Don't start again, J.B."

"Come on, where's your sense of humor? Didn't you used to have a less grumpy attitude, Irish? Learn how to have a good time; learn how to relax."

When they walked in through the front door, Happy Harry immediately closed his eyes. He had possibly put on a few pounds from the time they had seen him three weeks before. Breed closed the door behind him and pressed in the button to lock it. Del Plato checked down the narrow, crowded aisles to make certain they were alone inside Decor Discounts.

"I thought you would be more pleased," Del Plato said. Happy Harry still had his eyes tightly closed. "At least friendlier. You have no idea how annoying it can be, really, everywhere we go, people with their eyes closed and not a friendly word." As he spoke, Del let his mind wander. He pictured himself hang gliding. "I thought last time we had reached some degree of understanding. That was my impression."

Breed wanted to know if any progress had been made on the coffee table for Gail. He offered Happy Harry a stomach pill.

"When your landlord stops in for a visit," Del explained, "I'm sure you don't go into a shell like this. It just goes against me, this . . . I don't know . . . this standoffish attitude. Is business slow, is that it? We come in here on a pleasant Florida afternoon and we get the cold shoulder."

"With business I can't complain," said Happy Harry. He knocked on wood without opening his eyes. "But the truth is this, I wish I was back in New York. When I sold my business up north, I never thought the day would come I should say this, but I wish now I never did it. Look at me, gents, I can't open my eyes inside my own place of business."

Del Plato cracked his knuckles and flexed his legs. He looked up and down the aisles again. What did wind surfing involve? Was it something you could get the hang of in an afternoon?

"My wife, God bless her, she has a bowling afternoon; every day she rides a bicycle. For her, this is paradise. She talks on the phone back there a few hours a day, she puts out dried apricots and a nice spread of cheese and cashews when the canasta girls come over, at seven o'clock sharp every morning she's at health exercise in the swimming pool. But myself, I'm suffering. I'm no longer my own boss. I can't open my eyes to look what's going on. And it's not that I don't like you, gents, because I sincerely appreciate that you didn't put me in handcuffs. Which you can still do, don't get me wrong. I know that as well as I know my tax charts. I was in a pinch, I got involved with the wrong side of the law, and now you got the goods on me."

"I understand," Del said kindly. "You have the money for us?"

"I would have to call my nephew who lives in Emerald Hills to defend me. And I would not like to call him. He graduated John Jay with law, Glenn, and I shouldn't tell you this, but with Glenn you would be home free. You could throw the book at me and never have to worry, because with Glenn you could bring in the death penalty." Happy Harry squeezed his eyes shut even tighter. "Once I took him to a baseball game, in Ebbets Field, where Carl Furillo threw out a runner all the way from the Gimbel's sign in right field, and he made in his pants. Glenn, my lawyer. Maybe he was nine years old at the time. This is who I would have to defend me. I won't say he's a complete schmo—because he's still family—but you'll forgive me if I can't open my eyes."

"You don't have the money for us," Del said.

"You tell me what to do, the other people tell me what to do. You make threats, they make threats." Happy Harry waved his hand back and forth in front of his face. "I don't see what's going on. I'm not looking and I'm not seeing."

"Something is going on," Del said. "It's been one of those days, and you have nothing prepared for us. I ate a terrible lunch; I've been able to accomplish nothing the whole day."

"That Furillo," Breed interjected. "Did he have an arm or what? But what happened in '50? You had to close your eyes then too, didn't you? Robin Roberts, Ashburn. We took it right away from you bums."

"I was hoping you would have some money ready. We would be in and out, like I said. You didn't want to get up, that would be okay, you would only have to tell us where we could find five hundred dollars." Del all along had been thinking of his good mood as something fragile, which could shatter with the first unkind word or annoyance—something you had to protect and nurture and make new laws for, like an endangered species. But here he was, still in a relatively buoyant spirit, despite veal cutlet, despite a sort of hard time with what was supposed to have been a routine shakedown. What was that if not a pleasant surprise? "I don't know what I'm supposed to do now, Happy Harry," Del said. "I'm genuinely disappointed. What do you think we should do?"

"I'm not seeing, and to tell you the truth, I can't even hear." The furniture man put his hands over his ears. "My hearing is suddenly gone, gents. I don't know what else to tell you."

Breed bent over close and spoke into Happy Harry's ear. "Jim Konstanty. You don't hear me, Hap. I can tell how you don't hear me. August, September, 1950. You're completely deaf when I mention Granny Hamner. You don't hear Stan Lopata. Not a word."

"I'm having a hard time with Happy Harry's Decor Discounts," Del Plato said. "Where one time I had to take keys to an innocent piece of furniture. Where it had been clearly understood we had a mutually profitable agreement, what with the incriminating evidence and all. Where five hundred dollars was supposed to be waiting for us. Today. Inside an envelope."

"I can hear sound. Sounds I can hear, yes. Not words. Words I can't hear, and even with the sounds it's getting worse every second. I'm slipping fast."

"You can hear sounds, Hap? Grady Hatton, how's that for a sound? How about Curt Simmons?"

Del Plato flicked a speck of dirt off his shirt. Breed began opening and closing drawers.

"Is my nephew here? Glenn? That's not you, Glenn, is it?"

"No, it's Del Ennis, that's who."

"One Hannukah I brought him chocolate money like a good uncle. While I was sleeping on the sofa, what did I feel in my pocket but his little nephew hands, looking for my wallet. My lawyer. In Ebbets Field he pished in his pants. I can't open my eyes; I can't hear. I can't do any of the other things; I'm not even talking."

Deep down, Del Plato was the kind of person who could be enthusiastic about the sunset over Hollywood Beach and eat ice cream on the shore with no shoes on. He could enjoy himself on a cruise if he had to. He could see the overall picture. He withdrew his service revolver and pressed the barrel against Happy Harry's cheek.

"I don't feel anything," Happy Harry said. He wasn't moving his lips. "I lost all my senses. I can't begin to tell you what's happening because there are no words."

Breed said, "My partner's down to serious business now. How does this turn of events hit you, Hap? Pretty unhinged, huh?"

"I couldn't say, gents."

"It's scary," Breed said. "Authentic. I don't know for sure if you're aware. This Irish, you step on his toes and this is what he does. What a guy." Breed yawned into his hand. "What a cruise companion."

It was time to use less discretion, more force. Del Plato had always been gratified by the way his fingers felt around the grip of a handgun, the squat cold sense of force and imagination. He could get the same pleasure from watching color TV, or simply flying in an airplane: the satisfactions and the basic wonder of our sophisticated life. Amazing, how they could design things so well, so comfortably—technology. Steel and screws, with a plastic grip, and it was nothing until it was in your hands. Select-a-vision. Six-speaker stereo. The ultrathin wristwatch, with a silicone chip. It was great to be alive.

"What a harsh man," Breed said, beginning to fidget. "Is

this erratic behavior or what? I'd say it is. I'd say he's got his game face on, my partner, that serious-business face. Watch out when he gets that way. Stand back when he gets this winning on the brain."

Del watched how steady he was holding the gun against the furniture man's skin. Fingers didn't quiver, hands didn't shake. When his weapon was in its holster, it weighed him down and worked against his nerves, but when it was in his hands, everything was fine. He was calm, the other Del Plato.

"Nothing will happen," Del said flatly. He paused to think about his words. Then he went on in a more serious tone, because he decided this was a pretty serious topic he had just brought up. "Nothing will happen. We're all in the same boat, we all sink or swim. Nothing happens."

Breed went back to opening drawers—old sales receipts with furniture sketches on the back, orange washers, pens, paper clips, knobs, bulbs. "Nothing happens because we're going home," Breed said. "That's why nothing happens. Hap over here is unprepared; no coffee table for Gail; no five bills; nobody home; and I make a motion that we get something to eat right now. Because it's late for one thing, and for another thing I'm serious about this way you're behaving yourself. Our Brooklyn Dodger fan, for instance, happens to be a civilian. What's this gun shit? I'm hungry and sometimes I don't know what gets into you. I have to worry about you, Irish."

Del Plato closed his eyes for a moment and tried to make things disappear. He wanted Breed to disappear, with his conversations, with his mag wheels and metallic paint. Del wanted Happy Harry to disappear. Ethan could disappear too, with his $130 graphite rackets. He wanted his gun to disappear, and himself.

"Also I worry about my car. Because if it's only five hundred dollars, we could come back for that, for the money. My car is back there in an alley, is what I'm saying, with all kinds of junk and dogshit. And if we're planning to spend half the day in a furniture store, we could just as easily come back another time with *your* car, which you don't have to be concerned about if you leave it in a changing neighborhood."

Where would Del Plato disappear to? His eyes were open but he was staring off into a no-man's-land. He would disappear to the beach. It would be easy as anything to be the new Del Plato, who would wear push-button watches that kept the right time, who would have all his shirts facing the same way in the closet. A Del Plato who got out more, mingling with a new and improved crowd—a six-speaker crowd, a crowd that didn't eat goddamn burgers three times a week and get potato chips served up as a vegetable. A crowd where you wouldn't even think about marrying the same person two times. With fast, sophisticated girls, who wore name-brand perfume and more than one earring in each ear, who wouldn't be put off by the idea of a meaningless relationship.

"Can we go?" Breed asked. "Because you're getting that vacant look, Irish, and generally nothing good comes from that."

Del was smelling the air. It smelled like furniture polish. He took the gun barrel away from Happy Happy's face and walked up a narrow aisle to the back room.

"How's pizza sound? I could go for a pizza. Or chili, if you'd rather. I'll be accommodating, Irish. I'd just like to leave already because you're leading me into all kinds of weird things lately and you're not yourself."

On the office door was a sign that said DO NOT ENTER in four languages. PRIVATE. Breed was right beside him, shaking his head. Del read the sign a few times, testing his knowledge.

What languages were up there? German? Forget German. French? Denise had tried to get him to speak French, but Del had shown no aptitude or patience, and he hated to purse his lips in that faggy way. What else? Spanish? Spanish was probably easier, Del figured, especially if so many Cubans and Puerto Ricans could speak it. When Keri was younger he watched *Sesame Street* with her, spending time with the kid, which a father was supposed to do if he was any kind of father, and Del had picked up quite a few odds and ends like that. How to count to twelve in *español*, how to say *kids*, and *exit*, and *cooperation*.

Breed pulled the cord on a set of model mini-blinds, looking at Del Plato and still shaking his head. "I've seen you

looking better, Irish. You look skinny. What you should do—
You want to make it over for dinner or something? I'll give
Gail a call. She likes company. Not you exactly, but she won't
mind." He pulled one cord and the slats opened. Another cord
and they closed. "Tell me again how we won't get caught with
this bullshit business. I liked that line, Irish. I felt a lot of
confidence with it. It was with your delivery, I think."

Del hadn't learned how to speak Italian either. He was
slightly disappointed when he thought about it. He would
have liked to know more than one language, to be a bilingual
person. The old man wanted only English around the house,
none of that greenhorn talk. Del's mother had spoken Italian
when she took him shopping to the pork store and fruit man,
where Del carried packages wrapped in thick brown paper.
Now, if he had to, he could order a half pound of cappicola or
prosciutto like a pro. His mother continued to speak Italian to
the family whenever the old man was at work or having a few,
and to let Del have an earful whenever he came home late for
supper.

"I won't say anything about Denise, because with Denise
I don't know how you feel, with what's going on between you
and all, but the few times I was over for a meal, Del Plato, I
have to tell you the food was only so-so. Maybe she has other
attributes, but one time we had some kind of casserole thing
over by you and it was actually less than so-so." Breed withdrew his nickel-plated Llama .25. He closed his fingers gently
over the stock and placed his thumb on the safety. Almost as
an afterthought, Breed leaned over and whispered. "Irish,
what have we got ourselves here? You know something I don't
know, or what?"

"A hunch," Del Plato said. "Nothing would surprise me.
I'm beyond surprises." He also took a turn on the mini-blind
cords. Up and down, open and shut, amazing. Technology.

"I'll tell you what would surprise me. If we really knew
what we were doing, that would surprise me."

"It's not the money, J.B. I think you realize with me it's
more than just money. It's even more than winning. I'm not
sure exactly what yet, but it's some fucked-up kind of thing."

"We know that much for sure, do we?"

"I'm the first to admit it."

"I'm talking about getting caught," Breed said. "When you look at the odds, Irish, they are unquestionably stacked the other way."

"What does that have to do with us?" Del Plato asked. Then he put his ear to the office door. Nothing. "You have faith or you don't."

Breed stepped forward and opened the office door. Tommy Polio was inside, with the others. They had their weapons in their laps, in various postures and difficult angles. Obviously they had given considerable thought to these arrangements, where to be, what to say, the tone. Tommy Polio was by the desk, beside a section of one-way glass looking out on the store. Hooven leaned casually against the wall, with the sullen expression and that tilted sideways profile of a male model. Hector from Orlando, wearing headphones and a mini-cassette player hooked to his belt, straddled a seat by the door. Growling Felix looked on from behind the protection of a filing cabinet.

"I got a cold in my nose," Tommy Polio said for openers. "Don't come too close." He was wearing a new toupee which made him look years younger.

Breed looked at Del Plato for what had to be a long time. He stepped inside and said, "This was a very brilliant maneuver, Irish, to get us here. I'm very impressed."

"We don't need sarcasm, J.B."

"No, we need more optimistic remarks, that's what we need. We need more brilliant maneuvers."

Del Plato stayed where he was, just outside the door. He was trying to work on the old breath control. Here was a stress situation, and what he needed to do was become the other Del Plato. *Nice and easy,* he said to himself, breathing in, breathing out. The Del Plato who could sniff the air for danger, experienced and detached. Who could open a door and face up to whatever was on the other side. That Del Plato. The one who took the last shot in a ball game. The one who obviously had a lot more going on upstairs than this counterfeit Del Plato who had somehow managed to take over recently—a lax and semi-divorced man, who got into these brainless good moods where all he could think about was an ice-cream cone on the beach.

He would become the Del Plato who used to shave regularly and never left his clothes on the floor. Whose shoes were always together in pairs, who didn't fall asleep in his underwear at two in the morning with trivia-quiz movies on the tube. Because this current Del Plato was something of a disappointment. This new Del Plato sometimes looked at his own reflection and thought he was forty-five years old. The only green vegetable he was eating was the celery stalk they stuck in his Bloody Mary. He was not getting laid on any sort of regular basis. Was this the kind of person you would trust with the ball with time running down on the game clock?

"Up north I had two colds a year," Tommy Polio said. "My wife gave me tablets, I drank plenty of liquids twice a year; twice a year I got plenty of rest." He coughed and pounded his chest. "Now I'm a Floridian—no more Union City—but twice a year I still come down with something."

Del tried to recall when he was last on the beach for any length of time. He drove past it every day, but the only sunburn he got was when he propped his elbow out the car window. What did you do? You brought a blanket, a swimsuit, some money for the man with ice cream, and you were set. If you didn't have a swimsuit, you could roll up your pants. This was South Florida, where things were casual. If you didn't have a blanket, you could take one of those earnest, Bobby Kennedy-type walks along the dunes. There were clamshells to skim, washed-up jellyfish to poke with sticks, sand and tiny pieces of shells to pick from between your toes.

"Just as long as there are no threats," Breed said. "Because my partner here, he can't take it with those threats. It brings something out in him, I don't know, an optimism or something."

Tommy Polio said, "I was getting to the point, last time, where we could talk about our secrets, our misunderstanding. That's why I'm here now when I should be in bed. Last time we left one thing, I'm remembering, still unsaid."

"What he is—look at him—he's the kind of guy who don't

really care about what was up in the air last time, about secrets and telling names. And you can't provoke him either, because he just won't stand for that. He won't. He's a winner. Go
ahead, try to provoke him. He'll spit right in your eye."

Tommy Polio felt his forehead for fever. "What was that
supposed to be just now?" he asked. "Was that wit? I don't like
wit. I'm a simple man, I have simple taste, and there's only one
thing I want to hear from you. Nothing else."

Del Plato felt like he could use some air. It was too
crowded inside. All these people, all these voices. He could be
this Del Plato, or the other Del Plato, but when, really, was the
last time he had spent some time on the beach?

Daytona, wasn't it? Sure it was, Daytona Beach. And that
was what, years ago, with Denise and Keri. It all came back to
Del Plato. Strange radio stations and unfamiliar motel beds.
The Round-ups and Tilt-a-Whirls, cotton-candy stands. In-
flatable lobsters and Batman dolls. With cars parked right up
on the sand, on the beach. Miniature-golf courses, bikers, ice-
cream sandwiches and body surfing.

"We can end this thing," said Tommy Polio, "or we don't
have to if you'd rather be witty. To me it's nothing. I drag myself from bed with a temperature." He patted his new toupee
and then snapped his fingers. "Don't ignore me. Tell me the
name."

Joe Hooven raised his weapon and sighted down the barrel. He had it trained on Breed. Breed was nodding his head in
a noncommittal manner, staring over at Del Plato, who still
hadn't stepped into the office. Del Plato had a dreamy look on
his face, peering off dimly at nothing in particular.

Breed was actually impressed with the way Del Plato
could keep his mouth shut and his spirits up under pressure.
Extremely impressed. The earth could be bumped off its axis,
everything spinning not quite right, and Del Plato was a
mummy. Breed was thinking that was something you had to be
born with—a genetic business, like a full head of hair or a big
wang, nothing you could improve upon in your spare time—
and that tough mental stuff was something that couldn't be
taught in a million years. Del Plato happened to have it.

"Five hundred dollars here, five hundred there. Traitors and breakdowns. We had to put a hit on our own spiders. I'm losing patience."

Del Plato was still thinking fondly about Daytona. What a good time they had all enjoyed, as a family. And what a place too, with motorcycle races, with Wheels of Fortune. You could lie down on the beach and get run over by a car. Fried shrimp in a cup, vacationland.

"We're not doing this again," Del Plato finally said. Firmly. "The shakedown, the criminal behavior, me and my partner have given it up. At least as far as you're concerned, Tommy. We're out of this business, out of your business; we're out of it completely." He took note of the drawn weapons, the overall mood, the temper situation. But all of this was of more or less insubstantial consequence compared to the importance of going to the beach, even for a little while. The prospect had taken on an immense significance for Del Plato. He lived in Florida. Why wasn't he on the beach more often? Why didn't he have a sunburn, or a nice car? Everyone else in South Florida had a sunburn and a nice car. Del Plato had a sunburn on his elbow. He had a car that left blue smoke, and little leaky remains wherever it had been parked. What Del figured he had to do was make up a list of priorities. One priority was to quit this shakedown shit. "You'll never hear from us again," he said, with the authority of someone who has made up his mind. "We're too good for this business. We're gone."

Tommy Polio made a small circling gesture with his hand, trying to get himself started. "I could do something to your car back there," he finally said. "In the alley. I could have these people I know work on it. They take off the tires, they take out all the little wires inside and even the catalytic converter. What they don't want they set on fire."

"You're not talking about *my* car," said Breed, trying to give himself that same dreamy look, that same faraway glazed expression Del Plato had, as if he were in a dentist's chair, for instance, and could care less about the drill and injections and wads of cotton inside his mouth. "Come near my automobile and we're talking about a major conflict. If you're trying to pressure my partner, really, scratching my car may not be the best way of going about it."

Del checked his breathing. Nice and easy. He told himself it was that time.

He turned around abruptly and walked away. Everyone watched for a few long seconds. It was a very unexpected thing to do. Del Plato walked in his normal, unhurried pace toward the front door. Down the narrow, crowded aisle. Past Happy Harry, who was still slumped beside his quiet cash register. Beyond the massive wall-unit displays, with their sections for liquor, good dishes, and the latest in electronics. Across the sales floor. Turning the door handle. Opening the door. Gone.

Del just followed his feet. He wasn't really thinking of anything, not a thought in his head. Just time to get the show on the road.

When Del was on the street, it was gorgeous out. A little on the brisk side, but sunny and warm, a diamond of a late afternoon, a chamber-of-commerce day in the Sunshine State. He could hear voices behind him, commotion.

He turned east, to the water.

Breed came up beside him. "Irish, wait up." They were outside, crossing over to the beach block. An insurance office, a men's store, fruit shippers. Breed scanned the street behind them. Tommy Polio and all three gunmen emerged from Decor Discounts. Hooven led the way, firearm at his side. They also turned east. Tommy Polio had one hand upraised to keep the wind from his new hair. There was a jewelry store, a travel agency, pinballs, Ice-Cream World. Felix had a gun right in front of him.

Del Plato was going to get out of the felony business. That's what he had told Tommy Polio, and he meant it. What did he need it for? Del figured what he really needed was a rest, or even a new place to live for that matter. An easier life. An unsuburban life for a change, an un-Florida life—where you didn't have to get in your car and drive all over simply to buy something as basic as aspirin or ice cream, where you didn't have to face up to the daily strain of Turf Builder and

black stuff on your ferns, and whether or not your water
heater was wasting electricity while you were asleep. Where
the Sunday *Free Press* came on Tuesday. Where you ran out
of places to take your kid every other Saturday. He could
leave that. He could walk out the door and be gone.

Del Plato stopped short on the street to pat his pockets.
He was outside Ice-Cream World and had remembered why he
was there. He asked Breed for a dollar. "Can I get you something, J.B.?"

"No."

Del went to the takeout window and bought a double
scoop. Then he paused to look at the ocean from where he was.
He could see the surf but couldn't hear it. He could smell the
water. Whitecaps tumbling evenly and thick, shattering
against the flat bright sky, and he started walking again to be
closer to the beach. He cupped his eyes and surveyed the ex-
panse of water, bathers by the shore, Hobie Cats.

Del Plato told himself he had to get a bathing suit. He
told himself he had to get a steady girl friend. He told himself
to get a smarter job, and a haircut while he was at it. Everything was possible. The best things in life were free. Del Plato
was one person among many millions, and everyone had the
same ideas. *You get what you pay for. Coffee boiled is coffee
spoiled. Don't talk to strangers. Aim always for the back rim.
It takes two to tango.*

All true, right as rain.

On a public bench, where the sand began, Del Plato
paused again. Breed held the ice cream while Del sat down to
remove his shoes and socks and roll up his cuffs. He took off his
shirt and tied the sleeves around his waist.

"I'm going to take a walk on the beach now," Del said.

"No shit. How nice."

Breed looked behind. The hoodlum kid with the radio also
had a gun out. Breed frowned and followed his partner. He
unbuttoned his shirt and tugged the shirttails out of his
slacks—a small concession.

"You don't know what you're doing, do you?" Breed
asked. "You got no explanation for this shit." Breed realized

he hadn't been on the beach himself in the longest time. Another thing he didn't like—the beach. Sand in your hair, green water. "You know what it is with you, Irish? You're acting mysterious, that's what you're doing. Right now you're putting on this whole mystery personality. The enigmatic Del Plato, he comes and he goes. The fucking optimist. The cruise man."

The beach was relatively crowded. It was late in the day, but vacationers were everywhere. One or two kites hung motionless in the sky. A white yacht was off in the distance. There were towels and limbs and radios and coolers.

"You'll have to tell me," Tommo Polio called behind them. He was twenty feet away. "One name is all. Sooner or later, I'll find out."

Del Plato continued walking. People were in the sand, sleeping in the daytime.

Hooven, leading the pursuit, came to an area where children had brought buckets of water from the ocean's edge and carved out an elaborate system of moats and tunnels. Hooven walked right through it, intent on not losing ground and also not that impressed with tunnels. His gun was in his right hand, only partially concealed.

"What's wrong with you, mister?" called one of the kids. "That really eats it, mister."

Hooven paused but didn't turn around. Mister? They meant him, didn't they? Asshole, Baggie, mister. Everyone was talking down to him all of a sudden; everyone had names.

A mud ball struck Hooven in the back of his trousers. He turned around to survey the damage. Mud.

What were they, like twelve years old? Which only proved what kind of justice there was in the world, if these twerps could annihilate an eighty-dollar pair of sailcloth slacks and the most they would ever look at was like malicious mischief or something, going to bed without chocolate milk, and it would get tossed out of any juvenile court before it even got that far. But hey, if he protected his personal property and bopped one of these little dudes with some of the same beach shit, or made a kid eat sand, or threw one in the ocean, or shot one in the kneecap, or strangled a little sucker, then forget it, then the whole world would come down on Joe Hooven for sure. The whole world would be calling him asshole and mister and talking to him like that.

Up ahead, Del Plato continued stepping carefully through a maze of lounge chairs and ringtoss, weaving an intricate path among brightly colored beach blankets with pictures of anchors and hula dancers and maps of the Gold Coast. There were plastic bags of fruit, lightweight folding chairs, souvenir playing cards.

"What I'd like to know," Breed said, "are you going to be a partner or an enigma? Because a partner makes conversation. And one partner always stands up for the other partner. Whereas an enigma mopes around all day and don't know shit about human nature. He goes for a fucking walk on the beach."

"I sense a little hostility, J.B."

"No hostility. Not any more than usual. I just feel a little stupid on the beach is the thing. Talk to me, tell me what I'm doing here."

"Nothing happens to us. Everything is perfect. It's a beautiful day and we'll never get caught."

Del Plato felt as if he could stand on a surfboard and do whatever surfers did in the water. He could water-ski on his bare feet, swim like the dolphins and lifeguards, do anything. He was free, he was eligible; everything was possible.

Breed also took off his shoes and socks. "You tell me what it is," Breed said, brushing grains of sand from his feet, then stumping along behind Del Plato. "Is it a Jewish thing or what, but I can't take two steps in my bare feet. I get splinters, I get pebbles, and it's too hot for me out here. Show me someone with no sandals on and I'll show you a non-Jewish person. I think I'm bleeding already."

Tommy Polio and his men had cautiously skirted the moats and tunnels. They stopped where Hooven had stopped, looking ahead.

"These people come down from the Midwest—Pennsylvania and Ohio—where they've never seen the ocean in their lives, and look how they can walk around without shoes and without problems."

Del Plato asked Breed if he felt like going for a swim.

Back by the more-crowded section of the beach, Tommy Polio and his men wiped their brows and watched Del Plato and Breed slip off into the distance. The cops were holding their shoes and socks; they had their shirts off. Del Plato and Breed, tramping along through remote strands. Heads up, facing the sun, sharing ice cream. Having a ball for all anyone knew about it.

Chapter

10

The first time he caught James Lloyd's elbow in his throat, Del let the matter slide because it was a rough game they were playing. Both men had been hustling after a loose ball when suddenly Del went down as though stricken with some kind of jungle poison, his hands at his throat, gasping for air, blue. He was shaken and stunned, and it was moments later before he was finally able to focus on the dark and impatient faces of basketball players hovered above, telling him he was all right.

"Accident," James Lloyd said. "It's our ball. You okay?"

Del slowly got to his feet and glared at James Lloyd. He reminded himself that things were bound to happen—the inadvertent elbow, the clash and discord of ten bodies going full tilt, leaping, crashing the backboard. Soon as he got his hands on the ball again, Del banked home a running one-hander.

"Happy birthday," James Lloyd said as they started it up again toward the far side. "Ain't you the lucky one today?"

Del could afford to be big about it because that afternoon at the academy gym he was on fire, pumping in jump shots,

passing crisply, scooping smooth, twisting drives through the
hoop. It was one of those basketball days for Del Plato when
everything turned out right. The ball always made that nice
satisfying sound for him on the hardwood floor, its full, com-
pact thud echoing back off concrete walls and the long
wooden-bench tiers and high metal-grated windows. He was
tuned in only to the raw, loose rippling of his muscles, the heat
of his own skin. Del could do anything. He had more than half
his team's total baskets, and he was absolutely eating up
James Lloyd.

"Run it back," one of the players shouted. "Push it up.
Let's move."

They had been running full court for almost two hours.
Everyone was tense and sweated, and even though the windows had been cranked open, there was no air. The walls were
slick.

For the longest time Del had been trying to convince himself to get back into some sort of shape. He needed to exercise
again. Since Denise left, he had been slackening off terribly,
terribly. Too often Del had been picturing himself with a divorced man's heart and a divorced man's temperament, with
the looks and posture and even the unhappy smell of a divorced man, someone who should have been living in a furnished room, among the downtrodden and jobless, a swivel fan
and a half glass of bourbon beside his narrow bed. Living from
laundry in a laundry bag, taking his meals in a cafeteria. Sitting alone on Thanksgiving. Somehow he had gained eight
pounds.

The few times he did run a game or two at the gym, Del
woke up the following morning stiff and incredibly sore. He
was an athlete; he needed a regimen. Forty push-ups a day,
and forty sit-ups. Then up to fifty. Just like the old days. A
proper diet and eight hours' sleep. In two weeks he would be
like iron.

James Lloyd dribbled the brown ball toward the other end
of the court. He had made up his mind to go right back at Del
Plato, one-on-one. James Lloyd believed he should have been a
professional basketball player because he had such a profes-

sional-sounding name. James Lloyd. It was the name of a fancy passer, a playmaking guard with a trim mustache and his own fan club. To James Lloyd it was a cruel joke he was only five feet ten inches and had never played beyond high school.

"Look up," Fast Calvin called from underneath. Medlow was also hungry for a chance. "Heads up now."

But James Lloyd was not giving up the ball. Del was certain of it. Once an idea churned in James Lloyd's head, there was no talking to the man, only wild-ass schoolyard moves and elbows. It was a question of pride; manhood was on the line. He was being shown up by Del Plato, and to James Lloyd you had no pride or manhood if the shooter you guarded was constantly playing you for a chump. James Lloyd was predictable that way. He would heat up and mutter and finally fly off the handle, resentment welling up for only so long before he would burst into cheap shots and fury. His temper managed to work in these measured cycles of agitation, like a washing machine.

"Right back at you," James Lloyd said with a tight smile.

Del stepped up at the top of the key to cover his man more closely. James Lloyd did a neat little stutter step, followed by a 360-degree spin that even a professional guard might envy. Then he lowered his shoulder and simply rammed his way toward the basket. Nobody really liked James Lloyd.

Still, Del had no intention of going easy. Someone else might have stepped aside to let James Lloyd have his basket, but instead Del waited for his man to lift his eyes toward the hoop at the end of his long dribble. Del Plato had been concentrating on the cadence, timing each deliberate bounce, waiting to make his move. When James Lloyd began to bring the ball up to a shooting position, Del reached in cleanly to tap the basketball away. For a brief frozen moment nobody stirred. The basketball seemed to float freely. Then Del Plato took a step toward it. James Lloyd cursed, swung another elbow. Again it caught Del Plato in the throat.

James Lloyd picked up the ball, dribbled it. Del lay prone on the court. Thud, thud, thud. "Here it comes," James Lloyd

said above him. The ball went up, spun through the hoop. It
came down beside Del Plato. "There it is."

Del rose and blinked. He felt no malice, no pain. If it ever
came down to it, Del Plato figured he had his defense already
prepared. "Guilty," he would plead, staring the judge and
anyone else right in the eye. "Guilty, with an explanation."
He pounced on James Lloyd in a headfirst tackle. They
cracked to the court floor. Del whipped on a headlock.

Here I go, he thought, *fighting again. Guns and crime and
fists.*

That morning Del had taken a good long look at his life,
where it was heading and why. He was financially overex-
tended, in a constant state of fatigue and doubt, with poorly
ironed shirts and no urge to get up in the morning. He felt
displaced, unloved, and surrounded by a vague sense of mean-
ness that was coming from nowhere else but deep inside.
Where was a strong sense of order? Where were the rules? His
future was being steered now by someone else, not himself,
some immature and reckless driver out for a good time, full of
skids and senseless, careening turns. He had to regain control,
get rich, or smart, somehow find his way back to the warm good
graces of money and love. But how? What were his qualifica-
tions? Del had a very nice smile. He could crack eggs with one
hand. He could parallel park on the first try. But were these
the foundation of a solid new life?

He thought some more about Denise. Denise with a baseball coach, Keri with a stepfather. The day his wife had left
him, five months before, Del Plato could mostly remember
having been starved. All day he hadn't eaten. Unlocking both
locks after a day's work, Del had entered his own house cautiously, with a growing, tugging cop sense of something gone
wrong. Drawers had been emptied. Cabinets were open in the
kitchen. Her pocketbook and coat weren't there, no car. The
bathroom floors had been cleaned.

All Del could think about was being hungry. He had
eaten half an English muffin in the morning, some of Breed's
fries in the afternoon. Now it was late, suppertime, but nobody
was home, nothing prepared.

Maybe they had been kidnapped, or murdered. For a terrifying instant, driven by a shadowy dread and an acute hunger, he imagined Denise broken and lifeless, Keri in pieces. Del didn't know what to do first. All the way home he had been thinking about steak. He searched closets and beneath the beds. How could you admit to detectives that first you had whipped up a little something and read the sports section before you really noticed? They would question you, with dirty dishes on the table, contempt in their eyes.

In the kitchen, on the refrigerator door, Keri's name had been spelled out in ice-cream sticks. Del Plato was starving. Inside the refrigerator he could find only colorless plastic bowls, a jar of mustard, sour cream, mystery stuff wrapped in aluminum foil. He was too frantic to wonder what the hell was going on, but he knew. Half a container of yogurt. No wife, no kid, no supper.

"Denise," he moaned. "Denise."

She had left him. Del slammed the refrigerator door. Keri's name fell off. A magnetic cookie broke on the kitchen tiles.

There was nothing to eat. What had she been doing in the kitchen cabinets? Taking boxes of cereal with her, for Christ's sake? How was he supposed to suffer like a normal person when he was so hungry? Only later did he find out his wife was in Montreal, with Keri, and she had been unhappy for some time.

Del flexed his muscles more tightly around James Lloyd's skull. His man groaned and seethed.

There was so much to guard against in this uncharitable world, which could swallow marriages and make children disappear from your life when you weren't looking. You had to draw some sort of individual line along the way; you had to make a stand. If a James Lloyd pushed and pushed, you had to push back. As a human being you had the choice, the ability, the perspective of choosing.

Del Plato felt as if he made a choice every day. Honesty was on one side, corruption and broken marriages on the other. Love was on one side, philandering on the other. Wisdom and ignorance, a good life and a bad life.

James Lloyd swung up wildly from underneath and man-

aged to connect, this one right to Del Plato's eye, another
cheap shot. Del continued pressuring, grinding. Not a word
had been spoken, only the heated grunts of struggle and the
squeak of sneakers along polished floorboards. Del heard himself breathing hard. He wondered briefly what it might be like
in James Lloyd's position. Everyone had secrets, everyone had
the same problem of choosing; the whole world with something
to hide, a universal bond of unshared guilt.

Del tightened his grip. He hadn't started this fight. He
flipped James Lloyd down hard.

Somehow he had developed this insatiable appetite for
funds, a new aspect to deal with, and the only way he could
deal with it was to give in. Some unfamiliar beast inside him
growled constantly to be fed—money, money, money. Del
Plato had no way of communicating, no way to deny or relent.
His only friends had no consciences, and for Del Plato each
new day had become mostly a series of distractions—eating
and driving, bills and TV. There was nobody to say this was
foolish, or that was dangerous. Here he was, dizzy with dollar
signs, and new rules seemed to come up every day. You had to
make adjustments; you had to keep feeding.

He wasn't a bad guy. Why he was doing this to himself?
Why wasn't he happy, or a better person? Even a simple game
of basketball, shirts against skins, and the whole match had
come to a standstill because Del Plato had drawn a line and
needed to keep this viselike pressure on James Lloyd.

Maybe love was the answer, after all. Breaking up, a broken marriage, an estranged family. His wife's lover going
through the leftovers of that increasingly more distant life—
touching Del's toothbrush or cuff links, examining labels,
making judgments. It seemed so long ago and so simple then.
You concerned yourself with a pension, how many kids you
might have, whether the babysitter could invite a friend over.
Where to go for good Chinese food, life insurance. Now Keri
was between dads, probably hanging out with scruffy adoles-
cents who smoked Marlboros and had no consideration for
math. Now Del Plato was dozing fitfully after midnight to
whatever was on the tube, while the rest of the world slept

soundly and dreamed the good and healthy dreams of solid citizens. At times he could feel a patched-together wall of values
crumbling down around him, falling in on itself like a cake
that had come out of the oven too soon. He was after a new car
and safe-deposit boxes. Did that make him guilty?

Fairly guilty, Del decided. *Pretty much guilty. Guilty
enough.*

But what about tow-truck guys who yanked away your
vehicle while you were getting your teeth fixed or something?
What about people who charged an arm and a leg to fiddle
with a goddamn carburetor, or American people from American companies who somehow convince themselves it's okay to
do business with our worst global enemies? When do you cross
the line? Lawyers stand up in court beside rapists and cop-
killers in new suits and they holler about technicalities, for
crying out loud. Adjustments all the time. You had to walk
through life like you would a revolving door, watching out you
don't get your heels clipped from behind, waiting for just the
right rhythm to jump in among the others—one, two, three,
now—so you don't pull while everyone else is pushing, all
alone in your own little compartment, faces floating on all
sides, going every which way, and even when you did everything right you were still only going around in circles.

He didn't want to be dragging James Lloyd in a headlock.
Del had been enjoying the game so much, relishing that singu-
lar feel of confidence that came when things functioned the
way they were supposed to. For a little while he had known
some law and order, the truest kind of harmony, when fifteen-
footers fell through and his moves came naturally, without
hesitation, from inside, and he never had to think about what
came next.

But now he was going to have a shiner, for sure. Skin burns
from scraping along the court floor, and a shiner. He grappled
with James Lloyd, tugging and twisting, turning around.

Other players had no patience for it. Medlow twirled in
lay-ups on the opposite end. They took turns drinking from a
cooler of ice water. One cop sat on the basketball, another idly
combed his hair. It was poor etiquette to interrupt a game.

They discussed vacation time, new assignments. They talked
about problems, football. A rookie cop had practiced the two-
handed draw in front of the only full-length mirror available,
which was inside the bathroom, and had accidentally squeezed
off a round. Now the veteran cops wore their vests to take a
leak. Someone had retired to open a liquor store. Someone else
was promoted.

Only Del Plato and James Lloyd were on the court, an
isolated thing, nobody cared. The fight wasn't their concern.
Human nature was something that meant you had to look out
for yourself. We all had it. Big children bully small children,
old people go into homes. That was human nature. Salesmen
turned back the mileage on used cars; you took towels from
motels.

"I'll hit you again," James Lloyd sputtered from below.
He was swinging crazily, off his feet, hopping up and down
and bent over. "You wanna fight, I'll fight. I mean it."

Del Plato felt and listened to the sound of his own throb-
bing heart, which pulsed and pounded out an indistinct but
troubling sort of violence. He was supposed to be calm; he was
supposed to be all right. But immediately this pressure seemed
to sink in his chest, falling down, down, cut loose now from the
flimsy strings and clamps of birth, dropping. How could he be
all alone? How could his actions be separate and distinct from
the rest of what was going on? Too much held the universe together, or else we would all be sinking or rising without reason, helpless as heavenly bodies, which were pointed in one
direction and would keep going that way forever, uncon-
nected, untouched.

Del squeezed once more. "Enough?"he finally asked.

"What?"

Then he let go. "Enough." They backed away from one
another without a touch or a look. James Lloyd took a moment
to straighten, then made a special effort not to rub any of the
parts that hurt. The other basketball players began to warm
up. Del Plato shook the stiffness out of his wrists and fingers
and stood off to the side to roll the kinks from his neck.

Crime was neither here nor there for him, not really.

Criminal behavior was always somewhere off on the periphery
of his being, a shimmering glint of color barely perceptible,
like water on a sun-baked road, which was right in front of
you, just ahead, but somehow never actually there. The shakedowns, the planned robbery, they had no place for Del Plato—
no context. He couldn't explain his behavior because he was
dealing with a mirage. Only the results were real, the profit.
Cash was real. Having was real. Not taking.

Medlow wiped the ball with someone's shirt. He tossed it
harder than necessary to Del Plato and told him to run it back,
they were losing time. The teams set up again, James Lloyd
jumpy and tight in front of Del Plato. He breathed sharply,
his face puffed up and ashen where Del Plato had been holding
him down.

"Just play the game," James Lloyd said. "Don't talk
to me."

"You got it."

"Don't talk to me."

Del brought the ball quickly over the center-court line,
passed it to the corner, got it back immediately. Everyone was
half-speed, waiting for the flow to return. He took two short
strides behind a pick, then backtracked and passed neatly underneath for a simple bucket. Del as easily could have hit the
shot himself. There was no doubt in his mind, he could shoot
over James Lloyd or drive around him, maneuver his way
through any defender. Del had never played so well before,
and this worried him slightly. His basketball game was improving as his personal life fell apart. Did that make sense?
Was that fair?

As if the earth had slipped a few degrees off its axis, Del
Plato saw himself a wandering victim of confusion, no longer
able to comprehend things. He himself might go out and shoot
someone, then turn around and score a hundred points in a
single game. Husbands and wives could love one another and
still find the time and patience to love other people as well.
Which strings were connected to what? Where were the corre-
lations and commitments, where were the parallels? Did divorce lead to unhappiness? Unhappiness to divorce? Everyday

objects were apparently still the same up close, but from a distance they had become increasingly more difficult to discern. What had been a comedy on TV turned into something tragic, or a commercial. People could solicit bribes and still be called up for jury duty. People could work seven days a week and still be a bad risk for a loan. People could cheat and lie and tattle on one another and still be invited to terrific parties.

James Lloyd had retrieved the basketball past the end line and started back the other way. Players loped slowly upcourt. Sharp breathing, feet, the hollow thud of an old ball.

Del Plato took long strides, anxious for the game's pace to return. He wanted to mix in with the flow, mingle once more with the steady rolling stream of action.

Fast Calvin came beside him. He patted Del Plato on the rear. "You play pretty good for someone with the white man's ailment. You can't jump and you're slow as shit, D.P., but you play pretty good. Yes, you do."

It was true. Del had lost track of his own points. He knew no score and had forgotten who was on his team. Everything seemed to go, and that was the only thing that mattered. Nothing else was like it. When you played ball, there wasn't a thing in the world more important, and when you were playing well, there was nothing better. Anyone moving with his skill and success had no reason to doubt himself about anything. Del was canning them from a distance, threading passes through traffic, snapping the ball on his dribble.

He would get his future together. Money, theft, whatever the hell was going on. He had secet plans for a more comfortable life, a more satisfied life. He would narrow the scope of his desires, take care of any major thing that had to be taken care of. These were his undefined plans, unvoiced and indistinct. That empty portion of his heart would be filled. But his goals, he decided, should always remain grand and undiminished, like dreams that slip away as soon as you open your eyes.

"People have to work for a living," his father had told him so many times. "What's wrong with the human race is they don't think. People been working through all of history and before, good people. Today we got teenagers with no-cut contracts. We got desk-job workers who take two hours to eat their lunch."

In the past, if he had found money in the street, Del's first thought would have been to wonder who had lost it. Now he would probably get on his hands and knees to hunt for more, searching through thick muffled turf for the distracting glint of silver or the right shade of green. He used to be the kind of person who had voted regularly, who had carried his trash until he found a trash receptacle. Now he was dishonest. Occasionally his plight would startle him, how much he had changed. The spooky, jolting shapes of right and wrong would loom before him without warning, sometimes in sleep, sometimes when he was busy thinking of an entirely different subject.

James Lloyd paused to check the alignment. Other players had crisscrossed ahead, apparently still pissed off at having had to wait so long. Del Plato kept his eyes on James Lloyd's stomach, because a player could fake and deke all he wanted—arms, legs, and head moves—but a defender would never get beaten by a stomach. Del's high-school coach had taught him that. It was a rule he would never forget. His high-school coach also had taught him to release a ball off the fingertips, and always to count your change after any purchase.

"How you doing?" James Lloyd asked, juking left and right, coiled. "You got one eye bigger than the other one. You know that? I think it's swollen."

Del saw things from the corner of his vision: Medlow pushing his way into the low pivot, Fast Calvin on the move. James Lloyd flicked his eyes in one direction and turned his head another way. Del fought the urge to smile. As soon as the pass left James Lloyd's hand, Del Plato had it. And before he could even marvel at what a wonderful game he was playing, he was already tearing for the opposite end of the court, all alone, on the run.

Del dribbled once between his legs. Nobody bothered to chase him. He took his last step at the foul line and left his feet for the hoop. For the longest time he hung in the air. Del

thought he might have taken flight; he had never soared so
high. The ball was suspended from his outstretched hand.
Gracefully he swooped toward the hole, poised in the air,
magical.

You steal something for the first time and expect the
world to be altered in some way, but it never is. Lie and noth-
ing happens. No sign, no secret, awful change. There was no
center, nothing to hold back for, no reason to sacrifice. Cheat
on your wife, break the law, take the Lord's name in vain. It
should mean the end of the world—a collapse of ethics, the loss
of family life. Del Plato had fallen. He was guilty. *The mist-*
thick surface of pain and conscience should have blown away
to point a terrible final finger. The sun should have gone black,
the stars and moon dropped from the sky. Mountains should
have toppled on us all, water taken us under. A panoramic
embrace. The end of the fucking world.

Del twirled the basketball very gently and it sailed
through the metal rim. Another basket. Even his teammates
turned away. He was playing a somehow superior game, scoring far too many points, floating with such lofty form the effort of basketball had been demeaned. He watched the ball
drop through and roll away. Everyone was at the other end of
the floor. It was the best game of his life. Del Plato stayed
where he was, under the net, feeling pale and strange and
empty, like a jelly doughnut where after a single unsatisfying
bite all the jelly has squirted out. He waited for someone to
come for the ball and start the action up again.

Chapter

11

B reed drank Manhattans, whistling "Come Fly with Me"
softly between his teeth until Del Plato asked him to stop.
The pool tables of the Quién Sabe Lounge were covered with
faded sailcloth and the lights above the tables were off; the
jukebox was plugged in. Joe Hooven was also having a
drink—Bacardi with crushed ice and lime—sitting on a folding chair out in the aisle. He wore white cotton drawstrings
without underwear, huaraches, and rimless glasses tinted to
change with the light. His shirt was brightly colored, with
mountains and sky and friendly wildlife all intricately embroidered by hand.

"These doctor types were discussing women the other day
on the radio," said Jewboy Breed. He had been on late duty
the night before and hadn't been home at all. "Maybe it was
yesterday. But I'm listening and listening, and I'll tell you the
truth, I'm amazed they can talk this kind of trash on the public airwaves. It was to me a very off-putting sort of discussion."

"What's there to discuss?" Del wanted to know. "What
kind of discussing?"

"Respect" had come on the jukebox for the third or fourth time. Del Plato tapped a finger to Aretha on the rim of his white wine. It was four o'clock in the afternoon, a Friday or Saturday. Del had been sitting with the same glass of white wine since two.

"Women are different," Del Plato said. "There's nothing to discuss. Take my word for it."

Breed wore his dark mirrored sunglasses indoors. "Here's the gist of it. A woman can have an orgasm from almost anything. Did you know that? You didn't, did you?" He chewed gum rapidly, which made his sunglasses go up and down. "I mean, what is it with these women? You try to please. Sometimes you bend over backward to be accommodating, or to try out a new move—I'm not ashamed to admit it's happened to me—and they're noticing something's crooked on the wall, or a fingernail broke. Now on the radio I hear they ride a bicycle and get off on that, which personally, Irish, I find more than a little bit scary. They breast-feed a baby and bust the nut. Honestly and truly, Del Plato, that type of information puts me on the defensive. It affects my ego. One lady called in and swore she was having one right that second, on the telephone, just from talking about it."

"I wouldn't know about any of that," Del Plato said. "I got my own problems."

"Don't we all? I'm nervous about what I learned," Breed told him. "I'll come right out and say it. What are we supposed to make of bicycle stuff? I'm a simple guy. I got a thing that goes up and down and I want to keep it that way. I don't need nuances and shit to interfere with my male psyche, which is something you never want to fuck around with."

Del Plato had ordered white wine because he didn't like it. To him that seemed a good way of cutting back. The pertinent question for Del was, would he be able to get tough with this developing paunch of his? Eight pounds was the immediate problem, although his head was flushed with concerns.

"All I know," Del Plato said, "is you look around and you find one girl, and for some reason you decide to live the rest of your life with her. That's what makes *me* nervous. A virtual stranger, and for her alone you open a door to everything you own, you sleep in the same bed with her. This is someone who might have a history of hemophilia or lunacy in her family. How do you know? But she laughs at your jokes, or you like the way she smiles, so right away you trust her with the keys. Half your children's genetic characteristics will come from this person, who maybe you went to the movies with."

Del squeezed a fold in his midsection and wondered what the problem could be with his metabolism, which had always been so dependable. Eight pounds. You stepped on the scale and either way you were winning or you were losing. They said a healthy body was a happy body. You got rid of eight unnecessary pounds and were on the road to recovery, or else you didn't get rid of them, and it would probably be booze and aspirin for the rest of your miserable, flabby life.

"Who decided marriage was the only kosher way to do things?" Del asked. "People seem to have a hard-enough time deciding whether they like boys or girls. How do you pick out the only one whose birthday you have to celebrate, and whose social security number you're going to memorize? You can go out with one girl who only wants to pay for her own dinner, while another will always tap you for an expensive entrée she won't take two bites of, and she'll even hit you for the fifty cents extra on blue cheese dressing. You tell me the secret. Which one is supposed to be love?"

Breed ate potato sticks from a can. "I see your point," he said. "In a little while, whatever you do anyway is going to be too much for her, or not enough." He appeared preoccupied, and wasn't paying enough attention. He was making jittery notations on the page of his souvenir jai alai program that had black-and-white photos of all the players. "I'm a little overwound right now," Breed said to Del Plato, snapping gum. "I'm a little tense."

"I can see. You're eating all the potato sticks."

Gene Pitney sang "Town Without Pity." The bartender turned up the jukebox volume because some girls had come into the Quién Sabe Lounge, and he was hoping to keep them inside by playing loud music. They had sat down, running combs through their hair.

Breed examined his jottings and didn't appear too happy

with what he saw. He had sketched a map of Olympia Jai Alai. Breed kept turning it over, examining all angles, as though the map were merchandise that had been reduced so drastically there had to be some glaring damage along the line.

Breed's greatest fears involved humiliation. He wouldn't object to even the stiffest penal sentence if a jury of his peers found him in the wrong. He would never crack under torture, or reveal a source. But what if he had invested in the kind of things nobody invested in anymore—like land in the Everglades, or mood rings, or eight-cylinder automobiles? What if he was getting himself mixed up with a deal that was way off the mark? What if somebody was taking him for a ride?

Hooven started to say something, but didn't. Hooven hadn't said a word in a long time. Del Plato, for one, thought it a very smart move on Joe's part. Hooven had his hands folded in his lap, gazing calmly above at rusty stains in the ceiling panels. The place was empty except for them and the girls who had come in, and two phone company repairmen who took a window booth where they could open the drapes and keep an eye on their service truck double-parked across the street. The squat jukebox glowed with tubes of green and pink neon, looking very lethal and expensive, like something you might find in a madman's basement.

"Personal feelings, okay," Hooven finally said. "But we got to put them aside, man. It should be obvious. I mean, hey, at this point. We got some conflict and bad vibes, but that's life, guys." He was still looking up at the ceiling panels, as though cue cards had been placed above him.

"I almost heard something," Breed told Del Plato. "Just now, a sound. An insignificant voice."

Del Plato thought it might be a good time to leave. He was not the best company, with his fuel-burning chemicals apparently on the fritz, and no plans for his future other than armed robbery. What would happen? He would become heavier, more unhappy, and soon he would have to learn what those numbers in a blood-pressure test actually measure.

When a phone rang beside the number-one pool table, Joe Hooven rose immediately and excused himself to answer it, leaving behind his Bacardi and ice.

"It's December and he wears white pants," said Breed, making a gesture with the little red sword from the cherry inside his Manhattan. "Look at him, your friend. In December you wear white pants if you work with pizza, or in a hospital. That's the way I was brought up, Del Plato. That's the way you were brought up."

"I'm here," Hooven was saying into the phone before it rang a second time. He spoke in a low, dry voice, the receiver propped against his shoulder. With both hands free, Hooven was able to drum on the Yellow Pages. The book had been chained down like something valuable or dangerous. "Everybody's in. But listen, listen, on Miami the numbers haven't come in so strong for me. Everybody for some reason is taking the points on this one, and me, I have to lay off because it's too much."

The bartender was checking his bottle inventory. He wore a shirt that had nice pictures of antique cars. Right off the bat Del recognized a Model T and a cream-colored Hispano-Suiza.

"I got nothing to say about who you do it with," Joe Hooven explained over the phone, "but I'm holding more than I got a right to be holding, so that's why I'm talking to you. Otherwise everything's cool." He opened and closed the phone booth door to fan the air.

Del Plato got up and went to the bar to bring back a bowl of peanuts and also to listen in. He wanted to get a better idea of what was going on with Hooven and telephone calls he would answer on the first ring.

"I got no idea why people are going with the dogs, and no, I can't wait for the points to change because I'm swamped. I got steady clients I gotta keep happy," Hooven pointed out. "If it's a favor, then okay, I could use the favor. As such. I'd appreciate it." Hooven flipped in a hurry through the pages of his notepad. "You don't have to say anything to Tommy. Just take my action, and if you need me, man, then call. You know where I am. I ain't going nowhere."

Hooven hung up and returned to the table, where Breed snapped his gum and refused to look at anything. Del Plato continued to stare straight ahead, into the mirror behind the bar of the Quién Sabe. He could see the stock of bottles, all shapes, sizes, colors. Bourbon, exotic liqueurs, costly brandies with names that were hard to pronounce. The bartender's shirt had a T-bird Landau in seafoam green, and another car which looked very much like Del Plato's own push-button Dodge. The mirror itself was large and tarnished, frosted along the edge with stencils of angels and clouds and curved horns spilling fruit.

Del Plato lingered for a while at the bar so Hooven wouldn't suspect him of eavesdropping, but Del didn't really care. One time when he was driving Joe Hooven through the parking lot of Olympia Jai Alai, so they could get a better grasp of escape routes and possible outside interference, Del glanced over to find Hooven fooling around inside the glove compartment, right out in the open. He was poking through Del Plato's personal stuff—old repair bills and sour balls, a knife, a fork and spoon, and road maps that had taken Del a long time to fold the right way. Yet, caught in the act, Hooven had simply shrugged and smiled, as though it were perfectly okay to snoop so long as you were up front about it. Then he had brushed his hair with Del Plato's brush.

Still, at their table inside the Quién Sabe Lounge, Del cleared a center space and made a big show of putting down the wooden bowl of peanuts. He took a sip of Hooven's Bacardi and ice. Everyone seemed absorbed in other matters. Del vowed not to touch a single peanut. Hooven continued to stare off at something nobody else could see.

"So how are things, Joe? How's the action?"

"Fine. None of your business."

Hooven reached for his pack of cigarettes and felt inside the plastic wrapping for one of the joints he had stashed away. He lit up with a slim gold lighter that was on the table from before.

The thought occurred to Del Plato that police work had perhaps not been the wisest choice for him. The same could be said of a decision to rob. But he became a cop because he was big and rugged, and because some decent part of him wanted to be a cop. He would look sharp in a uniform; he would help people. Now, however, Del Plato was in another place entirely.

He was like a newspaper article that starts off on page one, full of promising details and clever phrases, only to end up way in the back somewhere, buried among store coupons and hi-fi ads and depressing statistics of the economy.

Breed had taken a drop cloth off a pool table behind them and was racking up the balls. One of the young girls inside the Quién Sabe folded the cover properly as Breed picked up a cube of blue chalk and went to work on the business end of his cue stick as if he knew what he was up to. This came as a complete surprise to Del Plato, who had never seen Breed play pool before.

"Pennsylvania," Breed was saying to the girl. "When you say it like that, Pennsylvania, the state, that means you're from one of those small towns in Pennsylvania. Otherwise you would have mentioned a city, like Philly or Pittsburgh, or even Allentown." He twirled his cue stick on the green felt pad. "I know these things. Trust me. Otherwise you would have been from *near* Philly, or near Pittsburgh."

The girl glanced over her shoulder to see what her two friends were up to. They danced with each other beside the back door of the Quién Sabe, where a space had been cleared in front of the jukebox for customers to dance.

"We're all from there," she told Breed. "From near Allentown, actually. We have this time off from school, with the winter break and all."

"I'm Jackie Molson," Breed said. "How old are you girls?"

"Nineteen."

"From near Allentown, in Pennsylvania."

From where he sat, Del Plato judged her to be fifteen, sixteen. Probably her dancing friends were no older. He left Hooven sitting at the table and took the peanuts with him. There were three guys, after all, and these three girls. The one Breed was talking to wore tight patched jeans and a tube top with electric stripes. It depressed Del Plato to think that he might have to carry on a conversation with someone who was only fifteen or sixteen years old.

Breed set up the white ball and snapped out a quick, clean

shot that scattered the rack. "So here you are in the warm weather," he said, concentrating on his next move. Breed crouched behind the white ball and squinted down a sight line.

"I'm Cindy," she said, standing back a few feet to allow him shooting room. "It's really Cynthia, but I hate that, Cynthia. Don't you?" She wore a fragile-looking gold chain with Cindy written out in script, and a pair of lightning-bolt earrings in one ear. The other ear had three crescent moons. "My ex-boyfriend back home plays pool. He has one of these tables in his garage."

"You girls drive down here, Cindy?"

"Ina has this Buick that her dad lets her have. She's the one with a bathing suit on. Bonnie doesn't drive, so me and Ina did it in twenty-five hours with no sleeping."

Hooven fed the jukebox as "Respect" came on again. Del Plato, spinning his wine glass by the pool table, thought Hooven would have no trouble having a conversation with Pennsylvania girls who were entirely too young. He would entice them with elaborate stories of pot plants frozen for centuries in the Arctic glaciers, or Morrison still miraculously alive in the south of France. He would show them his unicorn ring. And of course the girls would fall for Hooven, with his long hair and his high-school English. A sophisticated person, to these girls, was one who drank beer from a glass rather than straight from the can. A sophisticated guy wore cool sunglasses, which changed color from one place to another.

Del was also troubled with the thought that white wine was probably just as fattening as beer, and if he kept ordering white wine he would eventually acquire a taste for that too, and then where would he be? No better off than before. He was also looking at Ina's bathing suit. She wore shoes with heels.

"How come you girls are not at the beach?" Del asked. "Where all the cute boys are?" Cindy was watching as Breed banged in a few shots. Del had absolutely no idea he could play pool. "Shouldn't you be out looking for boys?"

"What cute boys?" Cindy turned to her friends again. The two other girls were doing dance steps Del Plato thought had gone out of style years ago.

He wondered what Denise would think he was up to. He

was fairly confident, from the way they danced, that these were not nineteen-year-old college girls. Their arm-bending and hip-shake motions reminded him of something they might have learned at an older sister's wedding, when the hired band calls upon the very young and very old to mimic the dance crazes of past decades—"Everybody now, watch me, the hully-gully. That's it. And now . . . here we go . . . *pachenga time!*" It made him very uneasy. Having your name in the paper as a criminal was one thing, while being singled out for the whole world and your ex-wife to see as a man who had a conversation with fifteen-year-old girls was another thing entirely, and much worse.

"Hey, Ina, he goes to me, he goes, 'How come you're not with the cute boys?' So I go, 'What cute boys?' We're in Florida and we might as well be in Wilkes-Barre."

"Oh, my God, Wilkes-Barre." Ina stopped dancing to cover her eyes. "Please don't make me remember Wilkes-Barre."

"Ina and myself party a lot back home. Ina's mother—it's a scream—she looks and talks exactly like Edith Bunker."

Ina walked over carefully to join them at the pool table. Jewboy Breed had just sunk a purple ball. Ina helped herself to a handful of peanuts, and Del interpreted this as a sign. It would never happen, of course, but if it ever did come about, he would pair himself off with Ina, in her bathing suit and high heels. Breed would go with Cindy and her flimsy necklace. Hooven would get stuck with Bonnie, who not only couldn't drive, she also appeared to be much less experienced than her two friends.

"Some things I'd rather just repress," Ina said at the pool table, adjusting the top of her swimsuit. Del noticed her shoes were closed off at the toe, shoes from up north. She wrinkled her nose and said, "I smell weed or something, I really do."

Breed called out a number. Twelve. He clicked it into a corner pocket. Then he walked to the opposite end of the pool table and pointed his stick to the five ball, and that went down.

"You're good," Ina said happily. "He's very good."

"What do you guys do?" Cindy asked. "Are you guys salesmen? What do you sell?"

"I'm a ballplayer," Del Plato said. "A relief pitcher for

the Fort Lauderdale Yankees. Jackie Molson, maybe you heard of me."

"Jackie Molson," Cindy repeated. She had her arms folded in a defensive manner. "He's Jackie Molson and you're Jackie Molson. Is that a joke, or are you making fun of us?"

"A joke," Del Plato told her. "And the other guy, the one with the hair, he's an undercover cop. You can hardly tell these days."

"I don't believe you. If you want to make fun, that's okay. Go ahead."

Breed nudged in a deep-green ball, clearing the table with slow, smooth strokes and a deliberate motion. He didn't ask Del Plato to join him. Del was considering this as a challenge of sorts when Hooven came over with a fresh drink for himself. "Ladies," he said politely to the two who were there, with a slight bow. Hooven also picked up a cue stick and began to chalk the tip. Del was beginning to feel left out because it wasn't his sport. Pool always seemed to involve a lot of idle conversation and good-natured ribbing, where people acted like they were in a beer commercial, and Del never cared for that sort of camaraderie. One of the reasons he liked basketball was because you had to keep your mind on the game, and comments were limited to "Nice shot," or "Don't do that again." Then you took a shower and went home. You couldn't steal the ball in a game of pool, or trip your man from behind if he was giving you an especially hard time.

"You guys live here?" asked Cindy. "We can stay for as long as money holds out. Bonnie over there, dancing, she has this savings account, and she got the gas money to come down, so we let her, even though she's pretty much a drip, Bonnie."

"We wouldn't have invited her otherwise, quite honestly."

Del Plato reached for Ina's necklace, which had twisted behind her neck. It spelled out Ina in a cluster of clear sparkling chips. "If you girls are old enough, maybe we can offer you something to drink."

"If we're old enough? We drove down here, didn't we? I already said we were nineteen."

Joe Hooven took a long toke of his joint, then cupped it

behind his back. He pressed against the pool table and placed two quarters on the silver lip of the coin slot. Breed never looked up. He kept punching in shots, taking his time, measuring. Del Plato couldn't get over it. Breed had not mentioned pool, not a single time.

Hooven's voice was already higher than normal. "The dude for sure looks to be a shooter." He slipped the two girls a ten-dollar bill and asked them to bring back a few drafts and something for themselves while they were at it. "I shoot too, you know, although I ain't saying I can do anything with this killer over here. Not the way he's knocking them in."

Hooven smoked his joint right down to the very end, the part that could alter your fingerprints or set your mustache on fire if you weren't careful. He rolled the nub between his thumb and forefinger, then swallowed it.

"The man's a shark," Hooven said. "I got no chance. I'm out of my league with this cat."

Hooven took a fifty from the center of a folded wad of bills and set it faceup on the chipped wooden rail, where Breed could see it. This was exactly the kind of juvenile stuff which turned Del Plato off to pool-shooting. People were always hustling and making disparaging remarks. They pretended to be worse players than they actually were, until you were a point or two from victory, when suddenly they would convert shots they had missed earlier and there went your fifty dollars.

"To get the juice flowing," Joe Hooven said, "make things interesting. Because look at the way he walks them home now." Hooven tested the weight of his cue stick and took a few practice strokes in midair. "I mean I've won a few games, sure; I been lucky here and there. But this Breed, hey, he can psych out anyone the way he handles himself. The moves and all, the concentration."

Breed removed the fifty cents from the coin slot and put the coins on another table. He picked up Joe Hooven's fifty-dollar bill and let it drop to the floor.

"I don't hear anything," Breed said. "I can't hear you, rambling man, and I can't see you either. You're formless. Isn't that strange? Without form. What else can I say?"

"I don't get the humor." Joe Hooven winked at one of the girls. They were comparing prices off the drink menu. He seemed very much in control even though he had gone through a few cocktails and eaten the tail end of a marijuana cigarette. "You said that before, man, and it wasn't funny even then."

"Nonexistent," Breed said, lining up his next shot from a crouch. "Without words. Some kind of transformation took place; it's hard to explain. Without the capacity to be heard. Voiceless."

Hooven stooped to put the money back in the pocket of his white pants.

"Invisible. Out of touch."

"Go easy," Del Plato told him. "We've been through this before. Let me drive you home, J.B. We'll look at that map you were working on."

"Shapeless." Breed clicked in a relatively difficult shot. He angled in another off the cushion. "Remote. Far, far away."

"Funny man," Hooven said. He thumped his stick on a neighboring table. Breed continued to pay attention to his follow-up shot, an orange-striped ball hugging the side. "I try to like work around it, man. I do my best, J.B., I really do. But you piss me off."

"I hear a noise," Breed answered. "I can't quite make it out." His face contorted slightly, as though he had stepped in something and was now afraid to look. Breed didn't like it when anyone outside of the department called him J.B.

Hooven whacked his pool cue beside Breed's fingers. Hooven's face went tight. Breed stroked in the orange-striped ball.

The jukebox changed, and "Portrait of My Love" came on, Steve Lawrence. The phone repairmen were gone. When they had opened the door to leave, the failing sunlight had shot through sharply, and a hot, humid breeze had cut briefly into the lounge. It lifted paper napkins, touched Del Plato's skin to make him realize he was in a sweat. Looking at the bartender's shirt again, Del recognized a Reo and a white Avanti.

Bonnie had stopped dancing by herself and sat alone now with her purse between her feet. She was watching a small TV set on the bar, tuned to an old movie. Del overheard bits of dialogue and recognized the picture as something he had stayed up to watch a few nights before. He read a cocktail napkin. It said *Miami Dol-fans*, turquoise-and-orange letters, with a terrific-looking girl waving a pennant.

Del traced his fingertip along the rugged-looking embroidery of Joe Hooven's shirt. He could feel the various shades of mountain, with trees and a thin, straight river plunging down, lush grass in the valley.

"Some chick gave it to me." Hooven also looked down to admire the handiwork. He was buying time to control the tremble in his voice. "You got to wash this sucker by hand. The great outdoors."

"You don't look so good, Joe."

"I'm not, man. It's coming down on me from all sides." Hooven checked his ponytail for split ends. He took a deep breath and abruptly became amiable. "Remember I talked about sailing, Del Plato? On the ocean? With nothing but a chick and some tunes? Well I'm up for it, man. I am really motivated."

"Yeah, sounds good to me too. Try not to say anything to my friend."

"You're telling me? I don't need the hassle. I don't need any of the hassle, man." He took out his cigarette pack for another joint. "Maybe I'm telling you both to stick it, I don't know. I'm thinking maybe I'd rather put up with Tommy Polio and all of his shit."

"He's just nervous because he wants to do it. Ignore him, Joe. We're very close."

"Oh, sure." Hooven lit up again. They were standing near the bar and Hooven's glasses became darker. "With Tommy Polio, man, he whacks you out, and it's done. But Breed, he keeps like annoying you to death. I don't see how you put up with him."

"We're working on a definite date. We're on the details now. It's close, Joe, try to understand."

Hooven exhaled away from Del Plato's face, aware of good manners. He was angry, but Del Plato wasn't the one to take it out on. Hooven wished he were still with the band, where there were disputes, sure, but you could get high with a cat and sort it out; you could overcome. But this Breed was a Republican, and a prick, and there was no room for dialogue.

"What's that name he always calls me?" Hooven asked. His voice was climbing again, so he took another hit. "Baggie? What is that? That's a scumbag, isn't it? That's what he calls me, man."

Cindy and Ina returned with frosted mugs of beer. Del Plato's first thought was to turn his down—No, thank you, I'm on a diet—but it was up to his metabolism to put things in order again, and he would have to give his system a fighting chance. He deposited his warm white wine on a covered pool table and picked a cold mug off the tray. Why should he drink white wine if he didn't want to?

"Is that doobie for you alone?" Ina asked Joe Hooven. "I knew I was smelling pot. Back home we have this hippie couple who grow it in their living room—marijuana—and it's great. They're very careful. They feed only organic stuff to the plants and play Dan Fogelberg."

Hooven ignored her. He was busy watching Breed. Hooven took off his tinted glasses and wiped them with a corner of his embroidered shirt. If Breed called him a Baggie one more time, just once, there would be no dialogue. There would be revenge, per se, and nothing else. Maybe he would have to shoot Breed and burn his body inside a vehicle. Maybe he would get his hands on curare or something radioactive and put it inside Breed's stomach pills. The dude's hair would fall out, and his breathing would like stop, and then people would maybe learn not to go around calling each other names and creating hassles.

Breed missed a solid-yellow ball wedged against the cushion. It was Breed's first miss since he had racked them. Del Plato went to the table while Breed waited for the white ball to stop rolling so he could try again.

"J.B., you're getting upset."

"I'm getting upset. Yes." He shot at the yellow ball again and it still wouldn't go down. Breed seemed almost

pleased. "Disputatious. How's that sound? I'm feeling disputatious, and I don't think I'm responsible for anything I
may do next."

"Don't talk that way. We decided to do something, so
we're doing it. Right? We decided, didn't we?"

Ina had reached across to share Hooven's joint. She stood
now with one shoulder thrust forward, inspecting insect bites.
Del Plato looked her over carefully from a distance for any
signs of nineteen. He admired the way she held a marijuana
cigarette so casually, filling her lungs and not coughing, very
practiced, the tightly rolled number pinched between her fingers. But no way was she nineteen.

"I'm nervous enough," Del said. Breed was at the other
end of the table, moving quickly and quietly. "Let's split. To-
morrow's another day."

"It's just that with people, certain people . . . Let me get
this phrased the way I want to. You depend on people," Breed
said, head up now, pool cue at his side, "you rely on certain
people, and then what happens? Complete the missing part."

"I'll drive you home. I haven't been drinking."

"What happens?"

Del Plato paused, as though about to deliver the weighty
last line of a poem. "They let you down," he said.

"They let you down. How true, Irish. They disappoint
you."

Del Plato walked over and placed an arm carefully
around Ina's waist, then bent to nuzzle her neck. She held a
pink drink the bartender had whipped in a machine. Del was
surprised at how bland she smelled. A faint unwashed odor
came from her hair, not at all the beachy aroma he had been
anticipating. Del had taken her for a surfer, or water-skier,
someone with chlorine in her hair and an open attitude toward
sex, who would wear a bathing suit in a bar, who would smell
good.

"I have stuff over here," Ina said. She shivered and moved
away, taking Hooven's joint with her after she had worked
free. "I'm going inside to change."

The bartender had plugged in his vacuum and was going

over the thin, dark carpeting along the bar, anticipating a rush of late-afternoon business. Ina walked through a door marked VIXENS.

"We have a couple of Thai sticks in the trunk of Bonnie's car," Cindy said to Breed. He had left his cue on the pool table because he was having a difficult time with the remaining few balls. "Would it be cool to get high in here, Jackie? After your friend lit up, that was so neat. Back home we only get high in someone's car, or in my ex-boyfriend's garage."

"Jackie, Jackie," Breed repeated. From the open curtains where the phone men had sat, the dropping sunlight seeped across the tabletops, slanting in with a low, dry glow. "No, it would not be cool to get high in here. That wouldn't be cool at all."

"I think I'm getting a sore throat," said Bonnie. Her voice was new, unfamiliar, and everyone turned to see who was talking. Bonnie had come over to join the crowd. Some mysterious instinct had brought her to stand beside Joe Hooven at the number-one pool table. Hooven smiled at Bonnie as though he had been waiting all along for her to come over and stand beside him.

Outside the Quién Sabe, in traffic, a Chow-Chow-Cup van beeped with an angry, rhythmic insistence. Del was looking outside, watching the sunset through the open curtain. Breed's car was parked in front. Hooven's car was nowhere in sight because he was always careful about that, parking a few blocks away from wherever they had scheduled to meet. It was the start of rush hour. There were wiry gardenia bushes lining the entrance to the bar, and concrete squares where tubular weeds grew through the cracks. Across the street was a long, flat office building with red-slate tiles on the roof. Chiropractor's World. A sign said LOSE WEIGHT, STOP SMOKING, BE HAPPY, with a phone number. SAVE 100's OF $$$.

Ina came out of the ladies' room wearing a wraparound skirt through which you could see what she was wearing underneath. She also had a pretty blouse with a price tag still dangling from the sleeve. Ina carried a blue tote bag, her bathing suit wrapped inside paper towels.

"You like to get high?" Hooven was asking Bonnie. "What do you do for fun?"

It was too much for Del Plato. All the noise, gaining weight, girls, crime. Absolutely too much.

To make himself feel better, he thought about the ride home, taking Breed's sharp car back to the precinct, where Del would get his own, then coast along the beach at twilight and head out. Crossing the causeway over Biscayne Bay into Miami gave Del Plato a greater sense of travel than any truly distant voyage. Going over that pale-blue water was a pilgrimage. The roadway rising in an arc. Speedboats and fishing vessels, the salt smell, piping birds hovering over the bay. Huge white buildings ahead, an approaching shoreline, new things.

"We could use a place to stay," Cindy said, "We won't get in the way, just to crash. For a little while. Until school."

Del Plato found himself with a beer in his hand. Ina was looking at him now, trying to read something in his face. It made him realize he was staring.

Other families for generations had lived and earned and worshiped and died in one place. But in this Sunshine State there were no roots and no memory, no center. Del was witness to change all the time, a Florida of wet and dry, of seekers and second languages. The dislocated came and went, hoping to slide perhaps somehow south of darkness. This was where Ponce de Leon had spent so much of his life, checking things out. Now there were low sprawling cities stretched along the entire white coast—modern people in a modern world, proud of their air-conditioning facilities and an international airport—an intertwine of civility and the glut of construction, where the Atlantic itself looked oddly harmless and shallow, like the flat pond around a fountain gone dry, something the sun would soon take care of.

The phone rang again in the booth beside the number-one pool table.

"I'm here," Hooven said. "I don't see where there's a problem, because all I want is for my book to be clean. I don't bet, man. I can't put myself in that kind of situation, and I don't see why I have to like keep waiting by the phone. We're business people, dig it, and this is business. I'm not a gambler. I got too much on one team, so you're supposed to get me off the hook." They all listened to the sound of vacuum cleaning. "I would appreciate it, yeah. Yeah, I would show my appreciation. Regards to all."

Two young men with hiking boots came in and sat on barstools. The bartender shut the vacuum cleaner and carefully wound the electric cord. More people came in, with deep tans and clean shirts—three guys and two women. Del Plato took them to be chiropractors.

"So do you think it would be okay to stay anywhere?" Cindy asked. She was writing on the back of a postcard. Breed was showing Bonnie how to use the bridge for a pool cue. "I just want to go somewhere. I don't care."

"Wilkes-Barre," Ina said. "All over again. You'll see."

"Don't be so morbid."

Del Plato thought he detected a new scent on Ina. She had put something on when changing, a strawberry fragrance.

"We're leaving now," Del told her. Cindy glanced up from her postcard. She had been printing in large, even letters. "You wouldn't have a good time with us anyway. Find some cute boys." She had signed the card CYNTHIA, in green ink.

"Sure, okay. Just like that, find some cute boys."

The postcard showed two enormous grapefruits side by side in the sand. WE GROW THEM BIG IN FORT LAUDERDALE.

"A change of plans," Del said. "Nothing personal, a change of heart. We're not your type."

"Wilkes-Barre," Ina said. "I cannot believe."

The Beatles were singing "Michelle." Beer signs took on a wavy, liquid glow, even though Del had worked hard to remain sober. You couldn't get out of bed without dealing with unseen consequences and perspectives. Every choice, however simple and straightforward on the surface, came with its own dimensions and disturbing connotations. And Del could no longer be up for that. He just wanted to think about never having to work on his car again. He wanted to know how to cook noodles so they didn't stick to the bottom of a pot. The basics, the very

principles of human existence, he wanted them. The privilege
to be on the guest list, and to get thirty-five miles per gallon,
and to know somebody with tickets on the fifty-yard line.

The early evening had brought a plum-colored light of
sorts, and it looked much cooler outside than it had been.
Breed had picked up a well-polished cue stick and was holding
it by the wrong end.

Del Plato figured there was a plus side to his life, and a
minus side, and some blank spaces. High on the minus side
was a lack of sleep. Also, he wasn't getting any younger, he had
lost a wife and child, and he was capable of washing dishes
with Lemon Pledge without even knowing the difference. He
could uphold the law or break the law and nobody would care.
Waiters didn't pay enough attention to him in restaurants.

Breed came beside him, twirling the stick. "Sometimes it
just hits me wrong, Irish. I look around and what I see are all
these tropical plants, and it's like I'm in some foreign country.
Some foreign fucking country where I don't want to be, because they talk funny, and their hair is too long, and I got no
business being around. It's wrong for me, Del Plato. A made-
up place, full of bad ideas, and all kinds of assholes you can't
turn your back on."

Del took away the pool cue.

On the plus side were his personality and the staunch remains of his optimism. From an early age people had recognized in Del Plato the qualities of a natural leader. He could
win, he could accomplish. He could reach conclusions. He
wasn't afraid to fiddle around with a live fuse.

"Sometimes I get like this," Breed said quietly. "I got this
sensitive side to me, Irish, and it's a very shitty feeling. I look
around and it hits me—wham!—I'm driving and I'm driving,
and all the time I'm in the wrong fucking lane." Some chiropractors were at the number-one pool table. Hooven was at the
jukebox, talking to Bonnie. "The deeper side of me, Irish. It
burns me up something awful."

Del Plato was trying to find his own part in the small, un-
broken measures of each day. If he found money inside a safe,
was that the same as finding money in the street? Was a dollar

saved truly a dollar earned? Here he was, at an age when other people already had second homes and their personal accoun-tants. What did Del Plato have to show? He was a cop, and a criminal, spending his day with people who stubbed out their cigarettes in the butter dish and complained about lousy placekicking. Men who blew their hair dry and went to work with guns in their pockets.

It was a matter of money or morality. What small choice Del Plato had centered between ethics on the one side, cold cash on the other. They were essential but opposite needs, which no longer mixed in his scheme of things. And you couldn't actually touch morality, could you? You couldn't count it in your hands, or collect interest on it.

"Can you help us out?" Cindy asked him. "Come on, Jackie. We can't just eat peanuts all the time."

She looked as if she might cry. Del gave her ten dollars and turned to leave with Breed.

Falling asleep in front of the tube at night, Del often found himself wishing the same three wishes. That Denise hadn't left him. That he had a million dollars. That he could have the chance to do some things all over again.

Chapter

12

Del was attempting to identify some round golden crumbs at his feet. Pretzels, toast? Parts of a doughnut? Denise had never permitted eating in the living room. He picked up a crumb and held it to the light. He had on his good shirt, which he wore on these out-of-the-ordinary occasions—a striped one, with strong buttons. People often complimented the color, how much it did for him. Later Del would go home and hang it back in his closet, unrolling the sleeves and keeping the top button buttoned, unless something had spilled or he had already worn it four or five times, in which case he would have to send his good shirt out.

"It's such a crazy world," Del Plato said. "If you stop sometimes and think about it. Guided missiles, test-tube babies. The whole welfare thing. It's a mess all over."

"She's upset enough as it is," Ethan said. "Let's not get carried away with topics that don't concern us."

Denise had come home that afternoon with Keri, after ice-skating and a lunch of frozen yogurt, to find the sliding glass door off its track and startling empty spaces throughout the house. It had taken her a few minutes to piece together exactly what had happened. Had she and Keri somehow walked into the wrong house? Was this some kind of a joke, or a surprise party? What had happened to the door? Why was she finding it difficult to swallow?

"No wonder there's a crime rate," Del Plato continued. "I'm not surprised. The postal service the way it is. Whipped cream that stays fresh in the refrigerator for a hundred years. It's crazy."

At first Denise had hugged Keri and thought how very lucky they were nobody had come into the house after the sliding door slipped loose. The house was wide open. Then she began to get jittery. First it was the stereo system. Where was the stereo system? It wasn't on the wall unit. Even the wires were missing. Denise got the hiccups and began racing from room to room. No stereo system. Keri followed two steps behind, darting along with her mother, positive the whole thing would in some way turn out to be her fault. Gone was the television set, along with the remote-control transmitter. Denise thought of the real-silver silverware and dashed in a panic to the kitchen, frantic and in some way wounded. The food processor was gone, with all the attachments and wide-mouth feed tube. Denise's heavy silver tea set from an aunt who had lived in France. The vacuum cleaner, the can opener. Denise held her breath for the hiccups until she became weak.

Apparently they had come in from the back and loaded up just about every item of marketable value. They even had the nerve to drink wine, leaving drained glasses on the kitchen table. Denise was furious at the notion of them toasting each other, wearing gloves and other people's jewelry. They took the Cointreau. Thieves, thieves. One of them used the bathroom and hadn't flushed.

It had obviously been a professional job. The stuff was probably in another state. Del was a little honked off because he had gotten a haircut earlier in the day and nobody in the room had noticed.

"Let's get our story straight," Ethan told him. "We're all here. We inventory and then Denise can call this in as a robbery. I don't have to tell you that when an insurance adjuster comes, Denise should be prepared."

Ethan had been thoughtful enough to bring a small stuffed animal for Keri, a fat panda with steel balls rolling inside its eyes and a funny hat. Ethan kept it on his lap. To Del it looked like the kind of stuffed animal you bought out of somebody's pickup truck at a red light, but he himself had come empty-handed. On either side of Del Plato's chair were rectangular indentations on the carpet where the stereo speakers had been. This haircut had cost him twenty-five dollars.

A portable plug-in radio played rock and roll in the garage. Del had bought it for Keri when she got the mumps a few years back and was forced to spend a long time in her room, where she had her temperature taken and connected the dots in fun pads. All the buttons on top of the radio had been preset to rock stations. Keri was by herself in the garage, sifting through toys she had outgrown, or those with pieces missing— Chutes and Ladders minus the spinner, Miss Piggy with only one leg, a rusted sled they had been saving and saving for some family ski trip, Halloween costumes. Stacks of comics tied up with twine, jigsaw puzzles for ages three to five. For better reception, the radio antenna touched a window looking out on the side yard. Keri had never seen Del and Ethan together in her house, and the prospect of two daddies in the same room upset her more than anything.

Del Plato had stopped into a hair stylist earlier that day, without an appointment, and a woman filing her nails at the front desk frowned a while before she called over a skinny girl named Morgan. Morgan appeared never to have done more than washings. She carried a can of diet soda everywhere and told Del she was going to cut him in a Sean Connery. "Almost Roman," Morgan said, "a very classic look. You can comb it with your fingers in the morning." Del copied down her number after she rinsed him with an almond shampoo that had a special formula for what she called "pellicules" and had scrubbed his scalp with a breast jiggling inches from his face.

In the living room, music from the radio coming through, Denise had her arms draped behind the sofa back. Ethan sat on one matching chair, Del on another. The fabric of the living-room furniture was something you were never supposed to get wet or it would leave rings, a sprawling pattern of geese and cattails, in sere September colors, which Denise had spotted in a magazine while waiting in a supermarket checkout line.

"The insurance company will ask for a list," Ethan said, clearing his throat first, "but we can work around that later. It looks as if I'm taking charge, if there are no objections. Not that I want the job, but I don't see anybody else coming up with suggestions."

Ethan had brought along his dog, an eager young Irish setter named Rover, who scratched and drooled on his hind legs near the hall closet. Rover had to sit near the hall closet because of the ceramic tile, which made it simpler to clean up his slobber. Also, Keri was still shy around large dogs. An overbleached pair of Del Plato's briefs, the elastic long gone, hung from a doorknob above the dog's head. Del peered closely across the living room and saw they were his shorts, absolutely.

Del recalled how he used to do his calisthenics in precisely that spot where the Irish setter now drooled. He had worked out with the lady in tights on public television. Del Plato would get up with the first soft sky, fix a bowl of cereal mixed with fruit for Keri, even though she preferred to do it herself, then go through his routine of stretching and bending near the hall closet. Denise would soon waken to work in the garden, Keri would wait outside for the school van, and Del would read the sports page or flip through the calendar, planning ahead, with the stereo playing low and the windows wide open.

"How much do you think the hi-fi was worth?" Ethan asked. "A rough figure."

Del looked up with mild surprise. He hadn't been paying attention. The front door was now stained a new, deeper color. Had Denise done the work herself?

Del told him the stereo set had cost about five hundred dollars, but even this figure Del considered high. It hadn't been very good equipment. He didn't like music, and Denise was fond of anything played loud, so they got a cheap unit and held back their wedding money for home priorities—exterminating service, a ceiling fan, pop-up sprinklers.

"Say eleven hundred. Say you bought it two years ago." Ethan snapped his fingers for the dog to come over. "Don't do it if you don't want to, but I don't think I'm wrong. You're a cop. They expect it, the insurance. That's why the premiums are so high."

Details took on a painful presence for Del Plato. Round black nail holes in the foyer, spots where the wallpaper had rubbed thin. A large spill stain, smudges on the switch plate. They brought on a huge, leaden dejection. To Del Plato it looked like a different house. Had he really lived here for nine years? He fought an odd surge of sentimentality, as though he were revisiting an old school to find the stairwells unexpectedly small and narrow, or going back to a favorite fishing hole to discover all the fish had gone.

Del was always afraid of sentimentality. It was a false emotion, and could only get in the way of clear thinking. Greed, on the other hand, was real to him. Lust was real, revenge was.

Rover had bounded over and was panting by Ethan's feet. Ethan slapped its shiny flanks, the dog's coat sleek and thick. When the dog drooled on the carpet, Ethan whacked it on the head and the dog went back to the hall closet.

"I feel so exhausted I don't want to do anything," Denise said. "I wouldn't know where to begin. This should never have happened to me."

She wore a long, thin-striped caftan which Del didn't recognize. She sat across from him tight-lipped and distracted, like someone who had been trapped inside a stuck elevator. She studied Del Plato, trying to read any emotions in his face.

"You want me to go?" Del asked her.

"Maybe. It's the situation. Maybe I shouldn't have called you."

Ethan rose from his chair with his hand extended. He looked taller than Del remembered, broader, with the kind of loosely buttoned shirt bodybuilders wear when they're not showing off. How had he become so much bigger?

"I hope I haven't offended you," Ethan said. "It's a case of trying to do what's best for Denise."

When Ethan shook hands, he did so limply. Del Plato had been set to crunch a few knuckles. His father told him you could judge a man's character by the way he shook hands. "This is the way a union official presents himself," his father had said, locking grips with Del Plato in some visceral test of strength. "A shipbuilder meets a railroad man, they don't shake like fairies. Squeeze harder, or you ain't no son of mine. This is the way Victor Mature says hello."

They were standing in the living room close together, Del and Denise and Ethan. The radio in the garage kept drifting in and out.

"Nobody likes this," Ethan explained, "but when it happens, you have to prepare yourself. You have to make the best of it, which is only sensible."

"You're doing great," Del said. "I think I'm supposed to go now."

"I'm not sure about that," Denise said. "I called Ethan and I called you. Everything is missing. Keri won't come out of the garage. It's awkward, isn't it?"

Del sat down again. Denise went to the kitchen, where Ethan joined her.

The dog slept by the hall closet, near Del Plato's underwear. Del had drifted back to dreamy thoughts of calisthenics, early in the day, when he was alert, when he was trim. He would wake up in the old days and switch on the set, listening to the easy sound of exercise. Toe touch, leg lift, turn and stretch. He had a family, excellent credit, not even the trace of a gut. There was no free-agent market, and they didn't list the chemicals in breakfast cereal.

Denise would pick a grapefruit off the branch. Keri would take her vitamin. Now it was the grabbing, glittery flashback of these simple pleasures that could make Del most miserable— his little girl eating a decent meal, the three of them folding laundry on the weekend. Comparing prices in the dairy section, buying Girl Scout cookies from Girl Scouts at the front door. In his memory he had begun to see everyday acts as the truly good things in life. Each was a small blessing, the kind of conventional joy on which a sermon could be based. "The best things in life are free," a priest might say, gesturing broadly to his congregation, to Del Plato and the multitude of believers. The smallest satisfactions had given him faith.

But the best things in life had slipped away from Del Plato. He had been careless, and his assurance in the natural, neat order of the world was badly shaken. He told himself over and over that he really blew a good deal, but what use was that? Denise was gone. A woman who never had to go to the dentist. A wife who didn't have to call in her husband to kill some spider on the wall. Gone.

He could still fall asleep only on his side of the bed. At times during the night he woke up so alone he thought he might choke. The breath would turn hard in his throat, his eyes would water and swivel from one dark corner of the rented house to another, Del Plato still not able to place himself among the borrowed surroundings in the middle of the night. Here was the phone, here was a closet. His clothes on the floor, his blanket thrashed aside. Everything seemed temporary and trivial except for his inability to breathe. Objects were out of place to Del Plato, his day-to-day affairs mean and without purpose. He would have said he was working things out if anyone asked, but no one asked, and those who knew him well—Denise, Breed—knew him well enough to realize Del was having a lousy time of living alone and they would leave it at that.

But still Del had faith in himself. That had to be the most important thing. And inside his faith he felt the assurance of cool air and solid rock under his feet, as though he were in the vault room of some old-time bank, with marble walls and pillars and a huge, unshakable certainty about it.

And he was from Detroit, too, the black and gray of commerce, a city of Pistons, of concrete and metal. Smoke and smog fought in the air, a city of Tigers. Industry shoved away the weak. Factories and fire were at its center, hot steel in its heart. Lions lived there, rip-toothed and hungry. Red Wings, beaks and talons and blood. It was a place of engines, where people knew what it was to have dirt on their hands.

What did they celebrate in South Florida? They took

pride in their orange juice and flamingos and glass-bottom boats. Football players were Dolphins. Visitors came to see where Flipper goes to school, where Mickey Mouse is on salary to pose with their children, where the whole state goes bankrupt when the thermometer dips below thirty-two degrees.

Keri came in from the garage, carrying a coloring book with all the pages colored in. She headed straight for her room, not pausing to look at anyone, keeping her distance from the dog.

"How's it going, kid?" Del called.

"Fine, Daddy. Hi."

"You okay?" Ethan asked, reaching out an open hand.

"I'm fine. I just said so." She walked into her room and closed the door.

Who would Del Plato marry? Would he have more children, and how soon? This worried him. He would have to say the same things over and over again to a succession of marriageable dates, each of whom would remind him of Denise— his favorite color, his favorite movie star, how much income tax he had to pay, the first time he got high—until this repetition and put-on personality would force Del Plato to see himself as a boring and uncomplex person, doomed to a nightlife of brief flings and idiot grins.

Denise went into her bedroom. Ethan followed, carrying a legal pad and the stuffed toy.

Del took a deep breath and considered the fact that other people would think he was about to commit a terrible act. Olympia Jai Alai. They would be fast to draw the lines, other people. They would come up with their own quick, civilian conclusions, forever guiltless, thinking it was probably forgivable in the long run to rip off a crooked bookie—putting themselves in Del Plato's shoes for just that moment—and even shaking down a drug dealer was something you could live with if you had the balls for that kind of thing. But robbing a jai alai fronton? With guns? Out of the question. Why? Just for the money? A truly criminal activity.

Del actually could see the sense in that. Part of him could step back and take a different view of what was in the wind, the various doings and goings on. A guy thinks his particular gripe is somehow more important than the basic social order we all live with, then sure, there's a problem. The delineations of behavior get bent out of shape. Even so, human beings were fairly consistent at being good to one another. They stayed in lane on the highway. They usually made an effort to pay for what they wanted. They contributed to UNICEF and the Red Cross. And whether it was fear of getting caught or some innate goodness that kept most of them honest was irrelevant. The mainstream of life flowed peaceably. People were law-abiding, and were content to serve as constructive members of society. They obeyed signs. They avoided using the f-word in public. It's only when people decide to make a special case of themselves that a problem comes up. They become bigamists, or poets, or habitual lawbreakers, and where then was some voice from the sky to say no?

Disturbing notions had a way of irritating Del Plato. He would have to work up pleasant thoughts to buffer his gnarled conscience, the way pearls are supposedly born.

But other people somehow got through each day with the same grim knowledge. Other people might be fully aware that a separated wife was shacking up with some Little League coach, and still they could hold down a job. They could find a way to get eight hours' sleep. Del had to think of jump shots or a good meal just to struggle out of bed. He had to make a sharp mental picture of a tree, a family, a shiny car.

Why should he be having such a hard time of it? There were pressures everywhere, sure, but everyone had to deal with them. *Our trade deficit with Japan, lousy air, not enough fiber in the diet. And even the hidden urgencies take their terrible toll on us all, not just on Del Plato. We all die, for instance. We have bacteria living right on our skin. The universe itself falls apart, our common future spinning to pieces out there, with unspeakable black holes, and goddamn quasars, and conflicting scientific theories all over the place. That cold shroud of the atom is hung above every single soul.*

No wonder we can't get the story straight. We allow ourselves to be distracted by disappointment, by annoyances. The murderously mundane undoes us—speed bumps and junk mail, disc jockeys and the need for upgraded insulation. A new noise in the motor. They take us away from the really big issues. A populace that dwells on the inconsequential of course can't keep tabs on life's ultimate indecency.

But Del Plato knew he was also guilty of not thinking long term. He was thinking selfish. He was thinking small. Millions and millions of people, billions, going through the rituals and motion of mortality, breathing in and breathing out, and in this sigh of humanity Del Plato was in a deep rut, because there was nobody now to feed him chicken soup if he started sneezing, no one to sew back a loose button. He was thinking inconsequential. He was thinking narrow. So what if the earth swerved closer to the sun every day? So what if they had nothing to eat in India, or Chad, or wherever the hell it was people had nothing to eat these days? Nobody was going to wake Del Plato from his chair at three A.M. to say it was time for bed. No one was going to notice when he got a new haircut.

He went into Denise's bedroom, following the other two.

Her jewelry box—a heart-shape design with glued shells and a ballerina who turned on tiptoe to "Für Elise"—was upturned on the queen-sized bed. Denise's jewelry had been fingered through for only the good stuff. They had taken a half-carat diamond ring with a separate floater policy, and a brooch that had been in Denise's family for generations. They had taken gold, a Gucci key case Ethan had bought for Christmas. Sapphire earrings, Russian amber, and a commemorative coin from the Franklin Mint depicting John Glenn in orbit.

As soon as he entered the bedroom, Del Plato felt a thousand miles away. He really had no business being there. He was Keri's father and would always be Keri's father, but there were limits. Del would go. Ethan could write a long, inflated list on his legal pad. Denise finally would be able to call the police and flush the toilet.

The thieves left behind a strand of puka shells and a Timex. They left a Bicentennial coin from the Franklin Mint, a turquoise ring, and the entire collection of good-luck charms

Del Plato had been buying each anniversary. They were on the bed and on the floor—a jade elephant with its trunk up, an ivory *figa*, the hand of God, Buddha. A bear claw, a sand dollar. She had fortune going her way from across the globe. A wishbone, a pyramid.

Ethan asked if any money had been taken, and Denise explained all her money went directly into the checking account, to cover general expenses. She never had more than grocery money on hand, never more than a little extra, because her separated husband only worked for the city, and was already living way beyond all his means.

"We'll claim eight hundred," Ethan suggested. He wrote down each recommendation while he spoke. "In this drawer here, with these shirts. You kept cash handy because you were saving for a vacation. I'm not telling you what to do, Denise, but this is one way to approach your loss. Write the eight hundred off your taxes. When the cops come, make sure you get an investigation number."

"I'm sure it could have been much worse," Denise said. "I know it makes no difference, but I feel better it was professionally done. I honestly hope everything they took is in another state by now, like Del said before. There was nothing personal about it. Just that Keri and I weren't home and they were able to get inside. If it wasn't here, it would have been somewhere else. What's gone is gone."

"I'll be moving along," Del said.

"I hope they never get caught. I hope I never see anyone on the street wearing my earrings or diamond."

Ethan ran off the items. Clock radio, Toast-R-Oven, framed prints off the living-room wall. Cut glass was gone, the smoke alarm, a cashmere sweater. The Princess phone. Ethan said Denise was entitled to everything, of course, but at original value, less depreciation, and they killed you if you were honest.

"You had a camera, Denise?"

"No."

"One camera," Ethan said, jotting it down. "With flash, a big lens, and leather carrying case. Replacement cost for anything is sky-high. The more you claim, the larger your settlement."

Del Plato was wondering what she wanted from him. She had an Ethan. It upset Del deeply that thieves had turned up their nose at his anniversary presents. Denise had problems, too bad for Denise. He had gone into boutiques and jewelry stores with double doors and buzzers, and he had done so for a purpose. He was hunting down a little something, an exotic talisman of luck, a token of love for his wife, an anniversary gift.

"They took your television," Ethan pointed out to Denise.

"It was a good set. The green came in a little too strong, but it worked fine. What are you going to say?"

"Two sets. Both color, Sony. Those bastards." Ethan had his hands folded in front of him as though he were at a funeral. He wore a solemn expression to go with it. "Guy I play against just had his car windows shot out. I'm not saying he didn't come out okay, but still there's the expense, and the shock of finding broken windows. Twice he got hit in the Camero, and another time they got him in the Lincoln, but bad."

Keri came out of her room. She delayed for a moment in the doorway, and Ethan let her have the panda with a behind-the-back toss.

"Thank you, Ethan."

"You're a terrific girl. Don't let anyone tell you different."

She set the stuffed animal carefully on her bed, then closed the door and went for her radio in the garage.

"He collected, this guy. Said there were business suits from the cleaners in the backseat of his car. Took out his own car stereo, collected, then had it installed again. It sounds dirty, I know—I can hear how it sounds, and I'm not making any judgments about right or wrong—but this is the way one person handled it. That's all I'm saying. And he came out of it strong. Came away from his loss very nicely. All I'm doing is offering alternatives."

"You do it for me," Denise said.

"I will. I'm claiming as much as possible. But we can present a list from here to kingdom come and even that wouldn't be enough compensation. Who pays for the tension? No insurance company makes settlement on the stress Denise has to go through. There's not enough money in the world."

Denise sat on the edge of her bed and patted the place beside her for Del. "Ethan, would you leave us a few minutes? Thank you."

When Denise was alone with him, she patted Del Plato's hand, then moved her fingertips over raspy dark portions of his unshaved face—a cheek, the chin, his neck. She was being very tender.

Del didn't want to be alone with her. In the next room he could hear his daughter with Ethan, and the radio.

"I think we have to talk," Denise said.

"Shoot."

"I called because it's more than making a list. It's more than claims, this affair."

"Tell that to the coach. He's writing everything down."

"Nobody comes out here to rob a house. Why this house? It's very unpleasant to come home and find this, let me tell you. It's a threatening experience, and a very unpleasant one. It's not right."

"You lost me back there."

"I feel threatened, and suspicious. You know what I'm saying."

"I honestly don't. You said we have to talk and I'm giving it a chance, Denise; you can see what I'm doing. I'm giving this talk a fair shot."

"Why this house? That's what gets me. This isn't the type of fringe neighborhood where you get senseless crime or attract the wrong element. We protect our school district here. We have flags for the important holidays. I thought you might have an answer."

"It's a robbery, Denise. The crazy, violent world, you said so yourself. I don't think you can read more into it than what it is."

She rolled her eyes impatiently. They were not communicating. Del wondered if she were expecting some sort of miracle now that they were apart. They had never had much success with drawn-out discussions. Was that supposed to change?

"I won't phone you anymore. We've gone our separate ways," she said, and an edge of insult had crept into her voice. "You have your life and I have mine. Keri has her life. Fine. If she wants to see you, she's old enough. One-to-one, you and her."

"What do you think? You think *I* robbed the house."

"With you and me, Del, you and I, it's time for a clean break. That's what I would like."

"I was getting a haircut, Denise. I have witnesses. I have people who will stand up in court and testify under oath that I was getting a haircut."

"I'm going to marry Ethan," she told him. "I think what you're doing is getting into some kind of deep trouble. I think what you're doing is the lowest. I won't have any ties to you when they put you away."

They had never been able to have discussions of any kind. What was there to discuss? You eat in or you eat out. You go to the movies or someone's house. You get dressed up or you go casual. Theirs had never been a marriage, Del Plato firmly felt, based on verbal communication. Whatever strength their marriage had, Del Plato felt, lay in support, in understanding, in union. Happiness had nothing to do with talking.

Arguments, on the other hand, had a lot to do with talking. When they talked, they argued. But they weren't supposed to be on a debate team. They were supposed to be in love, married happily, where you could walk through the woods for two hours just holding hands and not say a word, and not look up at the sun to guess what time it was, or start in about lost deposit slips, or whether you could wash certain garments by hand rather than send them out.

"I stopped loving you," Denise told him in a pleasant way. She was actually smiling at Del Plato. *She always did have a lot of nerve*, he thought. "I make no excuses. We were together and now we're not." Denise had been able to knock on the doors of strangers, start up conversations with anyone nearby. She could ask salespeople for a better price or return merchandise to a store where it hadn't been purchased. A ton of nerve. He was the same way. "I don't know what else to say," Denise told him. "It's done. I suppose that's it."

"You don't have to say anything. You didn't have to say what you just did."

"I don't trust you, Del." She put her hand on his face again. "I want you away from me."

"What kind of trouble do you suppose I'll get into?"

"It doesn't matter. Big trouble." Denise took out a cigarette from a pack on the bed. She held her palm up for ashes. "Keep away from us. You have your own friends and your own life."

It made Del consider his own motives once again, but he realized he probably had none. No motives. It didn't seem healthy to have no motives. There had to be all kinds of underlying stuff he wasn't willing to admit to himself, loose inside, in his head and his body, pushing and pulling, giving him heartburn. Underlying stuff. Like the fact that he didn't have to close the door now when he went to the bathroom. Seamless stuff, dissatisfactions, which couldn't really float to the surface as simple and nameable, as ordinary as a motive.

"I don't want Keri to hear about it in school, whatever you're up to. Don't ask me how I know, but I can sense it. You're up to your neck. I think you're being very inconsiderate, to Keri and to me. They'll tease her and put gum in her hair. Whatever you're doing is unfair. She'll have to visit you in jail, with murderers and check forgers. Is that what you want? On Father's Day you'll be in with bank robbers and spitters. I want you to know exactly how I feel. You're being inconsiderate."

"It's not much of a talk, Denise. I'm sitting here and the anniversary presents I gave you are all over the floor."

"We went to a restaurant," she said. "Keri was sleeping over at a friend's house and you wore a tie. It was a Friday night. I knew that night something was wrong, terribly wrong. They brought us a big menu, a huge menu, very elegant. With us, something was wrong with us. And there was nothing on

the menu I wanted to eat. It had a gold tassel in the middle,
everything was gold letters. I kept looking at this enormous
menu; it was like something you could find hanging in a
church. I was so hungry, but I couldn't order anything. Moses
could have carried this menu down from the mountain. They
had musicians who came to the table. I didn't want veal, or
chicken, or *steak au poivre*. I wanted to cry I was so hungry.
But I couldn't order, Del, I couldn't choose. Something was
wrong with us. Your tie was wrong. If you held the menu over
your head, people would fall to their knees. It was the worst
time of my life." She held both hands over her midsection, as
though she still might be hungry from that night. "So I went
to my father. I took Keri to Montreal and when we came back I
changed the locks. I had to do something. You ordered wine
and I couldn't drink any. I was so confused. I put your clothes
and shaving things in a carton. The people next to us ordered
an entrée that had to be wheeled out on a special cart, with the
musicians. I remember it all perfectly. It was so unnatural. I
couldn't eat."

Del nodded all along. Nod, nod. A part of him felt like
hugging Denise, right then and there, patting her on the back.
Another part of him said he should have cut out a while ago. It
wasn't like her to be so revealing, and it wasn't like him to
listen.

"Can I ask you something?" Denise said.

"I suppose."

"Do you ever talk to your lawyer? I never talk to mine."

"I got this guy through work who puts me on hold. I
really can't talk to him very long." He stood up. Del Plato
didn't want to be in the room with her any longer. "It's legal
words with us from now on. Signing papers, Latin terms."

"Chin up," she told him, smiling sweetly again. "I'll
put this house up for sale and split it with you. Unless you
want it."

"That's okay."

"He gets along beautifully with Keri. And he's polite.
These days you don't meet men with manners. Half of them
are gay, and the other half grab you. We're going to Atlanta,

for a tournament. We'll get married as soon as the papers come through."

"Right."

"I've never been to Atlanta, except the airport."

"Nice town."

Del had never been there either. He went blank and dispassionate, trying hard to think long term. He was trying to think universal. The bedroom windows were open, and across the street he could see the results of new construction. It was quiet there, among the newly completed homes, fresh paint, and new appliances. A clutter of building tools lay in the circular driveway of a house directly opposite Denise's. A glue gun, a Rivitool, an aluminum yardstick. They were so noticeable to Del Plato, resembling carefully scattered stage props, that it was as if the entire community itself had been wheeled in as the opening set of some Broadway production—a musical, perhaps, or a mystery—with no big-name star and a need for realistic scenery.

"What if you get killed?" Denise said. She stood beside him, at arm's length. "Keri will have to visit a father in the dirt. She'll have to wear a dress and bring flowers. They'll put sheets on the mirrors or whatever, and she'll have a broken heart. Think of your daughter. You'll lose your pension and she'll inherit peanuts."

"You're right," Del Plato told her. He had on his stone face. "You're absolutely right."

It was the face he reserved for the roughest situations, tight times in the line of duty, the grim excitement of work. It was the face he held back for the worst traffic, or when you paid big money for theater seats and it turned out to be a stiff. It was his face for the hardest games, when he might get low-bridged off a drive or clocked underneath, when Del might get an elbow in the throat and still not give anything away. *You want me, you'll have to come in and get me.*

"I might not be pregnant. I haven't seen a doctor, but I can't drink juice in the morning and that's what happened with Keri. So I might be."

In the other room Ethan was explaining to Keri how a

curveball is properly thrown. "Fingers along the seams, snap the wrist down. That's the girl, way to go."

"How many friends do you think I have, Del? I can't talk to very many people. I'm telling you, because if I tell Ethan, he'll want me to go ahead with it."

"What are we supposed to be now? Are we buddies?"

"You're angry."

"Of course I'm angry. Go ahead with what?"

"With the baby. If I'm pregnant."

"For months we went through some bad times, Denise. We went through the same bleak stuff. We slept in the same bed, and when our bodies touched by mistake, we said we were sorry. But what bothers me is the way you've given in, Denise. People grow apart, sure, and sometimes they get divorced. But you treat this like you've been expecting it for the longest time. You just let it roll right over you."

"It's not a competition. We weren't married to see who could hold out the longest. I don't care what you say, Del; something has to change when you spend half your time at home going through the medicine cabinet for something to take."

"I wasn't that unhappy."

"You were. You gnashed your teeth at night."

"Everybody grinds their teeth. Babies do that, it's completely natural."

"You made sounds. You grunted."

"I did not." Del made sure to keep his voice down. He didn't want to be in the room alone with Denise and he didn't want to be having this conversation. "What's so bad anyway about a little unhappiness? It's a stage, Denise, unhappiness is a stage. Married people are supposed to live through various stages. You come out stronger at the end. Otherwise you can just chuck out an entire marriage every few years and it's nothing, no big deal, like an expired insurance policy."

"I was miserable. What are you talking about? I was in pain." She left, carrying ashes in her hand.

Del Plato felt oddly lighter, as though his body would topple forward of its own weight. He realized it was his gun. He didn't have it with him, and he missed it. The heft of his gun would have pleased him—an object with a center to it, a heavy, indisputable core to keep him from falling down.

He was pondering the chain of events again. That morning when he first got dressed, he had put on cutoffs and a short-sleeve T-shirt. Then it was time to leave the house, so he changed to corduroy pants. But a T-shirt didn't go well with corduroy pants, not really, so he had to change his shirt. And then, already dressed, he felt obligated to put on shoes and socks. That was a chain of events, one thing leading to another, an undeniable progression.

He saw himself as one simple person getting caught up in the momentum of inevitability. He was a mortal, a regular guy. He had a couple of questions, a few doubts, but Del Plato would swear he was trying as hard as anyone.

For some reason it brought his mother to mind. Del was confident she had passed away a happy, fulfilled woman, one who had done the best she could. Mostly what Del remembered about his mother was the great pride she had taken in her ability to shop. This was her talent; to wheel a wobbly steel cart down the narrow brick streets of Detroit. Del recalled tagging along. Dented-metal trash cans on the gutter edge, and chained dogs, and private homes with huge sunflowers that grew beside the stoops. His mother called herself one of the city's top shoppers, and would have entered herself as a contestant if there had been any way to prove it—on *Jeopardy*, for instance, if there had been a category for Groceries. To inquire about the butcher's children before she inquired about his meat, this was his mother's art; to pick out exactly five pounds of potatoes without a scale. Grandmothers with bright scarves on their heads and their own rickety carts would ask her to sniff a canteloupe for them, or nod solemnly to her judgment of the asparagus.

She knew if strawberries were genuinely in season, or if only the choice ones had been wedged up top to fool you and when you got home you would find only small, squishy ones underneath. She knew what to do with vegetables most people had never even seen before. She knew the cuts of beef, all the grades, and where they came from. She knew the thicknesses of spaghetti. She knew what grits were actually made from.

One time, when his mother lay in a hospital bed without a clear prognosis, the shopping fell on Del Plato. A Jewish fruit-and-vegetable man came away from a group of customers in heated discussion over screen stars who were really Jewish despite their names. The man patted Del's shoulder and smiled in a wise, burdened way, and said he would pray for Del's mom. Then he deliberately didn't charge for a sack of bananas, saying, "Go, go, be well," slipping them in with a sad wink, as if he and Del Plato were pulling a fast one on somebody who wasn't there.

Del could hear activity in the living room, and when he got there Keri was tumbling, doing cartwheels and somersaults to Ethan's applause. He was on the second page of his list.

"I could double-check the approximate values," Ethan said to him. "Up to you. Denise phoned in the complaint just now; they're sending out a patrolman within the hour. I think we're prepared, but that's the least of it. You live with this kind of jumble. I don't have to mention the kind of setback it can be for regular people. Financially, mentally."

Del just stood there, looking Ethan square in the eye for no good reason.

"Thanks for coming," Ethan said, holding out his hand. "I think it's a good thing we were both here."

Del took it a second time, and again they shook without any of the usual up and down motion, no pressure, like snobs. He kept staring at Ethan, although for the life of him he couldn't figure out why.

"Keri, I'll see you, kiddo," Del called.

"Bye-bye, Daddy." She was upside down, standing on her head against the sofa back. Ethan's dog watched nervously, hoping to hear its name.

Denise pulled Del aside toward the hall closet. It seemed to him everyone else was having a decent-enough time. Rover sniffed the cuff of his corduroy pants and moved steadily higher. Keri was having a decent-enough time, Ethan, Denise.

"When we were first together," Denise told him, "nothing had impact. Can you remember? We were full of hope, we were inexperienced. The most important thing in the world for me was to be a size five. Love, happiness, they were no big deal. But we've grown, each of us."

"I think I may have already heard this part."

"Now I find myself wanting some things we never had together. I would like furniture you don't have to assemble yourself, for instance. I would like curtains made to order. A new set of china, with gold along the edge. Permanent things, Del. Can you appreciate what I'm saying?"

"Yes, Denise, I can."

She opened the front door for him. He looked for the wall clock to check how late he was running. "I'll talk to you, Denise." The wall clock wasn't there.

Del went over a few things as he got into his car and started it up. He considered his broken family. Why did he have no motives? Why hadn't somebody taught Ethan how to shake hands? As he pulled away, Del passed a patrol car with a single patrolman inside, coming out to make the report. He passed neighborhood activity, kids on bikes, neighbors with tools. He decided to wave at everybody he saw. Everyone waved back. Men waved from ladders, women in pools, toddlers on tricycles. He honked his horn and turned corners, and people stopped what they were doing to extend a friendly hand. "How you doing?" Del called out his car window. He didn't recognize a face. "Not bad," strangers responded, "can't complain." He drove through sections he hadn't been through before. Men with rakes, women pulling weeds. Boys and girls. "How you been?" Del Plato called to each, a smile on his face. Maybe they thought he was running for office, or he had just come home from the army.

He saw even more new homes, heavy equipment and materials. He saw a tree with sneakers dangling from its branches. The early-evening moon hung white and small over a field, a reckless cluster of tangled growing things. It was getting close to supper. He turned left on one corner, right on another, waving, caught in a weave of fraternity, steering his way through a maze of welcome.

"Good to see you," Del would say. "Putting on a few pounds, aren't you?"

Del would go home and kill the evening. He'd have dinner out—maybe fried clams and a couple of drafts in a local hangout. He'd see more faces, people who washed their cars on the weekend and would wave if you waved to them. In his rented house later he'd put clothes in the dryer that had been sitting wet in the washer since yesterday. He would look out the window, see which of his neighbors were home, what they were up to. He'd thumb through a book, or do the *TV Guide* crossword puzzle in two minutes. Perhaps he would go for a drink, a single drink, with plenty of ice. Eventually Del would call it a night for himself, and fall asleep.

But then he would wake up, at three in the morning, feeling as though his day was supposed to begin. Wide awake, his eyes clear, the house dark and empty and his head spinning with useless bits of information.

He could sneak into the houses of everyone he had waved to. Del Plato felt certain of that. He could take their stereos, their wall clocks, their children's toys. He was capable. But how could you explain that to people? He was a decent person, without motives, without a mean bone in his body. But he could lift their wallets. What good were buzzers and police locks and policemen when fortune was geared to slip you a fast one? He could take their gold-rimmed china, their heirlooms, their dollars.

There was nothing like three in the morning for feeling miserable. Del Plato could see it coming.

Chapter
13

The tablecloth was a smooth white linen, with delicate, laced flowers put in along the border, expensive as all hell. In the center of Hooven's table stood a shiny-white skinny vase with two purple flowers inside. It was that kind of restaurant. Everything was first class, and probably from France. The purple flowers might have been flown over. Even the silverware stood out, polished by hand more than likely, piece by piece. Joe Hooven was willing to bet you could pick up a knife or fork at any table in the place and not find a single clump of food stuck anywhere on it. The wine goblets at each setting had the thinnest stems he had ever come across. They might have dated back to the Middle Ages, or have come from some Fifth Avenue address where even the salespeople took three vacations a year. Primo stuff all around. He was wondering if there was some way he could get the wine glasses out of the restaurant afterward.

Fifty bucks a head, Joe was thinking. *Without wine. Without the tax, without tip. They'd change your napkin one time, big shit, and give you a single scoop of sherbet before the main course.*

If he had brought a lady with him, she would have a handbag, and he could sneak a few wine glasses in there, just shove them in with her sunglasses and six lipsticks and whatever else chicks felt it was necessary to have with them, per se, everywhere they went. Pictures of some best friend's kids, pills, a brush with hair all stuck in it. She wouldn't even have to know nothing, the chick. She could be eating her French food with her spotless silverware and he would wrap the wine glasses inside a napkin from another table while she was going on about this or that—her job, her abortions, the equal rights thing—and he would jam the shit in her purse. Over and done with.

Women like that anyway, the intrigue. Petty stuff, they always went for that, the low level. He would say to her, "Don't look now, babe, but you're carrying something for me in your purse." And she would giggle and hold her bag with both hands, and probably remember that moment the rest of her life. It got girls excited in his experience, a little stepping out of line. If you like walked the check or drove too fast, man alive. And if she went and got caught, hey, the chick could always pull some weeping act out of the hat—they were good for that too—and say this guy did it, I swear to God, the whole thing was Joe's idea. That's what she would say.

He looked up as Del Plato and Breed came in, finally. There was a chandelier when you walked inside with so many crystal things hanging off it that you probably needed six good workers to get the thing cleaned right. Del Plato and his friend. They would go through two bottles of wine. They were twenty-five minutes late.

Hooven looked away, pretending not to notice them or be upset. But they were dressed, two cops, like they had just come off the bus from Winnipeg, and he had told them, specifically, he had spelled it out in plain English, that this was no ordinary restaurant, it was a ritzy restaurant, where people who built shopping centers came for a bite to eat, and it wouldn't be against the law to look halfway decent when they decided to show up. Winnipeg, which was way the fuck up in Canada, where all they did was hit each other with hockey sticks and

eat steak for breakfast, and for sure that's where these two
gumballs looked like they just stepped off the bus from. It had
to be that they enjoyed being so excessive.

A sweet young thing up front offered Del Plato and Breed
a couple of house jackets to wear while enjoying dinner. She
rolled up the sleeves and pointed them to the table where Hooven had been waiting for twenty-five minutes, with nothing to
do but gawk around and make believe he wasn't disturbed to
be sitting alone so long. He could knock off the tax when it was
time to figure out a tip, but he wondered if he could knock off
the wine as well, if that was totally uncool. Or did you have to
leave something separate for the dude who popped the cork? It
might be a place where they added in the tip, and didn't even
tell you, or else it was written out in fucking French somewhere, which nobody could understand, and you ended up
leaving *two* tips. And then on your way out they'd give you a
dipshit mint from France and on your way home, when it was
too late, you'd go over the tab and think, hey, no way it could
be that high, man, no way.

Del Plato, at the entrance, took a good look around the restaurant. In a coppery-tinted mirror he caught a full shot of
himself, head to toe, thinking he looked pretty goddamn good
in the borrowed jacket.

"We have these dates," Del Plato was telling Breed.
"Dates with exceptional people, me and you. I'm describing
something we might look back on in our later years, J.B. Dates
with Bianca Jagger, okay, and say Sigourney Weaver, when
she was in *Alien,* with those little white panties she wore at the
end. Anyway, we're coming on strong, with drinks, and funny
stories, and there's lots of chemistry. Are you with me so far?
Try to picture this. They have these terrific outfits on, and
their hair is all wild."

"We don't get to the movies too much," Breed said. "You
pay good money to get in, there's always jerks sitting near
you. The movie's about Chicago, they say, 'Oh, look, we were
there. We ate in a restaurant not far from where they're
standing right now.' I hate that in the movie theater."

"You're not listening."

"We're on a date," Breed said. "Bianca Jagger and some movie star I never heard of, with white underwear."

"And they're crazy about us; we can't do anything wrong. But after we leave the disco, J.B., then what happens? Tell me."

"I'm still listening."

"They have a headache. That's what happens. Me and you, we have to take a cab back to the hotel by ourselves." Del tugged at his coat sleeves until the cuffs were just right. "The night's over. The fun is over. I mean we had a very nice time while we were together, the four of us; we hit it off very well. But still the whole experience is a little deflating. It's not quite what it could have been."

Breed spotted Joe Hooven at the table, looking away. "Joey," he called with a wave, but Hooven was deaf.

"Undeveloped," Del said. "Missed opportunities. Could have been this, could have been that."

"I forget what we were talking about exactly. This is our life of crime?"

"You got it."

"Fair enough," Breed said. "But tell me something. On that date before, which one am I with?"

"Take your pick. It's not the point."

"I realize it's not the point. But I know Bianca Jagger. That other one, Irish, I didn't see *Alien*. I don't know what she looks like."

"Nothing comes of it. That's the main thing."

"Which is what I'm getting at. So I could go out with Cheryl Tiegs, too, for that matter, nothing comes of it. If I'm not getting laid, Irish, I don't have to strike out with somebody I never seen before. Cheryl Tiegs I know is gorgeous. *She* could have a headache as soon as the next one."

"Fine. Cheryl Tiegs has a headache. *She's* the one walks out on you." Del picked up a wine goblet at Hooven's table. He ticked the rim to hear it ring. "That make you feel better?"

Jewboy Breed closed his eyes and said, "Plain white panties. Are they silky?"

"Very attractive. But it goes nowhere. The relationship

has barely gotten off the ground when it collapses, for good."

After a moment Joe Hooven looked up from his setting at the table. He wiped his mouth with a corner of the napkin spread across his lap, though he hadn't eaten a thing. Hooven was attempting to catch Del Plato's attention. He wouldn't even nod to the other one, Breed, that's what Joe decided. He wouldn't say two words to Breed or even glance his way like one time. It had to be Breed's idea to come late, to dress up like they were from fucking Winnipeg, in Canada.

Del Plato took a seat with a view of the lake. Hooven watched as Del took in the other diners, the linen napkins, the prewar china. Joe felt confident that Del Plato would be able to get it, the overall ambience, fifty bucks a head before you even started any serious addition.

They were on the upper level. It was more expensive on the upper level.

"The thing never culminates," Del Plato said quietly. He nodded hello to Hooven, then turned back to Breed. "It's super at first, everything is, but the kicker never comes. It doesn't go, this relationship. This crime."

Hooven had no idea what they were talking about and he didn't really care. They weren't looking at him, so they weren't talking about him, so it didn't concern him. The place was crowded but quiet. Hooven wore a white hand-tailored suit, Jamaican cotton, and he was hoping to get through the meal without globbing up the fabric.

Gentle waves rippled the grainy sand below them. To Hooven even the birds flying outside the restaurant seemed cleaner, somehow a shade more classy than regular birds as they chased each other in and out of berry bushes and the tall, blond grass touching on the shallow lake. These were sophisticated birds, who had nothing to do with the riffraff that hovered above the roof of an everyday diner or one of the fried-fish joints. When he made it, for real, this is where he would take his meals. With his sailboat outside, dual cabins, with true friends.

A tanned captain in a crisp cutaway stood a few feet off at the edge of the portico. Another tip.

"You talk about our life of crime, Irish, so can I. We stiff out on a date, that's one thing. But we can't go into this jai alai like gangbusters and there's no control. We're looking at a large degree of embarrassment, you and I. Do you agree with that, or what? Because somebody discharges a weapon, let's say, anybody, and what are we looking at? I'm talking about me and you."

A waiter, bowing, asked if they would care for a cocktail. Breed said, "Not yet, Jack," and as the waiter backed off, Joe Hooven got this very bad feeling. They were talking about him. The meal would not go well, and the rest of his life would be for shit. He said these words to himself, and in his mind they took on the slow, odd inflection of authenticity, a weird accent all its own, like he was at some spooky seance and the fortune-teller was holding his palm and trying to break it to him gently.

"What if we have to shoot a cop?" Breed asked. He had his arms folded belligerently. "It's the realm of the underworld, Del Plato. Are we ready for that? Because it's a thin line we walk every day, but once we're that far on the other side ... Need I elaborate? In two seconds we're out of control, and whatever we walk away with, there's a very thick price tag comes with it. I'm talking the actual event."

It was the middle of the afternoon, and the weather was perfect, seventy-five or so, nothing but sun and soft sky. On the lake were boats you had to pedal by the hour, and orange rafts, the sun's huge reflection, and on the shore at the opposite end were black barbecue pits dug in among the sturdy palms. Across the way, beside a footpath that led to the benches and charcoal, a steep, dusty slope was visible through the burned, sun-withered leaves of banana trees.

"There are vicissitudes, Irish; there are vagaries. Olympia Jai Alai is full of ups and downs, and what we got to do is try our best to be prepared."

"And we're not prepared," Del Plato answered.

"Definitely not. Not with the jai alai. I'm raising some points which it would be stupid not to raise, because I see nothing but sudden dips in the road for us. Things happen,

Irish, I'm telling you, things happen all the fucking time, and if we don't cover ourselves, we're unprepared. We go in and we try to wing it, terrific, but somebody isn't where he said he would be, or a shot rings out, and suddenly we got a revolution on our hands." Breed had his eyes closed, his beefy arms folded. "You see what I'm getting at"

"I'd say yes," Del told him, "but no, I don't."

"Joe Hooven." Breed pronounced the name carefully, with lots of contempt. Then he looked at Hooven and kept on looking until Hooven looked back. "The man is a vagary, Irish. The man is a definite vicissitude, Joe Heavy. Also an asshole."

Hooven pushed back his chair. He had wrapped the napkin from his lap around the knuckles of his left hand. Del Plato reached over and touched Hooven lightly on the chest.

Breed said, "I see you and it's like I just bit into something rotten. You know that feeling, Joe? When your face shrivels up, when your stomach does these flip-flops. Do you think that's a pleasant feeling, Joey? Well, it's not, it's not at all pleasant."

He leaned back to smile at an elderly couple across the terrace. They sat side by side, old people, facing the lake. A silver bucket of ice, the well-tanned table captain three steps away. Breed had a dazzling smile when he put his mind to it. "How's the food?" he called to the old guy, who nodded back approvingly, but was either too well-mannered to speak with his mouth full or else was the kind of shopping-center builder who didn't want to get into a discussion with Breed across the entire room. There were museum-size oil paintings on the wall.

"I deserve this," Hooven said.

"Ah, Joey, don't be so hard on yourself."

"I try to like elevate your taste, man. I bring you somewhere and I'm fucking picking up the tab. But you come on with that cop mentality, with that blue-collar mentality you always got, man, and I should have knew better. I should have known it. With that no-collar mentality."

"Joey, it's a joke. Where's your sense of humor? Look, you can't help it if I got this hard-on for you. Come on, Joey, say it's no big deal. It's just an aspect we got to recognize by

now—we got to live with it—that sometimes I get a little vola-
tile when you're around. Where's the crime in that?"

A relish tray was placed on their table, the flowers taken
away.

Del Plato was staring off dreamily toward the lake. He
saw himself pedaling a boat, while the sun went down, gray
and pink, and the smell of pine needles drifted softly over the
water. It was a cool and peaceful hour of the day, the way Del
saw it, when children from all over ran for the ice-cream truck
and grown-ups at home sat out on the lawn with their feet up,
in the shade of some tree as old as their house. Out on the
water Del would be alone, possibly rich. Possibly taking some
time off from an otherwise busy schedule. It was hard to say,
hard enough to imagine. In any case he would stop pedaling
and just float, cut loose, leaning back to watch the sun descend
and thinking how terrific it was that he could still appreciate
these things—the water, the sun going down, an innocent hour
of the day.

"You're extravagant," Breed was telling Joe Hooven.
"Everything about you is. Your hair is extravagant; it's much
too long. Why do you wear your hair so long? Why do you talk
the way you do?"

A sense of loss stirred Del Plato, the loss of many things
at once. He could have been falling, suddenly weightless and
free, or even drowning. He could have tumbled from the boat
and have been drowning in that lake. People were pointing at
him as he went under again and again. Children were made to
watch him go down, as a stern example of what would happen
to them if they weren't careful. Del fought a lightness in his
chest, flutters in his stomach. So many lost things, so much
lost. His belief was gone, his family was gone. And as he gazed
out the window Del realized clearly the lake was very far away
from where he sat in the restaurant. An idyll of franks and
lemonade, the dirty jokes in mixed company, it was so very
distant.

"Joe Heavy," Del could hear beside him, "let me put it to
you this way. Do I look like the kind of person, someone who
would—oh, I don't know how to phrase this properly—the

kind of person who would hurt a friend? Do I strike you as that type? I'm asking you a question."

"No."

"No, I don't look like the kind of person who would hurt a friend. That's not the answer I was looking for, Joey. Not the correct answer."

We had faith to get us through those dark spots outside our simple human understanding. Eternity, death, gold futures. But life itself, Del thought, *life is what's truly beyond us.*

"Fifty thousand dollars," Del said. "Each. Forty thousand, thirty, something like that. I wish you guys would get along better. Thirty or forty or fifty thousand dollars, each, that we never have to pay taxes on. Everything else becomes secondary. Money that can grow."

"I hear you," Breed told him.

"I know you do. One big thing brings us together." Del Plato gave a thumbs-up sign to Breed, one to Hooven. "We all want the same."

"I just want everything out in the open," said Breed. "You're still on that discussion with good and bad and shit, aren't you, Irish?"

"I'm thinking about the aftereffects. After we got the money, and it's done."

"Conscience, in other words. This bullshit smacks faintly of conscience. Is that what you're driving at?"

"All I see is more and more. I don't think I'm ready for that, I really don't."

"You can back out if you want to, but listen to me, Del Plato. Watch me while I'm talking to you. Conscience is one of those things for kids, a sketch pad. You lift the magic slate, everything is erased. Presto, you're free and clear. Believe me, Irish, everyone learns to live with conscience. People are very adaptable."

"Yeah, but I look at myself now, I see bad deeds. I don't go to church, and now I'm moving all the way on the other side. Where does it stop? People become junkies, right; they get divorced six times. They lose their willpower. It's always

a progression. Look at Vietnam. One day you got your toes in
the water, just for fun, just fooling around, and the next thing
you know you're out in the middle of the ocean, and how you
got there is a story nobody wants to hear."

"Vietnam?" said Hooven quickly. "What are you talking
about, Nam? I got a buddy, man, a good friend, he was almost
killed in that Vietnam. It was some scary place. On *Quincy* the
other day they had these two dudes—like vets?—one with no
feet, and the other one who was totally out to lunch because of
what happened over there. Fucking war."

Even on that flat cool water Del Plato wouldn't be able to
shake the feeling he had hitched a long ride in the eye of a
hurricane, untouched himself, but in front of him and behind
him and on both sides would be the whole world speeding
along, all of nature a rushed and wind-tossed mess.

"It's a dollars-and-cents thing," Breed told him. "I know
what you're going through, Del Plato. I can feel it myself. But
me, I take a realistic view of the situation we're in, and the
only reason I'm going along, the main reason, is for the bucks.
I been through it, the whole scales of justice responsibility
you're into, and I've come out of it. I'm your friend. And what
I realize now is that I never needed all those petty obsessions I
was always having. I didn't need to cut salt out of my diet, or
run five miles a day. I didn't need *tae kwon do*, or all that carrot juice I was drinking. Because all along it was only money.
What I needed right from the start was more money." Breed
held his arms open, like the statue of some statesman in the
park. "And it's always money, Del Plato. Always."

Joe Hooven looked up from the wine book. He had his own
problems. If he ordered a fourteen-dollar wine, which is where
the wines started, then the restaurant people would think he
was also from Winnipeg, just like the turkeys he was sitting
with. From way up north, Canada, where they thought popcorn was an okay vegetable to serve with a meal. Where everybody had like two pairs of the same exact desert boots, and
they put these 747-size tires on their Jeeps, and even a six-
year-old kid knew what an alternator was. But even if he went
for the middle-level wines, forty simoleons a shot, these cops

would never know to appreciate the texture or whatever. They would just go through three or four bottles, easy—dusty bottles, from a cellar, the kind of wine that sophisticated people could sip and discuss for twenty minutes like it was a religious subject or something—and in the end it would all fall on Hooven.

He went through a practiced motion of removing a cigarette from an art deco cigarette case he carried in the inside pocket of his white suit jacket. Hooven didn't like to think so much. Not about wine or problems or anything. He bought his cigarettes at the airport duty-free shop. He tapped one in the center of his palm before lighting up.

"With me," Hooven said, "all right, I thought we had something going that wasn't too hard and wasn't too complicated. You made scratch, I made scratch. Now we got something else and it should be the same way."

Breed knocked the cigarette out of Joe Hooven's mouth. Hooven touched his lips where the cigarette had been. He saw it on the floor quite a few feet away.

"You don't realize," Breed was saying to him, "you have no idea how you rub me the wrong way." Breed turned to Del Plato and said, "Jerk taps his cigarettes. Did you see that?"

Hooven, outwardly calm, got out of his seat to retrieve his cigarette. James Bond smoked the same brand. One time a neighbor's cat had kept him awake by howling all night, so Hooven left out a saucer of milk and vodka, which killed it. After a club manager had hired a different band, Hooven poured a two-pound bag of sugar into the guy's gas tank. Some things just had to be taken care of in a private way.

Hooven lit the cigarette as casually as he could and decided he would go for the forty-dollar wine selection. Life was short.

"We're doing it," Del Plato then said flatly. He placed a hand on Breed's shoulder. "We got Jackie Molson over here with his pass inside the fronton, we got a Saturday matinee lined up. I took the liberty of making notes. Saturday sound good for everyone?"

Hooven worked at untangling his hair with his fingers.

"Isn't this sort of like rushing things?" Saturday? Hooven wasn't at all prepared for anything so final, so definite. In a million years he would never be able to make heads or tails of these cops.

"Rushing things?" Breed had pulled his chair close to Joe Hooven. "Rushing things? Soon as this is over, Joey, then I'm finished with you. How's that rushing things? Think before you ask stupid questions."

Del Plato said, "So that's it; we're decided." He was a bit surprised to hear himself speak, but it was very simple, actually. "I been very discreetly checking the place out. I been looking things over, and what I got detailed makes sense for us."

In a way he expected them to back off the project, coming on with some shaky but earnest arguments, as though Del Plato were on the basketball floor and somebody with a law degree thinks a back court violation has been committed. Del thinks otherwise. Suddenly the air is filled with contention and words like *contingent* and *whereas*, and everyone on Del's side is right away backing off. His witnesses change their story. They start to equivocate on their support, and what happens is that he's come this far, and he's the one holding the ball, and some guy with a diploma has taken an opposing point of view.

"Saturday," Hooven said in a tight voice. "That's like right around the corner. You come here, you guys, the two of you, with your small threats and the way you behave, and you tell me Saturday. Just like that." He glanced around to see who was listening. His voice was out of control. He wanted to be like forceful, and instead he had to hear his own voice shoot way up to a level that could like bring porpoises to the surface. "This is my idea. My idea, man. I said let's take off Olympia— didn't I?—it was my plans. And now you give me Saturday, this Saturday. You been checking things out."

"If you're saying no," Breed told him, "say it right now. Do us that favor. Because this is not the place for comments, Joe Heavy, or your shithead observations."

The three of them sat around the small round elegant

table, waiting for tempers to settle. Only Del Plato appeared unperturbed. He was making his choice of crisp things inside the relish tray. "Saturday," Del said after a brief silence. He chose a white clump of cauliflower.

Jewboy Breed repeated the word, "Saturday," as though something profound had been uttered, and very quickly an aura of finality came over them, and there wasn't much left to say. Breed reached for a carrot wedge. Then it was Hooven's turn. He said the word too, "Saturday." He went to the tray and came away with a rippled slice of cucumber.

Del, thinking that sometimes he could really amaze himself, raised his hand and made a big show of snapping his fingers. The table captain stepped forward.

"I'll have a Pepsi, pal," Del said, completely confident. "No ice."

"I'm getting us a wine," Hooven told him. "Hang on a second, man, I got a thousand wines to look at." He made a hand signal to the table captain that everything was smooth. "This is a class joint I take you to, Del Plato. You don't drink soda here."

"Perhaps a sparkling water for monsieur?"

"Perhaps not. Perhaps a Pepsi."

There was a sigh and a bow. "We do not serve a soft drink, monsieur, I regret. We can recommend a chilled light wine with which monsieur can better enjoy his choice of menu."

"You can?"

"Of course."

"I can recommend something too. There's a Seven Eleven down the street, I bet. Why don't you go out and buy me a Pepsi? Send a busboy; here's a dollar."

"Go get him, Irish."

Del said, "My cousin over here is spending a healthy amount of hard-earned cash on this food. I have a right to enjoy it. Right? I don't like wine. I like Pepsi."

"Unless we order fish," Breed said happily. "Then we would want something lighter. Perhaps a Fresca. Joey, am I right, Joey?"

"It's very funny," Hooven answered. He tried to catch the

captain's eye, show some kind of understanding. A waiter in a place like this earned twice what any cop could make. "I'm like very amused, with your behavior and all. With that mentality."

Someone else in a sharp tuxedo had made his way over, and whispered in private to the table captain. The new guy had a purple flower in his lapel and a handkerchief folded just the right way inside his breast pocket. He approached the table and bent forward beside Del Plato.

"We seek a Pepsi for monsieur. My name is Lucien, should the gentlemen wish to order soon." He came to Hooven, who had closed the wine book. "May I help with the selection?"

"Lucien," Breed said. "Lucien. That's a nice name. What's that, French?"

"Yes, it is."

"Let me ask you something, Lucien. You have ice tea here, don't you? It's not the kind from a package, with all that sugar in it?"

"No, monsieur."

"You swear?"

"Monsieur may try it, complimentary." Lucien looked like he had been wearing a tuxedo all his life. He had silver hair and a thin silver mustache. When he raised his hand, a waiter in a black suit came over.

"I don't know if I can trust you on that," Breed said. "I'll tell you what. When you go out for my friend's Pepsi, you can bring back another one for me. Fair enough?"

"As you wish."

Del Plato was mulling over what he had to gain and what he had to lose. The pros and cons melded together as he weighed them in his mind, until all he could envision was a bulk. It took the shape of a room. The room pressured him, closing in.

He was going through the motions of robbery, doing the work. It was so foreign, so unreal. This was nothing to rush into, with one on-the-spot decision you might come to regret too soon. It was a complex problem, taking in such related matters as ethics, and marriage, and the goddamn pursuit of happiness. It should have been worked out with freshly sharpened pencils and clean paper, like a trigonometry problem, with all the needed tools and preparation to solve a tough one.

But there was no answer, really. Or one answer. For Del Plato, only one. He figured he could lay out the problem—filling in the little formulas and figuring all the angles with a protractor—but still for him there would be only one answer, whether he was prepared or not.

Do what you got to do. It would always be the same conclusion. Do it. Just do it. Fate was too big, too thick, and inside that hard, dark shell a simple soul could bounce around forever between good and bad, like some dried bean inside a gourd, rattling from one dead end to another while waiting for something to happen, banging out a hollow two-step of indecision. So maybe he wasn't honest. *So? You got to do something, do it.*

Across the table Hooven was fidgeting with the wine book. "Monsieur?"

Hooven held up the book and it was taken away. He took a deep breath and shrugged. "What the hell," Joe Hooven said. "I'm having what my friends have. Bring me a Pepsi."

"The rambling man. The world, I'm telling you, is full of surprises."

"Pepsi for monsieur."

Del Plato told him to relax, so Joe Hooven leaned back and did his best to smile. He was about to tap a cigarette when he caught himself.

"What do you think?" Del asked him.

"Hey, what am I supposed to think? Looks like I'm here."

"Joe Heavy, Joe Heavy," said Breed. "*El Moocho.* This is the single biggest mistake you'll ever make in your entire life." Breed reached over to Hooven's cigarette case and helped himself to a smoke. "Let me tell you something, in case you don't already know. Joey, Joey. You are fucking in for it now."

Chapter
14

O n the morning he was to become a felon of the first order,
Del Plato found himself more alive than he had been in
months. He had a terrific night's sleep for a change, followed
by a working man's breakfast of three fried eggs, bacon, toast,
Cheerios, cookies, two glasses of milk, more cookies. No waver-
ing. None of those drawn-out bouts of maybe this and maybe
that, no decisions. This was it. He shaved and combed his hair.
At his side Del Plato held a slate-gray Samsonite attaché case,
the kind of thing an investment banker might own, which he
had purchased the day before—cash—specifically for the job
at Olympia. It was important to him that he go about this robbery in a businesslike fashion, unconfused, first class.

He read the daily paper inside his rented house, lingering
over dirty dishes, until Joe Hooven honked outside—one short
honk—and picked up Del Plato in a stolen car. Del took along
his gray case and the newspaper, locking the door behind him.
The news was all football injuries and possible trades. Del still
wanted to turn to the back of the sports section and look up
Friday night's figure at the local frontons.

"So how you doing today?" Hooven asked.

"Fine, fine." Del had never been inside a stolen car. It didn't surprise him that it was nothing special. He was going to work, no more than that. Del wore a brand-new shirt, the lines still crisp where it had been folded inside the cellophane.

They got extra keys made for the hot car—one for each of them, just in case—and drove to the fronton parking lot ahead of schedule, stopping off first at Gulfstream Savings, where Hooven pulled up to the drive-in teller and folded a check for five hundred dollars to be cashed through the tube.

"It ain't so much the dough as it is the getting away. I'm getting back to my music, man. Get far away from you, and the other one. Only reason I'm here, Del Plato. You need Mr. Green to live right."

"I suppose that's true," Del said. Hooven opened the canister. He shook out five hundred in crisp bills and an orange lollipop. "What are you doing?" Del eventually asked. "Don't we have to be somewhere?"

"This is a transaction, nothing. But Key West, man? I'll drink beer, you know, get high. Get laid. Get back to the basics."

Hooven had boosted the car that morning. He got up early even though he didn't like to. He had to hunt down a getaway vehicle, so he took a walk around his neighborhood, wearing a zip-up jacket with PRESTIGE POOLS on the back, sketching things on an eight-by-eleven pad in order to look busy. He drew rabbits because that's what he could draw best. Floppy ears, whiskers, big buck teeth.

A lot of people left their houses just before nine. Men going to work, women going to work, kids off to dance class. It didn't really matter to Hooven where people were off to because he wasn't planning to take very long. One entire family drove off in a Buick Regal which had been inside their garage. Husband, good-looking wife, two kids in soccer outfits. They left a blue Toyota Starlet in the driveway. Very good-looking wife. People felt better about leaving one car in the driveway. A potential burglar would think somebody was home.

Hooven tucked his ponytail into the back of his jacket and put his ear to the front door. He didn't hear anything. No radio, no TV, no vacuum cleaner, no one on the phone. He rang the doorbell. Nobody home. Hooven then checked inside the Toyota—and there, clipped to the driver-side visor, was the portable garage-door opener. He clicked it one time.

It was a few minutes past nine o'clock. If somebody had answered the door, Hooven would have scratched his head and said he was with the swimming pool company, and they were giving free estimates on installation in this neighborhood. Then he would have tried a different house. No problem.

Once inside the garage Hooven walked quickly to the electric eye on the far wall and clicked the door closed behind. All the tools he would ever need he found neatly hung on pegs. It was a very organized garage. Hooven put on his kidskin gloves, which were from Italy. Then he selected a hammer and slammed off the doorknob in two whacks. He stepped inside the house.

Car keys were right on the bookshelf. A key fob displayed the Toyota emblem. Hooven dropped the car keys in his pocket and nosed around some more. Above the sofa was a family portrait. The wife had looked a lot better when she was driving away.

Mixed in with the dish towels he came up with the checkbook. Hooven turned to the balance, $1,142, Gulfstream Savings. He tore out the last three checks from the back of the checkbook and replaced it neatly among the dish towels, just as he had found it. Easy money, it was always easy.

In the master bedroom he went through the drawers and found some dress-up jewelry hidden in a toothpaste box behind a pile of folded T-shirts. Cuff links, graduation ring. He decided not to bother. In the walk-in closet Hooven patted all the men's shirts until he discovered a lump in one of the pockets. Money. He shoved it in his jacket without looking.

So easy.

He took his pad and left by the front door. The Starlet was a nice-enough car. It started up right away. A full tank of gas. Cassette tapes too. Diana Ross, Kenny Rogers, Manilow.

Hooven chucked them all out the window as he drove off. The whole thing had taken maybe ten, twelve minutes.

On his way to get Del Plato, later, Hooven came up with the man's signature on some bills in the glove compartment. Five-thousand-mile service, new brake pads already. At red lights Hooven practiced writing the name. Then he signed all three checks, and the best two forgeries he made out for five hundred dollars each, payable to cash. At a gas station he pulled over to go through the phone book. One convenient branch of Gulfstream Savings was on the way to Del Plato. He'd stop there first. Another was located not too far from the jai alai fronton at Olympia. He'd pick up Del Plato and stop off at that branch also. All part of the profession—a treasure in every drawer, booty under the bed.

Del Plato didn't especially like the way Joe Hooven drove, but he wouldn't let it get him down, not the way he was feeling today. It was a beautiful weekend sky, blue and white and a touch of yellow. Del snapped on his seat belt—something he didn't normally do. Hooven drove too slow, that was the main problem. Who would have thought Hooven to be a bad driver? The man was a criminal, totally without scruples or honor, and he was driving forty miles an hour in the left lane when he should have been going fifty or fifty-five. Never looking at his rearview mirror. One foot on the gas and one foot on the brake, like an old person. It made Del Plato suspicious again. Maybe he shouldn't be getting involved with somebody who drove this way. Hooven had his hair pinned up in back and tucked together under a hairnet. Del wondered just how little he trusted Hooven, and if that was important or not, trusting Joe Hooven.

He was sure Hooven would sooner or later blab about the jai alai heist. He would talk it up in the company of thieves, the way a bee has to go crazy for the rest of the hive over a field of pollen. It would be too big a score for someone like Hooven to hold back. The man was unstable. He was a lefty, which was one thing, with weasel eyes that Breed had pinned from the start, and he drove too slow, much too slow.

Hooven relit half a joint he had pinched out earlier and

offered Del Plato a toke. Del didn't want any. As he drove, Hooven fit a dirty-blond wig over his natural hair. He slowed down and was oblivious to cars darting around him. The hairpiece matched the photo on Hooven's clip-on license, which had been issued by the Florida Gaming Commission to James Molson. Jackie. Hooven looked even more disreputable in short hair. He asked Del Plato to hold the jay while he checked himself out, looking in the rearview mirror for the first time.

Del Plato carried his off-duty .38 underneath a nylon jacket. Inside the Samsonite attaché case was everything else he would need. Del tried to picture just how much room $150,000 would take up. Would it fill a suitcase? Would it be too much for one person to carry? Could it be split three ways without extra trouble?

The parking lot at Olympia was already backed up with cars. It was after two o'clock, and the matinee program began at one. The heaviest betting, serious money, was laid down during the eleventh and twelfth games, the last races of the day, when the top jai alai players took the court against one another. Del forked over the buck and a half to the parking attendant because Hooven said he had nothing smaller than a fifty.

They took the long way around the parking area, just checking, trying to get a good scope of things, a frame of reference for later, when it counted. Then Hooven pulled the Toyota to the first spot he found around the corner from the main entrance. From there they could get through the easement and into the flow on Federal Highway without trouble. Past the antiques and filling stations, past the custard stands, nothing to worry about. Del checked his Fako watch. He was becoming a little hungry, perhaps a little anxious. They walked the long way, unhurried, timing themselves from the car to the main gate. They blundered through clumps of leggy brush, covering the possibilities, leaves upon leaves of mulberry and pokeweed, through puffs of foliage. Orange lantana, purple morning glories streaked with pink.

Breed was supposed to leave his car in the front lot of a Winn-Dixie, the Beef People, half a mile away.

Around back was another door the athletes used, and the

attendants who set out the shirts and towels and took care of equipment. It led to the locker rooms and showers beneath the playing court. Two guards were stationed outside. Hooven got ready to go inside. He would take the employee elevator to the second level, where he would change his clothes and report to work.

"We're doing this, man. Look me in the eye and say it."

"Don't worry," Del Plato told him. "We won't hang you up."

Hooven couldn't walk away; he was still there. "I want this to be over. I hate it already. You, me, him. It's too much, man." Hooven stood up straight; he threw back his shoulders. Then he reached out and squeezed Del Plato's arm with his left hand. Hooven was wiry but strong. "He's gonna like shoot me inside, isn't he? I got a feeling. Tell me the truth, man. Don't fuck with me now."

"Joe, come on, you're talking stupid."

"He shoots me, man, I'm telling you right now, it isn't fair. You tell him this for me, Del Plato. Tell him it isn't fair."

"You're hurting my arm, Joe. You're making a scene."

"I'll fucking never give that dude a day's peace. If I'm dead? If I'm dead I still don't care. I'll come back and haunt him, I'll haunt you both, you pricks; shoot me like that." He took the nub of his joint from between his lips and threw it down and squashed it. "I can make you suffer, you jerk me around."

Del wasn't really paying attention. He couldn't quite shake the nagging notion he had forgotten something. Maybe it was important and maybe it wasn't, but he could almost remember what it was and then it would be gone. Vanished. Poof.

"Pisses me off," Hooven said. "I don't know who you people are. I got like no idea what's coming next, what's important to you. I ain't made of iron, okay. I can't handle all this shit."

"I'm looking after things, Joe. Really, you can't take everything so personal."

"I take everything personal." Hooven, rocking on his

heels, poked Del Plato in the chest with one finger. Then he put his hands in his pockets. "Don't tell me what to do. You know? Don't tell me."

The vague, unremembered thing was just beyond Del Plato's grasp, a vast, urgent swirl without shape. What? Maybe it was something with the robbery. Maybe it was nothing with the robbery. But he couldn't think, he could only do.

Hooven finally went in. He showed the guards his employee tag and they wrote down his number. Del Plato turned the other way, heading back to the main gate, breathing evenly. Spikes of sunlight pounded down in a slow smothering heat as he approached the entrance.

One day it would come to Del Plato, this vital fuzzy thought he couldn't quite put a finger on. He was sure of that. Probably it would wake him in the middle of some absolutely silent and black night. The silence would wake him. And then he would sit up in bed and an ominous recognition would come to him from out of the haze, like the voice of Christmas Past. What could it be? Had he overlooked somebody? Had they left behind some obvious sort of clue? Fingerprints? A change of clothes?

Two guards in uniform tore tickets in half and directed the crowd that was filing through turnstiles. Inside the lobby was a booth where somebody sold the daily programs. Both the entry guards had holstered revolvers. Del Plato paused by the glassed-in admission cashiers beside the wide white gates going in.

Del Plato bought a regular-admission stub. When he saw a large group entering the building, he stepped in to mingle with them, then went through a middle turnstile and handed over his ticket and walked into the jai alai lobby. It amazed him that he could be so regular, appear so normal, slip right in with the millions when he had a gun at his side and sin on his mind. If it was crowded when he walked through the high-columned gates, painted white and gold, marble under his feet and over his head, Del figured they would be less likely to pull him aside for any reason. Light streaming down in thick, broad beams at once blinded him; he had been looking up. He couldn't recall the place having been so splendid. It was like a palace. Huge and white, and wide open, immense.

Del couldn't think of himself as a bad person, no matter what. He was an optimist, that's what he was. If anything, a fighter despite the odds. And even if they proved him dishonest, at least that would show he had hope as well, and aspiration. Del would lie and cheat, but for a purpose—to become better here and now, to have more. He held that in common with dishonest folks.

He figured the afternoon crowd at six thousand. There were people in the balcony and people in the loge seats and people watching the overhead closed-circuit screens as they stood tightly grouped in the lobby. Each game's total wagers were counted and wrapped and then stacked upstairs, where Joe Hooven was working.

Del's judgment was weighted with so many different things. This was an irrevocable move. When his mother finally died in the hospital, wearing a nightgown he had bought for her earlier that day, he mostly recalled having been disappointed. The phone rang at night, his father had picked it up and thanked the doctor for calling. Del's eyes immediately filled with tears of bitterness. Why hadn't she fought harder? He was expecting her to be well. Each day she grew more bloodless and shrunken and tired, but people also got well. His own mother, why hadn't she pulled through? A week in the hospital and she went under. Going peacefully of all things. In her sleep, without a whimper.

Del felt about his mother's death the way he knew his father always felt about him. Disappointment was the one emotion they were able to express at home without difficulty. And failure stayed with a person. Del Plato knew. It penetrated deep to the bone, clung to the skin, remained like the heavy, bitter smell of smoke after a burning. They could hope for more, the way he saw it, but couldn't really expect anything. The Tigers never won, the Red Wings never won, the Pistons never won. Workers were laid off. The government took your money without asking.

Who wanted to be honest? That had nothing to do with goodness. Honest meant you had to be satisfied with what you

already were. Unsuccessful. Small. If you were honest, you
were content to wait your turn in another place, another lifetime, because you didn't have it in you to face up right here
and now. Honesty was a deficiency, like rickets, or beriberi,
only no medical care or vitamins could help with something serious as that. You had to cure yourself.

He took his attaché case to a corner of the arena, below the
large tote board that flashed betting odds for the upcoming
race in yellow lights. It was the eighth game of the afternoon
schedule, and the lines at the betting parlor windows were ten
deep. To Del Plato's right, at the base of a long, sharply de-
scending row of shag-covered steps, was the square court itself.
Concrete floor and the tall green wall in front, and the players
in game shirts tossing the pelota back and forth against it.

The five-minute bell went off. There was a sudden flurry
of money changing hands, a buzz of motion. Del listened to the
sound the ball made on the jai alai court as it ricocheted off the
wall. A player scooped it off one bounce in his wicker-weave
basket and flung it back. Pock, pock. Del rested against the
back block of seats on the mezzanine level, away from the rotating cameras. Pock. Pock. The players casually catching the
ball, lofting it back, warming up.

There was more of a fuss when Jewboy Breed came in. He
wore a red Santa Claus outfit with a fake white beard, giving a
yuletide laugh to the admission guards as he bulled through
the turnstile, wide and jolly, his .25 high-chrome Llama with
the custom grips tucked out of sight in his boot.

"Yo, Santa!" a college kid called. All the way through the
turnstiles the kid held hands with a girl who was still oiled for
the sun. "It's Santa Claus! You bringing me something for
Christmas, Santa? I been good."

Breed quietly told the kid to fuck off. He was trying to get
his bearings inside the fronton.

Once inside, Breed fit in better among the busy crowd. He
noticed Del Plato across the wide terrazzo floor of the lobby,
but didn't let on. Del was watching the game down below. Red
number one was on against blue number two. When the pelota
hit wood, out of bounds, making a different sound, the referee

raised his small red flag and number three in white ran on the court to return serve.

Breed hung around the Big Q window. The cashiers dialed out the betting combinations and the results were fed into a computer upstairs. Yellow lights on the large tote board kept humming and new numbers spun out. Perfecta, superfecta. Win, place, show. The daily double. Trifecta. Bet cashiers wore red coats and shiny-red cummerbunds and they knew how to count in at least two languages. They stood by their bank trays during match play, checking individual takes, until state-hired deputies wearing tan regimentals rolled in a steel cart to transport all the locked-up goods upstairs, by elevator, where Hooven and other counters would then parcel the revenue— separate it, wrap it, stamp it, stack it high in thousands.

The five team, in black, was in the midst of a long rally with yellow six on the jai alai floor. Breed winked at an Olympia Fronton Wager-ette, who wore seamed stockings and ruffles on her behind. "Season's greetings," Breed said to her as she walked past. "Ho, ho, ho." She was getting drinks for some heavy bettors in preferred seating. Breed watched the way she walked; it was more interesting to him than jai alai. She had red sequins on her outfit and a push-up bra. Her eyelashes were like the fringe on beach umbrellas. Breed thought he might be falling in love again.

The yellow front man, an American, took the pelota off a short hop and whipped it quickly at a sharp, pinched angle into the left corner, where it rebounded on the court and headed toward the retaining net for an apparent winner. But the front man on the five team had anticipated this *ramate* shot, and scrambled to the out-of-bounds wood to intercept the kill in time. He then heaved it high off the wall, just below ceiling level, to give himself time to regain position.

The crowd gave five a brief round of applause. Breed walked across the far end of the lobby to where Del Plato was standing.

Now the back men had the play, trading deep, skidding returns which shot off both front and rear walls. A player would balance the pelota in the scoop of his cesta, take a few shuffle steps for momentum, then rocket the ball with the

three-quarters delivery and wrist-snap motion of a baseball
pitcher firing one in.

It was a long point. Both teams were getting tired. People
in the betting audience were on their feet, hooting in English
and Spanish. When a front man scooted back to take the ball
on the fly and rifle it back, there would be the opposing player
to leap high and retrieve the carom. Both teams wanted the
point.

"*Shalom,*" Breed said. He had come up behind Del Plato.
Del didn't flinch or turn around. "What do you know?"

"This isn't for me," Del told him. "I don't especially want
to do this, I decided, so I'm going home now. I changed my
mind."

"Make jokes. Only you got that quality, Irish, a real tech-
nique. You make jokes at the most inappropriate fucking
times."

Breed rested a foot against the mezzanine rail. He patted
his boot to make sure his gun was still there. He didn't mind
the red suit so much, or even the droopy, annoying hat that
went with it, but all this standing around wasn't such a good
idea, not for Breed. It didn't fit his temperament.

"Everything okay?" he asked.

"So far as I know."

A front man, exhausted, finally took a little off his return
and simply lobbed it into deep court, just beyond the second-
service line. The opposing man sensed a chance to put the ball
away and came in on the run to slash his shot deep and hard
down the left wall, *contada,* but when he turned, spinning his
torso to fling it back, the ball simply plopped out of his cesta,
like an egg from its nest. And for that brief, suspended moment there wasn't a sound. Then the referee blew his whistle
and dropped his flag for the next team. Brown seven came on,
front and back players, running.

Breed fluffed his thick white beard. "One thing," he said.
"How do you even know it's here, this money? I mean we're
not taking off Happy Harry now. These people have been in
business a long time. How do you know what they got? How
are we supposed to find it?"

"I have faith in money," Del told him. Points were registered on the scoreboard above them. "It's here, J.B. Even if I can't see it, I still believe in money. Look around, it's here."

"I don't know why I talk to you." Breed fixed his broad black belt and turned the other way. "I don't know who I got less confidence in, you or Joe Baggie. I have to tell you the truth."

A different Wager-ette appeared, also good looking. She wore spike heels and the seams of her stockings were off-line.

"If I were to plan a holdup," Breed said, "I'd have it different. I'm here because I said I would be here when you asked me from before, but if it was me, I'd have us in and then right out. Because the more we putz around in here, the more time we have for a fuckup. You know my way of thinking, Irish, don't you? You remember?"

"Where somebody gets the short end."

"Nobody gets the short end," Breed said loudly. Then he lowered his voice and came a little closer. "Okay, maybe one person gets the short end. Somebody gets screwed. But it ain't you, Del Plato, and it ain't me, so what do you care?"

Del kept his eyes on the court. He hadn't glanced at Breed even once.

"Saint Irish, my partner. You're too good for this world, I'm telling you. Down here we don't deserve you."

Del Plato watched the games with mild interest. It was a difficult sport, jai alai. The words meant "merry festival" in Basque, but they played it with a rock-hard ball, going a hundred miles an hour, and men in crash helmets. Yet it had its own lilting language, which you could probably whisper to your date over wine. He wasn't a betting man, but the competition alone would have brought him back. At home he could watch bowling from the Firestone Open, or high diving off the cliffs of Acapulco. The sport didn't matter. The heightened intensity appealed to Del Plato—that elevated moment of awareness when there was no world beyond the immediate need to come in first.

He propped his gray case against the wall, closing his eyes. He would rob this place and become wealthy. They would move after money for the tenth went upstairs.

Del Plato thought about Denise. One time she had hit him. It wasn't that long ago, but it seemed another lifetime. Right at the start of their bad months together, when he began taking an enormous interest in *The Cisco Kid* after midnight so he wouldn't have to lie stiffly in bed with his eyes wide open, feeling her galling heat beside him under the sheets—bothering him, the sting of her skin when they touched. Del would arrive home and wonder if it was too much to hope for Denise to be already asleep, so he could unlock the door, shift around with only the hall light on, eat a quiet sandwich alone. Rub his feet, relax. Not have to ask how her day had gone, or have to tell what had happened to him. Words weren't easy.

That day Del had been in a pretty rank mood. Someone in the precinct lockerroom had made a comment about pussy-whipped, and Del was thinking about that on the way home because he was on the outs with Denise, and one thing led to another in his mind, until by the time he got home, late for dinner, he had worked himself up to a good frenzy. And after some small banter, sarcasm back and forth—nothing really— she suddenly reached out and cracked him one with an open hand. Hard, above the ear. He could only look at her, speechless, stunned.

What the hell was her *beef? Who knew what the hell* she *had been thinking all day? What was going on here?*

Denise then went around looking at her hand like it was something she had never laid eyes on before, going on and on about how bad she felt. But how could you tell how bad anyone really felt? It was done. That's the way it happens. The incident itself takes a second. Whap. And it wasn't one of those things that you could step back and view in any reasonable terms. Denise just knocked him—swock!—and his head swam.

She held both her hands to the place on his head where she had struck him, all hugging and frantic, and when she asked if he could forgive her, he didn't have to think. "Sure. It's okay." But who *was* this woman? If she was capable of doing that, to him, then human nature was beyond understanding.

"Sure," he had answered, "it's okay," smiling stupidly in her direction, with the phony smile you put on for a camera. Only the person taking your picture isn't familiar with the shutter release or something, and you're left there with a painful, stupid grin waiting around for a click that might take forever.

Inside the main hall of the gallery, on the far end of the sports complex, forty feet beyond the betting island and adjacent to the refreshment counter, was a white steel door with a sign bolted on. FIRE EXIT ONLY. It was always locked on the lobby side with a Citadel rotating plate. On the other side of the door was a staircase going up one flight. The upper level maintained the employment office of Olympia Jai Alai, the central computer room, a permanent on-premises suite for the Florida Gaming Commission, restrooms, and the square-shaped accounting office where Jackie Molson was licensed to work on a fill-in basis. Hooven wore a pocketless red jumpsuit with his ID clipped to the collar, regulation dress for all accounting room employees. He got eight dollars an hour and Blue Cross.

Besides Hooven, there were three other counters inside. They worked at a long flat table, with cashier trays from downstairs, a rubber tip over each thumb for sorting through the funds. They had machines for checking stacked piles of money, one with an ultraviolet light for detecting counterfeits. Wads of wrappers, clumps of rubber bands. There was also an eight-foot-high safe with its doors swung open, and a four-tiered supply shelf where the counted batches of money were placed in small, neat stacks of ten thousand each. Checked, double-checked, and stamped. The guard upstairs, wearing his chocolate-brown turn-out coat, was watching the second half of Alabama-Texas.

When money from the ninth race had arrived and been arranged, Hooven excused himself to take a leak. Through the men's room he sneaked out into the upstairs hallway. On one wall was an oil painting of Frank Sinatra, and then a long row of photos of celebrities posing with management. Hooven stole past the elevator doors, which were guarded on the two lower levels by security men who had the only tubular keys to operate the elevator. Hooven paused under a clock in the upstairs corridor and stood next to the upper-level emergency door. FIRE EXIT ONLY. Hooven pulled a four-inch strip of nylon packing tape that had been wrapped around his ankle. It hurt like hell to tug it off. He taped closed the tongue of the self-locking upstairs door and took the steps two at a time until he was at the bottom. Then he cracked open the downstairs door leading to the fronton lobby. He opened it just wide enough to seal that too, with tape off his other ankle. The door pressed flush without a sound.

In the brief seconds he had the downstairs door open, Hooven heard the clamor and rush of excitement outside. It had sounded to him like a party. The swell of voices, the smell of tobacco and sweat, and Hooven wasn't really anxious to go back upstairs. He wanted to go out there, for maybe just a minute or two, in the jai alai lobby with everyone else, in his red jumpsuit. Soak it all in, the atmosphere and the tension. But he did just what he was supposed to do with the door, which was to block the lock notching so Breed could use the stairwell and take the money and probably not even give Joe Hooven half a chance once it was done.

He flew back up the stairs three at a time. He had listened as both steel doors, top and bottom, swung shut behind him without snapping locked. He went through the men's room back to the accounting room, took his corner of the money table, and busied himself with paper. All he was supposed to do now was not act nervous. He was supposed to stand around and wait for things to either fuck up after the eleventh race was underway, or else it would all go smooth as silk, whatever. That's what he was supposed to do.

Hooven kept on counting. It wasn't up to him anymore. He eyeballed the tightly wrapped stacks already on the shelf tiers and put the purse at a hundred grand, give or take a touch, which sure beat a lot of other ways you could find to pay the rent. People did worse for less; he wasn't complaining.

The guard continued watching his small screen. Nobody had missed Hooven upstairs. The other counters were people who only knew a co-worker by the name of Molson, who wasn't very sociable but he did his work well enough and paid for a round of soft drinks every once in a while. A nice-enough guy, with short blond hair, who punched in and went home.

A few minutes later some state deputies stepped out of the elevator and knocked on the door to the accounting room. Texas had the ball in Alabama territory, third down and long. The guard inside looked at Hooven, who was closest to the door.

Hooven opened up, and they rolled in the cart of bank trays which had accumulated for the tenth match. "How's it going, gentlemen?" Hooven said as he let the money in.

Next time it would be for real. Things were going down. Lots of action, lots of what they were here for.

At three-thirty-five on the watch of the person standing next to him—a nervous older woman with pencil scratches all over her tout sheet and calculations no one else in the world could possibly understand—Jewboy Breed massaged his padded belly and took a casual stroll across the lobby floor. He figured he had been on his feet almost an hour, and he was a car cop—he wasn't used to being on his feet. Breed stood a comfortable distance from the upstairs fire door. He heard the two-minute bell sound for the eleventh race of the matinee program—a singles game featuring the eight leading point scorers to date over the course of the jai alai season.

A convoy in full dress tans had just wheeled money boxes from the tenth game into the elevator. They were going up

"Love your suit," the woman said behind him. She had followed Breed to the other side of the white hall. "Can I rub your beard for good luck? Would you mind? I need a change."

Breed leaned over to make it easier. But the woman was looking at him very intently, and this made him nervous. A witness? That's what he would get for being a nice guy. Why didn't she just do it and fuck off? What was this scrutiny?

The woman finally backed away, but only to get a better look, puzzling over something. Finally it hit her. "Christmas is the twenty-fifth," she said happily. From inside her blouse she removed a balled-up handkerchief that had been squirreled in her brassiere. "I like the way you look; I felt something in that beard." She unfolded the handkerchief to her reserve of wrinkled twenties. "The two-five quiniela is showing two-to-one. I'm putting my money on you, Santa. Don't let me down, please. Two-five for me." She hurried away before the betting parlors shut down.

Breed then held his ground beside the fire door heading up, leaning back with his arms folded and his eyes riveted straight in front of him.

Two minutes later, when Del Plato came out of the men's room with a mask on, Breed pulled at the doorknob, popped inside, and yanked off the tape. He let the door snap to a close behind him and reached into his Kris Kringle boot.

Inside the downstairs men's room, Del had turned his jacket inside out so a different color was showing. Then he snapped open his pebbled-gray businessman's case. Del took out a rubber Richard Nixon mask, which he stuffed into one jacket pocket. In the other pocket he stashed a giant size tube of Krazy Glue and his .38. Inside the case he also had a burlap sack with a twist tie to keep it closed. He unknotted the tie and slammed the case, then snapped the locks and left.

He had fit the mask over his face by the time he was through the second door of the men's room. Del worked at the eyes so he had a clear field of vision.

The Llama wasn't an authorized off-duty weapon, but Breed liked to have it for dirty work. It could never be traced, for one thing, and also he really enjoyed the detail etched into the grips. It showed craft. They didn't make small arms like they used to. The gun butt was of monster trees, and a cliff dropping straight down into choppy water, all done the old-fashioned way, by hand. The sun or moon engulfed the whole scene, nature out of control, on the loose. Earth, air, water. The gun itself was fire. Breed could appreciate the art, the effort involved.

He removed the tape upstairs. At the first door he came to he knocked twice. ACCOUNTING. NO ADMITTANCE. Sounds from the lobby below rose in soft murmured currents, like a tide, the push of cheers, pull of dismay.

"Eleventh race," Breed called out in a clear voice. Hooven

had explained clearly the way it was done. "Come and get it, ready or not."

The door to the accounting room swung open from inside. Hooven. Breed stepped in. He leveled the barrel of his weapon in classic target style at the guard who was watching football on the small screen just beside the door. Hooven immediately closed up shop.

"Happy holiday," Breed said. "Don't nobody move. Nobody breathe, nothing." He took away the guard's handgun, told him to put his hands on his head. "Don't press any buttons. Don't make me nervous. It's Christmas, I don't want it where I have to kill someone, fucking Christmas and all."

Action was already hot on the competition area. They were hammering it up just above the dead line, one against one on the court, bolting the pelota against the front wall, and the crowd was on its feet.

Del Plato stood sideways with his gun partly hidden behind his left arm. Latecomers hurried through the turnstiles into the general-admission area, but the crowd was already in by now, and Del had planned it this way. Those inside weren't leaving until the eleventh match had been decided.

One guard took stubs at the main entrance. The other guard was near the seats, watching them play on the court below. Pock, pock, a mix of yells and groans from the people in seats. Cashiers at the bet windows were busy clearing their trays for the final race. The lobby floor was crammed with torn tickets and crushed paper cups, the lobby itself dense with noise, packed.

Del Plato came within five feet of the lone turnstile guard before he swung his left arm free, revealing his shiny Police Special. The guard went ashen and let his mouth drop open. He was about to raise his arms when Del Plato told him quietly not to do that.

"This is a protest situation," Del said. He put down his gray briefcase, leaning it against the entry barrier. Del held the gun close to his body so no one else could see. "Act natural. We have this whole thing planned."

The guard was very cautiously trying to look around. What were the other fronton people up to? He had Dick Nixon here, armed.

"We're concerned citizens. No more nukes. You hear me?"

"Sure, mister. What are you going to do?"

"We're gonna change a few things. And we're saving the manatee, too." Del took out the Krazy Glue. On the smooth stainless-steel top of the nearest turnstile bar he squeezed a few small drops. Just as the instructions said, for best results. "Put your hands on that. You ever see a manatee?"

The guard moved his hands hesitantly toward the clear tiny globs of glue. He shook his head no.

"Of course you haven't. There are almost none left." He helped place both the guard's palms flat on the droplets and told him to press down. "We do this all the time, don't worry. We never hurt anyone if we don't have to. The manatee is almost extinct, and all because people come down here and they have no regard for other living creatures."

Del squeezed more drops on the floor. The guard was getting the hang of things now and stepped into place.

"They poison the atmosphere; they would run their speedboats right over a helpless manatee. That's the attitude. Can you lift your hands? Try to lift your hands."

"They're stuck."

"You wouldn't kill one, would you?"

"No, I wouldn't. Honest, mister."

Del nodded. The guard couldn't move his arms or legs.

Carefully, Del Plato pinched two more drops on the confused guard's lower lip. Del lifted the bottom part of his mask to demonstrate how both lips were to be pressed together. After the guard did as he was shown, he couldn't move or make a sound.

"It doesn't hurt or anything, does it?" Del Plato had slipped the gun into his jacket pocket. He wouldn't be needing it again.

The guard shook his head side to side. No, it doesn't hurt. He couldn't budge: his hands stuck to the counter, his shoes glued to the floor, lips absolutely sealed.

The other guard was fifty feet away, watching the game. Even if he turned around, he would only see his partner at the proper post, guarding the only way to get in and out of the arena. Nothing out of the ordinary.

The jai alai players were hurling the pelota with the same drumming sound. Fans shouted out numbers, clapped their hands, stamped their feet.

Del Plato took his gray case and started for the mezzanine seats. Everything was moving, going along fine.

Jewboy Breed held a position behind the seated guard. He could also keep a close eye on the three other counters. Padding Breed's red Santa coat were two extra-large Glad bags, for leaf and garden, heavy duty, green on the outside, black on the inside. With his free hand he tossed these to Joe Hooven.

"I'm gonna be keeping up a steady stream of conversation," Breed announced. "Mindless stuff, just to keep you from thinking up anything dumb, so no one gets unnecessarily shot."

Hooven punched open one of the bags. He went to the shelf tiers where all the counted bills had been systematically arranged for pickup. One at a time, ten thousand each, Hooven tipped in the money stacks. He started with the top left corner and worked across in tidy rows, back the other way, like someone eating corn.

The guard had his hands way up and his eyes locked in on the TV screen. Breed asked if he knew what the score was. The guard could only gulp.

"The football game. Who's winning?"

"Don't know."

"Okay, look, I feel a little erratic up here. Unpredictable. I don't know. The thing is I got the gun, I got the responsibility, and I'm not sure I can handle it. So all of you, listen up, why don't you lie down on the floor? Because otherwise I'll get even more nervous, and let's not even think about that."

A fourteen-year-old kid worked his way to the turnstiles. A minor, no admittance. But he wanted to get inside the fronton, and he held a few folded singles to show the entry guard what it would be worth.

"Nobody's looking," the kid said. "What's it to you?"

The guard was craning his neck backward to see where Del Plato was, what Del Plato might be up to. The guard twisted his face, trying to whisper to the kid hoarsely, with his lips closed, the way an amateur would throw his voice.

"And I got a friend too," the kid said, trying to pick up on the guard's signals. Maybe they were being bugged and he wasn't supposed to mention any actual numbers. The kid reached in his pocket and added two dollars. "Is this okay? It's all I got."

The guard bobbed his head furiously toward the inside part of the lobby. He made muffled noises and no move for the money.

"Gee, thanks a lot, mister." The kid whistled and five boys the same age appeared. They each said thank you and tore through the gate, past the frozen guard, hurrying through the lobby and down front for seats where none of the ushers would bother them.

Del had walked at a regular pace to the head of the right-hand aisle. Everyone was watching the court, an exciting match. *"Chula!"* people shouted, standing and clapping. *"Ramate!"*

One of the sequined Wager-ettes had her back turned. Del glanced at his Fako until two minutes had passed. Behind her he stooped and clicked open the gray attaché case. The burlap bag was undone. When he nudged it with his shoe, a four-foot rattler slithered out. The snake was toothless, without venom, but what the hell. It raised its head and flashed its tongue, and curved toward the darkness of the seats.

Del Plato didn't wait for the screams. He left the briefcase where it was, walked quickly past the betting island to the front gate.

He stood behind a white marble pillar, watching the emergency door. He had ducked under a short thick arch and emerged again into the soft light of the hall. Del felt absolute peace standing there. He was totally satisfied and calm when the first rising shrieks cut through.

Hooven had started in on the unstrapped money spread evenly across the accounting room table. Hundreds, fifties, twenties. The three other money counters were crouched under the table. The guard was under too. Tens, fives, ones. Everyone faced the stripped shelves in back. Hooven flicked in a separate section of Canadian money, held together with a rubber band. Blue traveler's checks, green ones, yellow ones.

"He's going next door for more," Breed told the men on the floor. "I'm going to be out in the hall, fellas, and I'll be a wreck. Because we don't know what the fuck we're doing, and I could get excited. . . . Pow, pow, and shit, you know what I mean? Kerboom. So don't set me off. I'll be right outside. I'm armed and I'm very nervous."

When they were at the fire door, Breed gave his car keys to Joe Hooven. Breed took both bulging sacks and slung them over his shoulder. Hooven kept holding out his hand for the gun. Breed just looked at him. Breed with his red boiler suit and his beard and his bundles, the gun, and the unflinching smile of a psychopath.

"Pow, pow," Breed kept saying all the way down the stairs. He was having a great time. He motioned for Hooven to go first. Joe had one hand on the rail to steady himself and he held his breath all the way. "Here it comes," Breed said behind him. "Right now, Joey. Fucking boom."

They hit the lobby just right. Breed and Hooven heard screams and opened the door to a swarm of people in a crush of arms and confusion. Folks flew from the aisles. Panic, giggles, people everywhere. It was serious, but not really so serious.

"Snake! Snake!" Del Plato was chanting. "Snake! Snake!"

Security guards dashed across the lobby floor, uniform and plainclothes. They were there to prevent panic and the dangers of a wild throng all wanting out. Guards could care less about a goofball in a Santa suit, or some freak in red overalls, or Richard Nixon looking around. Guards pushed their way through customers and did their best to restore some order.

Del Plato stood sentry beside the turnstile guard, who couldn't signal for help or do anything. The guard heard the clamor behind him and could only wonder what this hubbub would do in the long run for the manatee, which was probably related to the whale or baby seal or some such animal that didn't know how to take care of itself.

Breed bounced across the bustling lobby floor, past the payout booths and gift shop, the two bulging sacks of jai alai money draped down his back. Hooven was right beside him. They had done it.

"Pretty good," Breed said to Del Plato as he hurried through the gate.

Breed was out first into the late-afternoon air. Then Hooven ran free, bursting out into the open, past the valet parking, then darting ahead and around the side with Breed's car keys in his fist. So easy.

All guards were on the mezzanine level. Calming down customers, applying crowd-control techniques. Del Plato left the fronton with the gun in his pocket. He cut out after one final look behind. Once outdoors, he whipped off the mask and felt the warm rush of Florida sunlight on his face, in his hair, all around, filling his lungs with a long, deep breath.

Everything was easy. Del loped effortlessly around the corner. The sky was gorgeous. Webbed with color, a filtered membrane of paling pink light that laced the far horizon. Everything made sense. The sun and moon were in their houses, the world was a good place to be. Everything fit together. The whole strange flow of reality was compressed into just this kind of tight moment, when you stepped outside of the endless ebb and pull. When one thing was definitely right, and another thing was definitely wrong, and the decision was all up to you.

Hooven had started up the stolen blue Toyota. He was waiting for Del Plato in the lane against the curb, the back door open. Breed was in the passenger seat, stripping away his red suit.

Del Plato was in no hurry. Everything had a purpose to

him, a clarity. Yes and no, right and wrong. When it was seventy-five outside and sunny, when grass was green as money and people knew what to expect. What a perfect world it could be. One marriage to last forever, life smooth as jump shots. When the world was right. When the beauty of it was all around you and the whole fucking universe rang so true.

Del got inside the car. Hooven nailed it. He had his long hair out and shaken loose, nosing the vehicle into the two-lane blacktop behind the fronton and away. Hooven immediately swung a right, not stopping at the stop sign, across the median to U.S. 1, and then a screeching left heading south.

"Holy shit," said Breed. He peeled off his cotton beard, unstrapped the extra padding around his middle. "I'm amazed. I'll tell you the truth, I'm amazed." He spun around to check through the rear glass. No sirens yet. He pocketed his weapon. Both bags of money were in the front on the floor between his legs.

It wasn't quite four o'clock. Hooven gunned the engine.

They zipped along in the far lane. Del Plato left his mask on the backseat with the Santa outfit and a change of clothes for Hooven. All three of them kept their eyes on the road, listening.

"Everything okay?" Del asked.

Up front both Breed and Hooven nodded. Easy, easy.

Half a mile down, Hooven veered sharply into a wide crowded parking lot on the west side of Federal Highway. Del Plato opened the door and came around to the driver-side window. They were outside Ice-Cream World, where Keri was celebrating her eighth or ninth birthday party.

"See you around," Del Plato told them. He wanted to say more, but didn't really know what to say at this point, or how to say it. "I'll catch a ride later."

They were right on schedule. Del straightened up and looked himself over for any signs of criminal activity. Did it show? He couldn't quite walk away because something was still troubling, way back in his head, and he didn't know what it was. When he walked inside Ice-Cream World, would Denise be able to see something in his face, his eyes? The small forgotten thing would not take shape. It throbbed like a splinter under his skin—a tiny bit of nothing as soon as you reached it, but until that time it was hard to get your mind on something else.

Hooven stared straight ahead, gripping the wheel tightly. Breed leaned back laughing, his hands behind his head and his feet on the money. He wore a striped polo shirt with a flesh-colored Band Aid across the left pocket. Breed peeled off the Band Aid to reveal the name stitched on. "Calvin Klein," he said to Hooven. "Are we swanky, or what? Let's get out of here."

Once Del Plato had stepped away, the blue Toyota roared off. Easy money.

"Troy, get your fingers away from there!"

"Sit down this second, Brookie! I will not repeat myself!"

Ice-Cream World was chaos. Keri's party was taking place at table four, the blue table, which sat twenty and had to be reserved six weeks in advance with a 50 percent deposit. Other birthday parties were going on at tables one, two, three, and five. Three mechanical bears and a gorilla who looked like Elvis were playing "Heartaches" on center stage under flickering bright lights.

"Daddy," Keri called as soon as he walked inside. She held out a shiny-blue rebel cap and a noisemaker. Denise waved hello from the head of the table. She dipped a knife into a dish of cold water and sliced off a chunk of ice-cream cake for him.

He had forgotten a gift. What kind of father was he? But Del Plato was almost relieved as he stood there empty-handed, the kid coming to him with a thick piece of cake. Maybe this was it, the nagging sense of something to remember he'd been fighting all day. No present for the kid. Now it came to him. Now, when it was too late. He was a terrible father. Was this the soul-searching mystery that had been trying to surface?

Denise saw the problem. She smiled across thinly, not bothering to call to Del Plato with all the noise inside, and he knew she would still cover for him. She would still make good, explain to Keri about devotion, and the love of a father. One day Del Plato would explain it himself, a father to his daughter. He would tell Keri about the true-blue wisdom, the things he himself and countless generations had also come to realize. The best things in life are free. One thing leads to another. He would take her up to the rim of a higher knowledge, where you could think these things and feel proud of yourself for no other reason than having thought them.

But table four was heaped high with shiny wrapped boxes, satin bows, and he had come up short. One layer of filling was chocolate, the other pineapple, with blue icing. He could make out a tiny portion of Snoopy's nose on his piece of birthday cake. Keri was probably crazy about Snoopy.

"I'm so glad you could be here, Daddy."

"My pleasure, angel."

Again that politeness. They were probably sending her to private school, where they wore uniforms and played field hockey, and the kids grew up to become astronauts. He would have to schedule a good long talk with her. Get together with his little girl on Saturdays, go to the movies or a mall.

Keri showed him where to sit. Next to Lance's mother, who was also wearing a rebel hat. Del Plato asked Lance's mother if she had any aspirin.

Breed told Joe Hooven to pull up behind the north wall of the plaza, where his car was parked from before beneath the white-and-red Winn-Dixie sign. Breed had dumped his boots into the backseat and was now in his Cardin socks. He had nothing to say to Joe Hooven. He wanted to go home, take a shower, see Gail, have a snooze.

Joe Hooven reached below the driver's seat as Breed bumped open the passenger door of the blue Toyota. Hooven had stashed away a gun. When Jewboy Breed stood up after stepping out into the lot, Hooven lowered the long black barrel and held it pointed dead on.

"Let me tell you where you're going now, man. Let me tell you."

Breed stared back, doleful and listless as he spotted the

weapon trained steadily at his heart. The car door was open. Breed was half-reaching inside for the green-black sacks of money they had robbed.

"Pow, pow," Hooven said. He was smiling widely, with his hand extended, as though prepared to greet an old, old friend. "Now you're dead, man. Just to see that look on your face. Like boom."

"Eat shit," Breed told him. "Moron."

Breed grabbed for both bags anyway. The rising ground-out whine of motors came roughly from the busy road behind them. He began to smile. He could see the humor in a situation as well as the next guy. When the coyote, for instance, got an anvil dropped on his head, or flattened himself against a painted tunnel which the roadrunner had just whizzed through, Breed could be amused by that. It was irony. He could appreciate irony.

Joe Hooven fired twice as Breed lifted the money. Thunk, thunk. Two shots ripped into the seat inches away from Breed's face. The explosions made him back away.

"A dream come true, man," Hooven said. "Greatest moment in my whole fucking life, right now. Touch my money again."

The smell off a shot hung in the air, powder and heat and the night coming on, drifting across the length of Florida lawns and the dense, dry grass outside. Both bullets had sunk in the upholstery. Hooven was beaming and so was Breed.

Hooven fired once more. Thunk, in the seat. Neither one moved.

Then Hooven nailed the pedal and the car lurched up, accelerating away. Breed stood where he was, hands in his pockets. He considered alternatives, and the irony of this twist. He could race to his own car and chase Hooven through the streets. One possibility. He could unsnap his revolver and try his luck from this distance. Or he could be philosophical about the whole thing, the whole funny development. Hadn't he seen it coming all along?

It was Del Plato's fault. You couldn't trust a man with weasel eyes. That's the way Breed had felt from square one, that was his position. You could never trust a man whose shampoo had all the ingredients of a salad dressing. You sat next to Joe Hooven, Joe Heavy, and when you sniffed the air it was green goddess. And he had told Del Plato, told him so all along.

Just before breaking out into the chopped mainstream of traffic, the blue Toyota came to a sudden, complete halt. Out the driver-side window came one of the plastic trash bags. The lumpy sack was knotted at the top. It tumbled one time as it hit the ground and came to rest against a Police Athletic League dumpster for recycled clothing. Hooven beeped and drove away.

Breed shrugged, still amused, and went to get it.

Some of the kids rushed to the front window to see cop cars streaking up Federal Highway, lights flashing. The rest of them stayed to watch Bernardo the Magician, on a raised platform with cutout stars and balloons taped to the drapes behind him. He had come all the way from Century Village to entertain the young and old at Ice-Cream World with wonders he had learned in far-off lands. He had climbed mountains and crossed deserts, lived without the Sunday funnies or even a decent pair of shoes on his feet, all for the sake of his craft. And now he needed two assistants. The birthday girl, and someone else.

After Bernardo it was time for presents. Then everyone would go home.

"Troy! Where are your fingers? Do fingers belong *there?*"

Del was hanging back, on the periphery. The magician was looking right at him, he wanted Del Plato to come up. Del didn't know what to do. Keri was already on the platform, peeking into the magician's hat.

Ethan pushed back his chair and went up instead. The birthday party people, when the magician instructed them to, gave Ethan a polite hand for volunteering, which seemed fair.

Del Plato sat back and tried to bask in the afterglow of a job well done and his daughter's good time. Soon he would be defrosting Swanson enchiladas, drinking more than he should, putting dirty dishes and glasses into the dishwasher till there were enough to be done. But now he was here, having robbed lots of money.

Bernardo was making hard-boiled eggs come out of Ethan's mouth over and over again when Jewboy Breed pressed his face against the glass outside. Del was disappointed because he could see the trick. Ethan had to sit on a stool with his eyes closed while Keri waved a magic wand over his head.

Del Plato met Breed at the side door. He kept looking at Breed, fixing him with one eye, then the other, like a bird. Del Plato hadn't even known he was thinking of what could possibly go wrong until his knees quivered and suddenly bubbles of air were coming up in his blood. Maybe Breed's car wouldn't start, with all its extras and fuel injection. Or they had been spotted back inside the fronton, and now it was over. Everything could have gone wrong.

Breed dropped his plastic green bundle and searched outside for a place to sit. He had no shoes.

And Del was wondering what he would have to do now. Walking outside, waiting to hear some terrible verdict. He'd have to stand around like this, trying to look regular for the rest of his life, like nothing exceptional had ever happened, another face in the crowd. Yet inside he was falling as though from a huge height, no foothold, no balance, off the edge of the earth and tumbling down into the dark, uncertain lawlessness of himself. And that would be it, a thump and thud from deep inside, deep as the heart—the truth, the whole truth—forever and always, just like now.

Chapter

15

I f he had right away splurged on a new set of wheels, Del
Plato would have run the risk of drawing undue attention
to himself, so instead he went out on a different limb and had
the Dodge repainted. And it wasn't cheap to get that original
tropical blue. On S.R. 84, past the pyramid and converted
warehouses and the cinder-block factories, Del found a res-
toration specialist who said it was an investment, a hedge
against inflation. If you were driving around in a Dodge with
push-button transmission, then you were driving around inside a gold mine. It was up there with the '68 Mustang and the
Corvair; rich people in places like Scottsdale and California
were paying top dollar for the real McCoy. The guy who did
the work was from Cleveland, and he and Del talked football a
bit before they talked business. Who was smoother, Lem Bar-
ney or Warfield? He offered Del Plato twenty-five hundred for
the car as it was. But he could deliver it immaculate.

All the rust spots were sawed out; the holes refilled with
fiber glass; both windshields taken out and then put back. The

automobile was compounded top and bottom, two coats of paint. Then it was all rubbed in by hand to a lacquer finish, three hundred dollars in itself, until Del's old car gleamed once again with turquoise purity and some high-gloss chrome, full of grace, and a bird with pink wings screwed down on the hood.

Del had the engine steam-cleaned, all belts replaced. He went for a new alternator, new motor mounts. For parts Del figured they probably had to send away to some 1960's car museum. New seats, front and back; heat cracks in the dash were touched up; four new blackwall tires with raised lettering. He thought it well worth the money to have his car saved.

Del was driving south on I-95, Jewboy Breed in the passenger seat and both of them busy thinking. Breed had just finished responding to a call in Coral Ridge. Some guy had rented a two-bedroom house with a deep-water slip. He paid first and last month's security in cash, three thousand dollars, and signed a one-year lease with no pets or children. Then the guy advertised the same house for rent, listing a phone number only, at nine hundred dollars a month. A bargain. He wound up taking first and last month's security deposit from ten different tenants before skipping out with the rattan patio chairs the original landlord had left behind. The police were called when ten people with rent receipts all tried to move in on the same day.

The first thing Breed wanted to know was whether the guy who took their money had long blond hair and weasely eyes.

But it wasn't Hooven. Breed was disappointed. He returned the squad car to the station, where Del Plato picked him up and offered a lift in the unscratched Dodge. Del was now able to keep the needle pinned at seventy, the hot port of Miami shimmering far off in the distance as they drove.

"Gail got me these briefs the other day," Breed said, running his hand over the new seat covers. "These European-style shorts. You know which ones they are? The kind with no fly."

"Are you wearing that?"

"I'm not saying. Maybe it's just me, because I can't speak

for the whole male population, but for myself I don't like to wear those things. When you got to pull everything down just to take a leak, that's what I'm talking about."

"You're wearing those things right now, J.B., aren't you?"

"Lay off. Because to me, I don't know, it's an unmanly thing to do. Okay? Which Gail don't understand. She threw away my Jockey shorts and she bought me this fashion shit."

Del Plato's half of the Glad bag had counted out to somewhere in the neighborhood of $45,000. Breed had $45,000. The *Herald* and the *Sentinel* ran the robbery total at $165,000. If you could believe the correct numbers were given out by Olympia management, that meant Joe Hooven was off to the races with $75,000.

"To me it's the same thing as I'm wearing panties," Breed said, "and it makes me feel funny. Unless maybe she thinks I got one that's too big to fit through regular underwear. What do you think, Lucky, you got an opinion? It's a problem the way I see it, no fly."

On either side of the road were squat white structures set one next to the other, randomly spaced, like building blocks which hadn't been put away. The sky was a bleached color, the sun somewhere above them. Del kept his original Saint Anthony, and the dice which hung from his rearview mirror for luck.

In the backseat of the car Del Plato had another brand-new briefcase, this one made of tooled leather, with rawhide stitching and lots of natural grain. Breed ran his fingertips over the leather. Then he brought the briefcase into the front seat, setting it flat across his knees. He was so sure it would be Joe Hooven back there, on the Intracoastal, taking people's money. It should have been. Breed had been planning what he would say, what he would do, when he finally caught up. How he would do it.

"For the ladies is who they should be redesigning underwear for," Breed said. "Like with this Velcro stuff, for instance, they could be making brassieres from that. Because me, say I meet a willing girl, I still haven't got it down yet with those snaps and hooks, all that European shit. I need two hands to get the job done. But the girl's got one of these Velcro bras on, one little yank and—hello—they're both free. Makes more sense than pussy underwear."

Right outside Ice-Cream World, flush from the take, when they excused themselves from the birthday party to lock themselves inside Breed's hot-dog car, with the smoked windows so nobody could see what they were doing as they thumbed through their share of the heist—the money Joe Asshole Hooven thought on a whim he could drop out the car window— right then and there Jewboy Breed shook a fist and vowed this was it with robbery for him. No more for him, never again.

"This is what we get?" Breed had asked, disgusted. He was unhappy with the weight of his share, like when you order steak in a restaurant and they give you some skimpy portion of meat that might have come off the kiddies' menu. On the spot, feeling vengeful and cheated inside his car, Breed swore he would go straight. "This scotches it for me with the strong-arm shit, I'm telling you. We're so smart, me and you, and he's such a Baggie, and look what happens. It could break your fucking heart."

Right away Breed began dreaming about a chance encounter with Hooven, just bumping into him on the street somewhere, totally unplanned, the best kind of surprise. Or hunting Hooven down, that would also be okay. The way Steve McQueen did, in *Nevada Smith,* when he tracked down Karl Malden just to shoot him in the knees and leave him there. That kind of getting together, because even crime didn't pay, not enough.

Inside Del Plato's briefcase was a cut of the Olympia loot. Breed snapped it open to check inside. Four thousand five hundred dollars of Del Plato's share, a matching grant from Jewboy Breed. They were on their way to Happy Harry's Decor Discounts, in Hollywood. The windows were open a crack and wind whistled in, howling above the new smooth sound of the converted pistons. It was New Year's Eve. Still the early part of tourist season, but a time also to put things into some sort of perspective.

"He's gonna get caught," Breed said after a mile or so of silence. They came over parched hills and the airport. Del turned off and took the service road ahead, then swerved toward the beach. "They'll catch him, sooner or later. I just want you to know, in case you didn't already. He'll give us up."

"I don't want to talk about that."

"Just passing the time with you, champ, that's all. What's the matter, nobody ever taught you how to make small talk?" Breed had been very reluctant to fork over 10 percent of his jai alai swag, but Del Plato had been insistent, acting all sullen and standing around with his arms folded until he finally got his way. "What would you rather talk about?" Breed asked. "How about winning? That appeal to you? The competitive aspect, coming out ahead. We could discuss that again."

Del Plato turned into the dusty alley beside Happy Harry's. On the white brick wall of the building between metal roll-up doors, some kids had chalked in a crude square stickball box. A pitcher's slab of blue marked the sidewalk edge as they left the car and came around, hurrying across the weedy pavement. Del stooped for the split half of a rubber ball at his feet.

Taped on the inside of the front windows were brown paper bags. The delivery door was blocked off with plywood strips hammered down by someone who wasn't a carpenter, with the rusty bent end of nails sunk half into the wood. ALL MERCHANDISE DRASTICALLY REDUCED! EVERYTHING MUST GO! LOST OUR LEASE! OUT!!

"Knock, knock," Breed said, coming through the front door. Del carried in the briefcase of money. "Look who's here, Happy. It's us, the long arm of the law."

Everything inside seemed shiny, newly polished. The entire clutter of decorator pieces was arranged now by order of bigness. Placed up front was the least-imposing wall unit, but then Del and Breed had to weave through deliberate avenues of increasing size and stateliness and higher tickets, until by the time they reached Happy Harry's desk in back the lanes were narrow and the furniture dark and enormous. They were dwarfed by Lucite and wood-grain Formica, boxed in by dress-

ers and headboards, the type of steep-sloped canyon an Indian
scout would warn the cavalry not to ride into. The aisles
weren't wide enough for more than one at a time.

Stacked on Happy Harry's desk were half-empty contain-
ers of Tic Tacs and a display rack of interior-design magazines. Del offered his hand and asked what the story was with
paper bags on the windows. Del was full of resolutions. He had
resolved to make a better first impression. Clean fingernails,
haircuts on a regular basis. Less booze. He would try to be
more polite.

"Lost our lease," said Happy Harry, who leaned forward
across his desk to also shake hands with Breed. "I wouldn't lie.
The other day I ask my wife—God bless her she works so
hard—I ask her for a copy of our lease. She tells me she don't
know where it is. So naturally, gents, I look around myself. I
look everywhere, but there's no lease." He opened a desk
drawer and moved his hand inside. Paper clips, an empty soda
can, pens. "It's not in the drawer, not in the safe, it's lost. We
lost our lease."

Del sat on the edge of the desk. "So how's business?"

"Picked up. We're supposed to be healthy, wealthy, and
wise, in that order, so I can't complain. But I suppose you
didn't come here to have a talk." Happy Harry had gained a
little more weight. Above the white collar of his working shirt
his neck and face were a bronze-red color. He also sold sun-
lamps. He stood up behind his desk and steadied himself
against the store stock. "I would like to be honest with you. I'm
content right here. No matter what happens. Indoors I feel
safe and completely content. I got pictures of my loved ones
right in front of me; I got a portable TV that works off batteries if you need it. This store is my one home. Here is my
castle. I can call up for meals and they deliver to my desk. I
got an alarm system with ultrasonic gizmos on the roof and
underneath your feet. I got hookups with police and fire. I got
peace of mind."

Del and Breed edged past, single file. Del Plato had a firm
grip on the money-filled case. "Sunny Side of the Street" came
over the easy-listening station. Del knocked on the rear door,

Tommy Polio's office. It wasn't locked. He entered the small room and stood inside, silent and oddly serene.

Tommy Polio was sitting down alone. He wore a thin suit and a tie, examining a sheaf of current invoices. Behind the glass partition the telephones were unattended.

"Where are the boys?" Breed wanted to know. "You got the gang working for a living now, or what?"

"A new thing," Tommy Polio said. He told them to come inside. "You see the way it is in my kind of business, I get a lot of turnover. Never the same faces. They quit on me; they go to jail."

Del Plato put his briefcase on the table beside all the bills due. "I brought this for you," Del said. He had made other resolutions as well. It was high time to shape up. "I've been going over a few ideas, personal stuff." He would put his house in order, learn to live with himself. Every decision was an important decision.

"Even when we were having our differences," Tommy Polio told him, "even then, I could see I was dealing with an honorable man."

"It's money," Del said. "I want you to have it."

"Money," Tommy Polio repeated softly.

"Take it."

Tommy Polio snapped open the briefcase and looked inside. He didn't let on if he was pleased or displeased.

Breed stood by the door. Under his uniform he still wore his regulation bulletproof vest, which he had been wearing all day, and it was annoying him. When he adjusted the collar, steam rose up and fogged his sunglasses. The money they were giving away to Tommy Polio also annoyed Breed.

Tommy Polio sat back, his hands folded in his lap. "I honestly like you, Officer. But you stand before me now, and I know in your heart you still have something to say." He left the briefcase where it was on the desk. "Say it, son. I'll forgive you everything. Just sit down and unburden yourself; tell me what's really troubling you. Tell me the name."

Breed saw this was nothing for him. He backed off toward the office door, then quietly stepped outside into the showroom. Del Plato had his arms folded and was looking away. It was quiet and still.

"Basically you're a decent man. I won't force you to tell me. You'll feel better if you do it yourself."

"What I told you last time still holds, Mr. Parrajo. We won't be bothering you again. You do what you have to do, and when you have problems, it won't be from us. That's the truth."

"I believe you. But you have something else to tell me."

"I can't do that."

"We're alone, Officer. Whisper the name. Confess."

Del Plato stood there a long time. Tommy Polio lifted one pack of green bills from the briefcase. He pushed other packs inside to see what color wrappers they had.

"You have nothing else to tell me?"

"Nothing you don't already know."

Tommy Polio raised one hand. With the other he covered Del Plato's offering. "Then you may go in peace."

Del edged back and walked right out. He closed the door gently behind him and kept going, from the narrow end of the store to the more open spaces ahead, past Happy Harry, past Breed, feeling his way through the confines of these things all around him until he was finally outside and walking away.

Del Plato could already feel a drop in temperature outdoors. Winter months were coming up fast. More birds had arrived south. He noticed them above the murmurous folding waves, perched on poles and on the pointed arc of new roofs by the ocean. Tourists would be coming each day, and rain, and cool breezes, and a much-needed time for roots to grab in the wet smell and blended air of this Florida, with its hustlers and rubber alligators, its stand-up comics and Canadians and sharks of the shuffleboard court. They were all here for something. They all wanted something.

Del Plato decided he wasn't responsible for the whole human race; he couldn't be. He was one person, no more and no less, one guy acting alone, that's all. Whatever he did, he did it himself. Absolutely.

Breed caught up with Del Plato outside, in the alley, next

to the stickball box. Del was standing a few feet away from his car, admiring the paint.

"Come on," Breed said, "I'll drive over with you to the Quién Sabe, teach you how to shoot pool."

Del Plato unlocked the car doors and started up. He took pride in the low rumble of his rebuilt engine. As soon as he turned the key, he had it going. It was amazing to him the way things could be set right. The car had hundreds of thousands of miles, a hopeless machine, yet still there was room for hope. He punched the button for reverse and backed into the street, then away.

"I think Hooven showed some character," Del said. "He could have taken you out back there, and Internal Affairs would have come after me. He had all the money. He could have six other names for all we know; we'd never find him. We never will."

"If you did it my way, we wouldn't have to look. We wouldn't have to think about where he is, or what he's wearing. What alias he's using these days." Breed started to reach for the briefcase of money, then remembered they had given it away. "We could have been looking very carefully at the money-market situation," Breed said, watching trees and phone lines fly by. "We could have been looking into bullion, and futures, and land. But he showed character, your friend."

"He really likes me, Hooven does. And Tommy Polio back there likes me. And so do you, J.B. What is it about me that everyone likes so much?"

Del Plato pulled alongside the front steps that led up high to the 01 Precinct. Breed got out. He kept the car door open, standing on the sidewalk with his back to Del Plato. Thick dark clouds had formed over the water, moving inland.

"You don't think we'll see him," Breed said.

"No."

"Neither do I. But let me tell you what I'm really fantasizing. I'm driving along, alone, when up in the sky I see colors, a rainbow, and the thing is it's not even raining. There's no rain. Just a sky full of these tremendous glowing colors, and the whole thing fills up my windshield. It's beautiful, Del Plato. This is like God is talking to me. So I follow it. I keep driving. And at the end of the rainbow, when I get there, standing right underneath this miracle, I see the Baggie. He turns around. And what he does, he just looks at me. He sees me. That's my vision."

Del Plato pulled away from the curb. He tugged the door closed and drove quickly across side roads toward his old house. He kept some after-shave lotion in the glove box, which he spread over his palms and on his neck.

Red spots had come up on Keri's back, Denise had informed him, possibly chicken pox and possibly nothing more than bug bites. Ethan and Denise had promised her a new bike with wide-traction tires and a whip antenna if it was actually chicken pox, because then they wouldn't have to worry about chicken pox for the wedding, which was a month away. Her lawyer said the divorce would be all right by then. Both lawyers were invited. Denise's father was flying down, and all of Ethan's family. He had never been married before.

Del went over his feelings on his way to her house. In a way he was relieved to realize he could no longer be in love with Denise. She was getting married. *Look at Medlow,* he told himself as an example, *who had become so wimpy on the court as a result of falling in love again with the same person.* It apparently took the best out of a guy, the same as putting in a fifteen-hour shift would, where all you could do afterward was nibble food and slump along and tell everyone to leave you alone. Denise and Ethan were celebrating their engagement, at the old house, in the backyard, on New Year's Eve, and there was no reason Del Plato shouldn't have a good-enough time.

The new homes on Denise's block were now complete, solid single-family units with artfully coordinated rooflines and elevations. There were fairly large American flags in the swale, held up with rocks pushed together, and flags advertising a low mortgage rate. Cars were doubled-parked in front of Denise's house; others trailed out the driveway and into the street. Del left his farther along. He didn't want anyone opening a heavy car door right next to him, chipping the new finish.

He came around the side of the house, past the coiled hose and tarpaulin-covered lumber that had been there since they took title years back. All the gates were swung open. It smelled like a barbecue. The Doors were playing from inside. Replacement speakers the insurance check had paid for were in the backyard. There was a faint trace of gardenias in the air, from a neighbor's garden, and viburnum, but mostly it was food on the charcoal and the music turned up high.

"Glad you're here," Ethan said as soon as Del came through. "I mean it, I really do." He pointed to the cooler and told Del Plato to help himself. "We have Bud and Lites, rum and Coke, we might have champagne left too. Take your pick. It's a happy time for me, and for Denise. Enjoy yourself."

Del recognized neighbors. Most of them he hadn't talked to even while he was living there. He noticed some raised eyebrows, quizzical looks, an occasional nod in his direction. Others turned away to avoid eye contact, as though Del Plato carried some dread disease, the ex-husband. He was aware, but didn't really mind. It wasn't important.

He picked out a Coke for himself and looked around. He and Denise had never given a party. A few times the subject came up, even got so far as the planning stage, but then it was always one thing or another, and then a simple dinner for two other couples would seem like plenty, more than enough. They were never much for parties. Denise would drink and get sleepy without getting drunk. Del would drink and make plans with other cops that he could never keep—skydiving, a canoe trip down the Snake River, salmon fishing up north.

Keri met him with a hot dog. She had it done up with all the works, the way he liked it. She was wearing her Little League uniform, a brand new one for the play-offs. She turned around to show him the back. Above the number they had given her was her very own name, sewn on in bright-blue letters. On the front was the emblem of a roaring vacuum cleaner.

"Are you having a good time, Daddy?"

"I always have a good time."

She was beaming at him. But then her smile began to fade as he ate the hot dog and there wasn't much to say. He was her father, but it was going to be hard. They both seemed to realize this at the same time. They stood there, apart from the noise and voices. Del was trying to tell her things with his eyes, gently. Keri kicked dirt from her rubber cleats.

"You're getting so big," he told her. His hot dog was gone in a few bites. He offered the soda, but she didn't like Coke.

Del set the can down on the grass and lifted Keri by the waist then, hoisting her high above, as he had done many times before. And he held her there a long time, his arms out and open, smiling up. The warm smooth skin under the uniform of his daughter was all he could feel. She was there, floating in his hands, his little girl, the sweet, careless weight of his love.

"I've got to go now, Daddy."

"It's okay, kiddo."

"Put me down."

The garden was edged by rough, wild hedges not doing very well after the dry season. A bramble of small rude leaves and peeled-back scuffled branches. Kids played soccer against one fence. Keri went to join them. Music pounded as Del walked around in his old backyard, holding an empty can of pop and the napkin from his frankfurter.

The new TV inside the house was tuned to a ball game, and neighbors drifted through to keep tabs on the score. Del knew very few of the people, which was fine with him. They were Ethan's people, or friends of Denise he never got around to meeting. He smiled in his even manner at everyone. They were celebrating an engagement, having a good time.

Walking along, Del Plato was thinking that he probably had more cash than anyone at this party.

Alone, he lay back on the high thin grass to gaze at the sky. Clouds drifted just beyond his reach when he stretched his arms to get them. He felt indestructible. Sunlight poured down; nothing could touch him.

He had his head pressed to the ground, his arms out wide and holding on. From that position Del could feel the earth tearing through the universe, with him and everyone else on board. If he let go, his body would rip free, probably rise on its own. It wasn't a pleasant sensation. He was dizzy from breathing in and out.

When he was younger, Del Plato had been terrified of the sky. He had been to church, and that was bad enough. Those huge dark walls, like the hall of some giant, with all the candles, and a fearful drone of prayer. But up in the clouds, above the clouds, it was even worse—a ghost lived there. A ghost who would watch everything Del Plato did and everything he said, a man with thorns on his head and spikes in his hand, blood all over.

Ethan hurried across the patio to hug some new guests. Then he removed a bottle of champagne from a wooden barrel filled with ice. He peeled the foil and called for attention, then called Keri to his side as he worked the cork with his thumbs, a tiny bit at a time. Keri wore her fielder's mitt. "Get ready, here we go." Finally the cork popped loose and shot up. People applauded. Champagne flowed over. And Keri said, "I got it, I got it," turning in circles under the catch, her glove held steady in the sun high above.